DOUGLAS DUNN

Boyfriends
and Girlfriends

faber and faber

LONDON · BOSTON

First published in 1995
by Faber and Faber Limited
3 Queen Square London WC1N 3AU
This paperback edition first published in 1996

Phototypeset by Intype, London
Printed in England by Clays Ltd, St Ives plc

Douglas Dunn is hereby identified as author of this work
in accordance with Section 77 of the Copyright,
Designs and Patents Act 1988.

A CIP record for this book is
available from the British Library

ISBN 0-571-17710-7

Douglas Dunn was born in 1942 and grew up in Inchinnan, Renfrewshire. He was educated in Scotland and at the University of Hull. His first book of poems, *Terry Street*, was published in 1969, and his sixth, *Elegies*, was selected as Whitbread Book of the Year of 1985. He has also received the Somerset Maugham Award, the Geoffrey Faber Memorial Prize, the Hawthornden Prize and a Cholomondeley Award. In 1991 he was appointed a professor in the School of English of the University of St Andrews, where he is also Director of the St Andrews Scottish Studies Institute.

Contents

ACKNOWLEDGEMENTS

Some of the stories in this collection first appeared in *Grand Street* ('The Boy from Birnam' and 'Mulwhevin'), *The Listener* ('The Political Piano'), *London Magazine* ('More than Half the Way'), and *A Roomful of Birds: Scottish Short Stories 1990*, Collins, 1990 ('Toddle-Bonny and the Bogeyman'). 'Orr Mount', 'Needlework' and 'Boyfriends and Girlfriends' first appeared in *The New Yorker*.

Orr Mount

Everybody knew Monty Gault. He was the local small-time builder, joiner, and handyman. No one round about the town of Dryfask thought twice about whom to get if they wanted a wall built, a floor laid, or a door hung. He could do anything connected with houses. When the Hendersons moved into Orr Mount and ran into trouble with the big contracting firm they'd hired from Glasgow, it was Monty they were advised to call for help.

'It's a funny thing,' Monty said to John Henderson, 'but I haven't seen this house up close since I was a boy.'

Orr Mount was a house about a mile west of Dryfask and 400 yards off the road, at the end of its own private lane. It was a substantial stone building in terrible disrepair, set in a garden that had surrendered to the encroachments of the woodland that hid the house from the road.

'I've been let down,' John Henderson said. 'It was two weeks ago before those fellows even made a start and did the damp courses. Now they're telling me it'll be July before they can come back.'

'You mean you accepted this estimate?' Monty whistled at the list of estimated costs that Henderson handed him and groaned at the total. 'Are you bound to this?'

'There were harsh words,' Henderson said, 'but my wife gave them the heave. Anyway, that's the estimate you've got to beat.'

'I'll work it out on paper,' Monty said, 'and let you know.'

'Could you give me a rough idea?' There was a quiet but worried urgency in Henderson's voice. 'My wife's annoyed that it's taking so long,' he said, almost confidingly. He sounded like a man who had been blamed. 'We're living in squalor.'

'I'll be cheaper,' Monty said. 'A lot cheaper. Frankly, I wouldn't have the brass neck to ask a price like that.' He slapped the estimate sheet. 'I'm a one-man band,' he went on to warn. 'I can start right away, but there's a lot to do, and it'll take time. I can do it, though. Stonework, roofing, joinery, electrics – no problem, Mr Henderson.

I'll need help from time to time, but day labour's not hard to come by round here.'

Henderson was in his mid-forties – a few years older than Monty Gault, six inches taller, and greying but without distinction. He looked as much at home in his blue business suit as Monty Gault did in his faded off-brown dungarees and ancient jacket.

'It's a fine house,' Monty said, but Henderson looked at it without showing pleasure or any pride of ownership. He looked at it as though it amounted to nothing more than a drain on his bank balance and months of inconvenience until the work on it was finished.

'I didn't know the folk who lived here,' Monty said. 'I pass your road end often enough, so I used to see their car come in or out. They were the sort of people you know by their make of car. I didn't even know they'd moved,' he said. 'I thought maybe they'd changed their car. I'd forgotten it's so big a house. I hope you got it cheap, Mr Henderson.'

'At the time, I thought it was a bargain,' Henderson said. 'But yesterday the wind slammed the back door and five slates fell on the doorstep. It's been empty for over a year.'

Monty cast his eyes over the roof. He noticed a woman he took to be Henderson's wife withdraw from an upstairs window when he looked up.

'When can you start?' Henderson asked.

'As soon as you like,' Monty said. 'Don't you want a price first?'

'As long as you're a lot cheaper,' Henderson said, 'you can start tomorrow.'

At least three months of guaranteed income was a windfall that Monty Gault had not expected. Nor was it often that he had the satisfaction of renovating an entire house, he told his wife that night.

'I've a funny feeling about that job, though. There's something I don't like there.'

'Steady work,' Mary Gault said, 'and you're complaining?'

'It's Henderson. I didn't take to the man.'

'That's you all over,' Mary said. 'You're happiest when you're working for someone you like, and then it shames you to take their money.'

Quick and capable at what he did, Monty enjoyed an appreciative cup of tea with his many occasional employers. He liked his days to be neighbourly and sociable. On longer jobs, his temporary near-membership in another family gave him pleasure. He revelled in their talk and gossip; he was often delighted by the eccentric routines of different households, moved by their sadnesses, and dispirited by their tensions. Orr Mount and its occupants were outside the circle of shared local personality and behaviour – they were tucked away from the life of the district – and Monty was unsure what he'd find there.

The following morning, Monty parked his van behind Orr Mount, curious to meet Mrs Henderson for the first time.

She greeted him at the back door. 'You know, of course, that we were let down?'

If anything, Mrs Henderson looked more on edge than her husband. There was a depressed kind of determination about her that Monty thought might be a response to the discomfort of her surroundings. The kitchen would have been modern in 1920; its obsolescence had brought a heavy, dark shabbiness. Everything in the room was makeshift, and utensils were still mostly packed in tea chests and cardboard boxes. 'It's filthy,' she told Monty. 'How could people live in dirt like this?' She glanced around her with disgust. 'I want you to start with the window frames.'

'Window frames first?' Monty asked. His ordering of priorities was different. He had come prepared, he told her, to make a start on the roof, some of which had grown a green patina. Here and there on its slipped slates there were distinct patches of moss. A sycamore sapling had taken root in the guttering. 'Then, after the downspouts, and a bit of pointing, I thought the rewiring, Mrs Henderson, followed by an all-out assault on this mess in here. The kitchen speaks for itself,' he said.

But she was firm. 'You don't have to live with the draughts in this house. No, the window frames. They rattle every time there's a puff of wind. *Then* the roof. But we'll see about that once you've shown me what you can do. You *can* make window frames?' she asked sternly.

'Oh, I've made a few in my time,' Monty said, trying to laugh off his surprise at her question and her manner – both of which insisted that Mrs Henderson would stand for no nonsense. 'I take it you're the boss,' he said. 'I like to know who I'm working for.'

'No, you're working for Mr Henderson,' she said.

3

But Monty was unconvinced. Why, he asked himself, do some wives pretend that their husbands are the masters of the household when it's as clear as day that they aren't? He had seen the relationship many times before. It was one of the facts of life that kept him in work: wives nagging their menfolk to fix things around the house, and then – when it dawned on them that their husbands wouldn't, or couldn't, do the work themselves – urging them to get Monty Gault in to do it.

'Well, I like my hot cups, Mrs Henderson,' he said. 'I'm an old-fashioned tradesman. I'll work better for a steady flow – tea or coffee, but tea's preferred, a touch of milk and no sugar.'

He spent the morning measuring the windows. Through the glass he observed in passing much of the work ahead. Floors dipped visibly where the joists were rotten. Naked light bulbs hung on the ends of old braided electric wire. Damp patches greyed through paint and paper on walls and ceilings. At each symptom of neglected husbandry, Monty winced in consternation.

He was on a ladder finishing with the upper windows when he looked into a room and saw a child in bed with bandaged eyes. Gauze and bedding obscured most of the child's face, and Monty could not tell if it was a boy or girl. Apart from the child's bed, a chair, and a small table, the room was raw and unfurnished. Monty stood frozen on his ladder and, through his slow shock, tried to understand what he saw. He checked over his measuring, and came down to find Mrs Henderson.

'I was frightened I'd wake him up.' He felt he should have been warned. 'A noise at the window, and him with his eyes bandaged – that'd scare anybody. Did he have an accident?'

'He's blind,' she said. 'They tried an operation on his right eye. They did something to the other eye, too. I should've told you he was up there.' She poured tea for Monty. 'He's been at home with us for the past week. We couldn't postpone the operation – a thing like that can't be put off because a builder drags his heels and lets you down. And we couldn't stay on in our old house. We'd sold it, and the buyers needed to move in. We were tied to a date. Robin's thirteen. I knew the operation would be a waste of time.'

'Has he always been blind?' Monty asked solicitously.

'No, not always.' Her tone made it clear she did not want to talk about her son. 'I know exactly what I have in mind for this house,'

4

she said. But having changed the subject, she said, 'You're probably wondering why we took the place, with all its problems.'

'It's none of my business,' Monty said. 'I'm just the hired help.'

'Good,' she said. 'I'm glad you know where we stand. It's difficult enough as it is without tradesmen carrying tales about us.'

'You weren't keen on me doing the work here, were you?' Monty asked.

'You're a bit too local.'

'Am I fired?'

'Robin will be much nearer a very good school for the blind. In fact, he's been a pupil there for almost a year. Living here saves me forty miles' driving a day. How long will the window frames take?'

'I don't know,' Monty said. 'A week to make, maybe more. And a week to set them in. Give or take a few days,' he said.

'I want replicas of the original windows. Exact copies, and the best materials.'

'His eyes were bandaged,' Monty told his wife that night. 'Great wads of gauze and surgical tape. Sound asleep. He didn't move a muscle. I was really shaken.'

'You always take other people's troubles too much to heart,' Mary said. 'That'll be why you've been hard at it out there until the back of eight.'

'There's a lot of window frames,' he protested. 'It'll be twelve hours a day until it's done.'

'Make it last,' Mary said. 'We need the money.'

Protected by plastic sheeting and tarpaulin, glazed, neatly primed and undercoated, the window frames arrived at Orr Mount on Saturday morning.

'I was wondering where you were! I was getting ready to come and find you,' Henderson said. His tone was more irate than he could quite bring off.

'What's wrong?' Monty asked.

'Where've you been?' Henderson said.

'Me? Where'd you think? I've been in my yard, busy making your window frames.' Monty opened the back of the van.

'That surely isn't all of them?' Henderson said truculently.

'It's a wee van,' Monty said, pointing out the obvious. 'I'll have to go back for the rest of them.' In the past, he had endured inspections

of his work by half-wits and incompetents, but Henderson's insin-
uation of indolence, or dishonesty, or the one excusing the other,
was new to him. It rattled Monty. He turned round and saw Mrs
Henderson approaching. Monty said to her, 'I'm sorry, Mrs Henderson. I thought you understood I'd have to get the wood milled and
then make up the window frames on my bench. That's the sort of job
I do in the yard.'

'I phoned,' she said. 'Three times I phoned you.'

'The phone's in the house,' Monty said, 'and Mrs Gault goes out to
work.'

'I hope the wood is properly seasoned,' she said to her husband.

'Is it?' Henderson asked, passing on the suspicion.

Monty pulled a window frame free of its wadding. He was losing
patience. 'Tap that,' he said sharply. 'Go on, tap it.' Henderson
rapped on the wood. 'Should they bend, buckle, or rot, you know
where to come. Now, is that a perfect copy of that window over
there, or is it not?'

Mrs Henderson began counting them. 'Where are the rest?'

'Maybe I could have got them all into the van, Mrs Henderson, by
squeezing them in, and scratching the undercoats, and risking a lot
of broken glass on that bumpy joke you call a road. Now, I think the
three of us ought to have a wee talk. There's someone round here
thinks I've been swinging the lead, and I don't like it.'

Mrs Henderson walked away and left her husband to apologize.

'We hadn't seen hide or hair of you the whole week,' Henderson
said, venturing an explanation for his previous ill temper. His right
leg trembled, his heel throbbing on the matted grass.

'I could see you were in a bad mood when you came back to
collect the second batch of frames,' Mary Gault told Monty later. 'I
suppose you just stood there and took it?'

'I did not,' Monty said. 'I gave them a piece of my mind.'

'Tipped your forelock and said "Sorry," if I know you,' Mary said.
'They want you on the cheap. I expect they've made you think
they're doing you a favour. Did they pay you?'

'Monday,' Monty said.

'Eight or nine o'clock every night this week, and you have to wait
until Monday?'

Monty spent the following week installing the window frames.

'They make a difference,' he said to Henderson, who pretended unsuccessfully to show an interest.

'It wasn't easy,' Monty went on. 'I hope you don't think that the man I brought in to lend a hand was a matter of handouts to my pals. I needed him for the upstairs windows. How's your son, Mr Henderson?'

'They're taking the bandages off in a few days.' Henderson sighed. 'Hospitals.'

Monty said, 'I can well understand how you haven't much heart for the work that's on hand here.'

'I feel bad about putting a boy through an operation like that,' Henderson said. 'All that hope, for nothing.'

'Still, you did it for the best,' Monty said. 'Well, once I've got these frames painted, I think the roof's next.'

'You'll have to ask my wife,' Henderson said. 'She's got it all worked out.'

'You might try putting your hand to the garden,' Monty said. It sounded like homely, rural advice. 'It could help take your mind off things.' Henderson's look made Monty feel that either he had said the wrong thing or Henderson's troubles were inconsolable.

Before he went home that evening Monty walked over the front garden, searching for an impression of what it must have been like under a conscientious owner. Weeds and wildness blended into the woodland at the garden's edge. Posts of a rotten fence were swamped by billows of runaway roses. An invasive bramblebrake, its briars and tendrils freshly green, crept towards unpruned shrubs. Daffodils and narcissi survived and bloomed here and there in the rampant neglect.

'You've a big job ahead of you here,' Monty said to Mrs Henderson, who had come out to him from the house. 'Have you any plans for it?'

'First things first,' she said. She looked around her with loathing. She picked up a forgotten rusted trowel from where it lay embedded in the grass and threw it into the brambles. 'Ugh,' she said.

While Monty painted the window frames at the back of the house, Mrs Henderson painted those on the ground floor at the front. He was disappointed; he had hoped for her conversation. He went round to see how she was doing.

She wore a head scarf. Her hands were spotted with paint and a small smear marked her face.

'Oh dear,' Monty said, noticing that her green sweater had recently touched wet white paint somewhere. 'There's the spot,' he said, pointing to the sill, where wrinkled paint was furred with strands of wool. 'No, don't touch it. Wait until the frame dries, then sand it down lightly and then repaint it. Apart from that, you're doing fine.'

After a moment, he went on. 'I saw your boy reading a book in Braille in there. That's wonderful. He showed me a bit about how it works. God forbid I should go blind, but if I did I ask myself if I could master that.'

'Shouldn't you be working?' she asked.

'Tea break,' he said. 'Mind you, I expect no tea right now, but it's time.'

'Am I taking the bread out of your mouth by doing this?' she asked.

'Would it make any difference if I said you were?'

'Robin's all right by himself, you know,' Mrs Henderson said. 'He likes reading. He manages better than you think. Manages us, too.'

When the windows were finished, Monty worked on the roof. He cut out and replaced rotted timbers, renewed slates, rebuilt the chimney stacks. He was hanging new gutters one afternoon when a car drew up at the back of Orr Mount and a woman got out. The mossed and weedy gravel was not to her liking; she seemed to set her feet down carefully as she walked round to the other side of the car. The passenger, a girl Robin's age, had already stepped out and stood waiting. She took the woman's arm, and they crossed the runnelled surface together, the woman warning the girl when they approached tufts of long grass near the back door of Orr Mount. The woman looked up, and Monty waved to her. She smiled halfheartedly. Monty suspected he had been too familiar.

Not long after they had gone inside, Monty heard a piano being played. The music went on for over an hour. The tunes were familiar, yet somehow the piano sound seemed unusual.

'It never crossed my mind that it was the two of them playing at once,' Monty said to Mrs Henderson when the guests had left and he went in for his tea. 'At first I thought it might be the wireless.'

'They're not prodigies, you know,' she replied. 'A lot of blind children learn to play the piano.'

'Well, I think it's marvellous. It had a nice swing to it.'

Mrs Henderson did not share his enthusiasm. 'Four hands thundering away at a pop song isn't my idea of music,' she said. 'They're taught to play at school – that was one of the reasons we wanted Robin to go there. I know he plays Mozart and Chopin for his teacher, because I've heard him. But at home all he wants to play is these awful songs he picks up from the radio. Are you musical?'

'No, but I can dance,' Monty said. 'To play music for dancing is a wonderful thing to be able to do. It's like being able to make people laugh, if you know what I mean.'

'Dancing's changed a lot since my day,' she said.

'I'm fifteen years out of date,' Monty said. 'So, thank God, is everyone else in Dryfask – at least of my generation. We have dances at the community hall once a month. You should ask Mr Henderson to take you. You'd enjoy it – everyone's very friendly.'

'I don't think so,' said Mrs Henderson. 'When you're finished outside, I want you to start on the fireplaces.'

'What about the rewiring?'

'No,' she said. 'The fireplaces.'

A look at each room challenged him with how much work he still had to get through. Cardboard boxes stood on the floors among the dust-sheeted furniture in the front rooms, where Mrs Henderson had already begun stripping wallpaper. Monty watched Robin help her by pulling at a loose flap. The boy looked up with his sightless eyes as he tugged at the layered wallpaper, which peeled vertically and then rose in a drizzle of old plaster.

At home, Monty told his wife, 'She watches me make good the stone and brickwork in those fireplaces as if she's dying to have a go at that, too! It wouldn't surprise me if she could do it. Talk about organized, Mary! She's got a whole list of what needs doing, at least six pages long, and she's very firm about how she wants it done.'

'And that sticks in your craw,' Mary said. 'You who like to be your own boss.'

'I don't understand it. Those old marble mantelpieces were lovely, but she's had me rip them out. "Careful," she says. "I've sold them to an antique dealer." Old jobs out, and what comes in instead? Older ones! But very nice, Mary. Beautiful old wooden fireplaces, stripped down to the timber, and she says she'll polish them herself. I'll say this for Mrs Henderson. The woman's got taste.'

'She can afford it,' Mary said.

'I dare say,' Monty said. 'Henderson's a civil servant, but he must be pretty high up. Still, if they were that rich, they wouldn't have come down the market and asked Monty Gault to work for them.'

Henderson came home one late afternoon while Robin and the young girl, Gillian, were playing a tune Monty had asked them for. He found Monty humming along as he screwed in a new wall socket.

'Do you think she's asking for too many outlets?' Henderson said.

'If there's one thing I've learned,' Monty said, 'it's to do what your wife tells me. She's a very practical woman, and she's nearly always right.' He consulted his diagram. 'Now, if I've got this wrong there'll be an almighty bang that'll blow the fuse box off the wall and through the roof.'

Monty's exaggeration drew Henderson to glance at the diagram, but he pulled back in incomprehension. He looked uneasily at a rugged channel gouged up the wall to lead the wires to the floor above. It looked like a ghastly, irreparable error.

'Personally,' Henderson said, 'I felt we should've got a proper electrician to do this.'

Monty frowned at him. 'I thought those days were over,' he said curtly but confidently, making his remark sound one of sorrow rather than anger.

'As long as you're sure,' Henderson said.

Monty lay down to winkle a wire under the floorboards. 'I know a man who'd do that garden for you,' he said. From his prone position, he saw Henderson's leg tremble and his heel beat on the floor at twice the tempo of the tune from the piano. Monty got up and roughly began prising a floorboard loose with a crowbar. Nails sprang free, and the board split.

'Rotten timbers,' he said. 'They were ready for the bonfire anyway. This man I know could go through that jungle in no time. Shall I ask him?'

'No,' Henderson said. 'The garden's my responsibility. I'll get round to it.'

'Suit yourself,' Monty said. 'It was just an idea.'

'I wish they'd play something else,' Henderson said. 'Four hands on a piano just rams home the mistakes. It gets on my nerves.'

'I like it,' Monty said. 'They're playing it for me. Your boy's as bright as a button, and he and Gillian make a good team.'

'They're very close,' Henderson said impulsively. 'We find it worrying. Gillian's his only friend, you see. And she's as blind as he is.'

Puzzled, Monty put his weight on the crowbar, and another floorboard creaked upward with a *ping* of nails and the destructive noise of wood tearing. 'But the two of them get on fine,' he said.

'Of course, we can't really discourage them,' Henderson said. 'It's just a bit upsetting that they're so inseparable. The Hepburns feel the same about Gillian. When you're bringing up a child who's blind, you're thinking about the future all the time. It's not easy for a boy like Robin to make friends with sighted children.'

Rich summer growth made more conspicuous than ever the tumbling, nettled, indiscriminate verdure of the garden at Orr Mount. Monty was dismayed. In Dryfask, unkempt gardens and shabby houses were taken as signs of the demoralization of their owners – symptoms of what was known locally as 'falling out with yourself'. Two months of mild evenings had passed, he reflected, in which Henderson could have made a start against the years of neglect. Nor had he laid a hand on the house.

'Paint-stripping coming on well, I see,' Monty said to Henderson, in the sly hope of shaming him. 'Slowly but surely. It's a heartbreaking job your wife's taken on there.' Days and days of Mrs Henderson's fastidious work with a scraping knife and a noxious-smelling chemical had turned out to be in vain, for the bottom inch of the skirting-boards on the ground floor was revealed to be damp and rotten under the layers of paint and varnish. It was like watching an archaeologist.

'But we're getting there,' Henderson said.

'There's light at the end of the tunnel.'

'As they say, it's very often the lamp on an oncoming train,' Monty said.

Henderson's worried uselessness bothered Monty. It was bred into Monty's bones that a man should neither be so lazy nor feel himself so superior as to shy away from turning a hand on his own property. Still, he thought,

It is the business of the wealthy man
To give employment to the artisan.

Work was getting harder to find. The longer the Orr Mount renovations lasted, the better it was for him. He hoped, too, that his performance in these substantial repairs might lead Henderson to offer him the lighter job of painting and decorating.

But when Monty saw Mrs Henderson tackle the tousled and thorny wilderness around Orr Mount he felt guilty at hoping for more work through Henderson's laziness or ineptitude. Mrs Henderson stooped down and snipped savagely at the rugged grass with a pair of garden shears. Monty turned away from the window with contempt for her husband's handlessness. The click of the shears slowed and then jammed altogether on a resistant divot. He could imagine the strain in the woman's arms, the impossible task of driving through those matted tufts with mere heavy-duty shears. What was called for was a strong man with a scythe, or something mechanical. Better still, the lumpy, repulsive meadow that the lawn had become ought to be dug up and re-turfed.

Monty continued with his plastering, expecting at any moment to witness Mrs Henderson give up in despair. But each time he looked out of the window she was shearing as vigorously as ever, and getting nowhere. He watched as her elbows shot up at each side with the action of her gigantic scissoring. Her arched back rose and fell with the effort.

After almost an hour, Monty could bear it no longer, and he went out to her. 'Honest, Mrs Henderson, if you want to do that, you should get the right tools for the job.' Smeared with wet grass and mud, the blades of her shears ripped viciously at a heavy tuft. 'You'll be at it this time next year,' he said, trying to make a joke of it. 'You'd as well gnaw at it with your teeth as pluck and pull with that. You'll never do it.'

She turned round and looked up at him. Her face was flushed with effort, and the strain of her labour, and her thoughts had made her face hard-favoured and bitter. Her cheeks ran with tears. She stood up breathlessly, wiped her face on her sleeve, and threw the shears to the ground.

'Many's the man who'd look at that mess and run a mile before he'd work a spade on it,' Monty said. 'Mrs Henderson, there's a pal of mine who'd transform it in a week. It'd save you both a lot of trouble.' His tone suggested he understood that the garden controversy expressed some profound matrimonial obstacle between the Hendersons. 'Would you like me to ask him to come by?'

'No, I would *not!*' she said angrily. 'How dare you interfere? I know who'll do this garden, and it won't be your friend.'

It was clear that Mrs Henderson's anger and her tears were not those of weakness or self-pity but of determination. Embarrassed and apologetic, Monty knew better than try to console her. When she walked away, he left it at that and went back to work.

Nor did he mention Mrs Henderson's tearful and violent gardening to Mary. Still, he couldn't help complaining to her about Henderson. 'He's spending money hand over fist on the house, I'm working miracles inside, and outdoors it's like an Amazonian nature reserve. God knows what wild beasts are roaming through that undergrowth.'

'I don't see why they don't get a man to do the garden,' Mary said.

'Actually,' Monty said, 'if I got the painting and decorating I wouldn't mind doing the garden myself. It'd finish the work nicely. I'd get a real kick out of that.'

'I don't care what you do,' Mary said, 'so long as it means steady money. I'm getting used to being able to pay the bills.'

'I'd like your advice,' Henderson said to Monty a few weeks later. The contracted work was nearly done. 'I want the kitchen floor laid with quarry tiles, can you recommend a reliable tiler?'

'How about me?'

'Can you? Surely you haven't had much experience of tiling?'

'Have I let you down yet?'

'To tell you the truth,' Henderson said, 'I'm looking for someone to do the decorating.' It sounded close to the offer Monty had hoped for, but he waited to be asked directly. 'I told Mrs Henderson I wasn't sure if it was quite your line of country.'

'Are you asking me?' Monty said.

'It's too much for us to manage on our own, what with me at work . . .' Henderson said lamely.

'I can do it,' Monty said.

Mrs Henderson's excitement and satisfaction at the progress made on her house, and the faint sound of the piano downstairs when Robin was allowed to play, made Orr Mount a happier house than Monty had known it. It was as if the incident in the garden had never happened, that animal clack of shears and furious tearing of grass. There was no forgetting it, though, or the fact of the garden, with its vegetation as energetic as ever. Very soon, Monty thought, the Hendersons would be sleeping in a bedroom that was in mint condition. But when they got up in the morning and drew the curtains, the lively, wicked overgrowth – all that strangled greenery, dripping with dew – would stare at them in challenge.

Henderson, too, was in a better frame of mind. He came home early one day. 'I collected the curtains,' he said proudly.

Monty helped him unload, and Mrs Henderson set off towards the back door with her arms laden with fabric. 'Where did you put the rods?' he asked Henderson.

'I couldn't get them into the car,' Henderson said, apparently unaware of the importance of his omission. 'They're long things.'

'Your wife'll be furious! She's dying to get these up. The rods are plastic – you could've bent them.'

'Some of them are wooden poles,' Henderson said stubbornly.

'We could've done without the poles, for the moment – they're for the sitting room. But we need the rods *now*.' Monty was openly exasperated. 'Look, I'll go and get them. Where's the receipt?'

Henderson fished a piece of paper from his wallet in silence. He was clearly offended at Monty's tone as he went on. 'You've got a roof rack there, Mr Henderson. You could've tied the rods on to that if you didn't want to bend them. You don't think!' Monty got into his van, leaving Henderson expostulating quietly.

When Monty got back with the rods an hour later, Mrs Henderson was cooking dinner.

'I know it's late,' she said, 'but do you think you could put these up in the bedroom?' It was a cold and formal request, without a hint of thanks in her voice.

'Never mind,' he said to himself as he sat on the window ledge upstairs, forcing the hooks through slots in the curtain tape. 'So long as we keep the peace.'

It was already dark when he got into his van. He looked up and saw Mrs Henderson pulling the curtains shut, then opening and closing them again. She did this several times. It was now a better window than the one at which he had first seen her, he reflected.

Sitting down to his own dinner, Monty told Mary, 'I know I'm far from perfect – '

'You can say that again. What time do you call this to come home, without so much as giving me a ring to warn me?'

' – but you wouldn't last ten minutes with that man Henderson. Now, there's an imperfect man for you,' Monty said.

'At least,' Mary said, 'he's got money, and he gets home at a decent hour.'

'The story of my life,' Monty said. 'I oblige folk by staying a bit later to get a job finished, and when I get back here I'm nagged for it. Mary, I'm a handyman. It's my business to be obliging. Will you never understand that?'

When it came the turn of the sitting room at Orr Mount, Mrs Henderson helped Monty move the furniture into the hall – everything except the piano. 'No, it's too heavy to move,' she said. 'It would block the hall. Leave it in the middle and cover it with a tarpaulin. Frankly,' she said, 'I'd as soon see the back of it.'

Monty glanced at her in surprise, but she was looking elsewhere. 'It takes up a lot of room in this house, one way and another,' she said.

It was near the end of the school holidays. Robin sat in his room upstairs or at the kitchen table, where he read, his fingers feeling over the sheets of text, his head turned thoughtfully to one side.

The boy missed playing his piano. His mother was in town ordering furniture, and he came into the sitting room where Monty stood on a stepladder, painting the cornices in deep concentration. Robin reached under the tarpaulin and played a loud chord.

'You gave me a fright, Robin!' Monty cried.

'Will you be finished in this room soon?' the boy asked.

'Give it three or four days,' Monty said. 'I'll be as quick as I can. I miss the sound of your music. But your mother told you to stay in the kitchen. If she catches you in here, there'll be trouble.'

Robin ran his fingers over the keyboard. 'Do you know where the wireless is?' he asked.

'Isn't it in the kitchen?'

'I can't find it,' the boy said.

'Come and I'll help you look for it.' Monty climbed down and put his hand on Robin's shoulder, meaning to guide him, but the boy led the way.

The radio was on a shelf too high up for Robin to have reached. Monty wondered why Mrs Henderson had put it up there when she knew that Robin liked to listen to it.

'Where was it?' Robin asked.

'It was on the chest in a corner,' Monty said, hoping to deceive him. 'There were things in front of it.'

'What things?'

'Cornflakes, washing powder,' Monty said, improvising an answer from packets he saw elsewhere in the kitchen.

Robin walked across the kitchen and put his hand on the packet of cornflakes. He lifted the packet and shook it. 'You reached up,' Robin said. 'Was it up there?'

'Are you supposed to be studying?' Monty asked.

'She hid it. She didn't want me to find it,' he said.

'Then if your mother doesn't want you to have the wireless, maybe I shouldn't give it to you. She must have a reason,' Monty said.

'You can say you didn't know I wasn't to have it,' Robin said.

A new bathroom was installed, and Monty's last job was tiling and painting it.

'Unless we've missed something,' he said to Mrs Henderson as he washed, 'I think that's it.'

They walked into the sitting room and she gave him a glass of sherry. 'I won't sit down in these overalls,' Monty said, conscious also of his working shoes on the Persian rug. He put his glass down and stepped off the carpet, kneeling to run his hand over the mellow glow he had succeeded in bringing out on the old parquet floor. 'I knew this floor had life left in it,' he said. 'It's come up a treat. It must have been hidden under those old carpets and underlays for years, just waiting for someone like you, Mrs Henderson – an appreciative owner who'll take good care of it.'

'There are one or two lumpy bits,' Mrs Henderson said. 'Otherwise I'm very pleased with it.'

Pictures now hung on the sitting-room walls. Rugs and chintzes brought a bright, complacent richness to the large room. There were books in the bookcases, and ornaments had come forth from the tea chests and boxes that had once littered the unkempt interior.

'This room has class,' Monty said. 'I like it. It has taste.' He waved his arm in a survey of the sitting room. 'I've done the heavy work, but I can see now what you had in mind all along. I must say, though, that it's a pity, a great pity, about the garden.' He smiled cautiously. 'I don't want to interfere, Mrs Henderson, but I've a living to earn. I'm making you an offer.'

Robin ran into the room, leading Gillian by the hand. 'My mother will be back for me at five. Is it all right?' Gillian said.

Eagerly, Robin asked, 'May we please play the piano for a bit?'

'No, you may not,' Mrs Henderson said. 'I'm speaking to Mr Gault.'

'Don't stop them on my account,' Monty said.

'Please, Mummy!' Robin said, put out by the delay.

'Go ahead then!' Mrs Henderson said angrily. She turned back to Monty. 'You *are* interfering,' she told him quietly. 'I'm sure you mean well, but the garden's not for you to do. No longer than fifteen minutes!' she shouted crossly to Robin, who made no acknowledgement. 'Did you hear me? Robin! Fifteen minutes and no more!'

'I'm sorry,' Monty said. 'I knew it rankled, but I thought maybe I'd be helping you out. And helping me out, too,' he added. 'I don't deny it.'

'I'll send my husband over with the money he owes you,' she said.

'It's not for me to talk about what's wrong here,' he said. 'But you're not trying, Mrs Henderson, and neither's he. You're making a big mistake. I wish you all joy of your house. Take care of it. There's twenty years of my hard-earned experience in the work I've put into it. And it would've pleased *me* to see it finished.'

Four young hands ventured on the first bars of a tune. As Monty left the house, he heard Mrs Henderson shout, 'Will you shut up that racket!'

Driving off, Monty saw Henderson's car approaching his own van on the narrow lane that led to the Dryfask road. He stopped in the middle of the lane, so that Henderson had to stop, too. He got out of the van and walked to Henderson's lowered window.

'You've the swankiest house in Dryfask, and the nastiest garden I ever saw. That won't be gardening; it'll be pioneering. You've got pixies in your orchard!' he shouted, exasperated, as Henderson stared at him incredulously. 'Do yourself a favour, Henderson. Get it done, and fast! Get it done before it's too late!' He started to return to his van but stopped and went back to Henderson. 'I'm talking about your garden. Can you wield a scythe? You'll have to learn!'

Henderson leaned on his horn. It was an angry, demented noise that howled over the countryside. Once back in his van, Monty Gault retaliated, and pressed on his. Their vehicles were almost nose to nose before Monty swerved and pulled up beside Henderson. 'If you need me,' he shouted, 'you know where to find me!'

Needlework

Mrs Esmée Boyd-Porteous had been sending donations for over a decade to the orphanage run by the Catholic convent of St Justina's. When she finally managed to visit the convent, during one of her rare shopping trips to Glasgow, she asked if there was anything more she could do. She was told that the benefactors of St Justina's sometimes took a girl for the summer.

'Oh, but I'm so extremely sorry!' she cried. 'That never crossed my mind. Yes, of course!'

'You should have brought the Morris,' Mrs Boyd-Porteous said now to her husband as they waited in the car outside the station at Dumfries. Her impatience had led them to be early. 'The Bentley's much too ostentatious. This enormous car will do nothing but harm to her state of mind.'

'I doubt it,' her husband said. 'A ride in a Bentley ought to be a treat for any girl.'

"She isn't coming to us to be initiated into your crass notion of "treats",' she said.

'I wish you'd calm down, Esmée. Don't get so excited.'

'Is it to be held against me,' she said, 'if I'm looking forward to young company at Mickleyaird?'

A protective feeling towards his wife, and a high regard for his peace and quiet now that he was living in semi-retirement, prevented Ronald Boyd-Porteous from taking his grumbling too far. The pair often had words together that brought them to the brink of bitterness, but he halted any conversation with his wife in which dissent threatened to expose what he suspected was his failure as a husband. More and more, he felt it was his selfishness that had stunted their marriage. 'Well,' he said, with a dry realism that Mrs Boyd-Porteous did not appreciate, 'I imagine she's hoping for a spectacular boost to her standard of living. That's what I'd be hoping for.'

'Your answer to everything is always money.'

It was a familiar criticism. 'Now, now, Esmée, that's enough of that,' he said lightly. He tapped the clock on the luxurious dashboard. 'The train might be a few minutes early,' he said, and reached for the car door.

At one time Ronald Boyd-Porteous had been among the youngest professors of civil engineering in the country. Profitable consultancies had enticed him from the academic life and into business. It was during one of his many absences from home that Mrs Boyd-Porteous announced, in a transatlantic telephone call, that she had become a Catholic. Whatever had hitherto crossed his mind as a possible explanation for his wife's polite and considerate listlessness, it was not a crisis of faith that was to build up to a wholehearted religious conversion. It took him a year to get over seeing it as more than an eccentricity. On subsequent trips away from home, he pictured his wife sitting at her desk writing letters of support to deserving institutions dedicated to the relief of misfortune, each with an enclosed cheque. He smiled with affection at the image, but it troubled him, too. He could tell himself that his wife now had plenty to do while he was abroad and preoccupied with the design and construction of projects costing millions, or absorbed in tiresome negotiations with governments and international agencies. Still, something was missing. He knew what it was but decided that the time had long passed to do anything about it. Instead of bringing up children of their own, his wife was a distant, anonymous supporter of young victims of famine, war and loss.

'I hope you won't overdo it,' he told her when they reached the station platform.

'Overdo what?'

The train pulled in from the north and passengers began to get off. People were being met by friends or relatives. It was a small crowd, but brisk and intent.

'I think that might be our Miss O'Hagen,' Mr Boyd-Porteous said, drawing his wife's attention to a girl of seventeen. She carried a coat over one arm and a suitcase in her other hand.

Mrs Boyd-Porteous waved and caught the girl's eye as if it were she who had discovered her among the flow of approaching passengers. 'Olive! My goodness, the train looks so *busy*! Did you have a good journey?'

The girl put down her poor luggage and shook Mrs Boyd-Porteous's hand. She was tall; her hair was dark; her eyes were lively with curiosity, and flickered with a temporary shyness. Her straight-

forward good looks were poorly set off by the old-fashioned floral
print of the dress she wore. She could have been taken for a daughter
from the sort of farm or village where people seldom travel beyond
the nearest small town – or, Mr Boyd-Porteous thought, for a girl
brought up in an orphanage.

'I had to sit among the smokers,' Olive O'Hagen said cheerfully, as
if this inconvenience had been interesting, if deplorable.

'Ronald,' Mrs Boyd-Porteous said, looking about distractedly, but
her husband was already walking towards the ticket barrier with
Olive's suitcase.

'I don't suppose you've been in a car like this before,' Mr Boyd-
Porteous said to Olive as they drove off. He half turned towards her
in the back seat, his voice rising pleasantly. 'It's my pride and joy. I'm
very fond of cars. Ever since I was your age and old enough to learn
how to drive. You could say it's one of my hobbies.'

'Ronald, please.' Mrs Boyd-Porteous often seemed to detect a note
of condescension that he could swear was not there. 'I hardly
imagine that Olive's very interested in cars.'

'Oh, but I like cars,' Olive said. 'My mother used to say I should've
been a boy.'

'Do you have any brothers or sisters?' Mrs Boyd-Porteous asked.

'No, just me. I was six when she died,' the girl said.

'I do so much look forward to getting to know you, my dear,' Mrs
Boyd-Porteous said, with that open and enthusiastic sincerity which
her husband found both laudable and irritating. 'And I do understand how you must be wondering what *we* are like. So if we seem to
be doing the wrong thing, then you must tell us. We're not used
to children at Mickleyaird. Oh, but you're not a child, are you? No, of
course not! St Justina's told us hardly anything about you. Your
name, your age, and the time of the train from Glasgow Central, and
that's about it. There's so much to do here. So much to see and do,
my dear. I intend that you should have a wonderful time.'

' "Mickleyaird" means "the big place". Is that right?' Olive said.

'Fortunately for us, the house is a bit smaller than its name
implies,' Mr Boyd-Porteous said, with a laugh that his wife found
disagreeable.

'I've been hardly anywhere. It was really exciting, being on a train,
and going somewhere,' Olive said. Her voice lilted on the thrill of

her day. 'I've been trying to imagine what your house is like, but I'm sure it's going to be a surprise.'

Mrs Boyd-Porteous was relieved at Olive's good-mannered confidence, and impressed: the girl seemed unsubdued by an encounter with a well-to-do couple in their fifties, to whom she was beholden even if, as yet, she had no grounds for gratitude.

Second thoughts about the wisdom of taking a girl from St Justina's had been introduced to Mrs Boyd-Porteous's mind only a few days before. Mrs Buchanan, of Forgallan House, was a co-religionist whom Mrs Boyd-Porteous seldom saw, but the two women had talked at a fund-raising sale for the benefit of a medical mission in Uganda. At one time, Mrs Buchanan told her, she herself had taken in girls from St Justina's. 'One felt tempted to use the place as a sort of employment agency – staff on approval, so to speak. I prefer to think that my motives were more disinterested. That, I suspect, was my big mistake.' A girl had tried to run off with a selection of the more portable treasures of Forgallan House. 'Honestly, it was so obvious – she might as well have written "swag" on her disgusting little suitcase.' Another, given the chance, would have run off with Mr Buchanan, she said. It crossed Mrs Boyd-Porteous's mind that the fault probably lay with Mrs Buchanan's husband, a well-known flirt, since deceased. 'Decency forbids me to go into what one of them did with my gardener's assistant. There was no end of a fuss. One has heard of holiday romances, which are all very well, but, really, in one's own home! No, Esmée. Surly, ill-mannered and ungrateful little madams. You might find yourself having to cope with an amateur *femme fatale* or a juvenile pilferer. If I were you, I should call it off while there's still time.'

'Well, yes,' Mrs Boyd-Porteous thought, as her husband turned into the long drive that led to Mickleyaird. 'Girls might behave like that in *your* house, but it is unlikely to happen in *mine*.' She felt her benevolent eagerness rise again, although she was less than fully confident of the weeks that lay ahead of her.

Gertrude Naismith had been the housekeeper at Mickleyaird for many years. She was a Presbyterian, and she resented her employer's conversion to what she called 'the Church of Rome'.

'You should be ashamed of yourself,' she had said to Mr Boyd-Porteous on several occasions. 'Your wife keeps bringing her Papist junk into this house, and what's worse is that I'm the one who has to dust her wee statues and wipe the glass on her holy pictures. I should get a rise in wages for having to wipe dirt off craven images,' she complained.

'Graven, with a "g", isn't it?' he answered mildly.

' "Graven", "craven", who cares how it's spelt? It's me who has to clean them!'

Exchanges of that kind were commonplace between Mr Boyd-Porteous and Mrs Naismith. 'And now it's to be convent girls, eh? What do you say to that? She's gone too far this time. I'm sure you must think so yourself.'

'As you very well know, Gertrude, I'm an agnostic. I haven't been to church willingly in years. We've had priests in the house often enough, and although you whinge at the prospect, you're perfectly civil to them when it comes to serving them lunch or tea or whatever. I think you're the sort of person who'd kowtow to *any* man of the cloth. Either that or you're a hypocrite.'

'A hypocrite? Me? Listen to who's talking! Who's the moneybags who never goes to the kirk but who aye coughs up when its roof needs mending, or last year when woodworm got at the pews?' Mrs Naismith said, with self-righteous triumph.

'You can hang your things in the wardrobe,' the housekeeper told Olive as she showed her around her bedroom. 'It's yours as long as you're here. And there's that chest of drawers and the dressing table. You've your own bathroom.' She opened the door to it.

'My own bathroom!'

'I don't suppose I have to teach you how to run a tap?'

Olive smiled at what she took to be a joke. 'Do you live here, too, Mrs Naismith?'

'Well, I don't live on the moon. Most days I'm here by eight-thirty, and I'm away at the back of six – later if they've got visitors. I live down there by the main road.'

The housekeeper had expected someone less winning, or a girl hardened by orphan's sorrow and institutional conformity. Had there been a mean, urban toughness to Olive's manner, Mrs Naismith would not have been surprised. Instead, Olive seemed to behave with a natural candour before the opulence and loveliness of Mickleyaird.

'It's beautiful,' the girl said, feeling the bedspread but giving no impression that it was too good for her. The comfort and prettiness of the room clearly animated the girl, but Mrs Naismith had to admit there was nothing vulgar in the way she appreciated its spaciousness, the elegance of its furnishings, or the wide view of gardens and woodland from the bedroom window.

'Mrs Boyd-Porteous is a kind woman,' Mrs Naismith said sternly. 'Too kind for her own good, if you ask me.' The housekeeper felt obliged to deliver her warning, even if Olive's manner had already suggested that it might be unnecessary. 'To a stranger, she's bound to look like an easy touch – a bit too generous, you might say. And with her having no children of her own, a person might just get it into her mind to take advantage. If that's your type, Miss, then I advise you to forget it.'

Olive's expression darkened with a look that Mrs Naismith decided was one of genuine hurt.

'Where's our church?' Olive asked.

'*Yours* is in Drumotter, six miles down the road. You won't find many Catholics here in Ferlie.' It was a statement of fact, but Mrs Naismith said it with pride. 'Don't worry. Mrs Boyd-Porteous is keen on her early Mass. We might even have the holy visitors. We've had a monsignor before now, not to mention bishops.' She pronounced the first title with flagrant inaccuracy, and hissed mild loathing on the second.

'I'm sorry. I took it for granted that you'd be a Catholic,' the girl said, embarrassed by Mrs Naismith's religious aggression.

'It's no skin off my nose, because the man of the house isn't a Catholic, either. By your standards, he's even worse than I am. Mr Boyd-Porteous is a heathen.'

'I suppose you're Church of Scotland, then?'

'And so was Mrs Boyd-Porteous before she changed her mind.'

'I see,' Olive said.

'I wish *I* did,' Mrs Naismith said.

Olive made a favourable impression during her first days at Mickleyaird. Mr Boyd-Porteous was entertained by the interest she took in his garden.

'What are these?' Olive asked him.

'Buddleia,' he said.

'And this one?'

'Veronica.'

'Is it named after St Veronica?' the girl asked.

'I've no idea.'

'It was St Veronica who gave Christ her handkerchief to wipe his brow when he was carrying the cross to Calvary.'

'Now, I didn't know that. St Veronica and her handkerchief? Somehow I never thought of them blowing their noses in the first century AD, but I suppose they must have done.'

'So many bees and butterflies!' Olive said eagerly.

'Buddleia for butterflies, Veronica for bees,' Mr Boyd-Porteous said.

To the mistrustful Mrs Naismith, Olive O'Hagen was a wonder: a convent girl with table manners! An orphan who did not bolt her food, let alone ask for more! Mrs Naismith's mythology was stood on its head.

'She's not at all what you expected, is she?' Mrs Boyd-Porteous teased the housekeeper with a sly but detectable moral swank.

'Don't come it,' Mrs Naismith retorted, with her customary disregard for the conventions of talk between an employee and the lady of the house. 'She's nothing like what you expected either. You went into a twist, like a cat caught in the rain, when you heard Mrs Buchanan's stories about the girls from St Justina's.'

'I am more interested in hearing what *you* expected,' Mrs Boyd-Porteous said.

'Thank God, but my experience of nunneries is non-existent. So how would I know what to expect? I'll say this, though. She cleans the bath after she's used it, and she folds her towels as neat as you like and puts them back on the rail. Laundry in the laundry box, and no clothes folded over the backs of chairs. Not that I'm one hundred per cent convinced that our Miss O'Hagen isn't a little actress,' Mrs Naismith said.

'You do not frighten me in the slightest,' Mrs Boyd-Porteous said. 'I'm sure you overheard her at lunch yesterday when Father Struan was here. She didn't *try* to sound particularly religious, and yet it was quite clear to anyone with eyes and ears that she is. What I hope you noticed, Gertrude, is that Olive was not in the least bit awkward or false.'

'I hope that place isn't training her for the nunhood, if that's the word,' Mrs Naismith said.

'Good gracious, no! Or – I don't think so,' Mrs Boyd-Porteous said, suddenly unsure.

'Well, there isn't a drop of make-up in her room,' Mrs Naismith said. 'Not so much as a wee bottle of cologne. The soap she brought with her isn't scented, and she still hasn't used that nice French soap you asked me to set out for her. And she's already in a convent, Mrs B.-P., even if it's an orphanage as well.'

'I hardly imagine that they'd *encourage* the use of cosmetics at St Justina's,' Mrs Boyd-Porteous said. 'Apart from anything else, there is the expense to consider.'

'She's quite pale,' Mrs Naismith said.

'Not, I think, as pale as she was when she arrived.'

'Peely-wally,' the housekeeper said.

'Gertrude. Unless a girl's cheeks were positively crimson, you'd call her peely-wally, as you put it. Anyhow, if that's your worst complaint, I'm glad. I do wish you'd give Olive time to settle in and get used to us. All of us.'

Although she had settled into Mickleyaird more smoothly than either the Boyd-Porteouses or Mrs Naismith anticipated, Olive greeted each new experience with an eagerness of heart that her hostess found disquieting as well as satisfying. The girl's exhilaration over gathering flowers and helping arrange them in vases made clear how thoroughly she had been deprived of pleasures that Mrs Boyd-Porteous had always taken for granted. She was cheered by Olive's excited gratitude and tender curiosity, but it led her to worry whether she had done the right thing in introducing Olive to a style of life the girl had never known before and might never know again. Donating money to distant worthy causes was one thing, but Olive created a special predicament: the *object* of Mrs Boyd-Porteous's charity was in the house. It seemed cruel to offer Olive a taste of affluence and then withdraw it.

Several times as they drove one day to visit Mrs Buchanan at Forgallan House, Olive begged Mrs Boyd-Porteous to stop the car so that she could get out to look at a ruin, or a view, or lean over the parapet of a bridge and stare into the clear water.

Forgallan House was older and grander than Mickleyaird. Its intrinsic interest, together with the declining fortunes of its owner, determined that the house should be open to the public – admission

£1.50 – throughout the summer months. Mrs Boyd-Porteous was apprehensive for Olive's comfort there.

'Forgallan House is somewhat *massive*,' she said. 'I've never been sure if it's Bunny Buchanan's fault or mine, or just the grandeur of the place, but I've never felt at home in Forgallan. It is not a welcoming sort of house, Olive. Please, be your usual delightful self, and we shall sail through this frightening experience. Bunny was terribly insistent that we should come, you know, and Forgallan *does* have the most intriguing little private chapel.'

They passed the notices that advertised the public visiting hours and the price of admission. 'Mrs Boyd-Porteous to visit Mrs Buchanan,' she told the caretaker, who manned a green shed where he took money, issued tickets, raised a barrier, and directed drivers to the car park. A gate marked 'PRIVATE' was opened to them. The attendant raised his cap.

'Don't feel privileged,' Mrs Boyd-Porteous told Olive. 'This is the former servants' entrance. The family have to use it when the house is open to the tourists.' As they left the car, she took a deep breath and said, 'Bunny Buchanan is such a bitter person that she brings out the good in one. Isn't that a terrible thing to say? Well, I've said it. I dare say we shall both leave feeling like saints.'

They were shown into a small, cramped sitting room that Mrs Buchanan used when the rest of the house was being trodden through by the paying public, of whom the lady had a low opinion.

'I can't think why,' she said, 'but they revel in viewing the rooms in which they suppose one actually *lives*. I've heard comments on the state of the upholstery, or the curtains, or that such and such a painting is not by who it *is* by. Some people, too, seem too take an extraordinary keen interest in what seems to be one's bedside reading. I say "seems", Esmée, because I take care to lay out rather serious historical or theological tomes, just to mislead them.' The mischievous humour of these remarks failed to force a way through Mrs Buchanan's lofty manner. 'Well, and how is this young lady's visit progressing, Esmée?'

'Oh, splendidly, quite splendidly!' Mrs Boyd-Porteous said.

'I'm having a marvellous time,' Olive said.

'Are you indeed?' Mrs Buchanan said. She had not expected Olive to speak. 'And what do you think of Forgallan?'

'I think it's wonderful, Mrs Buchanan.'

'Most of the house was built a hundred and some years ago, as you may have observed.' Mrs Buchanan's voice implied that she placed little conviction in Olive's grasp of architectural history. 'But the bulk of the west side was formed out of the old Forgallan Castle, the ancient seat of the Wotherspoons.' She turned back to Mrs Boyd-Porteous. 'I see, Esmée, that the standard of dressmaking at St Justina's has not improved.' She nodded towards Olive and the dress she wore.

'Actually, Bunny, that's an old outfit of mine that my Mrs Naismith altered for Olive.'

'Oh? Really?'

'Would you think it too forward of me, Mrs Buchanan, if I asked to see the chapel?' Olive asked.

'It's on the tourist route,' Mrs Buchanan said curtly. 'My great-grandfather – this, you see, is *my* house; it was not my late husband's. I am a Wotherspoon – '

'Do you use it?' Olive broke in, as if unaware.

'Use what?'

'The chapel.'

'Well, yes. My youngest daughter was married in it a few years ago. Do you remember, Esmée?'

'Oh, Olive, it was the most beautiful wedding!'

'Does Father Struan say Mass in your chapel?' Olive asked. 'Oh, Mrs Buchanan, a chapel of your own!'

'Olive is a very religious young lady,' Mrs Boyd-Porteous said with considerable satisfaction.

'And from St Justina's? I am amazed, Esmée. Next I shall expect you to tell me that Miss O'Hagen is preparing to take the veil. Are you, Miss O'Hagen?'

'No, I'm not,' Olive said. Mrs Boyd-Porteous detected a note of annoyance.

'What, if I may ask, do you intend to do? Do you have a career in mind?' Mrs Buchanan arched her brows in exaggerated interest.

'I didn't get a place this year. They said it was because I'm too young – my birthday was only a few weeks ago,' Olive said.

'A summer baby!' Mrs Boyd-Porteous cried. 'Olive, I didn't know!'

'But it's as good as guaranteed for next year. I've a place to study English at the University of Edinburgh.'

'University?' Mrs Buchanan said, in a tone of spontaneous disbelief. Good manners should have kept that under control, thought Mrs Boyd-Porteous, who was herself surprised by Olive's announcement.

'Olive is *extremely* clever,' Mrs Boyd-Porteous said.

'Obviously,' Mrs Buchanan said. 'The girls *I* took from St Justina's certainly didn't go to university. Oh, no! Wherever else they went, it certainly wasn't the University of Edinburgh. I could tell you a thing or two about the girls from St Justina's.'

'Bunny!' Mrs Boyd-Porteous said disapprovingly.

'Well, why not, Esmée? They gave me a great deal of trouble.'

Olive seemed to be included in Mrs Buchanan's dismissal of St Justina's. The girl rose and said stiffly, 'I would like to see the chapel, Mrs Buchanan. I'm sure I could find it if you were to tell me where it is.'

'It's not a particularly attractive chapel,' Mrs Buchanan said, resisting Olive's request. 'It's rather poky, to tell you the truth.'

'Oh, Bunny, no! It's perfectly delightful!' Mrs Boyd-Porteous interjected with gentle indignation.

'Actually, "hideous" is the word that comes most readily to *my* mind,' Mrs Buchanan said. 'Of course, I have never claimed to be a particularly devotional sort of Catholic. Oh, very well. I suppose you must, if you must.' Mrs Buchanan told Olive how to find the chapel. 'You'd better be quick about it,' she shouted after the girl, 'or Esmée and I shall eat all the cakes!'

When Olive was out of earshot, Mrs Buchanan said, 'I suppose she's eating you out of house and home. All of mine did. Eat, eat, eat ... Did I tell you? There was one girl, the same who rather fancied herself as a burglar, and she raided the kitchen, Esmée, in the middle of the night! Cook swore that the detestable glutton had grilled herself fifteen sausages! Fifteen!'

'Olive is very obviously *different*,' Mrs Boyd-Porteous said forcefully. 'And I think you were rude to her.'

'Me? Rude?'

'Yes, Bunny, *rude*. You showed her no consideration whatsoever.'

'And do you *believe* what she said about university?' Mrs Buchanan said with broad scepticism.

The chapel was small and cool. A religious tranquillity glowed in the varnish of its wooden panels and carved seating. Pools of red-and-blue light spilled from stained-glass windows and twitched on the stone floor near the altar. In the pews lay cushions and kneelers stitched over the years by women of the Wotherspoon family. A needlework Annunciation hung in a Gothic-arched frame; it was light and delicate, composed with obvious artistry. Other works by the same hand hung elsewhere on the chapel's walls among memorial plaques and devotional inscriptions.

Olive regained her equanimity in the chapel's calm, and walked about inspecting these fine embroideries and appliqués for some time. She thought them about the most interesting things she had ever seen. After a while, considering that she been away for too long, especially after her risky display of temper, she started to make her way back to the sitting room. Distant voices and the threatening resonance of hard heels on the stone floors added to her sensation that she was a trespasser or an unwanted guest. It was a feeling that she decided she was under no obligation to endure. Her face hardened, and she walked quickly away, not quite knowing where the corridor would lead. She came across a sign that said 'EXIT', and then, a little later, one that said 'TEAROOM'.

The café occupied what had once been a large storeroom on the ground floor. It was almost empty. Olive bought a cup of tea and sat down at a table. She felt exhausted with the effort of being good, well-mannered, and full of delight. She was torn between feeling comfort in Mrs Boyd-Porteous's jolly innocence and contempt for it. Well, if she'd gone too far, with Mrs Buchanan she'd have to find a way to put it right with the Boyd-Porteouses.

In a few moments she found herself the last remaining customer. 'We'll be closing soon, dear,' said the waitress behind the tea counter. Olive was rising to leave, and calculating her next move, when the two women appeared in the doorway. The mistress of Forgallan House set her hands on her hips in the pose of one displeased but unsurprised.

'Olive!' cried Mrs Boyd-Porteous. 'Where've you been? Did you get lost? We've looked everywhere for you!' Her tone was urgent but she seemed neither unhappy nor angry.

'I must see to the guides,' said Mrs Buchanan. 'I'm sorry, Esmée, but I'll say goodbye. I have so much to attend to.'

'I'm sorry,' Olive said to Mrs Boyd-Porteous in the car. 'I'm sorry if I embarrassed you.'

'My dear, how could I blame you? No doubt Bunny Buchanan will tell everyone she knows about your "bad manners", but in my opinion you were magnificent.' She giggled as she craned over the steering wheel before turning on to the main road. 'I rather love you for it. Buying your own tea in the café! Rather than talk to that haughty crone! My dear, I shall cherish it until the day I die. By the way, she doesn't believe that you're going to university. She thought you said so as a lie merely to impress her. Did you go round the entire house?'

'No, I didn't have time.'

'How can Bunny *bear* to run down that chapel?'

'I thought the chapel was lovely. And the needlework,' Olive said, pleased to move on.

'Oh, that needlework!' Mrs Boyd-Porteous enthused. 'By generations of Wotherspoon women, and Bunny Buchanan can't so much as sew on a button. Families! Oh, no, that sort of wonder does not run in families. How like you to have noticed it, Olive! It's so precious to me.'

'It was very beautiful,' Olive said.

'I do a little myself, you know,' Mrs Boyd-Porteous said. 'Embroidery mainly. I confess my deficiencies as a needlewoman, but if I may be so vain, I have mastered Florentine stitch.'

'Those cushions in your sitting room?'

'Oh, yes, they're mine!'

'Would you teach me?' Olive asked. Her tone was hesitant.

In the days that followed, Mrs Boyd-Porteous applied herself to teaching Olive her repertoire of stitches. They sat together on the sitting-room sofa or in an arbour outdoors. They visited a friend of Mrs Boyd Porteous whose skills in all forms of needlework were a byword in excellence. They made sketches from plates in books, and started work on an Annunciation of their own.

'She should be showing Olive more of the countryside,' Ronald Boyd-Porteous complained to Mrs Naismith. 'The girl didn't come here to learn how to sew.'

'Well, she's a good girl, and she's a sight handier with a needle than I am,' the housekeeper said. She smiled, a little sheepish at acknowledging her change of heart.

'Still, it's nice to see,' he conceded. 'They really get on with it.'

'Olive likes it here,' Mrs Naismith said. 'Maybe too much. She'll miss Mickleyaird something terrible.'

'Has she said anything to you?' he asked.

'She hasn't, but I'd say it was a fair guess.'

'That's charity for you. One lot gives, the other receives, and those who receive can be forgiven for feeling a bit jealous of what the givers have got.' He looked questioningly at Mrs Naismith, whose downturned mouth and raised eyebrows registered disapproval. 'I didn't mean it like that, Gertrude. Anyway, how can envy be avoided? It's perfectly natural. All she has to do is compare St Justina's with here. It's inevitable. She's too intelligent not to have felt it already. Surely?' he said.

'For a start, I don't think she *is* jealous,' the housekeeper said. 'I just work here, and I'm not jealous. She likes Mickleyaird. She loves the place. Of course she'll miss it. You can make that easier for the girl,' Mrs Naismith said. 'Make sure you ask her back for next summer.'

Ronald Boyd-Porteous was moved by the sight of his wife and Olive together in the garden or sitting room. At the same time, it made him uneasy over the decisions and indecisions of the past. For all his conscientious hard work, his chairmanship of committees, his international prestige in an important field, there had been an indolence in his life.

'You've become extremely fond of Olive,' he said to his wife during the dressing-gowned fifteen minutes before they went to bed. Outside, a warm August night had been cooled by the briefest of showers.

She turned to him from her dressing table, hairbrush in hand. 'I should think that you are, too, by the looks of things. I can't imagine anyone not being fond of Olive. I always knew that St Justina's was well run, but I had no idea how splendidly they could respond to a girl of her sensitivity. And perhaps we could help.'

'Yes, well, I imagine that she's their pride and joy. She'll have the resources of the Vatican backing her up, I should think.' Mrs Boyd-Porteous frowned with good-humoured impatience at her husband's flippancy. 'All the same, there's nothing to stop us from giving her a hand ourselves. Taking an interest,' he explained. 'Shall we ask her back next summer?'

'I've already taken care of that.' She resumed brushing her hair.

'The art shall not die,' she said, with a wave of her brush. 'We're planning some really quite *ambitious* tapestries.'

'It's very appealing,' he said with difficulty. 'Watching the two of you working away with your needles. Master and pupil. Or mother and daughter.' He felt the phrase linger on the air, the subject never broached. Even as he went on, the words 'mother and daughter' were what he heard. 'It's crossed my mind, over the past couple of weeks. I can't say I've been looking forward to it, Esmée, but I've been expecting you to ask – '

She put her hairbrush down and looked at him in her mirror.

Abruptly, he said, 'I'm going out for a smoke!'

Mr Boyd-Porteous did not stop until he reached the garden. He lit his cigarette. As he stood holding his lighter, he felt how moist and hot his palms were. He looked at the few stars in the cleared sky and groaned at the thought of his emergency. Rushing downstairs in his dressing gown and through the house to the garden was the most dramatic incident in his marriage. It was preposterous – he was an undemonstrative man! – that he should find himself standing on the damp lawn in his dressing gown. The scent of night-aromatic stocks went unnoticed. He could have avoided the truth by keeping to the discreet routines of his marriage; still, he was glad to have come so close to puncturing his restraint. He stamped on the half-smoked cigarette and climbed back upstairs, weary with his own weight.

He paused inside the bedroom door in a state of embarrassed sorrow. 'I know this is as likely to sound as selfish as everything else I seem to say, but I can't bear the thought of making fools of ourselves. Not after all this time. It would look like desperation on our part.'

'What are you talking about?'

'I know what you've been thinking. I can feel it. You want Olive to live here, with us – legally. You've been thinking about how to make official moves in that direction. Haven't you?'

His wife turned to him. 'You must think me extremely vulnerable, and very stupid,' she said, her words measuring sad surprise. 'To imagine that Olive could be my daughter? Olive is seventeen! She's ready to begin a life of her own!' He had trespassed too clumsily for it to be dismissed or forgiven as a simple misunderstanding. 'Is that your idea of starting a family – to adopt an adult?' She spoke with uncharacteristic bitterness. 'Did you honestly believe that's what I had in mind?'

'Yes,' he said firmly. He was sure his deductions were reasonable. 'The way you two sit together, laughing, sewing, talking . . . The way I've seen you *look.*'

She gazed at him with a kind of wistful horror. 'And you think I could be so pathetic as to want to adopt a seventeen-year-old girl . . . I wish you'd said nothing. After all, you say so little. I wish you'd left that subject dead. Unborn.'

'It was bound to come out sometime,' he said.

After a pause, she went on. 'I *did* think of it, but only for a second. Just like that – for one single moment. We have our own regrets, but we must leave Olive out of them!' Ronald Boyd-Porteous kept silent; he could see his wife's self-control slip from her grasp, and he was unsure of his own. 'It has nothing to do with Olive. She knows that she is welcome here at any time.' She switched off the lamp on her dressing table. 'And there shall be *other* girls from St Justina's.'

Postponing the Bungalow

Two years before, Agatha Bethune's circumstances were, in her own description, 'wrinkled'. 'You make it sound as if you're on the edge of the pit itself,' her old friend Kenneth Drumm-Sanderson said. 'Damnation seems to be just round the corner. You ought to give some thought to moving in here with me, at Magiskill. God knows, I've enough room. I can't vouch for comfort, but space – that I do have.'

'Kind of you, Drumm. *Most* kind of you. I was rather hoping that you'd make the offer. I'm probably sounding rather graceless and very much as usual. Aren't I? I can't help it, Drumm. I haven't a bean, you know. Not a brass farthing!' she said, half-swooning but at the same time amused at her own forthcoming penury. 'Still, I accept.' She took a bold sip of sherry and said, slapping him on the knee, 'You always were a good stick, Drumm. Magiskill, eh?' She looked around the sitting room which Drumm-Sanderson had spruced up for the occasion. 'I always *loved* Magiskill. Ah, yes, Drumm, the past! The glorious past!' She sank back in her armchair, both hands cupped around her glass as she spoke over its remaining contents 'Not much point talking about the past, eh, Drumm? Oh, no. No point at all. Your Pauline, my Jock, and now look at us! I wonder if they know Do you think they know?'

'I've never been entirely convinced about the after-life,' Drumm-Sanderson said. 'It's the chink in my theological armour.' He rose and refreshed her sherry glass. 'If things are as bad as you say, I don't see what else I can do, Agatha.'

'They're even worse than I've admitted. Offers for Lachrieglen were *very* disappointing. Lovely amontillado – lovely.' She took another brave sip. 'Prospective buyers probably got wind of my parlous state. Rumours, Drumm. Gossip and tittle-tattle. Anyone who's anyone in Scotland must have got wind of how Agatha Bethune's on her uppers.'

'I wouldn't say that, Agatha.'

'There's sweet Fanny Adams in the kitty, Drumm. Or there will be when I sell the house and pay off the bank. Somehow the price seems to match my astounding overdraft. I shall come to Magiskill with an out-of-date wardrobe and half-a-dozen tea-chests filled with treasured possessions I simply *cannot* part with, plus a dressing table I'd be utterly bereaved without.'

'What about your furniture?'

'All spoken for as far as the dreaded overdraft is concerned.'

'Oh, dear.' Drumm-Sanderson looked miserable. He was genuinely upset for Mrs Bethune. He had known her for decades. His late wife, Pauline, who had died fifteen years ago, had been Agatha Bethune's dearest friend. 'Rotten luck, Agatha. It really is. And not just yours. I'm thinking of mine, too. Still, one mustn't dwell on these things. Scottish fortitude, eh? We must be stoical. Not all our fault, you know.'

'You're a most refreshing man, Drumm. You haven't so much as insinuated that I've brought it on myself. You probably thought it, but you've the courtesy to keep it to yourself.'

Diminished resources emphasized Drumm-Sanderson's benevolent nature. He had always been known as affable and easy-going. His temperament struck almost everyone who knew him as precluding a career as a soldier, yet he had lasted for years as an officer in a Lowland regiment simply on the strength of looking the part when neither smiling nor puzzled. Military discipline was a ferocious curiosity as far as he was concerned. Shouting, stamping and barking on parade grounds seemed to him to be rituals invented by the stupid to impress the gullible. On active service – Malaya, Cyprus, Aden – he hadn't been frightened of the enemy so much as deeply concerned at why they were shooting at *him*, and why he was responsible for men who were shooting at *them*. He was the sort of man who loved and believed in his country without patriotism ever having crossed his mind.

He was tall and slender; his sixties saw no fattening of his waist nor stoop in his back. His presence could appear to be one of enfeebled refinement, but it was created by the age of his clothes rather than the onset of physical decrepitude. High cheek-bones, white hair, an outdoor complexion, small blue eyes and a small mouth suggested that whatever he said would be precise and truthful. He looked distinctive; his appearance was resented by some men who knew him, who spoke as if Drumm-Sanderson did not deserve his good looks, having done nothing distinguished. He loved his house and couldn't care less about the land and ancestry it seemed to represent in the minds of others. In any case, it had been built to celebrate money that had been new in the 1880s. His grandfather had been a distiller and whisky blender, described in his time as 'jumped-up'. It distressed Drumm-Sanderson that he and Pauline never had a child to whom Magiskill could be left.

Economy dictated that most of Magiskill's public rooms remained cold, empty and unlived in. From time to time he did his best to clean them. Agatha Bethune didn't help in these household activities, and Drumm-Sanderson got used to her handlessness in domestic matters. He accepted that housewifery wasn't part of her character. They inhabited a sitting room on the second floor because it was small and easier to heat than its spacious counterpart on the floor below. Logs were budgeted. Coal was too expensive to be considered. He was no longer capable of chopping, sawing and cutting wood on the scale necessary for plentiful fires, and it was years since he'd been able to afford to pay someone to do it for him. The central heating system had been out of commission for years.

Agatha Bethune gathered a travelling-rug around her shoulders and then tucked its generous tartan folds closer against her corduroy-trousered legs. 'I'm cold and I'm hungry,' she said bitterly.

'Toast?'

'Any more toast and I'll feel grilled!'

'Beans on toast?'

'I'm particularly sick of beans.'

'If you'd care for an early tea I could do some fish fingers,' Drumm-Sanderson said with gentle coaxing.

'I entered this world as a *privileged* child, and I'll leave it as an old woman malnourished on a diet of toast, beans and fish fingers. I simply cannot work out what went wrong.'

'Aren't you overdoing the woe, old girl?'

'How I *do* remember gastronomy!'

'I've always been a plain eater, I suppose.'

'Oh, come, come, my lad. As I recall, Pauline was an ambitious and accomplished cook. There was nothing austere about Pauline's idea of a menu.'

'Ah, yes. We were never wealthy, you know. About all my father left me was Magiskill. Pauline could make money *stretch*. My pension's adequate.'

'Jock could spend it almost as merrily as I could. Almost, that is, but not quite. Has the weather turned to the peculiarly awful since I moved in, Drumm, or am I imagining it?'

'It was a very uncertain sort of summer . . . '

'This winter's so sure of itself it strikes me as cocky – a reliable winter, I'd say. Bad and worse in roughly equal proportions.'

Outside the heavy falls of snow of the last few days were being rained on. Patches of earth were beginning to brown against the pocked white of the thawing snow. They spoke against a backdrop of drips and running water as cascades descended from the roof where there was a blocked gutter.

'I really must do something about the plumbing on the roof,' Drumm-Sanderson said anxiously. 'Leaks, then rot or the dreaded *Merulius Lacrymans*. Dry rot would be the end of me. We'd a gardener who use to call it Greetin' Muriel. Never heard it called that since. Have you ever heard the expression?'

'An early tea might help to cheer me up,' Mrs Bethune said. 'Could you add some scrambled eggs to the fish fingers, Drumm?'

On the first spring-like day of the year Drumm-Sanderson made a start on the vegetable garden. Economy, not enthusiasm, was the motive behind his horticulture. There wasn't much he could do with the rest of the gardens. They were too extensive for one man to cope with, let alone a man of Drumm-Sanderson's years.

Before he left the house he risked Mrs Bethune's scorn by saying that she might, if she felt like it, tackle a bit of housework. 'Yes, I might,' she said.'There's something about a decent turn in the weather that puts one in the mood for several hours on one's knees in a scullery.' Her irony amused him.

'You really are formidable. It's probably what I love about you.'

'For God's sake,' she said, 'don't talk about love, you pathetic ass.'

When he came back at lunch-time Mrs Bethune was in the kitchen with her feet up on a chair, drinking tea and reading a back issue of *Scottish Field*.

'Is there tea in the pot?'

'No,' she said. 'I finished it.'

'Cheese sandwiches do for lunch?'

'Actually, I could fair go a dish of trout, followed by duck, and perhaps a *filet mignon*, washed down by bottles of *Châteaux this-and-that*. Fat chance, I suppose. There's a man in your newspaper, Drumm, who says that sweet wines are coming back. Funny, I'd no idea they'd been away.'

'Cheese sandwiches?' he asked again.

He was back in the garden by 1.30. At four o'clock. when he felt too tired to continue, he returned to the kitchen, where Agatha Bethune was seated in the same chair with her feet propped on another.

'I've a confession to make,' she said.

'I could see that coming,' Drumm-Sanderson said with amusement.

'I'm not used to housework. It's so *boring*.' She looked at him, and said, 'I wish you'd tell me off, just now and again, Drumm. You should hurl insults at me. I deserve them. I started on the downstairs sitting room, but the sun was simply streaming in. I perspired like nothing on earth. Dust, dust everywhere! I practically choked on it! So I popped out to talk to the horses.'

'Your blessed horses, Agatha. I don't understand it. You muck them out with a will and groom like a fifteen-year-old stable girl, but turn your nose up at *dust* . . . '

'It's what one's used to. We can't all be as saintly and responsible as you.'

'I wish you'd stop calling me "saintly",' he said, trying to control his annoyance. 'Saintly, indeed! Never mind rebuffing my proposals of marriage, I'm forbidden a goodnight peck on the cheek. I doubt if there can be anything worse than to be in love with a woman who shows no affection whatsoever, *and* live in the same house as her!'

'Nothing, it seems to me, is more disgusting than geriatric lubricity,' she said scornfully.

' "Saintly" is not the word! Nor, I hope, is "geriatric".'

'I was thinking of your ecclesiastical good looks. You have the manners of an archbishop I once met – awfully nice man, but *he* picked at his food, too. And when you smile, in that way you have, after I've been irritating, you remind me of a hermit reciting his beatitudes. You *look* saintly!'

'Well, I'm not.'

'Anyway, I've told you a hundred times that I took a sort of vow after Jock died.'

'Best part of . . . how many years?'

'Seven,' she said, 'come September.' She poured some tea for herself. 'He was dead for only a few months before people round here began talking as if you and I *would*. You must have heard them for yourself . . . '

'Some vow,' Drumm-Sanderson said, forcing himself to scoff at her. 'It managed to include three round-the-planet cruises, months at a time in the south of France, and God knows what else. Unmitigated extravagance here, there and pretty well everywhere else!'

'I didn't vow not to enjoy myself,' she said coolly. 'Marriage. Amorous attachments. I swore off love.'

'Well, I'm in love with you, so you failed.'

She had never heard him speak before with so much trembling rage in his voice. 'No one believes me, because I dare say we never gave the impression of being lovey-dovey, but I was devoted to Jock.'

Drumm-Sanderson shrugged. It was certainly true that they never gave the impression of even liking each other. They used to snipe and snap across dinner tables. He couldn't remember Jock so much as holding Agatha's coat for her when they left. Jock seemed to exclude his wife from his conversation; he'd made a habit of interrupting her when she spoke. He had been the kind of drinker who walked away after a bottle of whisky and never got drunk. Instead of getting drunk, he died. That was how it had always seemed to Drumm-Sanderson. He was very suspicious of this 'devotion' that Agatha was harping on about. It sounded to him like retrospective story-making.

'Everyone, you know, is firmly convinced that you "live" with me,' he said. 'Yes, you're right. When Pauline died these same people were sure of it – a widower's year, and I'd be knocking on someone's door, wielding a bouquet. And when Jock died, they were sure it would be you.'

'I feel *sullied*! You're not a gentleman, or, if you were, you would make it perfectly clear that we are *friends* sharing the same house, and nothing more.' She shivered with the appearance of someone on whom a bucket of something disagreeable had just been emptied. 'Tittle-tattle! I feel like I want to vomit! Yes, go on, look ashamed! Or perhaps you'd prefer it if I took my sparkling witty conversation elsewhere, along with my diminutive so-called "pension"?'

'That's the last thing I want, and you know it,' he said. 'Then shall I invite them round for dinner? Or accept their invitations? It's because you never want to go that they've made up these stories. Agatha, they're convinced we're too besotted with each other's company to so much as cross the door!'

Agatha Bethune stood up, stamped her foot, and screamed. It had a visibly withering effect on the gentle Drumm-Sanderson. 'I won't stand for it!' she shouted.

Most of Magiskill's land had been sold off to various farmers when Drumm-Sanderson was still at school. Smaller portions had gone the same way before his father died. About ten acres of surrounding woodland were left to give the house the atmosphere of being at the centre of a substantial estate. Furniture, pictures, books and ornaments could have been sold, but it was a move that he resisted. When thoughts of raising money by selling off possessions crossed his mind, they were followed by memories of his father – unpleasant memories.

Agatha Bethune had mentioned the value of objects around the house. Lately, though, she was talking about what Magiskill itself might fetch. 'You could keep up standards in a smaller house,' she explained. 'You've got standards here, of course, but you can't afford to keep them up.'

'What are you talking about, "standards"?'

'Sherry before dinner. Or dinner, if it comes to that. You have such beautiful old crystal glasses and nothing to put in them. There are also the joys of central heating to which you have never been introduced.'

'We *have* radiators,' he complained.

'Ming dynasty radiators that work on the gravity system. *And* they're in the rooms that you don't use. I doubt if they'd work even if you could afford to run them.'

'Well, I read not all that long ago that a house like Magiskill in Scotland attracts something less than a semi-detached in the London suburbs. I'm not a snob, but . . .

'*I'm* a snob and I see great advantages in a bungalow in Pitfebbie.'

'Without my house,' he said wistfully, 'I'd lose ... I'd lose ... Well, I'd lose my identity.'

'It's certainly true that a new breed of middle-class *arriviste* is buying up the country,' she said. 'After all, they run it, so they're determined to get their whack. But your information is out of date. I wish I'd been able to hold out for a couple of years, because prices have gone *up*. The *nouveau riche* is competing for rural grandeur. You could sell, buy a bungalow, and live comfortably off the remaining capital.'

'I lashed out on a bottle of malt when I was in Pitfebbie this morning,' Drumm-Sanderson said, indicating the full decanter.

'I knew it. I could feel its presence in the room.'

'Want some now?'

'Yes, please!'

'Care for anything in it?' he asked, handing her a tumbler.

She looked at it carefully. 'Yes, Drumm,' she said. 'I'd like more whisky in it. You couldn't pickle a tonsil in what you've given me,' she said, protesting at his small measure.

'We'll have to make it *last*.'

'Drumm, do you want it to last *for ever*?'

He gave her more whisky. 'Cheers,' he said in a whisper. 'You know, all this talk about selling Magiskill, and buying bungalows, is pretty upsetting. I wish you'd leave it alone, Agatha.'

Agatha Bethune neglected the subject for a day. Her next line of approach was to mark illustrated advertisements in the *Scotsman*'s property supplement. Drumm-Sanderson noticed them and knew what her game was. Sometimes she underlined the asking prices and followed them with three exclamation marks. Clearly, she thought them the equal of Magiskill, or inferior, and was drawing his attention to sums ranging between £150,000 and half a million. Against one entry, she wrote, 'A nest-egg doesn't hatch by sitting on it!!!'

Faced with Mrs Bethune's hints and newspaper messages, Drumm-Sanderson chose to ignore them. He was appalled and amused by her tactics. From how she looked at him, he gathered that she was expecting to wear him down. She was confident that the information she was providing would force him to acknowledge the inevitable. 'If this is worth 220 grand,' she wrote opposite an advertisement, 'then M. is worth at least 50 gs more.' On the following week's edition she pointed out that a 'nice' bungalow in Pitfebbie wouldn't cost more than £50,000, which, she deduced, left '200 gs to play with'.

On a morning in late April Drumm-Sanderson was working in the greenhouse. He had been brushing a fall of flaked white paint from his seedlings after opening one of the roof vents with too much vigour. Mrs Bethune opened the door with a push of her foot, bearing a tray. 'Tea, Drumm?'

Never mind her civility, Mrs Bethune bearing tea to her friend and provider was a big enough novelty in itself. He feared the worst. Had he held out too long? Would his best ploy be to speak first, admit the practical wisdom of her advice, but deliver a firm *no*? Such thoughts ran through his mind, and his mouth was half-open to take the initiative when Agatha – she was very nimble – sat up on a table.

'I've just had a thought, Drumm. Instead of taking that old carriage out once or twice in the summer to trot me round the lanes in your usual state of witless *ennui*, why don't we put it to more profitable purposes?'

There was, he thought, an almost amiable self-confidence to her suggestion, but what she said was too obscure to understand at one telling. 'I can't think what you mean,' he said in a tone of dignified stupidity.

'Tourism,' she said with a hint of impatience. 'Last summer I couldn't help but notice how many tourists find their way to Pitfebbie. It's a kind of pit-stop for them. It's become a summer nosebag.'

He thought for a moment. 'No, not a lot to preoccupy the *touristique* mentality in this neck of the woods. Long may it continue.'

'Horse-drawn excursions at reasonable rates,' she said.

'Ah!' he said, as if it dawned on him. 'What?'

'Your landau, my nags, a round trip lasting, I'd say, about an hour . . .'

'I can just about stand being a lapsed laird, but I draw the line at being some sort of tout,' he said, trying to work up the vehemence necessary to dismiss Mrs Bethune's industrious notion. 'That *would* be coming down in the world!' He looked at a tray of emergent cabbages as if expecting them to agree with him.

'Oh, dear Drumm, you *have* come down in the world.'

'Not by that much I haven't!'

'What'll these be when they grow up?' she asked, nodding at a box of seedlings.

'Dinner,' he said. 'Really, Agatha, it's bad enough one's house and property being worth the equivalent of a bedsit in London West One without *touting* in the hope of paying one's way. You're confronting me with apocalyptic *peddling* so that I'll think of selling Magiskill as the preferable option.'

'Never mind the mysteries of the British economy,' she said. '*We're skint!*'

'Not destitute yet,' he said. 'When my father sold the distilleries, shares in the company that bought them were part of the price. God knows why, but for some reason he kept them. All too few left. Most sold off, and then one takeover for another. Six years ago I sold too many to the Japanese company that bought the company that had bought the company my father inherited. Not a large income from what's left, no, and not even what we *need*; but with thrift, we'll get by somehow.'

'We can lay on a very agreeable itinerary,' she said, disregarding his claims to solvency. 'First stop Barnshaugh Castle, followed by the enchanting dilapidation of Pitfebbie Abbey. Not much to see there, but it *is* delightfully ruinous. Then we round the whole thing off with a cantering circuit of Loch Febb. Home base will be Market Cross, where a board, properly done by a reputable sign-writer, will announce our times of departure. Five pounds strikes me a reasonable charge. That's twenty quid an hour. Capital outlay is negligible. On a good day we might even anticipate a hundred quid, Drumm,' she said with subdued cajoling. 'Think of that for a money-spinning idea!'

By the time she'd finished Drumm-Sanderson was mesmerized by the confidence with which she outlined a day's work when not a week had gone by without Mrs Berthune proving herself incapable of useful activity, other than care for her horses. 'The nags, as you accurately describe them, wouldn't stand for it,' he said.

'I know horses better than you, Drumm. My horses thrive on work. They've been denied it, and I'm full of remorse. And don't think I'm not up to it myself. When my heart's in it, I can go about a job of work like a demon.'

He wondered what 'job of work' in the past justified her assertion. Perhaps it was a lobster supper washed down by *premier cru* Chablis, or a particularly demanding hunt ball. It was a difficult reproach to make. It felt ungentlemanly and mean. But Drumm-Sanderson was desperate. 'I've good reason for keeping you and horses off the streets of Pitfebbie.'

Her smile was one of complacent viciousness. 'I was having a nervous breakdown at the time. Lachrieglen was sold and gone. I was refusing to accept it. My mind was very much bothered by having to feel dependent on the kindness of my friend . . . '

'Yes, I know! I'm sorry for having been so insensitive,' he said, angry with himself.

Two weeks after moving into Drumm-Sanderson's house, Mrs Bethune had taken off on a tall hunter, since sold. Men and women on horseback were not uncommon on Pitfebbie's streets. What was unusual about Agatha Bethune's urban equestrianism was its demonic speed and the unbridled gallop with which she tore down the Barleygait. Drivers braked; those who didn't brake in time rammed into the backs of those who did. Pedestrians scattered, leaving their shopping where it fell. Cattle being herded to market stampeded. They barged down High Street like the bulls of Pamplona. One ended up in the supermarket. Another, a hat dangling from a horn, entered the foyer of the public library and stood eyeball-to-eyeball with a bust of its benefactor, Andrew Carnegie. Were it not for fancy medical evidence at the private hearing in the sheriff's chambers, Mrs Bethune could have been faced with a hefty fine, or worse. As it was, insurance companies wrangled with Mrs Bethune's lawyers for months. Mrs Bethune didn't know it – the information was kept from her – but Drumm-Sanderson had paid a bill, parting with a block of his precious shares, plus a cheque drawn on his current account.

'Some sort of licence will be necessary,' he said 'If your name's on our application, fits will be thrown.'

'Your name will do just fine, Drumm,' she said. 'You're far too highly thought of for the district council to let you down. I mean, Kenneth Drumm-Sanderson, of Magiskill,' she said, overdoing the expansive sweep of her arm.

'The idea appals me,' he said.

'Then you'll do it?' she said, slipping off the table to her feet in a gesture of delight.

Wondering what he'd said that made her leap to a false conclusion, he tried to say no, but instead he said, 'Well, if you think . . . '

'Wonderful!'

Three weeks later, Mr Geddes from the district council's office in Pitfebbie phoned Drumm-Sanderson to say that although the application was unusual, it had been welcomed as a local initiative in the effort to attract and entertain visitors to the area. 'All, that is, except Mr Stravick,' he said. 'Normally if he objects, then the committee does tend rather to go along with him. Being your application, he didn't make much headway, of course.' Drumm-Sanderson winced at Mr Geddes's merrily deferential tone. 'I take it you know Mr Stravick?'

'Yes, I do,' Drumm-Sanderson said curtly.

'A mental note to be made here, I believe,' the official said. 'I wouldn't be too surprised if Jim Stravick puts one of his employees on the road with a carriage-and-pair. If you ask me, I think he saw your idea as just a bit *too* good. If you take my meaning. Then again, the committee might be perplexed, shall we say, were he to put in an application himself. On the other hand, he might be covered by existing licences pertinent to his taxi and car-hire line of business. They're long-established. Their paperwork might even go back as far as the horse era,' Mr Geddes said with a telephonic guffaw.

'You've been most kind, Mr Geddes, *most* kind,' Drumm-Sanderson said with fraudulent fulsomeness, raising his voice as much for Mrs Bethune's benefit as Mr Geddes's.

'Was that what I think it was?' Agatha said.

'Indeed. Your spruced-up carriage is now legal. Should all go well, I'll spend the summer looking like an antique postilion or Victorian coachman,' he said, walking away.

'I'll ring Archie Cooper,' she shouted after him.

'Who's he?' he called from half-way up the stairs.

'Our sign-writer! He's standing by and all ready to *go*!'

'Oh, my God,' he muttered as he climbed the stairs.

On the second Saturday in June, Drumm-Sanderson drove the carriage into Pitfebbie. He approached the town by an indirect route of lanes and minor roads to avoid the morning's shopping traffic. Drumm-Sanderson wore tails as part of his outfit as a coachman to the gentry of yesteryear. He had seen no good reason for this, but Agatha Bethune's chatter about 'image' and 'authenticity' had been relentless and he gave in. Mrs Bethune was attired in a riding outfit – cream jodhpurs, black riding boots, black jacket, white silk jabot and a black bowler hat. She had spoken about dressing in Victorian costume. 'No, no, I draw the line at Whistler's *Mother*!' Drumm-Sanderson had shouted intemperately, wishing he'd been able to muster the appropriate rage at the beginning, and put an end to the enterprise before it even began.

On the outskirts of the town, he took off his top hat and stowed it under the seat.

'Isn't it comfortable?' she asked.

'I feel like a Dickensian undertaker,' he said crossly. 'Agatha, I'm absolutely terrified! I've spent most of my life avoiding public show. Now look at me! Money isn't everything,' he said sternly.

'Don't look so sour. Smile. Smile,' she coaxed. A group of pedestrians stared at them. Agatha Bethune doffed her hat like a man.

A photographer and reporter from the local paper were waiting beside the board placed there earlier that morning by the sign-writer. Pictures were taken. Drumm-Sanderson found himself saying to the reporter: 'Old-fashioned things really do seem to have come back. How shall I put it? Pleasures of sightseeing at a gentler pace? People do seem to enjoy the style of the bygone age. Besides, Pitfebbie's been rather slow to offer itself to tourism, and yet there's no doubt that visitors find the place attractive. My hope is that we'll do some good for the old town. Surprised, actually, no one's done it before.' To himself, he said, 'Have carriage, will tout. Anything to keep warm in the winter. To say nothing of giving Agatha her chance to earn a shilling or two.'

Ten minutes later four customers paid their money and took their seats. It was like a royal progress. Ancestral respect for the families that populated the 'big houses' seemed to repossess the racial memory with involuntary deference. Cars backed off with circumspect obedience, as if the horses had the right of way. Crowds on the pavements stopped to look. Drumm-Sanderson was reminded of marching through the streets of London after the prime minister of a dominion had been met at Victoria Station and was being carriaged to Buckingham Palace. People with dogs held their leashes tighter. A stray ran in front of them, thought better of it and back-pawed to the side of the road.

Very soon, though, the news rumoured its way around town that Mrs Bethune was on the streets in charge of two horses and a coach. The fact that she was there at all was enough to encourage exaggeration. Her function, though, was to act as guide and commentator. For several weeks she had shivered in the library mastering the distressing history of Barnshaugh Castle and other antiquities. Much of what she needed to know was contained in old books unopened in decades. Pitfebbie Abbey, she discovered, had not been dissolved in a tantrum of Reformation vindictiveness as she had hoped. Its abbot had not been flayed, exiled, hanged or come to a sticky end of any sort. As the books retold, he had been given a brisk tutorial by John Knox to such good effect that he converted immediately, he and all his monks. To prove their sincerity they had knocked down the abbey themselves.

'Over this seemingly innocent turf charged the English forces, intent on plunder, pillage and Heaven knows what else. Imagine, if you will, the bannerets of the tiny and half-starved garrison, commanded by that redoubtable figure Lady Mary Wodderhead, in her way perhaps the staunchest friend of the Queen of Scots. Not one to let femininity get in the way of a good day's soldiering! As valiant as they come! From there she hurled boulders on the enemy as they placed their scaling ladders against the battle-scarred walls . . . '

While the four tourists strolled among the ruins, peering down through an iron grille at the awful dungeon, Drumm-Sanderson said, 'Laying it on a bit thick, aren't you? I've a vague memory of reading that the castle surrendered as soon as the English came over the hill.'

'This is business, Drumm. Minor historical episodes are up for grabs as far as I'm concerned. Shall I tell them that the Wodderheads were cowardly double-crossers? That Lady Mary ran off with the English commander?'

'She didn't,' he said. 'Did she?'

'As a matter of fact, she did,' Mrs Bethune said. 'And I sincerely hope that her progeny ended up as a long line of swineherds.'

'You should be careful of history,' Drumm-Sanderson said in an advisory manner. 'I've always avoided it myself. It makes people overheat. They get worked up and angry. I know a bit about that sort of thing. I was a soldier, after all; and as well as being a profession that makes history, I suppose, soldiering's something that puts one right in the thick of rather stupid events devised by people who really ought to have known better.'

Pitfebbie Abbey wasn't much of a sight to see except to those sensitive to monastic stone stumps and half a stone arch rising from

rampantly nettled ground. Again Mrs Bethune delivered a peror-
ation. Drumm-Sanderson shivered as he listened to her lyrical
account of alleged ghosts and the doubtful history that explained the
haunted nature of the place. Two middle-aged English couples from
Peterborough lapped it up as if they couldn't get enough.

They returned by Loch Febb. Drumm-Sanderson drew the carriage
to a halt to let his passengers look at the swans and watch the flight
of a heron. When they got back to Market Cross, one man tipped Mrs
Bethune a five-pound note. Four other people were waiting. As they
climbed aboard a man ran up to reserve the next trip for himself and
four friends. He was told that they could squeeze five in, if he was
happy to be slightly crowded. Drumm-Sanderson realized that he
was enjoying himself.

Business was brisk that first day, and every day for weeks after-
wards. It took its toll on Drumm-Sanderson. It was over ten years
since his last spell of gainful employment, when his job had been
with a public relations firm in Edinburgh. His function was to shake
hands with clients and offer them drinks and titbits. He gave these
events the presence of upper-crustness, good manners, class, a whiff
of another world, another time, when there had been more grace,
courtesy, and charm. He was like an old master on the wall of the
hospitality suite, except that he was alive and active. He was there to
impress, a sort of figurehead, which is what he'd always been. In all
the many jobs he'd had over the years he'd never been expected to
show competence or do anything – it pleased his employers if all he
did was *be*, as if he exemplified a sort of innocence, or a past time
when manners were more instinctively elegant, the pace slower, or
the urgency of business secondary and something that could wait
until more important matters had been taken care of, like lunch.

'I'm beginning to believe that the public think we're at their beck
and call,' he said petulantly.

'Well, yes, we are. Drumm, we're giving a service. Of *course* we're
at their beck and call,' Mrs Bethune said, explaining what she considered to be obvious.

'What about *our* lunch?'

'I'm hungry too, but doesn't the sight of money do *anything* for
you?' She opened the handbag in which she kept their receipts.
'Pretty healthy, eh? Three trips at twenty, one at twenty-five. Eighty-
five quid before lunch and you want to stop to eat?'

'The horses get fed. What about me? And you, you of all people – aren't you peckish?'

'I'm not passing up twenty quid for a forty-pence sandwich,' she said on a ripple of disbelieving laughter.

By late July Drumm-Sanderson was tired of his services to tourism and personal finance. It was all he could do to drag himself from bed in the morning. Their lowest takings in a day had been £100. In their best week they had grossed £1,000. Drumm-Sanderson was giddy on arithmetic. It depressed him. He'd rather have pottered in his vegetable garden. There were seedlings that had overgrown in their boxes in the greenhouse and would never become lunch or dinner because he lacked the time and energy to plant them where they should have thrived under the ministrations of his weeding, watering, and tending. The horses were beginning to complain: they were growing even less willing to face another day than Drumm-Sanderson.

Horse problems were soon solved by Agatha, who phoned a friend. 'Yes, everyone's talking about it. Fancy persuading Kenneth to get into such a stunt. Well done, my girl. It might show him a bit of the wider world at long last. Of course, I'll be happy to oblige. Always pleased to see a spot of enterprise along the lines approved of by our beloved leader,' Brigadier Scott-Perry said with what sounded like po-faced seriousness.

'For God's sake, don't say anything like that to Drumm, or he'll throw his hands up in horror,' Mrs Bethune said.

'Mum's the word. But when are we going to *see* you two? You've been hiding yourselves away for ages. Everyone's talking about it. Have been for months, and months. It's time you two climbed out of your love nest and showed yourselves.'

Agatha Bethune grimaced, thanked him for the loan of his pair of horses, and said she'd look forward to seeing his stable girl that evening.

'I've given it a lot of thought,' Jim Stravick said to Mrs Bethune. 'I mean legal vocabulary to the effect that you weren't to be seen dead near a horse in Pitfebbie. And there you are. And there you have been for weeks.'

'And nothing untoward has happened!'

'I merely suggest that there you are, holding the reins, contrary to a decision at law, madam.' There was a long-suffering reasonableness about Stravick's manner of speaking that maddened Mrs

Bethune. 'I have a duty as an elected representative of the people,' he said.

'I am *not* holding the reins,' Mrs Bethune countered tartly, giving him a good view of her hands.

'Oh, but as good as,' he said with the same benign manner. 'Your man's in there, and you're left in charge of the rig.'

'Major Drumm-Sanderson, for your information, is not my man,' she said, following her precise words with an intense stare that failed to provoke Mr Stravick.

'Then you're sitting *beside* the reins. The question is: what can we look forward to if the horses bolt?'

'Your concern,' she said candidly, 'is not only pious, it's a self-interested lie.'

Drumm-Sanderson appeared from the café bearing a tray on which were tea and sandwiches. 'Oh, dear,' he said when he saw Jim Stravick.

Stravick smiled as if he'd been passing the time of day with Mrs Bethune, which encouraged Drumm-Sanderson to smile back, although when he caught Agatha's glance he could tell that pleasantries had not been exchanged. 'A beautiful day,' he said to Stravick.

Quietly, the impression being that of a friend whispering well-intentioned advice, Stravick said, 'Given the lady's history with horses in this town, you're taking a bit of a chance leaving her in charge of the waggon . . . '

'Nonsense!'

'Oh?' Stravick said, with such benevolence that even Drumm-Sanderson could see it was a challenge he had to rise to.

'Give their flanks a good smack, if you don't believe me. These animals have been trained into a state of abject docility. It's a labour of love to get them to break into anything faster than a walk.'

For a moment it looked as if Jim Stravick was toying with the idea of startling the team into a panic and, with luck, an episode of sufficient drama to put Drumm-Sanderson and Mrs Bethune out of business. 'It isn't easy to stand by and see the law flouted,' he said. He walked off.

When they got home in the evenings, they fed and watered the horses, rubbed them down and settled them in. After that, Drumm-Sanderson found it hard to muster the energy to hold his knife and fork. 'My digestion's going. I used to have the gastric capacity of an armoured car, but any more of this reheated stodge from the fish-and-chip shop or the Chinese carry-out and I'll end up ulcerated,' he whined pitifully.

They were up early to attend to the horses, clean harnesses, rub brasses and give the coach a wipe. Wheels were greased and cushions plumped and brushed. Drumm-Sanderson looked longingly at the still-folded newspapers that were delivered from Pitfebbie at eight o'clock, knowing that he'd fall asleep over the front page at around 9.30 at night and never get around to catching up with the rest. The only television was in Mrs Bethune's bedroom. She seemed to watch it until very late. Drumm-Sanderson wondered where she found the energy.

A few mornings later, during a lull in business, Drumm-Sanderson opened his copy of the local newspaper. It appeared weekly, on Fridays. On the centre pages a news item reported 'A Prominent Citizen's Concern'. The subject of this concern was tourism. Drumm-Sanderson read it aloud to Mrs Bethune: ' "Mr Drumm-Sanderson has shown what can be done, although in a very small way. Yet this is the sort of activity that ought to be properly organized. Why hasn't the district council been in this line of enterprise?" It really is quite critical of us,' Drumm-Sanderson reported. 'It makes us out to be rank amateurs. Stravick, of course. Subtle, oh, very subtle,' he said. 'He's managed to mention your name – one, two, three, four times.'

Agatha Bethune took the newspaper from him. 'It says, "See Letters Page",' Drumm-Sanderson said. He put a finger in his mouth to chew nervously on a nail, but Agatha Bethune, despite the crisis, had the presence of mind to smack his hand. Reading from the Letters Page, Agatha Bethune intoned, ' "I feel perfectly entitled to call upon the owner of these horses and demand a new pair of shoes." ' She looked at Drumm-Sanderson. 'I always had a suspicion that dung would do for us before my disgraceful past. How very clever of Mr Stravick.' She read out the other letter to the editor. ' "I am becoming sickened by the obstruction to traffic created by the carriage which has become a lamentably familiar sight on our streets . . . " It goes on and on about how our horses frighten cars,' she said wearily. 'No wonder people have been looking oddly at us all morning. They read the *Messenger* hours ago.'

'Good morning!' Drumm-Sanderson called to a bystander, who stiffened, took offence and walked away.

'Do you accept Mr Stravick's gauntlet, slapped in your face?' Agatha Bethune asked challengingly.

'Is that what it is? I wouldn't go that far,' Drumm-Sanderson answered. 'Are you sure?'

'You'd do *anything* to avoid unpleasantness!'

'Give in to the likes of Stravick?' he asked incredulously.

'Businessmen like Stravick rule the country. For all I know they might even rule the world. Dig your heels in, Drumm. Show him that yesterday still counts for something. All you have to do is think of the tasteless hacienda *he* lives in. Think of the vulgar furniture he clutters it up with. The pictures he hangs on his walls!'

'Oh, Agatha, I know what you're driving at. It's sentimental drivel. I never had any faith in people like me being natural heirs to responsibility. Almost everyone from my sort of background that I ever knew turned out to be inept. I could name a score of nitwits and ninnies, some of whom actually wielded *power*. Some of whom still *do*, for Heaven's sake. They weren't unsuccessful, but they were *useless*. Some of them will actually be named in the history books, with *respect*. If I did anything right in my life it was refusing to be one of them. I'll fight Stravick, tooth and nail if needs be, but not on the respectability of yesterday.' He took a breath. 'Good morning,' he said to a by-passer.

'Who was he?'

'Mr McAllister in the Inland Revenue Office.'

'The *what*?'

'The tax man. I dropped him a line. Agatha, we're in gainful employment. I'd rather do this thing properly than have someone with E-two-R on his briefcase ringing the doorbell when the money's spent.'

'Oh, dear,' she said.

'Someone has to keep the books.'

'Books?'

'Accounts. You got us into this. If you don't keep books, Ernie Roberts the Second crops up on your doorstep asking to see them. That's one line of malicious approach Jim Stravick's been denied. The other I intend to do today. And that is, sign a statement swearing that you don't drive the landau and that it is entirely in my charge, your presence being that of guide and local expert. God save us if we're asked for an example of your expertise. We'll be arrested for misrepresentation of local history. I'm relying, you see, on getting into legal process before Jim Stravick.'

'I couldn't think of *everything*,' she said plaintively.

'Didn't expect you to,' he said, patting her white-gloved hand with his own. 'Don't suppose I have either.'

He noticed a change in Agatha Bethune's mood. He'd observed a softening in her manner several days ago and put it down to tiredness. From her gloomy, thoughtful expression, however, he suspected there was more to it than fatigue.

'You've never approved of it, have you? All along you've been going against your grain. You've been my partner in this, but you've done it for me. I've never been very good at saying "Thank you",' she said.

'I started to be won round as soon as I saw the first day's takings,' Drumm-Sanderson said. 'Being me, I might have been rather slow to make that clear.'

'All I can say is, putting you through what you obviously experience as an ordeal makes me feel quite poisonously selfish, and a bully, and someone who had no right to do it, and I think all the time about how you don't *deserve* . . . '

'Oh, wait a minute!' he said, his seriousness stiffening Mrs Bethune's expression into an expectation of the worst. 'Magiskill's on the verge of falling down. The water-heater in my bathroom's on the blink. Bills for this, that and everything else are extortionate. I know why it's the likes of Stravick who run the country. They're the only people who can fall asleep at night knowing they can afford to wake up in the morning. No, it wasn't a good idea you had, Agatha. It was a stroke of genius.'

'Not such a bad idea, you mean?'

'I said it was a stroke of genius, and I meant it. When the tourist season drops off, I intend to blow my share, or some of it, on a few essential repairs around the house. Anything in mind for yours?' he asked her.

'I haven't thought about it yet,' she said tentatively, still getting over his applause for what she believed he continued to deplore as 'touting', as a public confession of near-penury, an almost-heralding of the depressing fact that the last of the Drumms and the Sandersons was riding away from the world in the uniform of a nineteenth-century coachman carrying four paying passengers worth about one-sixth of his quarterly electricity bill. 'Are you telling me that some of it's mine?' she asked.

'Half,' he said.

'I thought it was *all* for Magiskill,' she said.

Drumm-Sanderson smiled approvingly, which disguised his amusement. 'Well, you can't tell me that you've been selfish, then,' he said. 'But it crossed my mind that you might have some little extravagance up your sleeve,' he said.

'Drumm! My extravagant days are over!'

'Not even a tiny extravagance? A short spree?' he said testing her. 'I saw a car the other week. It had one of those amusing stickers on the rear window. It said BORN TO SHOP. I thought of you, my dear.'

She looked at him with a winning defensiveness. 'Well, I can't say I'm not tempted, because I am, but I'm too determined about our winter comforts. Dinner on the dining-room table. Roast rack of lamb for Sunday lunch. The Aga fully operational and a cosy kitchen. Your library is one of the few rooms I know where you don a fur coat to enter it even if only for as long as it takes to find a book. Perhaps even a woman in, two or three mornings a week, to tackle the dust, grime and cobwebs, and the attentions of a plumber, an electrician, and perhaps even a heating engineer's expert opinion on your boilers.'

Drumm-Sanderson was impressed. He wondered if he was meant to be. 'And a few friends to dinner?' he asked. 'We could try to do it properly.'

'And a few friends to dinner,' she conceded. This time Agatha Bethune placed her white-gloved hand on his. It was unpredicted, an affectionate surprise, and its significance baffled him. 'Not, though, under present circumstances,' she said. 'I'm an absolutely dreadful old woman. You know that better than anyone alive. I take some consolation from the thought that I haven't always been so awful, but I suspect that most of the time I've been pretty bad. I'd make your life a misery.'

He wasn't sure what she was saying. Her tenses confused him. The phrase 'present circumstances' puzzled him. He thought he must be mistaken and on the verge of making a fool of himself yet again.

'I've got through the worst you have to offer,' he said. 'Haven't I? Anything else would be plain sailing. Or am I leaping to the wrong conclusion? What about your "vow" to Jock?' he said hesitantly, anticipating correction, or reversal, or rebuff, or a slap on the face. It wouldn't have been the first time she'd cuffed his ear.

'I didn't vow anything to Jock. Oh, I made a vow; but I made it to me. I took an oath of independence. I became a selfish, hedonistic little republic of my very own. Jock drank himself into an early grave,' she said with difficulty. 'I loved him, and he was worth mourning. But he wasn't worth a vow of perpetual fidelity, Drumm. If Pauline doesn't mind, I don't see why Jock should.'

Agatha Bethune looked to be having trouble keeping her emotions in check.

'You're agreeing to marry me. Is that right?' Drumm-Sanderson said, finding himself smitten with Agatha Bethune's near-tearfulness. He put his arm round her shoulder.

'What do you think I've been saying?' she said with an annoyance that was close to her usual manner.

'That's wonderful!' he said. He kissed her briefly and gently. 'It doesn't seem right that we should have to go back to work,' he said. He was dazed by what his 'present circumstances' had suddenly become.

'We have reservations,' she said sensibly. 'There are people waiting, and, like it or not, we're in a service industry. Let's not talk about it any more in what is, after all, a car park, and practically right next door to the public conveniences.'

She seemed better now, folding greaseproof paper and placing it inside their sandwich box.

'We might even manage to go somewhere nice for a week,' he said. 'To hell with the cost of it, a week in Paris, in October, would do us good.'

'Paris is dreary in October, Drumm,' she said. 'I know. I've been there in October.'

'We'll think of somewhere else,' he said, taking hold of the reins.

'I like Rome in October.'

'It would cost more,' he said prudently, although he'd never been in Rome and had no idea of what travel and hotels cost anywhere, let alone somewhere in particular.

'A Roman autumn would be *lovely*!' she said eagerly. 'Maybe even a week in Florence, and a week in Venice!'

Her enthusiasm was not to be dismissed, not even criticized with gentle reminders of Magiskill's repairs or getting through the winter without perishing of hypothermia or starvation.

Drumm-Sanderson mouth-clicked and his giddy-ups nursed the horses into the street. Tourists were waiting to be shown the romantic ruins of Barnshaugh Castle, Pitfebbie Abbey, and Loch Febb with its swans and herons and reflected sky. Beside him, Agatha filled his mind with Italian sunshine, hotels, restaurants, art galleries, gondolas and candlelight.

Nancy, Bruce and Percy

It was an eternal triangle – a man, a woman and a parrot. As such birds go, Percy was unexotic. Visually, he disappointed visitors whose experience of parrots was drawn from zoos or colour plates in coffee-table books. His blue-grey feathers left less than enough room for a display of his pinkish belly. His ruff looked like an ill-fitting avian toupee. Sagacious intolerance radiated from his piercing eyes. His beak looked a size too big. A tradesman employed to rebuild the brickwork in the fireplace had refused to continue with the job after only ten minutes of Percy's untrustworthy presence. Getting him out of the room against his wishes was just not on. Only Bruce knew how to sweet-talk Percy into a co-operative state of mind. Almost every twitch of his behaviour seemed calculated to demand respect – a shuffle along his perch drew attention to his claws; and when he screamed, he wanted you to notice his hooked, nut-smashing, fruit-tearing beak. Bruce Gifford loved the bird; he talked to him like a person. His sister Nancy loathed him.

'You're a fake! You're a pigeon in fancy dress!' Nancy pretended that she gave as good as she got. He hadn't assaulted her, but Percy's fits of aerial rage were hard to get used to, and there had been visitors who hadn't stuck around to try. It made the sitting room off-limits to anyone except Bruce and Nancy. Behind the closed door, you could hear him vent his fierce, tropical nostalgia in the draughts and silences of a Scottish middle-class sitting room in a house that had been built to accommodate ancestral conventions. Among such furniture, pictures, curtains and wallpaper, Percy looked like a colourful eccentric.

Nancy Gifford was forty-five and the former Mrs Hugh Hannah. When Nancy met her husband in 1964 he was a hard-living, rugby-playing advocate of twenty-seven. Nancy's mother was alive then. Hugh Hannah's brilliant prospects – that is, his father was loaded – dazzled Mrs Gifford into a state of maternal rhapsody that Nancy realized with hindsight should have changed her mind instead of confirming her choice. The animated widowhood of the late Mrs

Gifford was still being lived down by her children; but she could spot a catch when she saw one. Hugh Hannah's radiant future had twinkled from glittering promise into as whoopee-doopee and lucrative a career as Mrs Gifford predicted back in 1964. Law or politics, had he stuck with either, would have proved successful enough. Twenty years ago, however, Hugh Hannah entered television. He did current-affairs programmes, news reports; he knew everybody. He set up several of his own production companies. His face was famous. He inherited a fortune.

Popular, fashionable, elegant, intelligent and innocent, Nancy had been an ornament in Edinburgh's version of the 1960s. Looking back, she wondered where she'd found the energy to cope with late nights every night, jazz clubs, dancing, chattering dinners, her husband's well-heeled but weather-exposed sporting events, and the company of young men and women who behaved as if fame and fortune lay at their feet like shoes and when the time came all they'd need to do was pick them up and try them on for size.

Women in the late Mrs Gifford's circle of friends were known to have said behind her back that Hugh Hannah was too good to be true. His rugged handsomeness was a bit unusual, but its divergence from an orthodox standard of Caledonian masculine beauty was more than compensated for by delightful manners. In a man so big, athletic, and revelling in manly popularity, his charm towards women conveyed a brutal gentility, always tantalizing to women of Mrs Gifford's type, who were never married to it, although by that age she wished that she had been. She'd married the son of a minor shipowner, just in time to witness his father sell off the tiny fleet to pay his debts. After that, Nancy's father settled down to a life in which he plodded through the litigation, gains, losses, inheritances, tragedies and comedies of farmers, small-town shopkeepers and minor gentry. His legal training had been intended to fit him to assist his father in running the shipping line. Its precise relevance had never been clear to him. His father's alleged bankruptcy had been astutely controlled, however, and when the old man retired he still had a house to give his son, and enough capital to buy into a law firm withering under the prestige of its longevity.

Nancy woke up one morning to the belief that the rumours she'd heard about Hugh's extra-marital affairs were probably true. Her lack of distress surprised her. It didn't put her off breakfast.

Now mention of her ex-husband's name in the newspapers – it happened two or three times a week – roused neither resentment nor regret. When he appeared on TV – which he did, often, and still does – she made no special point of watching, although Bruce followed Hugh Hannah's regular programme. He admired his authority; he approved of his politics – Conservative, like his own.

'Rather good tonight, I thought,' Bruce said. 'He certainly put that trade-unionist in his place.'

'Oh, for heaven's sake! Call that "good"? Deep down he's still an Edinburgh lawyer. What can you expect? His profession, and yours, hasn't had an original idea since the early nineteenth century.'

'I don't blame you for disliking the man, but you have to admit that he's able. He's good at what he does,' Bruce said, extending an arm so that Percy could walk from his shoulder to the table beside his chair. 'I don't understand why he isn't in Parliament. A man like that would make a lot of difference. Not a prime minister. But a secretary of state for Scotland. It's what he deserves. It's what *we* deserve.'

'Oh, God, never, no,' Nancy said, performing her imaginary vomiting act into a bowl of pot-pourri.

For the past two months Nancy had nursed a hunch that her younger brother's absences from home weren't what he claimed them to be. His departures left behind an atmosphere in which she could detect the tell-tale stink of the clandestine. It was years ago, but she retained a very clear memory of how a man's back as he left the house could conjure up suggestions of erotic deceit. For a man of settled habits and confirmed hobbies – Bruce painted in water-colours, made model aeroplanes and read deeply in natural history, particularly on the subject of parrots – he appeared less annoyed than Nancy expected by the inconvenience of his regular trips to Edinburgh. When he complained that he would have to be away on Tuesday or Wednesday, or over the weekend, his displeasure sounded insincere. 'I'll miss the Attenborough programme, and it's about anthills,' he'd say dejectedly; or, 'Would you believe it? That last time I couldn't get the TV to work in my hotel room. It took thirty minutes before someone came with a replacement, and by then the programme was off the air.'

Nancy noticed a jauntiness in her brother's disgruntlement that reminded her of Hugh Hannah, particularly during the last few

weeks of their two-year marriage. She felt convinced that Hannah
was still up to his old tricks. A few months back she'd watched *The
Hannahs at Home* in the series where an upper-class twerp who wrote
books about country houses visited the titled, the distinguished and
the famous in the extremely worthwhile endeavour of justifying
how the other one-hundredth of the population live. Now a family
man with three children and a wife dedicated to flower arranging
and bullying the gardener, Hannah's genial relaxation looked decid-
edly shifty to Nancy Gifford. Either the second Mrs Hannah didn't
mind, just so long as the greenhouses were kept up to scratch, or
Hugh confined his sexual wanderlust to California, New York, Paris,
Berlin, Venice, Rome and other such places in which he seemed to do
business about every five minutes.

'I don't suppose it's crossed your mind that I might find this
painful to watch,' Nancy said.

'What?'

'I used to be married to him. Remember? And there he is, with the
three little Hannahs. He used to tell me he didn't want children.
Career, career, career ... "No children", he said. "Well, maybe
later." '

'It must be one of the most beautiful Scottish houses I've ever
seen,' Bruce said.

She didn't think there was much point in repeating herself. A few
minutes later, Bruce said, '*Is* it still painful for you, sis?'

'No, not painful,' she said. 'Embarrassing. Sick-making. Horrid.'

'Oh.'

Some bars of country-house Vivaldi blared from the set and Percy
shrieked.

'Don't you dare talk to me in that tone of voice!' Nancy shouted at
the parrot.

At breakfast a few days later, Nancy decided to confront Bruce
with her suspicions.

'I think you ought to tell me about her,' she said. 'Don't look as if
you didn't hear me!' She watchful a forkful of scrambled eggs fall on
his plate. 'I respect your privacy. You know I do. I didn't interfere
when there was all that fuss about Deidre What's-it. I let you get on
with it.'

'You did nothing of the kind!'

'A few words of sisterly advice were definitely called for,' Nancy said. 'I'm your sister. Your closest surviving relative. I *ought* to be the first person you tell,' she said bluntly.

'How did you know?' he asked cautiously.

'I guessed. Why be shy with your sister? Me, of all people!'

'I wanted to be sure.'

Bruce returned to his eggs. He cut one piece, then another, then a third, before putting his fork down in the gesture of a man who'd lost his appetite.

'You're thinking of marriage, but she isn't? Or she is, but you're in a state of maybe? What do you mean by "sure"? You've asked, and you're waiting for an answer?' Bruce rose to none of Nancy's speculations. 'He's a man and you're ashamed to admit it!'

'Don't be ridiculous!'

'Then it's a parrot!'

Bruce threw his napkin on the table.

'Does she paint?' Nancy asked quietly.

'Actually, yes, she does.'

'Does she have a name? Do I know her? I'm certain she lives in Edinburgh, but it would be nice to be proved right,' Nancy said, her voice shifting from the sisterly to the annoyed.

'You honestly guessed?'

'And I bet you told that blighted fowl, but you couldn't bring yourself to tell me. I'd like to know why. *Did* you tell Percy?'

'Anita McFarlane, and you don't know her,' Bruce said rapidly. 'She's thirty-six and she's an economist, in banking. Very senior, very highly thought of. She hasn't been married before, and she certainly isn't married now, in case *that* was worrying you.'

'How did you meet her?'

'It's none of your business!'

'Oh, shy, are we? You always were. I bet you didn't make the running. Did you?'

A habit of Nancy's that outraged her brother took the form of silent appeals to imaginary presences in the room. Disbelief drove Bruce from the table.

She jumped off her chair and followed him down the length of the hall. 'It's perfectly natural that I should want to know!' she shouted after him. He ran up the stairs taking them two or three at a time, a speed Nancy was incapable of matching. 'You're my *brother*!' Outside the locked bathroom door, she said, 'The later you left it, the more anxious I've been. Nothing much seemed to be happening in that department other than Deirdre Horse-face, and *that* was an unmitigated disaster! Bruce! I'm delighted you've met someone!'

'Go away!'

'You're pushing forty! It's high time you got married. I might be bad at showing it, but I'm happy for you!'

A bellicose parrot is a lousy companion especially if, like Percy, he taunts, as he did Nancy, with mispronunciations of her name. His shrunken vowels and swallowed consonants reminded her of the harsh propriety of speech shared by her mother and her cronies. They reminded her of Mrs Gifford's chronic bronchitis through which an increasingly vituperative personality had been expressed in gargled croaks. 'Go on, Mother, spit it out,' Nancy used to say, as her mother coughed while she tried to adjust herself into a comfortable position in bed. Mrs Gifford was disappointed in her daughter. Nancy's dismissal of Hugh Hannah was, in Mrs Gifford's words, no more than a gutless inability to take the rough with the smooth.

'Hanky-panky's only to be expected in this day and age,' Mrs Gifford stated. 'God knows, it was common enough in mine.'

'And some of it all of your very own, Mother,' Nancy said.

'You're trying to be insolent, but you won't offend me. Anyway, you know what your father was like. Can you blame me? I was never the sort of woman who sits at home with her crochet. "Would you care for a refreshment?" ' she said, mimicking the late Mr Gifford's ponderous hospitality. 'He was the meanest man I ever met. He kept the cheapest wine, the lousiest whisky imaginable, and had that ugly Irish girl serve them in the smallest glasses you ever put a lip to! And him with a cupboard full of his family's absolutely *delightful* crystal, which he would *never* allow me to put on the table.'

'You're being obsessive, Mother.'

'Hugh might still take you back,' Mrs Gifford said. She coughed. Nancy gave her an enamel dish to spit into. 'If you'd any sense you'd have turned a blind eye.'

'It wasn't only his infidelity,' Nancy said.

'Men get over their rampant phases, you know. He'll calm down. In no time at all he'll be as domestic as you like if that's what you want,' Mrs Gifford said before another strenuous outbreak of coughing brought her to a halt and Nancy returned the enamel dish.

'But what do you do?' Mrs Gifford said. 'You shame me; you trot back to Mummy. You embarrass me, deeply. You wound me with prattle about how you're going to get back the wedding presents from *our* family. You stupid woman! Anyone will tell you!' She broke off to clear her throat. 'If you try to divorce a lawyer, there's hell to pay! Wealth!' she said several times, working up to a whisper. 'Well, do something! Get me a drink!'

Nancy's confrontations with her mother failed to rattle her. When she'd woken up that morning, suspecting that the rumours of Hugh Hannah's faithlessness were probably true, the absence of sorrow was explained by the realization that she no longer even liked him. Even then, Hugh was scouting the opportunities of the times. When he was in town, almost every evening was spent entertaining, or being entertained; her objections were dismissed on the grounds of social and business necessity. She sickened of his money-talk, and of the contrast between his benign smoothness in public, and, in private, his monologues on the future, his ambition, opportunity, his speeches about how this was wide-open to take, and that was doomed to closure, while this was where tomorrow's lucre would be found.

Bruce left the house, slamming four doors one after the other.

'Percy,' Nancy said to the parrot, 'if I'd the courage, I'd throttle you. Then I'd put you in a brown paper parcel and send you to Hugh Hannah, of whom you've heard so much over the passing years. It wouldn't surprise me if you remember him. It wouldn't surprise me if you *liked* him.'

When Bruce came home, the first thing he said was, 'I'm not talking about it. Not one word more on the subject until I say it myself.'

'How very masterful,' Nancy said, with an impertinent curtsey as she opened the sitting room door for him. 'Some whisky, for your nerves?'

As always, Percy fluttered with welcome, then walked the length of Bruce's arm to his shoulder.

'Having thought of little else all day, other than, of course, the laundry, the vacuuming, the washing-up and what to have for dinner, I really do insist on a few questions,' Nancy said.

'I won't answer them,' Bruce said, poking his nose against Percy's beak.

Nancy poured herself a drink. Her crystal glass was one from her father's family stock, kept for years in a cupboard in the dining room. 'Pour your own,' she said. 'I flatly refuse to pour a drink for a man with a parrot on his shoulder. And a yo-ho-ho to you, too,' she said, raising her tumbler to Percy.

The parrot jumped up on Bruce's head as Bruce left the room.

'What about *me*?' Nancy shouted at the closing door. 'Where do *I* come in. Where do I *live*? What do I do for *money*?' She thought she noticed hesitation in the last few inches of the door closing. It seemed to her that Bruce's hand remained thoughtfully on the doorknob for seconds longer than he intended. 'If you haven't thought about *me*, then I think you should!'

Nancy approached her morning's housework with her customary reluctance. Apart from the kitchen and bathroom, both of which were modernized a few years before, nothing in the house seemed implicated wholeheartedly in the late 1980s. Much of the furniture looked as if it had turned its back on the present, or still lived in the nineteenth century. She'd read that the preferences of the past were staging a come-back. Glossy new periodicals were dedicated to this retrogressive fashion. She couldn't work out why. As if reading her mind, oak and mahogany sideboards, dressers and bookcases seemed to look at her with the smug satisfaction of those proved right. Redecorating, which had been done around the same time as the bathroom and kitchen, resulted in sprucing up the taste of her grandparents' generation, handed down to their children and their children's children. Anita McFarlane was still at child-bearing age. If Bruce and she married, there might be yet another Gifford to inherit the house and what it signified.

Bruce, though, was a Gifford. Brilliant at respectability, the Giffords had never been much use at marriage, sex or happiness, although why the three should always be linked struck Nancy as incorrigible wishful-thinking on the part of the married or would-be married population of the entire world.

Room after room told Nancy the same Gifford stories. There was the photograph of her grandmother who died in a swimming accident at the age of thirty-two. Photographs of her mother and father spoke of how two smiles could lie about love for the sake of a posterity recorded in the lifetime of a picture. He had been ten years older than Mrs Gifford, whose vivacity he'd endured with abject puzzlement. Her social energy left him gasping for breath. Mrs Gifford posed on the mudguard of a long-snouted car, the spoked wheels and white-wall tyres of which looked the embodiment of 1933; and twelve years later, with padded shoulders and her hair piled high on her head, she looked the portrait of a well-to-do woman-about-town on the wartime cocktail circuit, which she was. With Nancy at five years old, her mother looked proud, pleased, and on the point of falling off her heels. Mr Gifford stood several feet off at the side, stiff, worried, and more like the girl's grandfather.

Even the set of initialled napkin rings were sly agents of her servitude. Dead energy lurked in corners, under beds, in drawers and cupboards. High, at the back of the house, three tiny rooms lay empty save for an unmade-up single bed in each. They were where the live-in housekeeper had once slept, and Elsie, the Irish maid who'd doubled for several years as a nanny. These were forlorn rooms, empty spaces, tokens of sleep, exhaustion and reminders of a time, not all that long ago, of sturdy prosperity and a degree of comfort, being looked after, taking life for granted, that had by now come to seem preposterously remote. Enjoying that now called for the success, acumen and resourcefulness of a Hugh Hannah. The third room was where the housekeeper's timid little boy had slept. Leaving and entering the house by the proverbial tradesman's entrance at the back, Nancy had seldom seen her contemporary.

'You'll get indigestion,' Nancy said as Bruce wolfed his fish.

'I'm late, and I want a bath. Besides, I've never been dyspeptic in my life. Did you switch on the hot water?'

'Have I ever forgotten?'

He was hungry, and cross. It was Friday evening and he was leaving for Edinburgh after his bath.

'When did you take up smoking again?' he asked.

'Shows how observant *you* are,' she said. 'I've been puffing the odd drag on the sly for weeks.'

'People who kick the habit, then start again . . . '

'Isn't it time you outlined your plans, Bruce? I'm involved in them, whether you've thought about it or not. Or would you like me to enlist a lawyer and have him speak to yours? "I'm sorry to bother you, but my brother and I feel compelled to contemplate going our separate ways." "Any dependants, Nancy?" "Well, yes, George, I'*m* a dependant. And then there's Percy. You may remember he had a go at your nose once. Yes, Percy Parrot, the very same. I do *not* want custody of Percy." '

Bewildered by her fantasy conversation, Bruce expostulated wordlessly, then said, 'You wouldn't dream of asking George Symonds to act for you!'

'Except for yours, his firm's the only one in town,' Nancy said. 'And I like George.'

'George?'

'There is nothing wrong in how I competed for his affection with his fiancée. But didn't people think so? *Natter-natter.*' Nancy's hand mouthed like a gossip in full flight. 'Intellectually, George is about as quick as a sideboard, but he's pleasant. Where does he get those ties of his? *Always* beautifully turned out. And their house is a delight. That little wife of his must be awfully industrious. I say hello to her in the street. *No* hard feelings between us. Well, she got him, didn't she? She can afford to be magnanimous. Oh, I'd have no compunction whatsoever in asking George. He's been married for long enough by now to pity me. I couldn't choose a better lawyer.'

'It won't come to that. I've been giving you a great deal of thought.'

'How nice.'

He finished his glass of water. 'Is there pudding?'

' "Is there pudding"? There's *always* pudding! Can Anita McFarlane cook? She's a career woman, by the sound of her. Not that I actually *know* anything about her. Can she iron shirts, darn socks, and sew on buttons?' Her voice changed from the aggressively flippant to the quietly serious. 'Where are you thinking of living? Here, or there?'

'How could it be anywhere other than here?' he said, meaning that his law firm made it impossible to live anywhere else.

'This house belonged to Grandfather Gifford, but he didn't live in it. His two elder sisters did. When mother and father got married, the awful great-aunties were turfed out and for all I know sold into slavery in Ayr. So it became ours. Or it became yours. You're younger, but it became yours. So, what happens to me? Where do I live?'

'It's big enough for three, but . . . '

'My mind's at rest!' she screamed to an invisible third party. 'I'm going to be Cinderella when I grow up! Unpaid scullery wench, cook, general handywoman, and handmaiden to my brother's career! From Mrs Hugh Hannah to domestic toilet skivvy!' She turned and glared at Bruce. 'Buy me somewhere else. A flat above a hardware shop will do. Anything. I'll look for a job. I'm led to believe they're as rare as parrots' teeth, but I'll find one.'

'Don't assume that I haven't been thinking ... '

'I've been giving myself a lot of thought, too! Have you a photograph?' Bruce looked confused. 'Anita McFarlane, you dope! The Edinburgh girl-economist! I'm dying of curiosity! I know what I can do. I'll find a job in a posh little dead-end of a private girls' school. I'll teach them about men. A photograph? Haven't you got one? Bruce, this is the sort of moment that a sister takes very seriously, especially when her brother's acted since adolescence like an erotic nitwit!'

He took his wallet from his jacket and fished out a snapshot encased in protective plastic. He was anxious enough to nibble a fingernail as he watched Nancy examine Anita McFarlane's head-and-shoulders. 'Don't do that,' Nancy said, meaning the finger in his mouth. 'And don't let her see you do it, either.' She looked at the photograph again. 'She's very presentable. In fact, she's attractive. How come she's still single?'

'Career,' Bruce said.

'Is she tall, short, or what? You can't tell much from this ... '

'Quite tall, yes; about an inch shorter than me. I've never fallen for anyone quite like this before. I know I'm far from prepossessing and all that stuff. Mother used to say there were dependable types, types who were too-damned-dependable, and give her a totally unreliable gondolier any day of the week. I wish she'd never said it. I docket myself in the middle category.'

'Yes, well, she was married to one and resented it. On the other hand, I wouldn't accept Mother's word on any subject, especially men. Does Anita know that you have a sister?'

'Yes, of course,' Bruce said, offended.

'Then I suppose she's aware that I'm the ex-Mrs Hugh Hannah?'

'Nancy, anyone who's anyone knows that Hugh was married before. *Most* people know *who* he was married to. It's public knowledge. It's not as if it's a big country, sis. When I've been introduced to people, they've actually asked if I'm your brother. I mean, people in Edinburgh who remember you. Some of them are old friends of

Hugh's. I've never had the heart to pass on their best wishes, or whatever it is they say. To some people I'm the brother of the woman who used to be married to Hugh Hannah,' he said in a manner that made it clear he disliked the distinction.

'McFarlane? I don't recall any McFarlanes from that time,' Nancy said.

'Anita's father had you and Hugh to dinner once. You had them to dinner, too. He sees Hugh fairly regularly.'

'I don't remember them,' Nancy said. 'In these high-class circles which you seem to mix in these days, does it worry you that I'm Hugh Hannah's ex?'

'So many people talk about him,' Bruce said.

'I see. Well, I say "I see," but I don't really.'

'He's a tremendously popular man.'

'He's very famous, I grant you. No, I can imagine,' she said. 'It's probably wildly inaccurate, but I can imagine people I knew in 1965 – I mean, I can imagine what they're like now. Old scandal would die hard in that tribe. Well, not "scandal" exactly. Something tasty to talk about. I'd like to meet Anita, and I think I ought to. You ought to bring her here,' Nancy said, thinking that she was being generous.

'She's been already.'

'When?'

'That Saturday you went to see cousin Letty in Ayr,' he said with the look of a man making a confession.

Nancy puffed, trying to blow away her exasperation. 'All very hush-hush, eh? Are you ashamed of me?'

'No!'

'Showing her the house, were you?'

'She liked it!' Bruce said, as if it were a good thing to say. 'She went on and on about the furniture. She really liked it. She said she felt really comfortable with the feel of the place,' he said eagerly, thinking it would please Nancy.

'You'd better run and have your bath,' Nancy said.

'She took to Percy straight off,' Bruce said smiling with remembered pleasure. 'And Percy took to Anita. I was worried about that. It's not everyone who does, as you know.'

He had his bath, dressed, and came down carrying his small suitcase on which his father's initials were stamped in pocked and faded gold.

'Ask Anita to come *here* for the weekend,' Nancy said. 'Next week-end, or at least very soon.'

'I'll do that,' he said, fumbling in his coat pocket for his car keys.

It was raining. Nancy took an umbrella from the hall and held it over him as they trotted together to Bruce's car. Rain pattered excitedly on the umbrella. Bruce didn't notice that Nancy was getting soaked. She stood in the beam of his headlights as he reversed the length of the drive. Once he reached the road he flashed his lamps a few times before turning the car, and then – an unheard of event outside that house – he sounded his horn a few times before driving away.

Hazards of the House

A complicated existence is inevitable for those of us fated to live close to the ground. Self-defensive footwork and vindictive farce are staples in our art of survival. Exhaustive television coverage is all we need to perfect the miseries of our diminutive prestige and reputation for being puny, disposable, and, to use a loathsome word, vermin. Butchered, mortally wounded or concussed, we are dropped into dustbins or ejected through open windows in flourishes of domestic defenestration. Our ignominious endings fail to trouble human conscience. Instead, they seem cause for relief and congratulatory pats on the back. How they can call themselves Christians, Buddhists, Muslims or Hindus, or humanitarians, or whatever, is beyond the powers even of my incredible intellect to understand.

Before this present lot arrived I had an agreeable time working my way through a sack of walnuts. They were dumped in the kitchen by the housekeeper. Anything half-way towards being hoardable appeals to her peasant nature, even if it's at least thirty years since peasant priorities were truly at the front of her mind. The landlord is blissfully absentee. He is a scholar in the history of art for whom a house in this part of the world was a matter of great fashionable concern and finesse. Now it is a source of rent that helps him to support a house in Tuscany I never see him. His housekeeper lives 500 metres away. For some if not all of the year where I live is, therefore, relaxingly vacant.

Being as aboriginal as I am – almost – the housekeeper never throws a feminine fit when she sees me. '*Souris? Bonjour souris!*' she says. That's *nice*. She's around fifty, and heavily cosmeticized as if still unfamiliar with prosperity. She wears stockings with seams and has many love affairs. I know about this, because here is where she conducts them. Like most men in the village, her husband lives in his cellar, armchaired beside a barrel of Armagnac from noon until the hour of collapse. Everything in the village is run by women.

When she treads on a nut that I've rolled playfully over the floor the previous night, she knows exactly what I've been up to, and looks for me. My nocturnal Sisypheanism amuses her, even if she just calls it nut-rolling – I mean, what does she know of Albert Camus? Still, I mustn't condescend. She is a housekeeper; she understands that another nut will have taken its place by tomorrow morning.

Tenants had come and gone since April, but the most recent couple arrived at the beginning of July. There was a tiresome clatter of heavy objects outside the front door. Voices, spouting bad French with a self-confident disregard of grammar, of which only the filthy English are capable, entered with the housekeeper, and poor Madame Rougier kept up an appearance of courtesy and good-nature in spite of the odds against her. The couple enthused over everything they clapped eyes on, ransacking a phrase book to find a name for what delighted them. We're an up-market establishment. Visitors' voices tend to be shrill and ebullient. When not, they are shrill and critical. Being an old hand at observing them, I know that the delight will soon be punctured by a complaint. Usually it is unnecessary, but they seem under some sort of obligation to make it. 'Oh, dear, I don't think this will do at all, darling. Would you tell her, please?' The poor man quivered then tried to work out how to say in French that a dripping tap would have to be repaired as soon as possible. All it took was a turn of the wrist.

'Oh-oh,' I thought. 'Here we go again.'

Indeed, we went.

One reason why I live alone is that I have always supposed myself to be a peculiarly selfish specimen. Matrimony, fatherhood and brats have no appeal for me. Solitude and the life of the mind are what I need, but then I have always said that an artist should never marry. It is just my luck that I should choose an otherwise ideal place to live regularly swamped by hyperactive intruders. Perversely, I think I enjoy their antics; I relish my critical perspectives on their bad behaviour.

Scampering nervously from room to room, I scouted my comfortably overlarge estate for signs of the kind of people they were. Shifted furniture, strewn shoes and clothes, can, in a few moments, transform familiar topography into a threatening new continent. These people were downright menaces. She appeared to have a highly developed sense of the tasteful emplacement of furniture. Wardrobes, sideboards, beds and what-nots squeaked as they were heaved over the floors. You have no idea how these timber noises travel through the dry, woody darkness of my domain under the floorboards. My teeth were set on edge.

Showing oneself for the first time is to dice with death. There is an exhilaration to it, a sensory thrill. Philosopher I may be, but a Puck-ish disregard of alien attitudes makes me also a type characteristic of my species. One false move, an unexpectedly nimble tantrum on the part of one's opponent, and the result might be a squashed demise under any of the several vulgar tomes left around the house by its bookish proprietor. Imagine it – to die under the weight of a flashy survey of modern art such as the owner leaves lying around to prove the cultural worth of his premises! But yes, I admit to a self-conscious savouring of sheer heroism as I venture on these first steps of deliberate annoyance. I rushed into the middle of the living-room floor, then stopped, grinned, and, deafened by the woman's shrieks, made a break for it back to the hide-out from which I'd launched my charge.

My efforts – *heh-heh* – fairly took them by storm. Most tenants imbibe greedily on their first night, and these were no exception. False happiness was in the air. They were tipsy, but tense. With almost disappointing predictability, she leapt up on a stool. 'Geof-frey! Geoffrey!' she shouted. '*Do* something!' she commanded of her husband.

In no time at all Geoffrey laid his hands on a broom and began swinging it in search of something to strike dead. By then I was safely established in a cranny from which to observe his gymnastics. As often happens, he launched a face-saving explosion of activity against a corner, where, he lied, he said he'd seen me. It was a false sighting that made his wife's stool unsafe. She leapt from it to the table, heedless of the havoc she created to glasses, dishes and the remains of dinner. Geoffrey thrashed with the broom. A few moments later, watching his wife jump up and down on the table, he said, 'Hilda, for heaven's sake, it's just a *mouse*!' But I could see that I was more than that. It wasn't the first time. Remorse wilted my whiskers a little. Geoffrey gave up. He carried her out of the room. *Carried* her! She yelled to be put down. For the next half-hour she screamed at him. It was deafening. It was all about his general incompetence. As ever, I was in two minds. One part of me enjoyed the mayhem I caused. A mere pin-prick! What could I do were I to set my mind to it! Another part of me regretted their unhappiness. They'd brought it with them, of course; it wasn't my fault. But it was my destiny to act as a catalyst and bring it to a show-down. I'd seen it all before. The *déjà-vu* was crushing.

The following morning they gathered up their maps and guide-books and set off for a day's sightseeing. I concentrated on some jaunty sport with a few nuts, rolling them up and down the flag-stoned floor of the roomy kitchen with no end of enjoyment. It pre-pared me for more intellectual pleasures – the languors of philosophy, the anguish of lyric poetry, a contemplative memory of the perfections of Ronsard, Corneille, Racine, Diderot, Hugo, Flau-bert, Baudelaire ... Accordingly, I settled into a cushion like the small, ornamental voluptuary I have become. As soon as I heard their car outside, I was off. Vigilance, I knew, would be passionate. Not Geoffrey's perhaps, but Hilda's – he might come back with no thought of me in his mind, but I suspected that in her fraught, turbulent way she was hoping I might put in an appearance.

Quiet, remote, surrounded by spooky trees, a house plonked down in the middle of animal silences, it can be hard for city dwel-lers to get used to this house. A single, disruptive noise, such as that of a walnut rolled over a stone floor, can terrify these London strangers and keep them off their sleep.

A tell-tale blade of light shot through the space under their bed-room door. Hilda was probably at the sitting-up-in-bed-and-listen-ing stage, frigid with fright and imagining terrors such as the Axe Man of the Dordogne, Algerian rapists and the French Revolution. She nagged until Geoffrey re-emerged from the sleep of the over-exerted sightseer. I nudged the nut forward, then again, and, for the sheer hell of it, one more time.

Dressing-gowned and totally unconvincing, Geoffrey patrolled the house bearing the kitchen knife he had taken to bed as a precaution against the night. I almost died laughing as he tip-toed hesitantly before standing painfully on the hard, wrinkled testicle of a walnut. Hearing his cry, Hilda seemed to fear the worst, because she got up and slammed the bedroom door shut. From the noise she made it sounded as if she shoved pieces of furniture against it.

Geoffrey said soothingly, 'It's just the mouse. It's been shoving nuts over the floor. I stood on one. That's all.'

'Get it!' she shouted. 'Just ... *get it!*'

Padding about on his bare feet, Geoffrey did not look like a man intent on putting me or anything else to the sword. He tried the outside doors and reassured himself that they were locked. Keeping up with him, I observed the sane, tasteful and thoroughly élitist manner in which he glanced at shelves of paperbacks. They have their own pathos. Left by tenants, who might even have read them, they have been added to a hundred times, half-read by itinerant holidaymakers. 'I'm trying to fasten this window!' he shouted while browsing across the bent spines. How far these English are from Cartesian clarity, Bergsonian *élan vital*, or even simple existentialism. Do they have schools in England?

For me, nut-rolling is an exercise in existential ardour. A little more that night around the moment when they were ready to drop off could have driven Hilda crazy and egged on Geoffrey to mount a serious indoor safari. Somehow I didn't have the heart for it. There was an elegance to Geoffrey's melancholy that I fancied must be much like my own.

During the next week, however, there was nothing for it but to take time off from my philosophical studies and put in the occasional appearance. One tires so easily of Hume, Kant and Hegel. And as for Schopenhauer and Heidegger! Hilda wearied of shock and phobia. A braggart would go on endlessly about 'close shaves', that sort of thing. Flung plates, books, shoes, axes, pots and pans were all dementedly inaccurate.

'All I can say is that you're hopeless.' Hilda's accusation elicited a long-suffering shrug from her husband. 'Not that you were ever anything else.'

'Putting in a call to Tuscany over a mouse seems excessive to me.'

'I want you to complain!'

'Do you know who he is? He's on television.'

'I don't care if he speaks to the nation at Christmas! We're paying him! For this! For *mice*!'

Geoffrey went out and returned with Madame Rougier for whom an obtuse rodent is neither a problem nor a hazard of the house but a creature to be taken for granted. It was with no trepidation that I watched her open a cupboard and show the Wilmer-Maynes where the mousetraps were kept – English mousetraps, suitcased into rural France by the owner's wife many years ago. (Are there mice in Tuscany as expert as me? I hope so.) Hilda chopped up morsels of

Cantal, which, as it happens, is my favourite cheese. Baiting a trap, Geoffrey came close to amputating a finger. There's a lot I would do for a piece of Cantal, but leaping through snapping low-tech jaws is not one of them. My brain is not small – it is exquisite. Strolling beneath the business end of a guillotine is an act of suicidal lunacy that I forbid myself to contemplate. Hilda noticed an old packet of poisoned pellets retailed optimistically as a final solution to the mouse problem. What self-respecting mouse would consider eating what looks remarkably like rabbit droppings? Madame Rougier knew they were useless, and said so, but was either ignored or misunderstood. Dimwits put a lot of faith in these products. They never learn.

Friends of the Wilmer-Maynes arrived the following afternoon. They were just in time. I was beginning to suspect that if Geoffrey didn't catch me, his wife would very soon be at his throat.

'Surely, there's something wrong with it!' Dan exclaimed. 'It can't possibly be as perfect as it looks,' he said, wagging a finger, an action which led Geoffrey to look self-consciously at its bandaged counterpart on his right hand. 'What happened to your finger?'

'Oh, it's as peaceful, as idyllic, as it seems,' Geoffrey said.

'Such a gorgeous view!' Victoria said with a swoon.

'There's a restaurant about five miles up the road that's really worth the journey, not just from here, but from *London*,' Geoffrey said.

'Aren't you forgetting a tiny, itsy-bitsy, but thoroughly negative detail?' Hilda said. 'Our little, resident nuisances?'

'Mouse-trap,' Geoffrey said, showing his bandaged digit. 'We've a mouse.'

'Mice?' Dan said. His wife laughed. I smiled. It seemed to be the other way round with these two – the man loathed mice, the woman couldn't care less.

'There's only one mouse, Hilda,' Geoffrey said in a tone that to my keen ear summed up their marriage.

'Six, at the least, and the most perverse breed of mouse known to man,' Hilda said.

'I'm a bit allergic to mice,' Dan said, practically in a whisper.

'No, you're not,' Victoria said. 'You're terrified of them. It's as simple as that.'

'Well, traps set, poison lavishly distributed in all the strategic places. We shouldn't have any more trouble with mice,' Geoffrey said.

It was irresistible. Boldly, I dashed across the floor in an electrifying sprint.

All hell broke loose.

'Where?'

'There!'

'Where?'

'There, you fool!'

'*There!*'

Short, serious drinks were needed to help them calm down. Hilda was by now more angry than frightened, but Dan was a newcomer. No matter the other mice in his experience that had reduced him to a rigid impersonation of a man at the North Pole with no clothes on, he hadn't encountered *me* before.

'You'll never catch them with these,' Victoria said, holding up a trap. 'What you need is a good old-fashioned cat.'

Cats!

No sooner do you start feeling sorry for one of them, than the next thing you know he's agreeing that, yes, a cat might be the answer.

'Then Madame Rougier shall be instructed to acquire a cat,' Hilda said matter-of-factly.

'I'm ever-so-slightly allergic to cats,' Dan said. His wife hooted.

A conceited Persian swaggered into my domain on the heels of Madame Rougier, that obliging woman. I hoped she'd chosen the feline equivalent of the village idiot. It carried its tail high and ingratiated itself against their legs. Dan sneezed and went out into the fresh air. Well aware of the carnage it was employed to inflict, it took no time at all to boost itself into their favour. Up went its ears; its eyes flashed and then settled into a fierce stare while its white tail brushed the floor with purposeful swipes. It was staring at the wrong place and it knew it. Commissioned for a lethal task, it was doing what cats invariably do. It was applying itself to the business of rewards before shedding sweat on anyone's behalf. This was reassuring. All the same, I backed off with silent discretion.

The following morning, after the two couples left for the day, I emerged to reconnoitre and assess my enemy's weaponry. There he was, basking like a tyrannous Pasha in a sunbeam. He looked as if butter wouldn't melt in his mouth, or so I thought until I saw a dying lizard lying handily within claw range. Each time the expiring reptile twitched, he cuffed it, just to remind it that, yes, it was finished, and that he, its executioner, was highly delighted with the fact. These carpet-sharks are interested in one event, and it's dinner. Almost anything will do as a mid-morning snack, including me. They were starving the beast in the hope of getting its adrenalin flowing.

It prowled around the house like a private eye. It nosed here, there and everywhere, and it dozed with one eye cocked for signs of action. It preened its whiskers like a white hussar, as if trying to convince itself that it was dressed to kill. Its ancestors probably warmed themselves at the fire when Joan of Arc was burned. It worked out in the garden on hapless butterflies. The hairy gum-shoe, I wouldn't have been surprised to learn, probably charged a fat fee, payable in Swiss francs into a numbered bank account. It was a hit-cat. Or thought it was.

'Oh, he's doing his best!' Victoria said, defending the cat. It swanked and swaggered each time it presented a lizard, worm or little bird. 'What a *good* boy!' It would make you sick.

'Keep feeding the cat, lady,' I said each time it was awarded a plate. A fat predator can be avoided. 'Keep feeding the brute.'

Nocturnal nut-rolling was by then a pastime for a mouse with the death wish. Through sneaky loopholes I watched the barbaric feline prowl through the house as if it were his. He stalked like visual braggadocio, a real night-time Narcissus of death, gluttony and pain. He walked like a search party, interrogation team and firing squad all rolled into one fluffy sub-section of totalitarian malevolence. Occasional clouts on table legs were to remind any watching creature that they were dealing with an expert, and that he was *hungry*.

Fastidious as ever, both couples declared their bedrooms out of bounds to their furry protector. I decided to put all five of them through their paces. A swift passage across Hilda's face, under her nose, created what can be described as a localized, bedroom hurricane. Their mobility was phenomenal. Everything in the room seemed to move. Smaller objects actually winged through the air. Victoria and Dan were knocking on the Wilmer-Maynes's door.

Our whiskery friend darted into the room like the legendary reinforcements that arrive in the nick of time to save the beleaguered legionnaires from the terrible Riffs, or delectable Anglo-Saxon ladies from the rough attention of Apaches. Sideboards were moved, wardrobes shifted, in the hope of revealing me to their overfed assassin. By then, though, I was safely beneath the floorboards and savouring the satisfactions of having pulled off a successful hit-and-run raid.

Madame Rougier made a great show of being upset at the tenants' misfortunes. She advised them to really *starve* the cat and give it nothing to eat unless it produced a mouse. She was looking after her hopes of a tip such as visitors usually leave for her.

Still, I had the other couple to work on; pride prevented me from calling it a day and lying low. It was getting more difficult by the hour. Pride was working for the cat, too. It was in the cellars. It was everywhere. Treating it to a fiasco and showing it up as a dead loss were desperate measures needed to get rid of it.

It was a hot night and Dan slept with a leg sticking out from his bed covers. White, a toe-nail winking in moonlight, Dan's foot was a tempting target but a bit high up for me to reach. Prudence encouraged me to wait. A little later Dan's leg reached to the floor. All awkwardness of ascent now solved, I ran up Dan's leg.

Anguish rattled in his throat. Simultaneously, he was petrified and all over the place. Victoria called him names and said things that I suppose were unforgivable. She slapped his face in an attempt to recover his sanity from the boundaries of terror over which his mind had crossed. Geoffrey and Hilda were on the scene and trying to calm them down without stopping to think that they stood in need of a tranquillizer or two themselves.

Getting out of the room was not going to be easy, at least not from how the lie of the land seemed from the shoe in which I hid. Another guerrilla masterpiece had been achieved, but it was too early for self-congratulation. Out of the corner of an eye I saw the grim form of the cat sitting at the open window, having jumped up from outside. A cool, luminous figure, I couldn't stop myself admiring its poise. It was clearly taking its bearings before homing in. One to one, and I was outnumbered like mad. It poured itself from sill to floor. My heart beat a retreat down the length of my tail and left without me. That furry snatch-squad leapt at me in a milky movement and I shot forward, straight underneath him. It demonstrated on a sock what it would have done to me if I hadn't been so nifty in darting behind the skirting boards, which took heavy punishment from its frustrated claws.

No one was in two minds about it now; the gloves were off. 'But he nearly got him!' Victoria protested.

'I put it to you that this was a sock,' Dan said, holding up the tattered remains. 'A sock, before your beloved little Purrypaws mistook it for a mouse!'

The cat was sniffing busily around the sitting room, cheering itself on, and unable to admit that it had met its match.

'A mouse! All this for a *mouse*!' Victoria said with exasperated contempt.

'I couldn't agree more,' Geoffrey said. 'A harmless, innocent creature. Unwitting object of childish phobias and totally irrational obsessions.'

'The cat *goes*,' Dan said, having first braced himself to make this manly command.

The cat was carried away by Madame Rougier.

They sat in the sun, drank wine, read books. Some days they set off together to visit caves and castles. I rested up in the shadowy corners, re-reading Proust.

Their tenancy was nearing an end. On their second-last evening Geoffrey complained of having caught a cold. He stayed in while the others went off to the restaurant.

'Go on,' he said, when he saw me. 'Relax. Roll a nut!' I looked at him. 'No one else is here. They've gone out,' he said. 'You're perfectly safe with me.' He was drinking. 'All gone out for the evening,' he said, sweeping his arms in a gesture of relief and freedom. 'I like mice. Now I come to think of it, I've always liked mice. I used to have a mouse of my own. A white mouse. Up its little ladders, round and round on its little wheel.' He poured himself another drink. 'Cheers!' he said, sniffing, then blowing his nose. 'I almost always catch a cold on holiday,' he said. He raised his glass to me. 'I called him Maurice. Round and round on his little wheel. Up and down on his little ladders.'

Native Heath

Joe Crockett's elderly pick-up truck strained over the summit of Riecar Hill, where the twists and dips of the Old Eldrick Road level out into a flat, windy, desolate stretch of remoteness. Acres of boggy upland fill the eye with impressions of inhospitable terrain. It seems big, but isn't. Here and there a grassy ruin proves that at one time a few families grazed herds, coaxed a crop or two, or otherwise squeezed a livelihood from infertile ground.

A lone pedestrian that far up the Old Eldrick Road was an uncommon sight. Crockett was startled by the man in the near distance for reasons other than that he was there at all. Something about his shape, size and walk was reminiscent. Wary, curious, willing to disbelieve his intuition, Crockett let the pick-up continue at a prudent speed. His hunch crept closer to certainty as they drew together. Crockett eased to a stop. So, too, did the man on foot. Crockett felt like backing off, turning round, and heading back to Dellonburn to spread the news.

Surely George Barr should have recognized him by now? Crockett was confused. It was a long time since he'd seen George Barr. But even with a beard the face of the pedestrian was unmistakable. Barr's appearance had aged in a way that highlighted his remembered looks. He was too distinctive – the same black hair, copious black eyebrows, striking eyes, prominent nose, full mouth, the lean but broad-shouldered height of the man – for a beard and shabby clothes to hide or alter him.

'It's me! Brock!' Crockett called from the cabin of his small truck. 'Do ye no' recognize me? Brock Crockett!' he shouted as Barr walked past.

Crockett emphasizing his own nickname worked quickly on Barr's purposeful mind. Without wanting to, he found himself hesitating. He knew how near he was to Dellonburn and the last thing he needed was discovery or distraction. An encounter with a man who knew him well, whom Barr knew well, was what he hadn't bargained for. He stopped and waited as Crockett reversed along-side. When he looked up Crockett was standing there.

'I could hardly believe my eyes!' Crockett spoke with trembling affability. 'I said, "Naw, naw, it canny be George." But there ye are. It's you, large as life!'

The slam of the pick-up's door sounded to Barr's ears to have happened thirty seconds after the event. It was as if it coincided with Brock's forced, fumbling handshake. Barr smiled faintly, unable, too, to help himself from making a nod of acknowledgement.

'God above, George, but naebody could say ye look prosperous.' He looked at Barr's dirty clothes and his shoes that looked as if another mile would finish them off.

Barr felt like knocking Crockett down and walking over him. He wanted their meeting to vanish and become a cancelled incident. He wanted it erased from the air. He inched forward slowly and Crockett walked with him.

'Look, George, you know me. Was anybody better 'n me at makin' excuses? I'm supposed to fix some wee wife's washin'-machine in Eldrick. I could as easily spin ye down to Dellonburn, no problem. Would ye like a lift?'

The offer sounded too generous; it was made with a chuckle that Barr heard as unintended. How could a man in George Barr's condition turn down the offer of a lift? That was what Barr heard in the chuckle. Either that or Crockett's edgy slip of a laugh testified to an agitated insincerity. But Barr knew it was as bad for Crockett as for himself. He found Crockett's embarrassment satisfying and resented the minor pleasure it gave him.

Brock laughed again. This time it seemed to be at the absurd out-of-the-blue coincidence of their meeting. Barr opened the door to the driver's side of the truck. 'Other side, George,' Mouser said.

Barr turned powerfully on the step and winded Crockett with an angerless thrust of the flat of his shoe against his stomach. Crockett fell over, groaning with astonishment and worried about what might happen next. He was up on his feet before Barr managed to start the pick-up.

'Some o' us were worried about you!' Crockett shouted. He was frightened and offended at the same time. He banged his fist on the locked door. 'I didny deserve that! No' me! I'll drive ye there, if that's what ye want!' In Crockett's face Barr fancied he could read signs of frustrated remorse, pity, and the anger of a man disappointed with himself. 'Don't cause trouble, George!' Crockett shouted. 'For God's sake, no trouble!' he pleaded.

Barr jolted the engine and reversed the crotchety pick-up off the road, turning it round to face the direction of Dellonburn. Crockett sat down on the other side of the road and watched Barr drive off. He realized that Barr hadn't said a word. Eldrick was nearer. He began walking towards it as fast as he could. He had to get to a telephone.

From the sensations of walking, Barr found himself thrust into modernity as if he'd crossed abruptly from one century to another. Hilly roads, narrow, downhill bends, were disobliging to a man who hadn't driven in years. After a few miles he stalled on a steep corner he'd forgotten was there. After a few minutes of hopeless peering into the engine, he freewheeled the vehicle off the road, and left it there, its bonnet raised and its engine steaming with a faint hiss. There was still a reasonable chance of hoofing it into Dellonburn before Crockett made it to Eldrick. He began to run. He threw his small bag into a ditch.

Martin Binnie's nursery was shielded from the main road by a much higher privet hedge than when Barr had last seen it. Trimmings were scattered along its foot. Some had been raked into mounds, and the tool with which it had been done was propped against the neatly squared section where someone had recently been at work. Barr was in the mood to see this as evidence that the work had suddenly been left off, interrupted, perhaps by an urgent message. Therefore, he walked cautiously through the open gate and over the drive which pointed towards the nursery on one side and a house on the other. Two substantial greenhouses looked as if they'd been put up a few years back. Two others, lightweight metal structures covered in plastic sheeting, seemed more recent. Wheelbarrows, seed boxes, coiled hoses, tools, plantpots, and all the rest of it – Barr had been used to the place; despite its enlargement he could tell at a glance that it wasn't worked as well as before – too many bits and pieces had the appearance of lying there for too long. There was an atmosphere of indolence and neglect, with which the untrimmed remainder of the high hedge – by far the larger part of it – now looked in keeping.

Barr was wrong about Binnie rushing off the job after being told to expect an unwelcome visitor. He'd gone back to the house with his hangover, rattled that his hedge trimmer had packed up on him. From the kitchen window he watched Barr taking in the details of the place. First, the shock of seeing Barr forced him to sit down. His kettle switched itself off with a click. That innocent kitchen-noise was enough to trigger panic. Unlike Crockett, Binnie's grounds for disquiet and fear were more precise, more justified. Over the past two years he'd imagined what he'd say and do were Barr to turn up and face him. Now that it was about to happen his tormented forecasts of his own behaviour and emotions were all proved wrong. Instead, what he felt was relief, but with enough fear remaining for him to rush to a cupboard, take a bottle of whisky and drop back a serious slug of the stuff. He felt his hand lean among hardening crumbs on the board where he cut bread. Noticing the big bread knife, he hid it in a drawer.

No one thought ill of Binnie for saying in court what he'd seen and heard. It was inconclusive evidence; Binnie had admitted to 90 percent certainty, but he was too familiar with Barr for that small element of unsureness to sound other than local wishful thinking. Now, though, Binnie was practically ostracized in Dellonburn, but, curiously, they thought worse of George Barr, as if they refused to accept the real killer's confession two years before, when Barr was in the twelfth year of his sentence. For Binnie, the last two years had been difficult. He was a true representative of Dellonburn, puzzled and battered by mistaken malice while protesting innocence and decency. Having swallowed its own poison, Dellonburn either refused to spit it out, or tried but failed, enough of the toxicity remaining to suggest that it might be as indigenous as other, sweeter phenomena – a thousand acts of kindness, children singing in a primary-school classroom, the thoughtful, head-bowed sorrow of old men and women on Armistice Day.

Binnie heard footsteps crunch slowly over the gravel. He'd done nothing about locking doors. He took another swig. Dispirited serenity crept into and ended two apprehensive years. How would an apology sound? How would Barr take Binnie's miserable account of what had happened to *him*? – his wife unable to take any more of it, and gone, with their children; the contempt, evasion and sneering silences in Dellonburn.

When Binnie looked out of the window again it was in time to catch a glimpse of Barr leaving through the open gate. Binnie's absolute certainty of recognition reminded him of his evidence – Barr's back, fourteen years on, then a side view as he approached the gate, from all of fifty yards away. He ran the cold tap at the sink by the kitchen window and flushed water over his hands and face. 'It's come down through channels. He doesn't bear a grudge.' Binnie remembered what the local police sergeant had told him and Telford two years ago. 'You've nothing to worry about. I doubt if Barr's inclined to see here again. But any contact, or you two see anything suspicious, pick up the blower. And another thing. Tell me if journalists, nosy-parkers, sniffers, or people writing books about "miscarriages of justice" turn up on your doorstep bearin' pads 'n' biros.' It wasn't over yet. Binnie sat down and stared at the telephone on the kitchen wall.

Between the nursery and the town Barr passed houses that he'd never seen before. There were streets of them stretching back from the main road. They'd been there long enough for their trees and shrubs to begin to look mature. Just before the town itself was a supermarket set well back from the road behind an extensive car park. But now that he was almost in Dellonburn itself – the three familiar steeples – he wasn't in the mood for niceties of observation and contrasts of old and new.

Oliphant Street was close enough to his memory of it despite several modernized shop fronts and general up-datedness. He flinched from recognition by people whom he couldn't care less whether they saw him or not. He was conscious, too, of inviting it and prepared to disregard the shocks or comments which his undaunted presence might elicit.

Even if Binnie phoned the police, or Telford, there was nothing anyone could do. He was innocent. He was a traveller, passing through his home town; he had lawful business to transact. Or so he reassured himself. He stepped into Telford's newsagent's shop.

The young woman behind the main counter was too young to have remembered him. She would know about him if only because a violent crime reared itself out of the past two years previously. 'Miscarriage of justice', 'wrongful imprisonment', 'compensation' – among other younger inhabitants in the district, she might have wondered why older people refused to accept these terms as true, or why they saw the third as an offensive investment following unacceptably from the others, like a nest-egg hatched by wickedness, but theirs, not his. He paid for a newspaper with small change and smiled at her. She looked in two minds about smiling back.

At the back of the shop, behind another counter, an arch was hung with multicoloured plastic strips. As Barr parted these strings, the girl said, 'Excuse me!' He stepped inside.

Telford looked up from his coffee and biscuits. He stared at Barr who stood just inside the arch, two strips on his left shoulder, one red, one yellow; he brushed them off – and stared back.

'Don't you lay a hand on me! I'm warning you!' Telford stood up and backed further away, although there was nowhere for him to go. He went back to the table and, still staring at Barr, fumbled for the telephone. Barr heard the faint sound of the dialling tone. He smiled, and backed out of the room.

'I'm sorry,' Barr said to Telford's shop assistant. 'I don't kill women. Never have done. Never will.'

As he continued down the pavement a patrol car followed him at walking pace. Barr stopped, looked at the police car, then pointed across the broad, market area of Oliphant Street to the firm of solicitors where his business lay. He said nothing, and neither did the two occupants of the car. Once outside where he was headed, Barr waited a few seconds for the police to finish a U-turn and catch up. He pointed to the door then looked up the street at the clock on the County Hotel. It was 11.30. He'd made good time. He nodded to the sergeant, who'd taken his cap off to hang out of the car window for a closer look. Barr nodded again, as if to say, 'Yes, it's me. You're absolutely right.' He supposed that Crockett or Binnie had phoned them.

Several lawyers and secretaries looked in through the glass door of the office where Barr was asked to sit before the partner who'd inherited his file came in. 'I'm Archie MacDonald.' They shook hands.

'Son of?' Barr asked.

'Nephew.' He went to the door in answer to a knock on it. A secretary handed over a large wad of files. 'We did our best to trace you.'

'Bristoi. I'd a job there.'

'What as? The Invisible Man?'

'Builder's labourer. Different name. But I'm back being me again. They'd never heard of me there, anyway. It was probably a bit daft.'

'You didn't take the compensation.'

'I wasn't ready. I wrote with an explanation,' Barr said. 'I hope it's still there, Mr MacDonald.'

'Postmarked Harwich.'

'Friend of a friend was going there. I asked him to pop it in a post-box,' Barr said with a smile.

'Right. First things first. I'll need proof of identification,' MacDonald said, feeling silly at saying it. 'I'm pretty sure of who you are, George, but I need proof.'

Barr took several items from his inside pockets. 'Passport. Birth certificate. Savings account book. Bank card. Very respectable, eh?'

'I'm not being critical, George, but you don't look it.'

'I felt like a walk.'

'From Bristol?'

'I could've taken a train, or a bus. But I needed time. It's very hard to explain, Archie. I came the slow way to make sure I was doing the right thing. A long walk clears the mind and keeps it steady. But actually, I had my doubts. A slightly overwrought, big, loud voice in here was yelling "Don't!" Another one, the legendary still, wee whisper, was saying, "Get a move on, George. Go man, go!" I'm above-board, Archie. I'm who I say I am. Did you get my letter, addressed to your uncle?'

'I got it. Didn't say much. You're more or less on time, though. Give or take a couple of days.'

'Did you inform the heroic constabulary?'

'Didn't see the need. Why?'

'There's a police car outside your front door. But there's another explanation. I bumped into an old pal, called Crockett, up on the Old Eldrick Road. Around nine this morning. I'd a bit of a brainstorm, Archie. I pushed him over and drove off in his jalopy. Which broke down. Brock's no athlete and never was, but even he could've made Eldrick by fifteen minutes ago. I'm sorry to bring you bad business.'

'Well, it might depend on Mr Crockett,' the lawyer said apprehensively. 'Or why are they waiting outside instead of knocking on that door?'

'And I had a look-see at Binnie's.'

'God, you haven't made it easy for yourself.'

'Just to let him see me.'

'And that was all?'

'And I showed my face to Mike Telford.'

'Showed your face?'

'Stood before him.'

'And nothing you did or said could be interpreted as intimidation?'

'Couldn't be. I didn't say or do anything. This new police sergeant, Archie – is he Gary Cooper, or is he a nasty piece of dark blue pork and shiny buttons?'

'By and large, I'd say he goes by the book. But he won't use his own initiative. He'll go higher up. Having wiped mud off their faces once, they won't want a second time. Look, I don't like the idea of you wandering the streets here.'

'That's not my priority, either, Archie.'

'You know that the funds from the sale of your mother's house can be released to you?'

'I wasn't sure.'

'I'll start that in motion. The Home Office compensation will take longer. I'd take you home but it's a forty-minute drive. A bath! You need a bath. You look and smell bloody awful. Have you any money?'

'Twenty quid.'

'Doesn't matter. I'll sub you. I'll take you to the County.'

'I've no intention of staying over,' Barr said quietly and decisively.

'I'm thinking of a bath, and some decent togs.'

'I wouldn't say no to a bath and clean gear.'

The lawyer sent a secretary to see if the coast was clear. About a dozen people had been moved by the police to the middle of the square and a constable brought in to stand beside them. The car still sat outside the entrance to Archie MacDonald's offices. 'Wait there,' the lawyer told Barr. MacDonald went to the car. He told the sergeant he was taking his client to the County Hotel for a bath.

'Expensive bath, George,' the sergeant called to Barr as he walked the short distance to the hotel.

'First-name terms, eh?' Barr said to the lawyer.

MacDonald explained at the reception desk, but the young woman there said she'd have to ask the manager. Barr felt inspected and discussed as he stood a few yards away. He noticed Archie MacDonald hand over money and receive a key.

'He wants to know if we'd like a table for lunch.'

'Sounds like a good idea. I've a plan to catch the three o'clock bus. I know there is one. I checked it yesterday.'

'Fine. We'll aim for that, then.' As they climbed the stairs, the lawyer added. 'Bear in mind the possibility of a slight delay. Crockett?'

'Crockett.'

'Crockett, Binnie, Telford, and police reaction, George. I've a feeling that Sergeant Donaldson's waiting to be told what to do.'

'I hope I get my bath first.'

Barr threw his shabby garments out of the bathroom, followed by his shoes. He sank into the water, grateful for an unexpected break in the unfolding of his day. He was angry with himself for what he'd done to Brock Crockett. Knocking a man down and driving off in his pick-up was a crime by anyone's standards. He'd as good as handed himself back to the system. The lawyer had looked disappointed and annoyed when he'd listed the morning's misdemeanours. On the other hand he'd made no fuss about them. Or very little. He got to work with the soap. Later he stood up and showered into the bath's load of diminishing filthy water. He shampoo'd.

MacDonald sat on the bed. He looked at the shoes in which Barr had walked north from Bristol by an undescribed route.

Barr came out of the bathroom wearing a towel. 'Would you say I suited a moustache, Archie?'

'If I were you, I'd finish the job.'

'Steamy mirror,' Barr said. 'But I'll take your advice. That certainly beats mountain streams into a cocked hat. And you can say what you like about nature, but Lake Windermere's freezing. I've a dilemma here, Archie. One we didn't think about. I've taken a loathly aversion to getting back into that heap of sordid textile.'

'Yes, well . . . Perfectly understandable.'

'But do I go out wearing a towel?'

'I'll go. Do you know your sizes?'

'Thirty-one waist, thirty-three leg, forty in a jacket . . . Fifteen neck. Socks and drawers. Nine, shoe. Belt? Your choice of tie. It's a bit much. Can you take it out of what you owe me?'

'Sure. I'll write this down, though.'

As he left, the lawyer said, 'If I locked the door on you, would you take it bad?'

'You don't need to lock me in, Archie. I'll think of it as locking the police out until you get back. Although the hotel'll have a spare key.'

'I'll make it snappy.' The lawyer locked the door. Barr returned to the bathroom to shave. He wiped the mirror. The disposable shaving kit that came with the room was hardly up to the job. Wiping the glass with a towel, scraping hair from under his nose, forced on him a more disgruntled encounter with his face than he'd bargained for. He was hungry; he was angry. Even in the bedroom, away from the steam, he found it hard to get dry. The mirror on the dressing-table was steamed. Who he was, his name, his hopes, felt as if they could be discovered only after wiping away a wet mist that separated him from his life. He wiped the digital bedside radio-alarm clock and stared at 12.56 until it became 13.07.

The lawyer knocked on the door and then unlocked it quickly. He came in with plastic bags and parcels and then went back for others he'd left outside the door. 'The suit's tweed. Your size, and it was on special offer.'

'Kennedy and Company, Gentlemen's Outfitters. Well, well . . . Still in business. I didn't notice it when I went past. It'll do fine, Archie. Thanks.'

'Shirt?'

'Very nice.'

'Singlet, drawers, socks, belt . . . Tie?'

'Wearable.'

Barr stepped out of his towels and began dressing. 'What did you say to the good sergeant?'

'Told him what I was doing.'

'And?'

'I'm on tenterhooks, same as you.'

'Don't suppose you saw a menu?'

'Hungry?'

'Famished.'

'How long did it take?' the lawyer asked. 'From Bristol.'

'I started on 15 April.'

'Nearly three weeks.'

'Never again, though,' Barr said.

'Have you a destination in mind? A place to go . . . '

'A few vague thoughts, Archie. Nothing solid. Confidence is hard to come by. I'll just have to shift as best I can. I want to scout around and look for a town that suits me.' Barr slid the knot on his tie.

'God knows how anyone recognized you. The transformation's massive.'

'There were three didn't have to look twice, then,' Barr said. 'How much can I expect from the sale of 26 East Wynd?'

'Thirty-five thousand.'

'That much? Next door sold for seven when I went inside.'

'House prices,' MacDonald said. 'You wouldn't believe it.'

'How long?'

'Before you get on the bus,' MacDonald said.

Barr sat down and put on his new shoes. He walked around, scuffing the newness of the soles on the carpet. 'Not a bad fit,' he said. He checked himself in a wipe of the mirror. 'Archie, the man who confessed – Lawson. If he'd stayed in Dellonburn the night before in that guest house, why didn't they talk to him?'

'They said they did. Routine follow-up. They said he was interviewed in his home town. Lincoln?'

'Lincoln.' Barr pulled on the jacket of his new suit. 'He was obviously a very expert creep. Binnie and Telford see me chase my mother's dog out of the park, but they don't see the dog, too dark, but see me, hear my voice shouting at it, and next morning a woman's found dead in there. Never struck me as much to go on, but they go on it.'

'You knew her quite well, though?'

'Not well, Archie. She was a few years younger. Worst bit of all was her folks and friends sure it was me who killed her, not that rep in ironmongery. That's not over yet. I could imagine their hate. I always thought there'd be a letter. "Dear Mr Barr, Deeply sorry to have loathed your guts all these years, when we should've been hating . . . blah, blah . . ." Not a cheep.'

'Her folks moved.'

Barr shoved his shabby clothes into the bags in which his new ones had been brought. 'Even so, Archie,' he said. 'Even so. I mean, what about how I felt? I'd a name round here as a man for the ladies. God help me, I was skirt daft. That's why I'd done nothing about marriage. I was playing the field for all it was worth. I don't want to sound big-headed, or stupid, but *that's* really what came down against me. Take a look at Dellonburn. Fourteen years on and it still looks like a town that's never been fucked in. Not a happy place, Archie. And I'd hoped for a better impression this time. Same as ever. Look in Telford's shop. He's got a top shelf in there for solitaries. In a town this size! And he's the nerve to employ a girl to sell them. I hate this place. Archie, I loathe it. I'll wash my hands,' he said, stuffing the last garment into a full plastic bag.

They'd started on lunch when the sergeant arrived accompanied by two senior officers from the main town in the region. The dining room was almost empty. Without being asked, the policemen drew up chairs. 'A quick word, if we may,' the superintendent said. 'All right, Mr MacDonald?'

'Brock Crockett,' the sergeant said.

'Don't ask for a reason,' Barr said. 'I haven't got one.'

'Is it necessary, sergeant?' the superintendent asked angrily.

'I know about it. Is there a charge?' The lawyer's question drew a negative shake from the superintendent.

'Brock's weary legs reached Eldrick about the back of eleven, George,' the sergeant said. 'He rang his wife. Mrs Crockett rang me. I need to know where he left the motor,' he said to the superintendent.

'Half a mile before the main road,' Barr said.

'Your old pal's in the Eldrick Arms,' Sergeant Donaldson said. 'Not as thirsty as he was when he got there, I'm sure. I spoke to him on the blower myself. "George Barr kick me in the guts? Not George Barr! George 'n' me, we go back a lot o' years!" So who do I believe?'

'You've thought about media interest in Mr Barr?' Archie Mac-Donald said to the superintendent.

'I didn't hear that.'

'Plans, Mr Barr?' the inspector asked.

'Three o' clock bus,' Barr said.

'Good. Our concern is that he doesn't hang about Dellonburn,' the inspector said to MacDonald. 'The three o' clock bus will do just fine.'

The policemen stood up. 'Good luck,' the superintendent said to Barr, holding out his hand to be shaken. Barr got to his feet, his right hand gripping the table and remaining there as MacDonald rose, biting his lip with anxiety. 'The officers on your case have either retired, or moved on, or died.' He looked and sounded embarrassed.

'But I've heard enough about you to think that you'll give it a go. A fresh start,' he said.

'There's no such thing as a new life,' Barr said, his voice broken with a controlled but irrepressible rancour.

'Maybe not. There might be times when it's all we've got to work with – a handy delusion,' the superintendent said. 'I've gone over the files. The police work done on your case wasn't text-book procedure. Very far from that.'

'Are you trying to apologize?' Barr asked.

'It's not official, but privately, yes, I'm sorrier than you can imagine, Mr Barr.' He looked at the lawyer. 'Any help you need with Home Office paperwork regarding the compensation, then I'll be pleased if you get in touch.' He looked again at Barr. 'Good luck. I mean it.' He offered his hand. Barr shook it briefly then sat down.

As the policemen left Barr pushed his plate away, thought better of it, pulled it back and started eating again.

'Your pal Crockett sounds like a good man.'

'Always was. I'll never know why I didn't take the lift he offered. I was coming in on a dream.'

MacDonald wiped his brow with a napkin. 'Tenterhooks over, eh? I'd practically convinced myself they'd run you in on a charge of GBH and car theft.' He laughed and took a pull of his beer. 'Sergeant Donaldson looked seriously put out.'

Archie MacDonald gave Barr a cheque in his office. They set off for the bus-stop. A few locals still had the law firm's entrance under observation and a policeman had been left there to keep an eye on them. He followed MacDonald and Barr to the bus stop a hundred yards down the street.

'Say thanks to Brock for me,' Barr said. 'He used to drink in the Wheatsheaf.'

'Sure. I'll buy him a pint. George, your mother sent for me.' He was conscious of how Barr's reticence would permit little to be said on the subject. 'Your case was practically an obsession with my uncle. He used to visit your mother before he died. I didn't come into the firm until five years after your trial. Then I picked up where my uncle left off. You know, the visits to your mother. She didn't want you at the funeral . . . '

'I know.' Barr tried to wave the subject away.

'She didn't want any trouble . . . '

'Just leave it out, Archie.'

'Sure.'

'You wrote anyway. I thought it was your uncle. I didn't know he'd died, Archie.'

'No?'

'No.'

'Then I'm sorry . . . '

'Accepted,' Barr said.

'It's been quite a day.'

'A one-off.'

'I can't do much more without an address. Write soon. Or phone. I want you to keep in touch until that money comes through. No more anonymity, George.'

'I couldn't have done it without you,' George Barr said, indicating his clothes. 'I was making a right mess of it until I reached you.'

'Keep in constant touch. Right?'

'Will do,' Barr said, shaking MacDonald's hand as passengers for Dellonburn got off the coach.

'Where to?' the driver asked George Barr.

'A single,' he said. 'All the way.'

The Seven Farms

From the eastern heights of the valley – which aren't very high – you can see almost the entire course of the river. With the aid of patience and binoculars you could reach an almost exact count of anglers, bridges, herons and swans, except for a stretch of about half a mile where the bank is steep and wooded. Look left, to the south, and most of a town can be seen. Walk slightly further and higher on the quiet road, and then look right, and there's a good view of the small estuary. To earn a better view of the sea and the larger town beside it means walking and climbing for a mere ten minutes more. A lot of just about everything can be observed in a short space of time involving very little effort. It's a small country. This district is one of its many miniatures.

Several small villages can be seen. There are a few unpleasant exceptions but for the most part the red-roofed tiles of new bungalows look as if they've lost a battle with modernity and pulled back with a blush into the same eras as the older dwellings. Old men and women walk on that minor road in the summer evenings. Watching them in that state of mind which distrusts the complacency of the district can lead to the suspicion that a comfortable arrangement between yesterday and now might be what these elderly strollers hope to have negotiated. They look at the peaceful valley as if they've forgotten most of what's happened to them and almost everything they've read in the newspapers or seen on television. Experience and news rarely coincide there. A satisfaction of the place is that it's both attractive and unremarkable. Almost anything disagreeable, unsavoury or vexing can be understated by slow degrees until it vanishes.

Dr David Findlater was unsure of his reasons for choosing to go back there during his summer break. An unsentimental man, he was aware of having taken a decision that was out of character. He felt that he was behaving badly towards himself. Rootlessness was an explanation that crossed his mind; but he thought it a matter for contempt that he should have allowed even an instinctive fear of deracination to have disturbed his usual calm. Personal crises, of which he'd known a few, were always explicable, no matter the pain and sorrow they caused. It felt disreputable and silly that he should find himself returning self-indulgently to where he'd been born and brought up, a place he'd left almost thirty-seven years before at the age of sixteen. He took comfort from the knowledge that only he could tell what he was up to, except that he didn't know exactly. There was an introspective mischief about his half-intended, reluctant reunion with his past.

Part of the unsettling enjoyment he took from his costly suite of bedroom, sitting room and bathroom arose – there was no doubt about it – from the fact that the hotel had once been the house that dominated his father's life, his mother's, his brother's, his sister's, and his own. It was less than 800 yards from the house in which he'd been born and raised; and the house of the proprietor of the seven farms was now a hotel! Dr Findlater wished he could resurrect his parents to tell them that. Not, though, that they could be imagined for a single moment agreeing to be put up for a few nights in Strathuden House, hotel or no hotel.

In the summer of 1955, when the Findlaters left, they went with the momentum of rancour. 'Nothing else for it,' Dr Findlater's father had said. 'Strike out for new pastures.' It was like his father not to have said 'pastures new'. Had a farm-worker's irony been encrusted on that ornamental word 'pastures'? It wasn't appreciated that Findlater's father spoke out on the subject of wages and enlisted the union to help him. Gilnickie – yes, these toytown Scottish names! – wasn't farmed by a tenant like the others, but by a manager put there by the estate's owner. Some of the farm-workers on the seven farms agreed with Findlater, but only in private. Others thought him a trouble-maker. Life was made awkward. There were accusations of pilfering – hens, eggs, seed potatoes, tools and the like. 'Nothing else for it,' his father said, his laughing cadences lilting with resignation more than belligerence, his discontent disguised by a forced good nature. Dr Findlater remembered coming home from school on his bicycle to see the man who once lived in Strathuden House shout at his father, 'Look for a job in your own time, not in mine!' Findlater thought of his father as curiously undefeated and yet incapable of wrath; and, ever since, he'd tried to work out the puzzle of his father's temperament, one in which principle and conviction refused the temptations of acrimony or even vehemence put in its way by a vindictive opponent. But perhaps Dr Findlater was perplexed by his own equable outlook on life, having seen disease and death during most of his working days.

There was a clear view of the farm cottages from his sitting-room window. He'd looked at them late that afternoon with his binoculars, which, that evening, he'd then trained on the anglers, bridges, herons, swans and other birds on the river when he'd walked up the high road after an early dinner. Now that he was back in his suite he focused on a low terrace which had been knocked into one elongated house, re-roofed, rebuilt, with a substantial garden, and a garage added at one side. His plan had been to visit it earlier in the evening. Instead, he'd taken a path to the minor road that ran under the upper ridge of the valley. He was booked in for a week. He didn't want to rush. But at the same time he knew his planned walk was postponed by a memory. On the day he left with his family there had been an argument about a potted geranium which his mother had left inside on a window sill. 'For luck?' his father asked. 'It'll die of thirst. What's the luck in that?' 'No luck, or bad luck,' his mother answered with a malice that surprised him. 'None for him who's pushin' us off. None for them as come in after us.' He remembered the geranium looking like an emblem of a curse. 'Don't blame *him*,' his father said to his mother, his reproach sounding too reasonable. Findlater's brother and sister were too young to understand much of what was happening. 'He's been moochin' around for a place for months.' He meant the man who'd be leading his family into the cottage in a couple of weeks' time. Their opportunity arose from the Findlaters' misfortune. 'So?' his mother said in the spoken shorthand that existed between her and Dr Findlater's father. 'I'll find a place for it on the back of the lorry,' his father said patiently. Time and delays never seemed to matter much to him. 'I doubt if they'd want it,' he said to a look of his mother's that suggested they give the plant to one of their two neighbours. He'd wondered often what his father meant. Presumably the significance of a presented geranium would have come across like an insult – 'Remember us by this, when we're intent on forgetting *you*.' It ended up under the tarpaulin of the lorry from Annan, where they were headed – 'Far enough away!' his father had said contentedly.

His sister was squeezed into the cabin on her mother's knee, beside his brother and the driver, an obliging man who all that morning agreed to everything asked of him with a succession of 'Aye', or 'Fine', or 'We'll get it in somehow.' He and his father stood on the running-boards of the old, over-laden truck, holding on to the inside of the doors, one on either side. Men, boys and women were haymaking in a field – not one of Gilnickie's, but belonging to one of the seven farms, which meant the same landowner. No one waved. Once off the unmacadamed farm road they drove to the station in the town. For a family that had travelled nowhere on holiday, it felt like a serious departure as Findlater and his father waved to the truck when it left the railway station. There was a momentary sensation of the family being split up, and Findlater hadn't forgotten that imagined, more extreme circumstance, followed by several hours when he had his father's company to himself.

Inspection through binoculars from his hotel window hadn't prepared him for the elongated affluence of the house he thought he knew and which he now stood beside. It was as different from itself as Strathuden House from the hotel it had become. Each dwelling once had four small rooms. Now it had been made one house and even at close range he couldn't tell exactly how the interior looked. A large extension had been added at the rear as well as the garage for two cars at one side. From the growth of shrubs and trees Dr Findlater guessed that the cottages had been rebuilt ten or fifteen years previously, long enough ago, at any rate, for their opulent unfamiliarity to confuse the memory he had of them. 'Put this place away,' part of his mind said. 'Why did you come back when it was already behind you?' Elation competed with disappointment. He asked himself if he'd really expected to see the same cottages and evidence of the same living conditions he'd known when he was young. Through a half-open window a radio transmitted a voice and then the music of the here-and-now. He smiled at the involuntary mutation of the music into the sounds of his mother's wireless in the early 1950s after electricity was led into the cottages. Double glazing, neatly pointed brickwork, wisteria and clematis beginning to fade and wither, honeysuckle coming into full flower, roses, and the scent of grass very recently mown – it was years, but a distance of more than time, from his home, and yet it was where his home had been and, in a perplexing geographical sense if none other, where it still was. Between his memory and what he stood there and witnessed were years of occasional, sharp reminiscences, many of them happy, but all of them shadowed by the conclusive soreness of their last weeks there. Perplexed by the discreet turbulence he felt, Dr Findlater was conscious of an additional source of confusion which was as unlike him as confusion itself – envy. In the course of its social history, its promotion from the dwellings of farm-labourers to the single house of whatever comfortably off family now lived in it, the house of his birth looked like the house in the country of which he'd dreamt increasingly over the past couple of years. His hospital consultancy in London provided a growing nest-egg which a man who worked hard, lived simply and on his own had rarely had the chance to ponder, and never the time to spend. Property, like money, didn't enter his priorities. Now, though, he stood outside a significant house and coveted it: he felt mortified by a lapse of taste.

'Can I help you?' It was a woman's voice. She repeated her question. She was forceful and emphatic. Dr Findlater was jolted from his thoughts and it took him a few seconds to find where she stood in the garden, only a few yards in front of him but partly hidden by the long, loose branches of a buddleia. 'What do you want?' She was in her mid-thirties and dressed for outdoors in shorts and a loose T-shirt. A boy of about four stood beside her holding on shyly to her tanned leg.

'I didn't mean to startle you,' Dr Findlater said over the waist-high white fence. Instinctively, he took a few steps towards the gate. His straw hat, which he now held in his hand, his blue linen jacket, white shirt, silk tie, off-white trousers and polished brogues would have suggested to just about anyone that he was a man of a certain assured style which settled on him naturally or as a consequence of income or professional status, even if imitated unthinkingly – as in Findlater's case – from admired senior colleagues now dead or retired. But the woman's indignant self-confidence ignored the signals sent out by his demeanour and clothes.

'You've been looking at this house for ages and I can't think *why*,' she said. 'I take it you can read? Then it says in very plain words on the notice' – she pointed towards the road-end – '*Private Road*.' Her voice identified her as English. Dr Findlater supposed that after so many years in London a quality of sound more than an accent determined the nationality of how he spoke. What survived in his mouth was nothing like the voice of the place where he was born and brought up. He sometimes talked it to himself or to Scots nurses in the hospital, as if in mutual code or an agreed, shared, spoken cuddle. 'Private Road – it's a very clear phrase. Isn't it?'

'I'm extremely sorry to have . . .'

'Half the houses round here have been broken into . . .' she said angrily.

'Well, it's always been a private road,' he said. 'Or it always used to be.'

'We've been broken into!'

'But it didn't mean "keep out." It was more an excuse for the potholes, or a case of "on your own head be it." '

'Are you a local?'

'No. Not exactly. But . . .'

'Then I'll ring the police if you don't go at once.'

What someone else in the same position as Dr Findlater might have said would be along the lines of, 'I am an oncologist of international repute, a Fellow of the Royal College of Surgeons, a Fellow of This, That and the Next Thing, and I was born here.' Anything as politely rebarbative or assertive was beyond him. Instead, he began to back off, finding himself concerned for whatever causes underlay the woman's animated ire, her evident distress. He was used to disquiet in men and women; he'd had to tell them things about themselves which put their self-control under serious strain, with all sorts of predictable and unpredictable reactions. 'I'm very sorry. I'm very sorry, indeed.'

'Get away from here!' There was a unnerving control behind the ferocity of her snapped command.

Dr Findlater made a placating gesture with his hands, smiled at the little boy, and walked away. A moment later he heard a door slam.

Clearly, he thought, I look nothing like a thief. She's realized her mistake, but she's too proud to apologize. It's her manner. Besides, having been broken into, and robbed of God knows what, maybe with all sorts of unpleasant mess, she must be in a bit of a state. Understandable. Understandable, but bloody disappointing.

It was preposterous! Was that house, that road, the entire district, accursed? As soon as someone called Findlater appeared on the scene there was a struggle with someone laying down the law and exercising proprietorial rights. Could anyone escape from the significance of their original circumstances? To have gone back there was humiliating enough without being addressed as a possible thief – he couldn't remember a single crime of that kind in his childhood – threatened with the police, and told to clear off. He stopped on a stretch of the road that was shaded on one side by elder trees – 'boortrees', his father called them. The shade was welcome. What should he do? Listen to his silent, rueful chuckles, his deserved rebuff, and learn from them? Or give in to the resentment which he also felt? Odd, he thought, that the membrane separating private amusement from secret anger should be so fragile. Odder still that some of us seem so disgustingly sane that we can control – or think we can – the passion that turns one into the other or mixes them up.

He was diverted by details of the roadside. Elder-flowers, dog-roses, grasses, led him to stop. He looked closely at what were once familiar minutiae – stones of a wall taken down long before his childhood, signs of lapsed fencing (some rotten posts, a few rusted strands of barbed wire), spaces in the thick hawthorns through which he'd pressed himself many times as a boy. His memory was clear and seemed part of present reality. Of course it was.

He remembered a reasonably distinguished colleague saying, when drunk, as they tried to find a taxi, 'I wouldn't go so far as to claim that I am pre-eminent in the profession. But one of its ornaments? Does that sound fair?' To which, Findlater – wincing and sober – had forced an answer: 'Yes, Peter. Strikes me as more than fair.' At the time he'd felt that his colleague's vanity, insecurity, or whatever it was, deserved a kick up the backside. But why had that footling episode come back to him? He supposed it might be a substitute, or explanation, for the riposte he hadn't been able to make to the woman a quarter of an hour before. How could I say to a woman who's obviously preyed on by highly understandable anxieties, 'I beg your pardon, but in point of fact I'm as glowing an example of Local Boy Makes Good as you'll find in these parts?' She must feel bad enough without my rubbing it in. But his frustration was large; it overtook him and met him farther along the road, where he felt it necessary to sit down on a low mound of stones and try to cool off. Agricultural machinery was baling a field nearby but the sight of it was hidden by a walled bank topped with a hawthorn hedge through which crab-apple trees grew. His hands were fisted; his fingernails dug into the soft lower parts of his palms. He took deep breaths, rolled his shoulders, and shook his hands loose in search of relaxation. He could see the hotel in the distance – Strathuden House Hotel that had been Strathuden House. Greenhouses reflected the sun in silent salvos. Stands of timber looked majestic and permanent as if almost forty years hadn't made a blind bit of difference to the power and ownership of which they were tokens.

He began walking back the way he'd come. Am I hoping for a chance to clear up this embarrassment and put that woman's mind at rest as well as my own? Or am I too tired to go the long way round?

A sense of how livings are made from land lingered in him, even if it was a reduced, half-forgotten instinct, several pulses out of seventy-two. He was surprised at himself. He loved and hated the sight of expert agriculture around him. The baler drove by above him with its invisible noisiness.

'You've been looking at this house for ages and I can't think *why*.' How long did I actually stand there? Why did she say 'for ages'? Wasps crowded around their nest hung high in the hedge. A subdued, intent, obsessive hum whispered over the road; it was a miracle of intuitive diligence. Dedication and getting on with the job until the day you die. No beating about the bush for these little chaps. No fancy dithering, either, about whether you're a paragon or whether it's 'fair' to opt for the rank of 'ornament'. Why must some people insist on treating others as if they were servants? Or as if from the vantage of superiority? *Did* I hang about outside her house for as long as she said? What's it called? A 'raptus'? Busy medical scientists, with patients, research work on hand, students and umpteen honorary professorships, aren't prone to day-dreaming and losing a sense of time. He punctured his misgivings, then re-inflated them. Perhaps I did. I have to admit it – I was stunned by the changes to the place. I knew in advance it wouldn't look anything like my memories. Outside lavatory, getting washed at the kitchen sink, water heated on the coal-fired range, electricity only in our last five years (my father trimming wicks on the lamps, yellow light pulsing on the pages of a book). Why do I remember these things?

He wasn't yet visible from the house. 'You've been looking at this house for ages and I can't think *why*.' He could feel her voice, its pronunciation, as if it were just out of earshot. He was hot; his throat was dry and he sweated. He fanned himself with his hat then loosened his shirt under the armpits and plucked it from his chest in an attempt to air himself. Please, don't tell me I'm about to explain myself to her! I should never have come here. There was the straight road leading to the highway. The argument over the pot-plant. Standing on the running-board of a ramshackle lorry from Annan loaded with plain, simple belongings. Being dropped at the station with my father. His purse. He always carried money in a purse! The fares already measured and the exact sum handed over. An eternal gesture of a family reduced to its last few pounds. Fingers in a purse. An exact knowledge of how much was in it – counted, measured. So much for this, so much for that, and very little left over for anything else. The train to Edinburgh. My father in a green tweed suit loosening his tie in the compartment and saying, 'Might as well be comfortable. An hour to wait at Edinburgh Waverley,' and that information having been told to him several times before in the past few days. His father winking at him – 'It'll be much the same, only different.' No, can't forget it. But that's no reason to come back. A man, in my circumstances, from my background, my very precise background in terms of this place and that absolutely specific house, comes home ... And instead of ... instead of whatever, he feels a disgrace to himself! He feels ashamed! He feels disgusted because he let it happen. She's probably right. I was rooted to the spot. I stood outside her relatively remote house, where she's alone with a child, for what would have seemed to her an inordinately long time ... Or did I?

Once again he was astonished by the conversion of a three-cottage terrace into a single house. Only someone who'd known it intimately, who'd lived in it, whose eyes had grown up looking at everything around it, could measure the fullness of its metamorphosis from the homes of the low-paid to the residence of those who'd done well out of recent time. 'I wouldn't go so far as to claim that I am pre-eminent in the profession. But one of its ornaments? Does that sound fair?' 'Yes, Peter. Strikes me as more than fair.' Why are people vain instead of getting on with doing what they do? Why do they barge, elbow, malign and deceive each other? Why is honesty booted from the room in order to leave more space for self-interest? He approached the gate with his hat in one hand, fanning his face, and his handkerchief in the other, dabbing at his brow. Opening it would have been overstepping the mark. Yes, he thought, the only 'nice man' is one who agrees with you or does as you say, one who lets you be boss or allows himself a role as second best. 'Excuse me!' he called. 'Is anyone there?' To be considered 'kind' these days you have to be subordinate or servile. 'Hello! Hello!' Or you mustn't rock *his* boat, but when he rocks yours you say, 'Thank you, Peter.' An ornament? Then an incompetent one, and lazy with it.

He saw the woman at the window nearest him. 'Could I have a word, please?' he said, over-mouthing the words for the sake of the glass between them. 'There's been a misunderstanding!' She opened the window and he repeated what he'd said. He brought out his wallet and held up his card. 'I'm not a thief and I'm not selling anything!' he called out. He was shocked by how declarative and firm he was being. 'I'm a doctor, as it happens. This is my card. Do you want me to bring it to the window?'

She closed the window and disappeared. Oh, no, I hope that stupid woman's not about to phone the police. He was too tensed by the effort of speaking to her from the gate to reach conclusions about what to read from her face at the window. She came round the side of the house followed by her son.

'I'm very sorry . . .'

'What do you mean by this?'

'Maybe my card will reassure you . . .'

'I don't care who or what you are.'

'You'd a perfect right to feel spooked,' he conceded. She was looking at him with what he considered to be excessive concern. 'I'm sorry about that. But I was born in that house. I hadn't seen it in nearly forty years. I was surprised. Actually, more than surprised, but I don't know how to tell you . . .' She took his card and stepped back. 'It's very different. To be truthful, it was a shock to me. You see, when I say it's different, I mean much more than that. I mean totally, totally changed, and I feel as if my memories' – oh, no, what a soppy, wet word it sounds, accompanied by languuorous violins – 'have been stolen, or chastised . . .'

'Are you all right?'

'Fine. Yes. I wouldn't say no to a glass of water. The heat,' he said. 'Shock, too, I dare say.'

She ran inside at a speed that struck him as over-solicitous. He fanned himself briskly with his hat. 'What's your name?' he said to the little boy, who walked off and sat on his tricycle on the path.

The woman returned quickly with a glass of water and gave it to him.

He drank half the glass in a single gulp. 'Never a good idea to drink too quickly when over-heated. What they say in the films is quite right. Not that I've been crawling across the Sahara for a week.' He took a sip. 'When was it rebuilt?'

'In 1980, 1979 . . .' she said, thinking aloud. 'Twelve years ago. I think it was more or less derelict for a while.'

'And you've lived here for . . .?'

'Five years. Are you sure you're all right?'

'Fine.' He sipped more water. 'You said I stood here for ages. Did I?'

'Yes. Why would I say it if you hadn't?'

'There were three cottages. We lived at this end – there. Not like your house. Nothing like. All three tenants were farm-workers. Two of the families were more or less transient. Here for a year or two and then off. One day you'd have friends to play with, and then you wouldn't. A couple who lived at that end for several months had five of a family. Five. Not much in the way of toys, either, I remember. They used to play with old shoeboxes and Ostermilk tins, soap packets, and they'd a couple of biscuit tins, a gas mask and a soldier's helmet. I was very jealous of that soldier's helmet,' he said to the little boy. 'Very jealous, I can tell you! Thank you for the water.'

She opened the gate. 'Won't you come in?' He smiled, thinking that he heard her cross a verbal obstacle.

'I'd better get back before they finish serving the expensive lunch I've already paid for,' he said. He wanted to admit, 'If I'm in this mess by looking at the outside of the old place, can you imagine me browsing through your tasteful interior without cracking up entirely?' But he said, 'No, that's very kind, but I mustn't,' and hoped she'd see the truth on his face. 'Delightful child. You must be very proud.'

'He was born here too.'

'Ah. Another native of the house.'

'My husband's at home all day on Wednesday. I'm sure he'd like to meet you.'

He declined the invitation with a smile and a flutter of his hands. He walked away for a few yards, stopped, turned round, and said, 'Goodbye. Thank you for the water.'

'What does the "D" stand for?' She held up his card.

'David.'

She nodded.

When he turned to look back a hundred yards along the straight road, almost against his will, she was standing out on the road and her son was on his trike. She waved, and Findlater waved. 'Goodbye,' he said quietly. 'Goodbye.'

Boyfriends and Girlfriends

Kemshill Community Association organized 'social evenings' for every second Saturday during the winter months. Couples were encouraged to bring their children – a gesture that was unpopular with some but welcomed by most, especially by teenage girls still too young to be allowed to travel to dance halls; they looked after the children between 6.30 and 7.30, when whist, which bored them, was played. Nine o'clock was a late hour for children to stay up in those days, the late 1940s. Postwar social change, an earnest gaiety, a sober optimism filtered through to places like Kemshill – places that are minor, perhaps, but where more of the world lives than the headlines and passions of history would have us believe.

A drummer, an accordionist and a saxophonist struck up music for dancing after the tables and chairs had been cleared to the sides of the hall. Mr Hogg, who organized these evenings, sprinkled rosin on the floor to give the dancers a footing. For us children this provided the best fun of all: no one minded when, a sausage roll in one hand and a cake in the other, we tested the floor with sliding. Known as 'the purvey', the sausage rolls and cakes lay on long wooden baker's trays on a trellis table at one end of the hall, beside the tea urns and a crate of lemonade bottles.

We would sit at the side, listening to the band, watching our parents dance to 'Heartaches', 'I'll Never Smile Again', 'Fascination'. Sometimes, without actually asking, Dorothy Gordon made it plain that she wanted me to dance with her. That ten-year-old couple made a mess of it. I was all heels, knees, and elbows, and so was Dot Gordon, except that she was too proud to admit it.

Dot's mother was a war widow, a melancholy, short-tempered woman with dark hair. One Saturday night she burst into tears during a slow dance in the arms of Ralph Harvie, who had known her husband. For a moment, it did not surprise me; many of the tunes that our parents hummed or sang as they smiled and stepped around the hall sounded very sad. Their cadences probed wordlessly into a life of which I knew nothing. (Either that or the trio on the platform were miserable.) Yet just as often the sadness was dispelled: 'Deep Purple' and 'Remember Me' gave way to 'Puttin' on the Ritz' or Scottish dances. At the sound, the old wifies gathered by the tea urns perked up and trotted to the floor, calling on elderly husbands, who knew these dances and no others.

But maybe it wasn't the music that made Dot's mother cry. Ralph Harvie must have said something to her; they were talking and she ended up in tears. Women led her off the floor, and one of them threw an accusing glance at Ralph, who smiled with cautious embarrassment. My father was among the men who sat down with him. Ralph seemed to be explaining himself, and my father patted him on the back with a kind, sympathetic smile, much like the one he wore when he told Bert Nelson how sorry he was to hear about his mother.

Pity, concern, subdued anger and disguised anxiety – the whispers around the hall were unmistakably troubled. Even at my age, some native sense told me that something was going on, but that juvenile curiosity would be met with a reprimand or a lie. Dot looked worried, but she was put out, too; she resented the concern that was directed at her. No one was dancing. The musicians were talking among themselves. Mr Hogg beckoned urgently to them; I heard him say, 'Play something foot-tapping, for God's sake! You're being paid to cheer us up!'

Irene Gordon was a tragedy of the place. History and change intruded on Kemshill as much as anywhere else, if, perhaps, a little later, and they were as readily accepted, criticized, or rejected, or all three at once; but Irene Gordon, with her prestige as the only woman in Kemshill widowed by the Second World War – her daughter the only child made fatherless – was Kemshill's measure of great events. She was a statistic of sorrow; she was a favoured citizen. Women whose own men had also been in uniform must have looked at her and thought, there but for the grace of God. She was Kemshill's casualty.

Without going so far as to wear her Sunday best, Mrs Gordon would smarten herself up when she went to the post office to collect her widow's pension. Her usual style was one of principled shabbiness, so it was noticed when she did up her hair, put on a hat or a head scarf, and left her customary dilapidation behind for an hour or two. The post office was little more than a hut almost a mile from

Kemshill, half-way to Overrigg and next to the railway station that in those days served both villages and now serves neither.

During school holidays, we children often played on a hill that overlooked the Overrigg road. Sometimes we saw Mrs Gordon walking along the narrow pavement. When Dot spotted her mother, she used to leave us and run down the sloping field, shouting and waving. For all her calling, Dot had usually reached the hedge by the roadside before Irene Gordon noticed her.

'I could brain that man Harvie,' I heard my mother tell my father. 'He pesters poor Irene Gordon, and it's not just when he tries to dance her on a Saturday night. Some of the men round here ought to have a word with him.' My father scowled, but she went on. 'She doesn't want him. Why can't he take no for an answer?'

'I've heard of nothing that could be held against Ralph,' my father said.

'You have now, because I've told you.'

'Irene could do worse – a lot worse. The only woman he ever wanted, and she shuts herself up in the past! It's six years since Lawrie Gordon died!'

For almost a year, there was a probationary armistice between Dot's mother and Ralph Harvie. In the spring, she let him look after her badly neglected garden. So far, convention had prevented a local man from volunteering to rehabilitate the unruly place. A brother would have been appropriate, but Irene had none; of her two brothers-in-law, one – married to her sister – lived in Glasgow and did what he could on their several yearly visits, but he knew nothing about gardens. Her dead husband's brother lived nearby in Overrigg, but he never showed his face, and was disparaged in Kemshill as a man who failed in his responsibilities towards kin. A hand from a married friend of the deceased would have been respectable, as long as his wife visited the widow while her husband forked and spaded. But Ralph Harvie was an unmarried man, whose fond designs on Irene were common knowledge; when Irene allowed him to trim the high privet hedge in front of her house, the town took it as a sign of his progress with her. It became the occasion for benign gossip.

Ralph transformed the garden. He took the squeak out of Dot's swing and oiled every hinge on the premises. He painted the gate, repaired the fence, and planted the earth in anticipation of a harvest.

Ralph was a tall, slow, good-natured and pleasant man in his thirties. He had big grey-green eyes and enormous hands. 'Ralph's onions are usually so-so,' my father once said, 'but he grows the best leeks in the village. He keeps his mother's table well provided.' Like many men in Kemshill, my father associated gardening with decency. 'Hitler was no gardener. I'll tell you that for nothing. That's a *fact*.'

For all the conversations that people in Kemshill exchanged on the subject of Ralph's wooing, Ralph Harvie and Irene Gordon said little to each other. I played in the Gordons' garden almost every day – Dot was my best friend – so I had some picture of things there. Mrs Gordon would make tea for Ralph and bring it outside in a white enamel mug, but they seldom spoke, and when they did it was not for long, or about anything but the garden. Ralph never entered the house while I was there. If he did at any other time, I'd judge he would have knocked first on the door and then gone no farther than the kitchen. She used to place the tea mug on the doorstep outside the kitchen, and they'd exchange their few words there. Ralph Harvie scraped what was left of the worn and blistered paint from the three stone steps; fresh white paint took its place – broad parallel stripes on either side of the hollowed treads. At the time I thought it insignificant, the work he devoted to those steps, but now I don't.

My mother admitted that she might have been wrong about Ralph. 'It's a big step for a woman to take. But maybe it'll be a while longer before Irene's ready.'

'They haven't been out together,' my father remarked. 'Suggest to Irene that you'd look after the girl if she and Ralph wanted to go to the pictures.'

My mother looked askance at my father in his role as go-between. Whatever might be said in my father's favour – many things – as a romancer he was a die-hard Presbyterian.

Dot Gordon had fair hair and skin so light it seemed you could see the blood through it. Eager, energetic, nimble, she could make the crossover from girls' games to tree-climbing and apple-raiding with a naturalness that made the vigour of other tomboys look forced by comparison. Most of the girls around Dot's age did not like her, perhaps because she shunned the leadership they extended to her as her right. Boys distrusted her: she ran too fast, climbed with sure feet, and refused to admire bravado or take second place.

Once, when she and I were playing together at the humpbacked sandstone bridge that carried a minor road over the Kem Burn, a car stopped and a middle-aged couple got out and leaned on the parapet to watch us float bits of stick on the water. 'That's the most beautiful child I've ever seen,' I heard the woman say in melancholy praise.

Dot ignored them. The woman called 'Cooee!' to attract our attention. When I started to make for the bridge, she shouted to me, 'Is that your sister?' I said no, and she asked me to tell Dot to come over to her.

Dot put down the twig she was using to guide a piece of wood on the water and went to her. A herd of cattle was kept in the field there. On both sides of the Kem there were slopes of trodden, muddy and ungrassed ground where the cows came down to the water's edge to drink. A scab of dried cowpat floated past, and as it neared the bridge, where the current picked up speed, the sun slid from behind a cloud and turned the cowpat golden. The bridge looked so old that I thought I could hear it flake and crumble into the radiant gurgle of the stream.

'She gave me a half crown, and a shilling for you,' Dot said when she came back to me, confused by these gifts. She looked at the coins in the palm of her hand, puzzled by the disparity between them, and then looked back towards the car, whose doors we heard closing. She gave me the half crown. I gave it back to her. 'Don't you want it?' she asked.

'You said she gave it to you.'

'Money from strangers!' Dot spoke with bewilderment. I took the shilling; a child could get a lot for a shilling in those days. 'She said I was the prettiest girl she'd ever seen! I was terrified!' Dot giggled. She looked at the large silver coin. She bit on it. Together, we ran to the roadside where the car was pulling away. The woman was drying her eyes on a handkerchief. It was an all-important mystery – the woman crying, the money, the couple we had never seen before.

For the next hour, we scavenged for more imaginary boats to sail, and discussed how to spend our windfalls.

'If we go to Edwina Gregg's shop, she's bound to ask where we got the money from,' I said. 'Same with the Co-op. But they wouldn't care in the post office.'

'Mrs Graham's in the post office,' Dot said, 'and she knows me. She'll wonder how my mother could've given me a half crown.'

'It's not a lot of money!'

'You should know by now, Alec, that my mother doesn't have *any* money!'

'Well, I get a shilling a week.'

'I know you do, and you've already spent it, so Edwina Gregg would *know*. We'll have to walk to Overrigg, tomorrow,' Dot said.

Dot was invited to stay for tea at our house. In fact, she stayed until past nine o'clock, when my father walked her home. For several weeks, Dot stayed all evening on Mondays and Fridays.

At first, I took it for granted that Dot's visits were the outcome of my father's idea of providing Mrs Gordon with some free evenings for Ralph. But as far as I know, Irene Gordon never went to the pictures or anywhere else with Ralph Harvie. Early in July, he stopped looking after the garden. Dot was mysterious on the subject. When I asked where he was, she said sharply, 'How should I know?'

I never mentioned this to my parents. But one night when he came back from walking Dot home, I heard my father say, 'That Glasgow man has a car. I think it's a Riley.' From his tone I gathered that a Riley was quite a car.

'I feel sorry for Ralph,' said my mother.

'First you call him names for persevering, and now you're sorry for the man? Where did Irene meet this new fellow, anyhow? If you ask me, we shouldn't be looking after Dot while her mother's seeing somebody else!'

My father sounded angry. Genuine concern that Irene Gordon should have a second chance was being forced to fight it out with loyalty to a local man he liked.

'All she told me was she'd met somebody nice, and that she wanted to go out with him,' my mother said. 'I don't know what he does for a living. I don't know his name.' She sounded as upset as my father, but she seemed to be defending Mrs Gordon. 'And don't ask me where he comes from, because I don't know that, either.'

Most women were of the same mind as my mother: they would have been happier to see Irene Gordon accept Ralph, but they admitted with sisterly approval that she had a right to her feelings. Discretion or family ties required some women to take Ralph Harvie's side.

A few were scandalized. They accused my mother of harming Ralph by looking after Dot on those evenings.

'I thought it *was* Ralph! Why else would I have offered to keep an eye on Dorothy? And how could I refuse when I found it wasn't?'

Information about Mrs Gordon's boyfriend was gathered piece by piece in Kemshill. Some of it came from me. Dot told me that she had met him, that his name was Clifford Peake, and that he was English. She had kept this news to herself for long enough – that was the impression I got from the way she blurted it out. Several times I had seen women ill-disposed to her mother turn neighbourly charm on Dot, hoping for snippets of fact that her mother had ordered her to keep quiet.

She and I laughed at the strange, high-falutin English name. 'He has a moustache,' Dot cried,'and you should see the ring he's got! On this finger. It has a red stone.'

My father obviously disapproved of my indiscretion when I started to repeat what Dot confided in me – I could tell by the way he opened his mouth to speak, though he postponed it when my mother looked at him with a shake of the head that told him to shut up.

'You're as curious as I am,' she told him. After that, I refused to divulge what I knew, but they prised it out of me. I told them about the moustache, the ring with the red stone, the man's name.

My mother had already reached the decision that to look after Dorothy would be to implicate herself in the mistake she felt Irene Gordon was making. She had gone to Dot's mother and told her she could no longer help.

Several evenings of the week by then, Clifford Peake's car could be seen parked at a tilt on the bank across the lane from the Gordons' house. On those occasions when Mrs Gordon went out with him, it was to Glasgow, where they dropped Dot off with her aunt and uncle. Dot used to boast about Peake's car, its speed, its upholstery. She talked excitedly about the city. Some days she didn't turn up at school, because she was still in Glasgow. Mrs Gordon no longer shopped in the village. People said she didn't dare show her face in Edwina Gregg's shop or the Co-operative. They prophesied that very soon the Gordons would be moving. They reminisced about Mrs Gordon's parents, and mentioned her mother-in-law, still alive in

Overrigg; the word 'if' could be heard on doorsteps, in conversations at corners and outside the shops, in my parents' living room.

Those evenings when Dot had stayed to tea with us, she used to play my mother's piano. My mother could read music a bit, but she couldn't play by ear. Dot could pick up a tune from hearing it, but slowly, and my mother used to sit at the piano with her, teaching her popular songs. It was at these times, I think, that I first detected a change in Dot's behaviour. Always vivacious, she now began to look controlled and pert; her sense of fun seemed less irrepressible and spontaneous, and she appeared conscious of the effect she wanted to make. She had never been shy, but now she seemed willing to affect a charming timidity.

She seemed to have a superior adventure in her life. All of a sudden, she was being whisked off to Glasgow in a fancy car, treated with presents of sweets, new clothes, books, and a bicycle that was too conspicuous for her mother to let her ride it through Kemshill. From having nothing and a sorrowful mother, Dot found herself with plenty, while Irene Gordon dressed smartly and was cheerful, if apprehensive of what Kemshill was saying about her. Dot still turned up to play in my garden, and it didn't take much persuasion for me to go and play in hers. My mother warned me, 'I don't want you there if that man turns up. As soon as you see his car, clear off. Is that understood?'

It's not certain who first passed on the news that Clifford Peake was a married man. Dot never told me that, and I doubt whether she would have told anyone else, even if she knew. My father said the talk would have originated in Overrigg. 'Bad news always starts in Overrigg. I used to think that Hitler might've been an Overrigg man, but I grant you that even Overrigg men aren't *that* bad. Nearly, though.'

'This is serious!' my mother protested.

'It's worse'n that,' my father said, with a smile that disguised his feelings.

From the way my mother bit her lip and her eyes moistened, I gathered that it was the end of the world for Irene Gordon.

But the news seemed to make no difference to Mrs Gordon. If anything, it elicited a courage, or barefacedness, that drove her to visit Kemshill's two shops after an absence of several weeks, and to allow Dot to ride her bicycle wherever she pleased. Clifford Peake's Riley was parked there almost every night now. Dot had a day off school again – she was in Glasgow, with her aunt and uncle – but the car was noticed outside the Gordons' house that next morning. A few days later, Dot asked my mother if she could stay for tea.

'Did your mummy ask you to ask, Dorothy?'

'Yes, she was wondering, Mrs Haddow.'

My mother bit her lower lip and said, 'Wait here with Alec, dear. I'll go and speak to your mother.'

My mother was embarrassed, but Dot's smile was hard and worldly. When my mother reappeared with her coat on, Dot said, 'If you don't want me to stay, Mrs Haddow, just say so, and save yourself a walk.' It sounded impertinent – the remark of a girl older than her eleven years. Worse, to my mother, was that it declared how much Dot knew about what was going on.

Clifford Peake never drove through Kemshill when he went to the Gordons' house or left it at night. He took the narrow back lane that ran past the house and met up with the main road less than a half mile farther on. It was a poorly maintained road, worn thin by agricultural traffic; on summer afternoons around five, it was impassable, jammed with driven cattle, sauntering herd boys and their ill-natured dogs. Most of the time, though, it was deserted. Where the lane joined the main road, the junction was concealed by hedges raised on banks of earth.

Ralph Harvie waited there late one mild, wet October night. When Peake's car stopped at the dark junction, readying itself to nose into the main road, Ralph stepped forward, opened the driver's door, and pulled Peake out.

Gentle, amiable Ralph Harvie – everyone made a point of saying that they had never known him to raise his voice, let alone his hand. I read the newspaper reports and listened to my parents talk. The papers said Peake's head was crushed, not by one unlucky blow but by several. And Ralph himself had called for the ambulance, before waking the local policeman. But, like everyone else in Kemshill, my father refused to believe that Ralph Harvie had left his mother's house that night with thoughts of murder on his mind. In my father's analysis, all Ralph meant to do was warn the fellow off.

'The wrench they're talking about – it must have been in Peake's car. Peake could have come at him with it! Who'd believe that Ralph – of all people – would lie in wait for a man, wi' a wrench, intent on braining him?'

Whatever Ralph meant, events had run out of control. He was strong; he worked in the loading bay at the Rathett Paper Mill. My father expressed the gravity of the matter with his fierce and native 'Ach, ach, ach!'

We were involved: my parents had looked after Dot while her mother went out with Clifford Peake. Two detectives and a uniformed policeman turned up on our doorstep. They were cross-checking dates that Mrs Gordon had given them. I was told to sit in the kitchen, but our house was small, and I could hear without having to put my ear against the door.

'I've known Ralph Harvie for years, and he's not a killer. I'll tell you that for nothing!' My father was always telling people things 'for nothing'. I had never heard him speak with such anger as when he protested against going to Glasgow to testify for the prosecution.

'It's the law, Mr Haddow.' The detective's voice was bored with my father's assertions. 'The Procurator Fiscal might want your evidence in court. You're the man who can verify what Mrs Gordon's said.'

'Me? On the other side from Ralph Harvie?' My father's laugh, rough and incredulous, taunted the policeman.

'A man's dead, Mr Haddow!'

Irene Gordon took Dot and went to her sister's in Glasgow for the duration of the trial. It was well she stayed clear of Kemshill – those who objected to Mrs Gordon's choice of a lover were vociferous in heaping the blame on her head. Anyone who had granted her freedom to choose now changed his mind. But, being devoted to Dot, I was tormented by not seeing her, or knowing what she felt. Something had changed between us, something that no adult platitude or juvenile insight could utter clearly.

Ralph was sentenced to hang. The town was outraged. On appeal, the sentence was reduced to life imprisonment, and Kemshill was still angry. Laws were held in contempt. A neighbour of ours struck his wife, who left him. The local constable was ostracized, and had to be replaced. His stout adolescent son, known as Biscuit Belly, was beaten up behind the bus shelter, and he named the boys who did it.

The townsfolk went over the case in detail until the subject was exhausted. 'Ralph's mother can't take it in.' 'That poor Mrs Peake – what a story to hear told in a court!' 'This village was never in the papers – now look at us! Irene Gordon's seen to that!'

'They're laughing at Kemshill in Overrigg,' my father said. 'But then, that's what they're like in Overrigg. They've always been jealous.'

Dot and Mrs Gordon came back after the trial. Dot told me they would have stayed on longer with her aunt, but the two women argued all the time, and her uncle threw the Gordons out.

Tall, cream-coloured curds rose on the bolted seedstalks of the Gordons' rhubarb that next summer. Left unharvested the previous year, vegetables that Ralph had planted reseeded themselves, and now they ran wild; Irene Gordon had dug up no more than a handful of potatoes, and let the weeds smother the rest of the garden.

It was good to have Dot back again; I had been convinced she was gone for good. And despite the feeling in Kemshill, my mother encouraged me not to turn my back on Dot. For her own part, she sometimes gave me a basket of produce to pass on to Mrs Gordon, but these discreet kindnesses were as far as she would go. For the moment, she could not bring herself to resurrect their old friendship, although I imagine there were times when she thought she should.

I remember Dot's mother, that autumn, hanging her washing in the rain, tramping down the overgrown wet grass to get at her weathered clothes rope. It could hang there for days on end. Whenever she saw me, she scowled.

No one spoke to Mrs Gordon in the street. Shabby, unkempt, she looked the way she had before Peake arrived in her life – or she in his, however it was. To do her irregular errands, she ran the gauntlet of the houses and entered the furnace of Edwina Gregg's little shop. Some animosity fell on Dot from the young people, too, but she turned up her nose at the hostility and walked away. She seemed undamaged by the drama that afflicted her house. Her young dignity seemed very grown up to me. Neither she nor her mother seemed to mourn Clifford Peake. Ironically, the village that had deplored her interest in Peake was now incensed at her present indifference.

'I think she should move,' my mother said. 'It would be better for her and everyone else.'

'Overrigg would have her,' my father said, and my mother frowned at his flippancy.

'Lawrie Gordon's brother lives in Overrigg,' she pointed out, 'and his mother, too – old Mrs Gordon. That's hardly a fresh start!'

'Now, if they'd done what family should've done in Irene's circumstances, all this might never've happened.'

'Were you a friend of Dot's dad?' I asked him once.

'I knew Lawrie, but I wasn't a pal. Anybody wi' any sense waited to be called up, but no' Lawrie Gordon – he volunteered the minute the war started. Dorothy would've been a year old. He was on leave for two or three weeks, and then he was off to the Far East. And that was that.'

Secondary school separated me from Dot. We went to the same school, in a town ten miles away, but she made new friends; none of them were from anywhere around Kemshill. On the bus home one day, she told me, 'We might be moving, Alec. My mum's been to see a flat in Glasgow.'

'Soon? I don't think I'd like living in Glasgow.'

'Oh, no, it's wonderful! I used to love staying with my aunt and uncle! Now they're just as bad as the people here. They need somebody to blame, other than the man who actually did it.' There was no bitterness in her voice, only experience.

But indecision, indolence and depression kept Irene Gordon in Kemshill. Often when I called to see Dot, she was not there but visiting her new friends in the town where we went to school. When I did find her at home, we used to sit in the kitchen, and her mother would pass silently in and out, chain-smoking and brewing endless cups of tea – she put twice as many leaves in the pot as my mother did. Only occasionally – say, if the mobile shop from Overrigg sounded its horn on the lane outside – would she perk up, animated by an event that snapped her out of her contemplative lethargy. The house was a mess: unwashed dishes and piles of laundry cluttered the kitchen, and the table was never cleared. On it there was a breadboard, and what was left of a loaf. Stale crumbs spilled over the plastic tablecloth, with its holes at each corner where triangles of wooden table peeped through.

'Look at the state she lets this place get into!' Dot said to me. 'She's always complaining about it. I do my best, but look at it! Half the time she hardly knows I'm here. She forgets things. Well, when you think of it, what's she got to remember?'

Again, there was no resentment in Dot's voice as she described her mother's incompetence. Any mild indignation she might feel she made part of this comic state of affairs; it was as if Dot laughed at her own circumstances, disapproving of the near-squalor of her house and yet accepting it – one more feature of her life that made her different from the rest of us.

Over the next three years, I suppose I called on Dot a half-dozen times a year, finding her at home less often than not. It was a friendship I was unable to let go.

Dot was a figure at school; she was bright, and she was theatrical and lively. She was known for mimicry and music, playing the piano at lunch hour in the Senior Girls' Common Room, hammering out the hit tunes of the day.

When I succeeded in visiting her, I saw that Dot's mother took no interest in her progress at school. Instead, she seemed to take it for granted that her sixteen-year-old daughter would be cleverer than most. I noticed an arrogance in the way Irene Gordon lived with her misfortunes and poverty. There was a calculating sneer, too, in the way she looked at me. Her contempt was puzzling. Perhaps she saw me as a representative of my mother, her former friend. When she asked about my mother, she looked at me coldly. Maybe she meant me to feel that she considered my mother disloyal. But there was more to Irene Gordon's bitterness than that. Everyone else in Kemshill walked past the Gordons' house as if it did not exist, or as if they considered it a place blighted and effaced from the map.

When I saw Dot now, it was usually on the bus home from school. As we got off one day deep in a conversation she had started, I asked, 'Does she ever mention your father?'

'You certainly pick your moments, Alec!'

We were crossing the road opposite where Ralph Harvie had killed Clifford Peake. I apologized, and Dot laughed at my sincerity and poor timing.

'I'll tell you how to start a new scandal,' Dot whispered mischievously. 'If you're seen carrying my satchel up the road ...' She nodded towards the hedge; behind it, an unidentifiable figure was scything grass. 'No, she never mentions my father, or hardly ever. I wish I could remember him, though. I can't say I ever knew him.'

Irene Gordon was forty – Dot and I were in our final year at school – when she started to work, in the canteen at the Rathett Paper Mill. My father raised his eyebrows and showed the palms of his hands to heaven – or the ceiling – as he groaned at the woman's irresponsible folly: that was where Ralph Harvie had worked, and he had friends there.

Dot hated her mother's newfound jauntiness. 'I don't want to talk about it!' she said, when all I did was mention that the kitchen had been redecorated. 'The last thing I want's my mother making more bad feeling in this place when I'm getting ready to sit exams!'

'I don't see how you can be angry . . . '

'Look, no one can say that my mother's done much for me. We've hardly had two pennies to rub together since I was born. There was plenty of money, once – you know who I'm talking about. But she never took the trouble to earn anything before. I'll tell you why she's taken that particular job: she's trying to make life worse than it already is. It's taken her four or five years to figure out how to go about it. What's she *doing*?'

'Everybody says your mother's looking much better.'

'Huh! *Everybody says!*'

'Honest, I think they're genuine. You should be glad that maybe they're willing to change their minds – '

'They don't know what to think,' Dot said.

In the canteen, Mrs Gordon encountered a customer who discovered who she was. He asked sly questions about how Ralph was getting along. Some reports claimed that she was slow to retaliate; others said that she endured the man's provocation for less than a minute before she lost her temper. There was a violent scene, and the management invited Mrs Gordon to lift her insurance card and other papers and leave their employ.

When I passed the news to my father, he looked up from his gladioli bed – two dozen emergent shoots, neatly labelled – and listened. 'I'm sorry to hear it, but I can't say I'm surprised. That's why she went there.' He brushed aside my questions as to what he meant and how he knew.

I went to see Dot, worried about this new development. 'There are other jobs! There are plenty of jobs!' her mother told me gaily. 'You can tell your saintly mother that I'm not sorry about what happened. And tell her I won't need her baskets of vegetables this year. I can look after myself. Tell her I've changed in a way she wouldn't even understand!'

There were parcels on the kitchen table. Irene Gordon began to untie one of them. Dot turned abruptly away. I sensed that the two had been quarrelling before I arrived. 'Wouldn't you say I've been hard done by, Alec?' Mrs Gordon demanded.

'I think you should keep Alec out of this,' Dot said from the sink.

'I'm talking to you, Alec! Hard done by – wouldn't you say so?'

I agreed with her.

Dot rushed up behind me and began pushing me towards the door.

'Don't you send him away, Dorothy! Alec, you arrived in the nick of time! I was about ready to wring her neck!' she cried.

Dot went back to the sink. Her mother dragged a dress from its parcel. Tissue paper floated in the room and settled on the floor as Mrs Gordon held the dress against her. 'What do you think, Dorothy?'

'I think it stinks!'

Dorothy pushed past me, opened the door, and went out. Her mother scowled at me with vindictive triumph.

After the examinations, there was little reason to go back to school except for the company; I took afternoons off. Once, on the noon bus, I found Dot Gordon reading, and we spent that afternoon together in the Gordons' neglected garden. Then we spent several more afternoons there – leisurely, loafing, tea-drinking afternoons. Time passed very slowly.

'It's sometimes the back of eleven before she gets home, sometimes much later. I waited up on Tuesday night,' Dot said. 'She was drunk. I'm sure she's got another boyfriend. How'd you like it if your mother were seen plastered on the last bus? We had a terrible row, Alec. She tells me, "I've scrimped and saved and done without, for what? For you to go to university? Don't make me laugh." '

I had nothing to confess about either of my parents that might help Dot feel less exceptional. I felt safe, coddled in averageness, affection and security, none of which Dot had ever enjoyed. At best, I could have said that my father was a political half-wit who had recently devised a theory that the compulsory study of flower and vegetable cultivation in all schools world-wide would save the planet from the madness of its rulers. My complaint seemed too trivial to counter Dot's accounts about her mother. And besides, I'd begun to suspect that Dot enjoyed being exceptional.

'She isn't finished yet,' Dot said. 'In fact, she's hardly started. And I'll tell you this – I don't care what she does, because I won't be here to have to live with it.'

Dot planned to share a flat with other students at the university. She was determined to leave home. 'She's got another job, as a waitress, and she can't claim that she needs me. And I don't need her,' she said calmly. 'I mean, she won't help me, and no one else will. I'll just make my own way.' It was the unruffled determination of her attitude that agitated me most.

'Leave home now and you could make your mother do something daft,' I said anxiously. 'You'd blame yourself.'

Her patience with me, her suppressed laugh that recalled her mother's face as it prepared for a downright scowl, seemed to accuse me of lacking perspicacity. 'I don't even like her,' Dot said. 'She's never made me feel that she wants me here. She told me herself she can't stand the sight of me.' These were unforgiving words, and they disturbed me. 'I wouldn't tell you this, Alec, unless she already knew what I think about her. I've told her what I have in mind. You don't know the half of it.' I was ready to believe her. 'We haven't said a civil word to each other in months. Neither of us can be bothered to even try.'

It took several days before I brought myself to confide in my father.

'You'll be worried about Dorothy, but I wouldn't worry too much, son. After an upbringing like that, she'll stand on her own two feet all right. I'm as sure of that as I've been sure of anything else in this world. Anyway, Dot's hardly the first young woman to make a break for it.'

'Did you already know it had come to this?'

'No, I didn't, but I could see it coming.'

'How could you tell?'

He paused as he firmed a plant in a pot. 'When water runs off that glass,' he said, looking up at the roof of his greenhouse, 'then I know it's raining.'

'I know Dot better than almost anyone, and it didn't strike *me* as obvious.'

'No, nobody sees what's happening to somebody they're fond of,' he said, with irritating judiciousness. 'A twisted minx she'll grow up to be, unless we've a miracle, and miracles don't happen. It's you I'm worried about. I know where you've been every afternoon this week.'

'Don't go round thinking it's like that.'

'Maybe not, but you'd like it to be.' I turned my face away. 'Do something about it,' he said. 'And if you take my advice, it'll be a goodbye.'

When I next saw Dot, I noticed a playful tolerance in her manner. Occasionally she showed signs of boredom as I talked about books or movies. Her intelligence was quick and brilliant; it was unlike her to say so little. She seemed to be waiting for me to take a step that she had predicted weeks or months before. Now, and probably then, too, I had a sense of inevitable ending – that I would touch her, kiss her, and that doing so would break all of childhood like a sheet of glass. I felt that Dot was enduring my reticence, putting up with me, her eyes daring me forward with their keen blue challenge that said she would not make the first move, that it was all up to me.

When I kissed her, Dot's complicity was unmistakable; her willingness felt as real as my own. But after a minute or two she pushed me away and got up from the grass. Her composure was remarkable; mine was less so, but at least it was composure: my father had not forewarned me in so many words, but he had hinted at how it would turn out.

Dot said, 'I've too much on my mind to get involved, and you and I probably *would* get all mixed up about this.'

She seemed surprised that I walked away without clumsy, amorous talk. She called after me as I swung the gate behind me. It squeaked worse than ever.

Before Dot left Kemshill early in September, there were reports of arguments late at night between her and her mother. After she'd gone, the stories continued, supplied by evening dog-walkers and furtive drunks, the bearers of whispers. Irene Gordon was seen on the last bus, they said: sometimes accompanied by a man, often abusive, well dressed, made up, smart and tight. Over the next years her looks, rescued from the past, succumbed to time and age. As she withered into pathos, repentance and loneliness, my mother and a few of her friends took to visiting her again.

Ralph Harvie was released after serving ten years of his sentence. When he came out of prison he had the good sense not to settle in Kemshill. Before moving farther away, he stayed for a few months in Overrigg. My father's humour survived a little longer. 'Overrigg? But Ralph, you were innocent.'

'George, I was guilty. I killed a man.'

'But Overrigg? That's too much punishment.'

Ralph waved away my father's jovial efforts. 'I meant to kill him. I thought of very little else ever since the day I knew he existed.'

It was six years before I saw Dot again; she called my name across a street in Glasgow. It was as though she had just been on my mind; perhaps she always was. The pale fineness of her skin had gone. There were faint lines running from her inner cheeks into the corners of her mouth. She looked older and different, but still persisting within her was the outline of the indestructible friend of my childhood. Perhaps I was the only person alive who could see that. She kissed me on the cheek, and said I could buy her coffee. I bought her dinner. Then the rest of it started.

The Boy from Birnam

Jack Hogg made a name for himself inside a few weeks of arriving with his parents to live in the village of Kilhaddo. He was seventeen, dark, short, athletic, garrulous, and good at school without ever giving the impression of studiousness. Although he had a long history of being considered too big for his boots, Jack Hogg had managed so far to avoid the humiliation of being cut down to size. He came close to it on his first day at Malcolmstown Academy, a school in the town a few miles from Kilhaddo. He had a fight and won it, flooring an outsized bully with a lucky punch. A note from the games master at his previous school introduced Jack to his counterpart at Malcolmstown Academy as a daring centre-forward. After a game with the Second Eleven, Jack was playing in the First Eleven, mesmerizing the opposition and scoring goals.

'Birnam, eh?' the teacher said in Jack's first English literature class. 'That's where the trees got up and walked. "Until Great Birnam Wood to High Dunsinane hill shall come against him," ' the teacher quoted. 'We'll have to watch this man,' the teacher said teasingly to the class. 'For all we know, he could be descended from certain witches.'

Jack was popular with everyone except the former centre-forward of the First Eleven and the bully whose nose he had broken with that lucky right jab. Too small a place to have its own secondary school, Kilhaddo sent its cleverer children to Malcolmstown Academy. Jack Hogg therefore encountered Norrie Lamont on the school bus. He was bemused when Jack singled him out as a friend. Never in his life before befriended by the well-liked, Norrie, in his shy and untalkative way, basked in Jack's company, as if he had been promoted. He laughed more, talked more; and his parents noticed a new self-confidence in him.

'When I lived in Birnam,' Jack said, 'the older lads used to take the bus into Perth. Sure, the legal age's supposed to be eighteen, but there's always somebody who looks eighteen. They used to buy a few cans of beer and then find a quiet spot in a park.'

'Birnam must've been some place,' Norrie said. 'You're always talking about it. What's wrong with here?'

Jack ignored Norrie's critical tone. 'We could go to Ayr. Who'd recognize us in Ayr?' Jack said with a persuasive, wicked smile.

'No thanks. I'll wait until I'm eighteen.'

'Your problem,' Jack said, 'is an ingrown timidity.'

'My problem,' Norrie said, mournfully, but with a candour of which he had been incapable before he met Jack Hogg, 'is Sandra Connolly.'

'Bags of money, a flashy car and a posh accent – that's what *she* looks for in a boyfriend,' Jack said dismissively. 'You haven't a hope! I've seen Sandra's latest bloke – he's over twenty and drives a big Volvo. It's probably his old man's, but it's wheels. His folks're loaded.'

'You've been in Kilhaddo a couple of months, and you think you know everything and everybody,' Norrie said, by now familiar enough with Jack to speak back to him with the same worldly contempt.

'Forget Sandra Connolly. Take my advice, Norrie, and start directing your attentions to Mavis Murray,' Jack said, like a man of the world.

'Mavis?'

'Mavis sits in the French class looking at you like this.' Jack imitated Mavis Murray's big, bewildered eyes and open-mouthed doting. Norrie smiled at Jack's performance. 'Mavis is keen on you. Everybody's seen it except you. This Connolly girl's a lost cause. She walks with her nose in the air,' he said, making Norrie laugh with his impersonation. 'She thinks she's royalty. Give Sandra the go-by, pal.'

In June, when the examinations were over, and their results were expected in a week's time, Jack and many others in his year at Malcolmstown Academy absconded from school. Norrie refused at first, but after a day of pointless classes, he joined Jack in an equally aimless wandering around of Kilhaddo.

'I've got itchy fingers,' Jack said. 'I've a strong urge to guddle a few trout in the Tanno Water.'

'You must have the death wish!'

'Norrie, I'm getting tired of you. Every time I suggest a spot of adventure, you start talking like my old man. I've been up the Tanno on a walk, yesterday,' he said, implying that the risks involved in stealing fish from Tanno Water were overrated.

'You're lucky they didn't set the dogs on you,' Norrie said censoriously.

'The trout up there are this big.' Jack demonstrated the size of the fish he had seen in the stream that ran through Tanno Estate.

'They prosecute,' Norrie warned, 'every time.'

'How else is a guy to find a bit of excitement around here?' Jack asked impatiently. He looked at the clock on the post-office wall. 'The Ayr bus stops here in an hour. I've a couple of quid, if you have.'

'I don't want to go drinking,' Norrie said flatly.

'It'd be better than kicking around this dump waiting for the exam results. Norrie, Ayr could never be as boring as sitting here, watching you look in the chemist's window for a glimpse of Sandra Connolly!' Norrie turned away from the shop window on the other side of the street, where Sandra Connolly, in her white overall, was taking something from the window display to show to a customer. 'Very nice, I grant you,' Jack said, 'but she lives on the moon. We could go to Ayr and drown your sorrows.'

'All right, I'll come to Ayr,' Norrie said abruptly. 'But you can forget about drowning my sorrows. We'll go to Alloway. I'd like to see Robert Burns's house.'

'Sure,' Jack said. 'We could do that.'

They met at the bus stop an hour later and went to Ayr.

Ten minutes after getting off the bus, while Norrie was wondering about how to get to Alloway, Jack walked into a bar. He looked back at Norrie from the half-open door, urging him with tilts of his head to follow him. Angry, Norrie waited outside for several minutes before daring himself to go in.

Jack stood with a half-consumed pint of beer before him. Having been open for less than an hour, the pub smelled of a mixture of detergent, air freshener and the aroma of stale cigarette smoke and beer. Only a few old men shared the pub with Jack and Norrie. 'What'll you have, Norrie?' Jack said.

'Let me taste yours first,' Norrie said.

'Don't be daft,' Jack whispered at this offence to his manhood. 'If the barman sees you sip mine, he'll know it's your first. He might ask what age we are.'

'Is it strong?' Norrie asked.

'It's as weak as water. All this stuff does is make you pee,' Jack said with a boldness that Norrie found less than reassuring.

Meekly, Norrie accepted the pint that Jack bought for him. It was Jack's first time in a pub, too, but he suppressed any signs of its being an initiation. He was so easy and familiar that at any moment Norrie expected Jack to ask the barman what he fancied for the three-thirty.

Norrie and Jack drank two pints more. They talked about what university would be like. The barman appeared to have no inkling that they were under age. They bought four cans of beer to take with them when they left. 'Do you really think we should?' Norrie said, feeling the effects of three pints.

They drank their cans of beer on the beach. The afternoon was grey and windy. A policeman looked at them over the sea wall to which they had their backs, sheltering from the wind.

'Is it somebody's birthday?' the policeman said, startling them with his sardonic question.

'We're waiting for a bus,' Jack said sharply. 'It doesn't go until the back of five.'

'Good place to wait for a boat,' the policeman said. 'For a bus, though, this is the worst place in Ayr. Come next week, though, you'll be able to buy a ride on a donkey.'

'From the bus depot,' Jack said, irritated by the policeman's humour.

'What age are you?'

'Eighteen, coming up nineteen,' Jack said, lifting his can to his mouth.

'Is that a fact?' the policeman said disbelievingly.

'You'll have to take my word for it, because I've nothing on me to prove it,' Jack said. Norrie fidgeted on the sand at the sound of Jack's insolence.

'Are you eighteen, coming on nineteen?' the policeman asked Norrie, with the voice of someone who knew he was quoting a lie.

'We come from Kilhaddo,' Norrie said. 'The next bus is at five-five, so we bought a couple of beers. Is there a law against it? Of course I'm eighteen,' Norrie said, emboldened by beer, but part of him wanting to say, 'I'm seventeen. I'll come quietly, officer.'

'Put these empties in a bin when you leave,' the constable said firmly, 'and stop telling lies about your age.' He walked away.

'I think it'd be a good idea if we caught the seven o'clock bus,' Jack said.

'I'm not having any more to drink,' Norrie said.

'Nor me either,' Jack said. 'It's sobering up that's bothering me. How long does it take?'

'We'll go for a walk,' Norrie said, 'and get something to eat.'

The expression on Jack's face changed. He crawled along the foot of the sea wall through the fine sand sifted by the wind. Norrie watched him as if he had never known that beer could make you sick. He looked at the tide coming in, gulped, then crept away in the opposite direction.

Before they boarded the seven o'clock bus, both Jack and Norrie were convinced that they had shaken off every last hint or stink of beer. They blew on each other to test the smell of their breaths and pronounced each other clean. They slept on the bus and felt bad when they woke up. They washed their mouths out with water from the tap in Kilhaddo's minute Memorial Park. They were in their homes for about thirty seconds before their parents exploded with amazed wrath at the reek of beer on them.

'You swore blind that there wasn't a whiff of it on me!' Jack complained the following day.

'Then your nose must be as feeble as mine, because I came through the kitchen door and my mother could smell me at the other end of the living room. They blame you,' Norrie said.

'You mean *you* blamed me,' Jack said, smarting from the trouble there had been with his parents the night before.

'They say you're a bad influence.'

'Mine blame *you*.'

'That's hardly fair!'

'Does your old man drink?' Jack asked.

'No, but I bet yours does.'

'He'd one too many at my sister's wedding, and I saw him plastered at New Year, but he said last night that he'd never been in a pub. He walloped me on the nut,' Jack said, touching the side of his head. 'I've never seen my old man so *angry*!'

'Somehow I thought you'd've denied it,' Norrie said.

'I did. That's when he belted me.'

A few days after the relief of the examination results, Jack Hogg said,

'Are you still as scared to go up the Tanno? I'm telling you, it'd be a walkover.'

'I've told you before – it's Stalag Tanno up there.'

'I was taught by experts,' Jack said boastfully. 'When I lived in Birnam, I was taught by a *real* poacher. You can imagine the bailiffs they've got there, keeping an eye on the Tay. I saw plenty, but they never saw me.'

'Sure, you were good at it,' Norrie said, unimpressed. 'This isn't Birnam. I know their gamekeeper. Dunky Morton's about my dad's age, but he's cunning. Nobody from around here would be daft enough to try to take fish from the Tanno. Getting caught with beer on your breath would be *nothing* compared to being nabbed by Dunky Morton.'

Jack looked amused by each of Norrie's objections. 'I've seen this Dunky Morton. He must be twice the age of your old man! Somehow I can't see a gamey who looks practically superannuated catching *me*.' Jack laughed at the preposterousness of being run in by Dunky Morton.

'I'm not as fast as you. He might catch *me*.'

'Oh, come on, Norrie! Live it up a little! We've just passed our exams!'

'I suppose that at our age, they'd still prosecute. But it'd be a first offence. That'd be a fine. Wouldn't it?' Norrie said.

The watery dusk by Tanno's banks was darkened further by the woods through which the stream flowed. At several places it ran through shallow and narrow gorges, overhung with branches. Rhododendrons, run wild from the parkland surrounding Tanno House, encroached into the woodland and up to the banks of the stream. Jack's agility over the rough terrain showed every sign of having been well rehearsed. Norrie stumbled and fell. He found himself moving on all fours to clamber over obstacles that Jack surmounted with sly, silent leaps. In that aquatic, woody half-light, Jack looked familiar with clandestine movements and illegal purposes. 'Shh! Shh!' Jack said several times, then listened, until sure that what he had heard – Norrie had heard nothing at all – was innocent.

When they were near a pool where Jack had noticed a plentiful supply of trout on his earlier reconnaissance, he whispered, 'Say nothing. Do you get me? Not a word. Very, very quiet.'

'It's freezing down here,' Norrie said, rubbing his hands together in an effort to dispel the gurgling chill that came from the Tanno.

'Shh! I said, "Quiet!"'

A few minutes later Jack sat down and took off his shoes and socks. Norrie copied him, rolling his trousers up the way Jack did. Nothing was said. Jack lowered himself from a shelf of rock into the water, with a silent whistle as his feet touched the surface of the cold stream. He seemed untroubled by its depth. It soaked him over the knees, seeping into the rolled cloth of his trousers. He stood still for a few moments. Instinctively, he knew where to go. Because of the depth of the water in the pool, bending down to guide his fingers under the edge of a stone immersed part of his chest and his right arm as high as his shoulder. With a movement that hardly seemed to disturb the slow, dark flow of the water, he drew a trout to the surface by its gills, held it up, winked, and threw it on to the bank. Norrie heard it land on the grass. His face twisting with the inhospitable temperature of the Tanno, Norrie slipped into the water, unable to keep the same silence as Jack Hogg.

Norrie's efforts to guddle trout succeeded only in getting himself extremely wet. The sleeves of his sweater rolled down no matter how high up his arm he pushed them. Several times more he heard a soft rip of water as Jack threw a fish out of the Tanno. It was dark now, and Jack made no noise at all as he went about his wet, cold and illegal work with a ruthless skill that suggested there must have been men in the Hogg family, far back in time, who had kept body and soul together by poaching other people's fish.

Jack waded over to where Norrie stood shivering and feeling himself unlikely to catch anything other than double pneumonia. 'This is even better than Birnam,' Jack said, as he passed Norrie. 'Five! And two of them are enormous!'

'Let's go, then,' Norrie said.

'There's a great pool about 200 yards up,' Jack whispered excitedly.

'Honest, Jack – I'm freezing!'

'You must be joking! This Tanno's a trout's paradise!'

Jack gathered up his scattered fish and stowed them in a canvas bag. He picked up his sock-stuffed shoes and sneaked away on his bare feet. Norrie sat down, rubbing his legs and feet, trying to bring life back to them, and amazed at how immersion in very cold water could make him feel exhausted. He pulled on his shoes and socks and then set off after Jack. Before he left the clearing by the bank next to the pool, he listened, the way Jack had done before slipping under the overhangs of shrubbery and saplings. Nothing he heard gave him cause to believe that anyone else was within miles of the Tanno. What he was listening to was the overlap of dusk and night, and night consolidating itself. Something small scuttled under a bush. Looking back at the pool, a high edge of rock on the opposite bank, he saw bats dart and jerk in the open air.

Had Norrie not expected to find Jack farther upstream, he might easily have gone past him. Once in the water, Jack was busy in an elemental silence, his hands probing the stones on the bed of the Tanno with a delicate naturalness that could only be criminal. He was fascinating to watch. His stooped shape was at one with the water and the heaped greys and blacks of the foliage beyond the stream.

Jack caught three more fish and then came out.

'We ought to go,' Norrie said plaintively, uncomfortable in his wet clothes. 'You've caught enough trout for one night.'

'Where there's fish, I'll take them,' Jack said, the quietness of his voice adding to the mean intensity with which he relished the danger of poaching.

'You're a fanatic,' Norrie said, too dejected to be anything other than offhand. 'I don't know why you're so proud of it. They aren't your fish.'

'They are now, pal. How can a live fish belong to somebody? I don't care *who* says they own this land, they *don't* – and they don't own the water, either. They might as well claim they own these bats, or the moon up there. Feel the weight of that,' Jack said, handing the bag of fish to Norrie.

Norrie felt the sides of the bag. It was like a live creature fighting against all the odds for its life, but knowing it had already lost. He was still holding the bag when the beams of torches splattered with broken light on the foliage fifty yards away.

'Run!' Jack shouted, hopping as he pulled on a shoe.

Norrie sprinted along the bank of the pool until he ran into bushes and ferns. Behind him he could hear the voices of two women calling on him to stop. He also heard the dramatic splashes of Jack Hogg, who had meant Norrie to run into the pool, and put that obstacle between them and their pursuers.

'Geoffrey! Geoffrey!' It was a woman's voice, strident, piercing. Norrie stopped, suspecting that whoever Geoffrey was, he was ahead of him, waiting to cut him off. A rustle of bushes proved this hunch to be correct. Soon the leaves of the bushes ahead of Norrie were being covered and uncovered with sprinkles of light from a torch.

Norrie fought through branches and briars until he reached the edge of a narrow gorge through which the Tanno flowed. A whistle from the other side was Jack Hogg urging him to get across. Norrie swung the bag a few times and then released it. It vanished into the dark and Norrie heard it fall on the far bank. Whistling on Norrie Lamont was a waste of breath, Jack Hogg decided. His friend was the sort of Lowland yokel who had to be told what to do in words of one syllable. 'Over here, y' half-wit!' Jack shouted.

Norrie knew only too well that he was expected to get across the gorge, and had decided to plunge into it down the crumbling slope that fell away from his feet. But before he could work up the courage, Dunky Morton clamped his large hand on Norrie's shoulder. 'Don't struggle,' the gamekeeper said under his breath, but gruffly. His understatement was convincing.

'What's keeping you?' Jack shouted, irate with Norrie's squeamishness.

'I am!' Dunky Morton shouted back across the gorge.

Norrie heard first the loud flow of the Tanno below him, and then Jack Hogg scampering down the trail of his escape.

'Is this boy known to you?' asked an elderly woman, who carried a stick as well as a torch. 'Is he local, Duncan?' Norrie felt blinded by the torches that were trained on him. The old woman prodded him with her stick.

'If you'll leave this to me, Mrs Lowther, I'll do what has to be done,' Dunky Morton said, the only person there who was not in a flap, nor breathless, nor angry.

Norrie said nothing. He decided that the best course was to speak only when spoken to. He worried about what his parents would say.

'I think the other one must be clean away by now,' a younger woman said, kicking a rotten log with bad-tempered disappointment.

Geoffrey made noises that led Norrie to feel that the man was angry with himself for having let Jack get away.

'It's not your fault, darling,' the younger woman said consolingly, while the elderly woman inspected Norrie, and prodded him again with her stick. 'There really was nothing *anyone* could have done about *him*.'

'We ought to have brought the dogs,' Geoffrey said.

Norrie noticed that Dunky Gordon was keeping as quiet as he was himself. But the gamekeeper maintained a grip on Norrie's collarbone. Once or twice Dunky squeezed harder on Norrie's shoulder. It felt like a comment on what the others were saying.

'Well, is he local?'

'Oh, I know this boy's father well enough,' Mr Morton said. 'I'd have thought that you'd've had more sense, Norman.'

In the torchlit dark, Geoffrey, his wife and his mother-in-law looked as if they would have enjoyed a chance to let fly at Norrie with their feet and fists. The presence of the gamekeeper appeared to be holding them off. There was a sensation of nocturnal breathlessness, the feeling that a much more serious crime had been committed. It was as primitive as the natural skill with which only a little while before Jack Hogg had fished the Tanno with his bare hands.

Mr Morton and his apprehended culprit led the way. 'I'll see what I can do,' the gamekeeper said into Norrie's ear, 'but I'm making no promises.'

Outside Tanno House, Mr Morton said, 'I'll take the lad down to my place, ma'am, and give him a right good warning.'

'Oh, no! Either you do it, or I shall – but one of us shall telephone Sergeant Findlay.' The older woman was very determined. 'Lock him up in the garage until Sergeant Findlay gets here.'

'A local lad, and a first offence? The sergeant won't thank you for wasting his time, ma'am. Of course, he'd never say that to you – it'll be me who gets the sharp end of his bad temper. No, a right good warning,' Mr Morton said mysteriously. 'A warning such as he'll not forget in a hurry.'

Dunky Morton's hint that a 'warning' meant more than words went down well with Geoffrey and his wife. Mrs Lowther was not so happy with it, and Norrie thought she might have been, were she to deliver the 'warning' in person. Norrie trembled while she made her mind up. In the darkness, Tanno House, with its sixteenth-century tower, looked in its original time, before its owners learned how to speak with an English accent.

'No, I really don't think I want to make an exception,' Mrs Lowther said, released by her decision to the extent that she leapt several feet closer to Norrie. 'We always prosecute, Duncan. That is my rule – *prosecute*. If one doesn't, then it just happens again, and again.'

Norrie knew for a fact that it hadn't happened in two or three years. He wondered why she was making such a violent issue of a few fish.

'It's a long time since you had to prosecute anyone local,' Dunky Morton said in his quiet, almost affable manner. 'It wouldn't do you any good, and I'm sure Sergeant Findlay would say the same. A warning. A right *good* warning,' he said, with broad-vowelled seriousness.

'I see. Yes, well, I think I understand you, Duncan. Young man,' she said to Norrie, 'you have wantonly and brazenly stolen my fish, from my river. You are without any shadow of a doubt guilty of malicious trespass. I *should* prosecute you.' She slapped Norrie on the cheek. Dunky Morton stiffened, as surprised as Norrie. He tightened his grip on Norrie's shoulder. It was his way of advising Norrie that a slap on the face from a spry old woman was a lot better than being prosecuted in court for poaching, a crime against property which not much more than a hundred years ago was thought serious enough for its rascals to be transported to New South Wales or Tasmania. 'I won't have it!' She slapped him again, then prodded Norrie in the knee with her stick, and might have slapped him a third time had her daughter not led her away.

As soon as they were out of Tanno House, Dunky Morton released his grip. 'It's well known that a man who tries to take fish from the Tanno's an idiot. So who was the cheeky wee monkey who got away wi' the bag?'

'You don't really think I'd clype on him. Do you?' Norrie said.

'What worries me is that he's good at it,' Mr Gordon said. 'That was a fat bag, boy. How many?'

'Eight, nine ... I'm not sure.'

Dunky Morton whistled with outraged admiration. 'You tell 'm that if he tries it again, I'll be waiting. Go on, Norrie, tell me the boy's name. You'd be doing him a good turn. I'd have a word in his ear and put any idea of coming back to the Tanno right out of his mind.

It could save him a spot of very serious bother wi' thon Mrs Lowther.'

'Thanks for keeping Findlay off my back, Mr Morton; but I can't tell you who was with me.' They walked down the long drive through the estate to the lodge house where Dunky Morton lived. 'I don't think I'd like working for people like that.'

'I know who it must be! It's that boy from Perthshire. I was speaking to his father just the other week.'

'What about this warning I'm supposed to get?' Norrie said.

'Ach, just spread it around that you felt the toe o' my boot. It was a master of the craft who taught him, that's for sure,' Mr Morton said, convinced that it was Jack Hogg whose educated fingers had tickled the gills of Tanno's trout. 'It certainly wasn't you, Norrie. And it certainly wasn't from anybody around here that he learned how to guddle. That's who it is, though – that boy from Birnam.'

The following morning, Norrie said to Jack, 'No, I didn't "confess". I didn't mention you. What do you think I am? Dunky Morton *guessed*. He worked it out. He said it *must*'ve been you. That'll teach you. You shouldn't talk about Birnam so much.'

'The worst he can do is try to warn me off. But he didn't catch me. I've *never* been caught,' Jack said, his sly chuckle bragging his invulnerability.

'As good as, this time,' Norrie insisted.

'Aye, you – you were caught redhanded. You'd've been clean away if you hadn't stood there dithering,' Jack said scathingly.

Later that day, Jack Hogg came out of the Bonetti Brothers café and Dunky Morton confronted him on the pavement. 'It'd look pretty daft if you made a run for it,' Mr Morton said.

'I don't know what you're talking about.'

'Cheeky of mouth, too, eh? You've got cheeky wee legs on y' – I'll say that in your favour, sonny. Not to mention fingers that poke as cheeky as y' like in and out the gills of my trout.' Dunky Morton spoke with an amiably threatening tone so that Jack smiled as if he were being complimented. 'Cheek – that's what you're not short of.'

'You've got the wrong man.'

'Do you see this boot?' Mr Morton pointed to a boot, raised off the pavement the better to show its size. 'It's a ten-and-a-half. It's a heavy boot, but I can still swing it, if I've a mind to, if I've a just cause. This is called a hand,' he said, holding it out for Jack to inspect. He dwindled it into a fist. Jack sneered at Dunky Morton's four pebble-sized knuckles. 'I'm a placid sort of a man, but I'm very, very protective about the fish in Tanno Water, so when some young twerp helps himself to my trout, I get very, very angry.' The expression on Dunky Morton's face was benign, but slightly saddened; his voice made light of the threats it conveyed, which had the effect of making his promises sound more terrible. 'Very bad anglers. I've yet to meet a Lowther who could catch a fish. So there are trout in the Tanno all right, as you very well know. Eight or nine less than there were, mind you. Not my trout, to tell y' the truth. God's trout. Natural fish. The fruits of the water. And you've been in among them like a wee piranha!'

'I don't know why you're telling *me* this,' Jack said, and tried to step past the gamekeeper.

Dunky Morton caught Jack by the front of his shirt. He lifted him off the ground and shoved him, carried him, into the narrow alley between the hardware store and Bonetti Brothers'. 'This is a warning. Got that? A warning. It's to give you an idea of what I'll do if I catch you up there again. My big boot,' the gamekeeper said, suddenly vindictive, 'and my big mit. I'll kick y' all the way to the police station. Who taught y' how to guddle like that?'

'Never you mind who,' Jack said defiantly, almost choking as Dunky Morton raised him a foot off the ground on the end of his arm.

Mr Morton let Jack go and Jack slid down the wall, his elbow resting on the café's dustbin. Jack said, 'I learned in Birnam. Know where that is? They've got *real* gamekeepers up there.'

'Ach, Dunky Morton's bark is worse than his bite,' Jack said later, waving away the memory of his recent ordeal. 'He didn't frighten me. It makes it that bit tastier, knowing he's on his toes. He won't even see me, but he'll know I've been there. I'll make sure of that. The man in Birnam used to leave fish on the doorstep of the big house – that was his calling card. I'll make Dunky Morton hopping mad!'

Norrie flinched as he listened to Jack's planned revenge. 'You'll regret it if that Mrs Lowther gets her hands on you,' he said.

'I'm eighteen in a fortnight's time. I don't care what my old man says,' Jack proclaimed. 'I'm walking into the Bruce Arms, with dignity, I'm going up to the bar. Davy Laidlaw'll probably say, "Away y' go. Come back when you're old enough." And I'll say, "Wrong, Davy. I'm eighteen today, and I've left school. So let's have a pint of heavy – smartish, if you please." Dunky Morton? Dunky Morton doesn't scare me any. And I'll tell you another thing. Dunky Morton knows it. I was taught by *the* expert.'

'You'll grow out of it,' Norrie said calmly.

'That's the sort of shrinking, careful thing I'd *expect* you to say.'

'You'll be going on your own,' Norrie said. 'I had enough of that to last me a lifetime.'

'I saw Sandra Connolly this morning. How many blokes has she been around with this year? Four, is it? Is it four, or five, Norrie?'

'Shut up about Sandra Connolly,' Norrie said huffily.

'It might even've been six. Anyway, she's now being squired around by a farmer, prominent, I believe, in the Malcolmstown Young Conservatives Association,' Jack said mischievously.

'I said shut up about Sandra Connolly,' Norrie said, moodily belligerent.

'Mavis Murray is *very* attractive,' Jack said, throwing a pebble at a tin can. They sat in silence for a minute. 'I'll think about you next week,' Jack said, 'while I'm downing my second, or maybe my third pint in the Bruce Arms.'

'Great,' Norrie said, scowling at his own irony. 'I'll think of you, Jack – being sick as a dog behind a hedge.'

'Not much point asking you,' Jack said, with his pleasant, troublemaker's grin. 'You won't be old enough for a couple of months yet. Of course, if you feel like risking the parental wrath, you'd be very welcome to join me.'

Toddle-Bonny and the Bogeyman

For the sake of a conversation with Frank Irvine, it wasn't uncommon for Keith McMinn to pay his newspaper bill daily.

'I'll no' go bust because you don't pay me on the nail, Keith.'

'It was on my mind that I owed you for the paper, and, och well, I was passin' . . . '

'I've customers who pay their accounts when they feel like it – and I mean *seldom*. But even quarterly's all right by me. I'm an obligin' sort of man, Keith. How about weekly?' It was easy to feel exasperated with McMinn, harder to allow yourself to show it. 'I mean, I've known ye let it go the four days. Fortnightly? The perfect arrangement. Monthly's the average.'

Eight years before, a few days before she died, McMinn's mother made a list of what he should do to fend for himself. He was to stick to Fraser for fish, Armstrong for butchery, and Logie the grocer. Sorrow before the event bestowed on her advice an almost luminous privacy. 'I hate to think of you living on your own,' she'd said. Her uncertainty at whether he could cope was matched by McMinn's dread of independence. 'If it comes to the bit where you can't manage,' she said, 'then talk to Dr Broadie. There might be a vacancy somewhere. We haven't had to even think of it, but there could come a time when there's nothing else for it.' She spoke with difficulty, as if summarising a subject that was too complicated for both of them. He often remembered that afternoon. 'I want you to try,' she said.

McMinn reproached himself for falling short of his mother's instructions. His meals began as raw produce, but ended up undercooked, overcooked or as blackened disasters. From time to time he examined the frozen food displays in the supermarket that Logie's had become since his mother's death. He resisted their packaged blandishments and thought that those who didn't ought to know better. When he passed the Chinese carry-out he stopped and looked in through the plate-glass window, disapproving sternly.

For eight years his mother's list weathered the steam and fumes of the kitchen as it hung on the same nail as his calendar. It was a yellowing relic; it was also authoritative, admonitory, maternal and tender as it stated the memoranda of his life.

Anything that happened in Antynth was McMinn's business. He was that small town's classic pedestrian. With his mind fixed on its innocent disdain, he was an encyclopaedist of its trivial alterations and momentous changes. His gait was one of a depressed jauntiness. Children imitated it. He was unaware of the impression created by his clothes that looked as if another outing would see them fall apart.

'They tell me that girls are drinking pints now!' McMinn complained to Frank Irvine.

'Is that a fact?'

'Pints! Young women!'

'Don't tell me you've taken to visitin' public houses?'

'Me? No! Never!'

'Not a drop's crossed your lips? Do I believe you, Keith?' Irvine was teasing him.

'Only that once – the Labour Club's Burns Supper, 1983.'

'Will I ever forget it?' Irvine's eyes twinkled with kindly mischief.

'I'd no' blame ye if ye held it against me. I'll never live it down. I was a disgrace!' McMinn said.

'Don't say that, Keith. I mean, I'm no' a hypocrite. Once in a wee while I get plastered.'

It was McMinn's turn to tease, and Irvine was conscious of having placed the opportunity before him. 'Once in a wee while, Frank?'

'Maybe once a month,' Irvine conceded.

'More than that, though, if ye could get away wi' it! Once a month?' he said with broad disbelief.

'Credit me wi' a spark of responsibility, eh? I've a business to run!' Irvine said, exaggerating his defence of his reputation.

A customer came into the shop and Irvine began to serve him. McMinn waited by the counter but the newsagent said, 'Bye, Keith! See ye later.' It was a decisive farewell. McMinn had no option but to leave.

Joe Crossan said, 'It beats me how he manages. All on his owny-oh, an' big empty spaces upstairs . . . '

'Keith does all right. Not all there, but he gets by on what he's got, Joe.'

'It's more than a loose screw. He only has to breathe an' ye can hear the rattle!'

'Human nature's what ye might call a hobby of mine, Joe. Ye wouldn't deny that ye come in here once a day? What do ye buy? At *least* half a pound of Liquorice Allsorts. It's a lot of daily sugar. There are folk in the medical profession would say ye must've the death wish. Ye make me feel guilty. Ye're a confectionery addict, and I'm yer pusher!'

'Ye sell fags an' all,' Crossan said accusingly.

'Why no'? I smoke as well. I'm no' pious. I'm pointin' out that when it comes to windy spaces upstairs, you an' me haven't a leg to stand on!'

McMinn was walking along Shields Street on an evening in late April. A Rolls-Royce approached him at a stately speed and went past in a mechanical hush. A Rolls-Royce was a rare sight in Antynth. McMinn would have rushed to Frank Irvine's shop to report the news, but when he'd passed it a few minutes before he'd noticed Velma behind the counter. Any time she served him it was with looks of distaste. Fifteen minutes later, on Baird Street, beside the cement mixer and bricks, where they were building a new bank, McMinn saw the same opulent black car. A chauffeur was at the wheel. Two men and a woman sat in the back. Its windows were tinted, but not so much as to make the occupants completely invisible. You could see them, but you couldn't see them. You could tell that they were men or women, but you couldn't identify them.

The light was fading but several boys were still playing football on the waste ground beyond the broken fence that made Lawrie Street a cul-de-sac. McMinn spectated from the fence for a few minutes and then went through one of the gaps in its rotting posts on which black smears of municipal weatherproofing were still trying to fight off ruin. A close interest in local football was essential to McMinn's instinctive assessment of what Antynth was all about. He watched a thwarted dribble with his hands on his hips. 'Ach!' he said, turning his head away like a critical expert. 'Left foot!' he shouted. 'Try it wi' the left foot!'

'What'd you know about it?' the player shouted back.

'Toddle-Bonny!' another yelled in retaliation.

Years of parental guidance came to his aid. Ghostly advice encouraged him to walk away, around the edge of the imaginary football pitch. He crossed the waste ground to the disused railway line and site of the old station. Green shoots of fireweed sprouted by the long-abandoned coal depot. Two young men were racing motorcycles on the loose gravel. They braked so that their rear wheels swung on the guided weight of their machines. Each skid sliced the gravel and threw up a shower of tiny stones that rattled off shrubs and sheets of rusted corrugated iron.

Soon he was back on Shields Street. Once again the Rolls-Royce went by. 'What the hell're they playin' at?' He took off his cap and scratched his head, wondering at his own, spoken puzzlement.

Outside the parish church the car's brief halt seemed to indicate that it was taking a closer look. As it passed him, it slowed, and McMinn stooped to look into it. 'Who the hell do ye think ye are?' he shouted at the departing car, having failed to see its occupants. Its acceleration was virtually silent. McMinn felt himself dislodged by its power and glamour.

McMinn suspected his own opinions and conclusions. He acknowledged that his intelligence was slow. He resented the belief that the Rolls-Royce represented some sort of conspiracy. Pally Gray was among the few people to whom he could talk. He was in his early seventies and had been a close friend of McMinn's father. McMinn saw him once a week in the rooms of the local Labour Party Club.

'Pally, am I right, or am I wrong? No one in Antynth drives a Rolls-Royce.'

'Is this a joke?'

'No kiddin'. I saw a Rolls-Royce the other night. Even I can tell a Rolls from any other motor,' McMinn said, inviting Pally to take him seriously.

'A ritzy visitor from the other world,' Pally said, 'but not from outer space. Not common on these streets, but there're plenty elsewhere, and folks there go for drives, Keith. Keith saw a Rolls-Royce the other night,' Pally said to a man who came to the bar.

'Och, it would've been mine,' the man said.

'A uniformed driver, two men and a woman in the back,' McMinn protested.

'Interesting,' the man at the bar said, meaning the opposite.

Holding his lemonade and a crude brown-paper parcel, McMinn headed for an empty table.

'They don't call ye "Pally" for nothin',' Curly Pond said. 'How ye put up wi' that half-wit . . . '

'Son of my best friend, Curly,' Pally Gray said, savouring Curly Pond's nickname. He was as bald as a plate.

'Everybody liked Tommy McMinn, but ye have to admit that Toddle's manner would drive a saint to pugilism,' Pond said, attracting the barman's attention. 'Anythin' for you, Pally?'

'No, nothing for me,' Pally Gray said quietly.

At their table, McMinn said, 'I don't rightly understand it, but there was somethin' about that Rolls that really bothered me. Ye could tell. Ye could just tell, Pally. It was lookin' down its nose at me. It gave me the creeps,' he said, imitating a shiver. 'Put the wind right up me, it did.'

'Ye're tellin' me the difference between thirty thousand pounds' worth of motor car an' that pair of shoes ye're wearin'.'

'It was the car itsel',' McMinn said. He struggled with how to say what he meant. He seemed able to make the gestures that would have accompanied his explanation, but the necessary words eluded him. 'I don't know how to put it,' he confessed, his gestures now those of his disappointment in himself.

'Never mind, Keith. I think I know what ye're drivin' at. Contrast of wealth an' nothin'. Contrast of future wi' no future.'

'Maybe that, but no' just that only,' McMinn said. 'It gave me a very funny feelin'. Ye know, Pally, I think somethin' big's about to happen. Any rumours goin' the rounds?'

'None that I've heard,' Pally said.

'I might be wrong, then. It was just a feelin'.'

'What's in the parcel, Keith?'

'Do ye think Rick would take a dekko at this for me?' McMinn began to undo the string. 'It's my iron. It'll no' go.'

'Rick obliges everybody else,' Pally Gray said, leaving it unsaid that he didn't see why he shouldn't help out Keith McMinn.

'You ask him for me,' McMinn said with a persuasive grey twinkle in his eye. 'He an' me don't hit it off.' He handed over the iron on its bed of brown wrapping paper. 'String's handy stuff, eh?' he said, stuffing it into his pocket.

Pally Gray returned from the electrician's table after what seemed to McMinn a long conversation. 'He'll be over shortly,' Pally Gray said. 'Don't look so doubtful. Rick'll do what I tell him.'

McMinn smiled as his father's best friend took a long pull of his beer. For a few seconds he looked around the bar with confidence. Pally Gray was the wisest, most respected man in the Antynth Labour Party. He had been a town councillor for years when Antynth was a burgh, before the reorganization of local government that absorbed it into the district council. Pally Gray had served two terms as the burgh's provost. There were no suggestions of grandeur about Pally Gray, but McMinn basked in reflected glory.

'That Rolls-Royce,' McMinn said with a rush. 'It looked as it if owned the place. I'm rackin' my brains to tell you how . . . '

'What's the point, Keith?' Pally Gray said with a hint of impatience. 'I've told ye that I know what ye mean. A Rolls-Royce in a town that's got next to nothin' goin' for it can shock a man wi' a sense of the unreal.'

'As if it owned *us*,' McMinn blurted, as if against the obstacle of a stammer.

'I've been in a few Rollses,' Pally Gray said. 'The burgh's official car was never a Rolls, but always a very impressive ride. I'd find myself in other burghs, of course, and some used to run a Rolls-Royce. When a delegation of us went to Edinburgh, the secretary of state had us met wi' a Rolls at Waverley station. By then we'd sold the burgh motor, so we went by train. Couldn't do that now. Heavy traffic all the way to St Andrews House. For all the distance, we'd've been quicker walkin'. Not on, of course. Layin' on the big flash car's a bit like linin' the palm wi' silver, or talkin' ye round to a wrong way of thinkin'. A touch of the high-class that makes a man think he's on the side of the big people. The Sunday-best every day for as long as it takes to say aye to the wrong ideas. It got to me, but it didn't change me. Unlike some I could mention. All of a sudden they even started to *talk* different.'

'It's a goner,' Rick Williamson said, putting the iron on the table. 'It's passed on to the heaven of the small electrical appliances.'

'No hope for it?'

'Not a snowball's, Pally.'

'Where's my brown paper?' McMinn asked anxiously.

'I chucked it,' the electrician said. 'It was *dirty*. I should've checked the stamps. They were probably two monarchs ago. That was very old paper, Toddle.'

'It was my last piece,' McMinn said, sinking back on his chair.

'I can do ye a reconditioned iron for seven quid,' Rick Williamson said.

'Make it five,' Pally Gray bargained.

'Five?' McMinn said, coming back from the loss of his brown paper to meet the consternation of a bill for five pounds.

'Any idea how *cheap* that is?' Williamson said incredulously.

'All right, I can manage a fiver,' McMinn said with reluctance. 'But as soon as ye can, Rick. Without an iron I'll look a shambles in no time.'

'Aye, I can see it's touch an' go,' Williamson said.

'I'll be sorry to lose it,' McMinn said, holding the defunct iron.

'The diagnosis is death. Everythin' wears out, Toddle. There comes a time when ye have to grin an' bear it, then buy another one. This is a very old iron. I'm surprised it's lasted this long.'

Pally Gray drove McMinn home after the meeting. A lift was a treat that McMinn appreciated. It amused Pally Gray to notice the self-importance with which Tommy McMinn's son settled into the seat beside him. Outside McMinn's door on Ingram Street, Pally Gray said, 'I wouldn't mind bein' asked in for a cup of tea, Keith. Now that I'm livin' on my own, I sometimes can't be bothered to boil the kettle.'

'Oh, sure. Only too pleased,' McMinn said keenly.

Pally Gray asked himself in to check whether Keith still managed to look after himself. It was part of a promise that he had made to McMinn's mother eight years before. Every two or three months he was moved yet again by McMinn's imitation of his mother's way of keeping the house. Furniture was in the same place. McMinn brought the tea through from the kitchen on a tray set in the manner remembered from his mother's routines.

'Did ye get the gas fire fixed?'

'Gas Board did it,' McMinn said.

'I thought it had a healthier hiss. Social Security come up wi' the right contribution?'

'Aye. Took weeks, though. The man there doesny like me, Pally. No surprise to me if he's plannin' on firin' me off to a Home.'

'Ye know who to come to if he starts anythin' bureaucratic,' Pally Gray said.

'What Rick said's got me all worried.'

'How come?'

'About everythin' wearin' out. I've a vacuum cleaner, a refrigerator, an' an electric kettle.'

'Aye, it's a worry all right,' Pally Gray agreed. 'You make a lovely cup of tea, Keith.'

'Are you managing all right? I mean, now that Mrs Gray's . . . Managing all right on yer own? Och, ye know what I mean . . . '

'Kind of ye to ask. I appreciate it. I don't do too badly. Aye, everything wears out, including me. Some mornin's I feel as stiff as a table. I'm havin' trouble wi' the waterworks,' Pally Gray said.

'The waterworks? Ye mean these plans for privatization?'

'My waterworks!'

'Oh, that! I thought ye were talkin' politics, as usual,' McMinn said, risking a joke. 'Oh, well, ye know where it is when ye need it.'

When he was upstairs Pally Gray admitted to himself that McMinn kept his bathroom tidier than he kept his own. He took a quick look at McMinn's bedroom, too. No clothes lay scattered about, the bed was made, and, as always, Tommy McMinn's presentation copy of *Labour Politics in Antynth and District* lay on the bedside table. Before coming downstairs he tried the door to what had been the bedroom used by Keith's parents. It was locked, as it always was.

After Pally Gray left, McMinn washed the cups and saucers, the plate on which he'd presented biscuits; he rinsed the teapot and put away the sugar bowl, the milk jug and the tray. He shook the tray-cloth, then folded its linen lines along the distinct creases made by his ironing. He pulled out the electric plugs in the living room, then switched off the downstairs lights. He undressed and put on pyjamas. He washed and brushed his teeth. Before he turned in for the night he took the key to his parents' bedroom from the drawer in his bedside table. Inside, he put the dead iron on their bed. Other things lay on the covers – a letter from his uncle in Canada to say that his aunt had died; copies of the local newspaper in which were reports that he knew his parents would be more than just interested. Among these stories were the write-ups, lasting issue after issue for weeks, about the redundancies at the factory that made paper bags, where Tommy McMinn had worked almost all his life, and then its closure. Christmas cards from relatives, year by year, mounted up in a cardboard box.

'The iron wore out,' he said to the bed in the darkness of the room.

'Rick Williamson says everything wears out. He's getting me another one. Pally's all right. He's getting by, but he's got trouble with his waterworks.'

He left quickly, locking the door, and wondering, as always, why he made these reports to his parents, or kept the interesting numbers of the newspaper on their bed.

Among McMinn's outdoor routines was walking to where the road from Antynth feeds into the motorway. It was a weekly event. He visited McCluskey's snack bar in a layby just before the road ushered itself into two lanes before joining the north-south and south-north hurry of the thousands of vehicles daily for whom Antynth was a sign at the side of the road. It was three miles from the town. McCluskey's snack bar was a converted caravan.

'No one in a Rolls-Royce ever drives in here for a quick refreshment,' McMinn said to McCluskey. 'That's for sure.'

'This is a hygienic waterin'-hole. Tea I make's fit for *anybody* to drink,' McCluskey protested. ' "Freshly cut sandwiches" – that means what it says. No dirty tea-cups here. No unwashed spoons. I give a spotless service.'

'Occasional large cars, yes; but when did you last've a customer in a Rolls-Royce?'

McCluskey looked amused and suspicious, as if McMinn was about to catch him out on something. 'Who needs a cheese roll when they can afford a Roller? It'll be the straw hamper on the back seat, caviare, smoked salmon and the cucumber sandwiches – brown bread, very thinly cut, quick stroke of best butter ... And the wee mahogany cabinet, probably refrigerated, containing the champers an' glasses. Not my end of the caterin' trade, Keith.'

'I saw one in Antynth last week.'

'So what?'

'Ten-to-one it must've come off the motorway an' gone straight past ye. Seen any big black Rollses lately?' McMinn asked seriously, his features pinched and pouting, demanding an answer.

'Even if it was solid gold an' playin "Annie Laurie", what's a Rolls to me unless it stops an' makes me an offer? What's botherin' ye, Keith? Why're we talkin' Rolls-Royces?'

'I walk up here, buy nothin', and' ye notice *me*,' Keith said.

'How could I miss ye? Ye come up that road like a one-man hunger march. Keith, the sun's shinin'! Why the raincoat? It's cryin' out for a decent burial. Donate it to the raincoat museum!'

'It said on the forecast, "occasional sunny periods",' McMinn said.

'Aye, *sunny* periods!'

'What comes in between "sunny periods"?' McMinn asked victoriously.

'Rolls-Royces?'

'I saw one!'

'Big deal. Look, how long do ye plan on wastin' my time . . .?'

'It's no' as if ye're doin' a lot else, Jim.'

'That's right, hurt me. I tell ye what, Keith. As a matter of interest. Personally, I'd find it a fascinatin' statistic. Away to that footbridge over the big M and count how many Rolls-Royces go by in . . . in an hour. That's it, a nice, round time. There's a cup of tea an' a ham sandwich in it, on the house.'

'Ye want rid of me,' McMinn said peevishly. He thought about McCluskey's suggestion. 'I don't have a watch, Jim.'

'Doesn't have to be an hour, spot on,' McCluskey said.

'I've a watch, but it was my dad's. I keep it for special occasions. Forty years' service in the Pokey Works. Gold presentation pocket watch. Are ye havin' me on, Jim?' McMinn asked suspiciously.

'Me? No way, Keith.'

'I'm hopeless at time. I could be there all day an' I'd still think it was less than an hour,' McMinn said.

'Och, I'll tell ye how long ye've been there when ye get back,' McCluskey said.

Big transporters roared under the footbridge, leaving the scent of diesel fuel that added to the day's fumes. A little shower began then stopped before McMinn could decide whether to run for shelter. In the time he stood there no one else appeared on the bridge which carried an ancient bridle path over the gorge cut by the roadbuilders through the low hills. Steel netting restrained shale and boulders on the escarpments dug through the local ground. Cars, trucks, tankers, vans and a military convoy raced under the bridge. Towards the end of his notional hour he spotted a Rolls-Royce, but it was beige, not black. He crossed to the south-facing parapet and watched it draw into the fast lane to overtake. Very few vehicles turned off for Antynth. Just as seldom did a car appear from that direction to join the motorway, either to head north, or, once over the flyover, to melt into the traffic going south.

'One Rolls, beige, an' it rained,' McMinn said.

'Just the one, ye say? I'm amazed,' Jim McCluskey said. 'Only rolls I'll know'll have ham or cheese in them. Bring on the tourist trade. Ham roll an' tea comin' up, Keith.' As he spread an opened roll, he said, 'So what was this Roller ye saw in Antynth?'

'Who knows?' McMinn said. 'It's a mystery.'

'Mr Mortgage, Lord Bank-Loan or Sir Humphrey Income-Tax,' McCluskey said. 'Read the papers. There's money everywhere except here. Mustard?'

'No, no mustard,' McMinn said. ' "Occasional sunny periods"? I told ye what that means!' he said, and McCluskey permitted him a moment of triumph.

A few evenings later, McMinn saw the black Rolls-Royce again. It drove past him on Shields Street and then stopped. McMinn hesitated, believing from how the car slowed, then drew to a halt ahead of him, that it was waiting for his approach. Its engine was still running. McMinn moved towards it carefully. By the time he reached it he half-expected a door to open and someone to step out with a full explanation. Sodium glow from a streetlamp prevented him from seeing through its yellow reflections and into the car. 'Who are ye?' he said to the window. He slapped the dark glass with his hand. A face, seen as if it were under water, looked out at him. 'Who the hell are ye?' McMinn asked angrily. He felt himself inspected. He was convinced they had stopped to look at him. Gleaming under the streetlamps with polished authority, the car drove off past Frank Irvine's shop and McMinn trotted after it.

'Before ye ask me if I've seen a black Rolls, the answer's yes,' Irvine said over a pile of unsold magazines that he was tying up. 'Tell me all about it, Keith.'

McMinn breathed hard after his haste to get there. 'I don't know, Frank.'

'An' here's me thinkin' that if anythin' happens in this town, then Keith McMinn's got all the answers.'

'Don't talk to me like that!'

'Like what?' Irvine said, matching McMinn's offended tone.

'As if I'm no' here! Ye talk to me as if I'm a lot younger than I am.'

Irvine hesitated over the half-tied knot held by his forefinger. He pulled his string tight. 'Tell me about the Rolls, then.'

'People that drive them cars don't answer questions from the likes of me. Or you,' he added.

'Can't think what I'd want to ask them,' Irvine said.

'First time I told ye about that car, ye didn't believe me,' McMinn said.

' "Mystery Rolls Seen on Shields Street." Sorry, Keith. It's in the same category as "Woman Gives Birth". "Keith McMinn's Iron Pronounced Kaput." '

'What?'

'Same category as,' Irvine said. 'It's not news. Its trivial stature's practically momentous. I didn't disbelieve ye, Keith. I didn't think it mattered. I still don't.' He was annoyed. He threw the bundle of magazines on the floor.

'Somebody high an' mighty's in that motor,' McMinn said, irate that Frank Irvine, like everyone else, shrugged off its visits to Antynth as of no consequence. 'I know what people say about me,' McMinn said.

'Oh? Sure you're no' imaginin' it, Keith?' Irvine said absent-mindedly as he measured more twine from a dispenser.

> 'Toddle-Bonny lives in a tent
> His bum's at the front, his legs 're bent
> Toddle-Bonny's the bogeyman
> An' 'e drinks 'is tea from an old tin can.'

McMinn drew back from the counter. 'I've been hearin' it since I was ten,' he said.

'*You* said *that* to *me*,' Irvine said. 'No' me to you. Remember that.'

'Ye'd heard it before, though,' McMinn said. 'I'm a decent, honest *man*!'

Irvine shook his head sadly.

'If you'd my life,' McMinn said, 'ye wouldny think it such a comic turn.'

'Mine's no' all that hilarious, Keith,' Irvine said. 'I'm tired. I've been on my feet since five this mornin'. Velma's got the flu. My eldest son's got a drink problem in Edinburgh, where I hope he'll keep it. Lorna's set her heart on marryin' a bloke wi' green hair, an' he wears so much studded leather it'll no surprise me if their kids turn out to be suitcases. Keith, look at these unsold magazines. Business's *lousy*. What's this for?' he said when McMinn placed some coins on the counter, and began counting more.

'Newspaper bill,' McMinn said.

'Ye paid it this mornin'!'

On Wednesday evening at the Labour Party Club Pally Gray delivered McMinn's lemonade and said, 'All of a sudden the Ghost Rolls is no longer a subject to baffle the mind. It belongs to a man by the name of Mussonwell.'

'Mussonwell? Mussonwell?' McMinn said, repeating the name until convinced that he hadn't heard it before.

'A Midas of hard times. He's bought a castle not twenty miles from here. A man for whom "slump" means the crock of gold at the end of the rainbow. For us it's a bucket of somethin' else entirely, but for Mr Mussonwell it means labour desperate enough to come cheap, an' deals made wi' unions.' McMinn's aghast facial turbulence invited Pally Gray to say more. 'A man whose principles might have to be endured if his interest in Antynth comes to anything. I hear things on the grapevine. Not as much as hitherto, but I have my sources. I hear, for example, that our esteemed Tory MP is cock-a-hoop about Mr Mussonwell takin' over the Pokey Works as premises for a new enterprise of his. No doubt development grants'll pave the way, to say nothin' of political jiggery-pokery – forgive the pun. Not paper bags, of course. Mr Mussonwell's interested in makin' deodorized insoles for footwear.'

'Pally, what's a pun?'

'Forget I even mentioned it. What's important is that Mr Mussonwell's mentioned the figure of fifty jobs.'

McMinn looked thoughtful. 'I don't like the sound of it, Pally.'

'Fifty jobs is fifty jobs. Fifty jobs is fifty wage-earners. This town's as poor as the tinker's granny. Five more years of bad luck and we'll live to see sagebrush blowing down Shields Street. I expect an acrimonious discussion at tonight's meeting.'

'I *knew* there was somethin' to that car!'

'Too true,' Pally Gray said. 'Fifty jobs puts jam on toast. Fifty jobs puts whisky in water. Mr Mussonwell's no philanthropist, but he comes bearing gifts. It'll be some meetin'. We've a hothead or two who'll see cause for a fight in this.'

'I don't like the sound of this Mussonwell,' McMinn said.

'You're no' too keen on his car, either. But the town needs a shot in the arm, and Mr Mussonwell owns the shot.'

'Right, Toddle. That's a fiver ye owe me,' Rick Williamson said, placing an iron on the table. 'You dig in to yer purse, an' I'll be back in a minute.'

'Are ye all right for money?' Pally Gray asked McMinn. 'Sorry I asked,' he said when he saw McMinn's expression. 'I understand how ye feel about Mussonwell.'

'What can we do about it?' McMinn said. 'Nothin'. I feel clean out of objections, because I know they count for damn all.'

'It's a question of takin' the bad over the disgustin',' Pally Gray said.

'Thanks, Toddle. Happy ironin',' Williamson said, picking up his five pounds.

'Capitalist,' McMinn said, pronouncing the word the way his father used to emphasize it.

'Me?'

'Aye, you.'

'Pally, tell me – what've I done to deserve this?' Williamson said.

'Keith's a bit rattled over this Mussonwell affair,' Pally Gray said.

'All right, Toddle. I'm in business for myself, but that doesn't mean I'm anything *like* Mussonwell,' Williamson said aggressively. 'Call me a capitalist again an' I'll iron yer face so flat ye'd think it was pressed in a laundry! Understand, Toddle?'

'Uncalled for, Rick,' Pally Gray said.

The incident was beginning to attract an audience. Williamson said, 'Yer half-way to capitalism yerself, Pally. No' hard to guess what ye'll be sayin' tonight. The ex-provost's analysis. Take the jobs and like them. It sticks in my craw, Pally. Our party's got the representation in Scotland all sewn up. But when it comes to exercisin' its muscle its power's about as nifty as a fused plug. Ten lousy Tories out of seventy-two MPs've fused it! Aye, but yer a Westminster man, Pally. Ye'd too many pals in the House. Ye'll follow the party line till the day ye choke on it.'

McMinn suffered to hear Pally Gray spoken to as if he no longer counted. Voices muttered an agreement with Williamson's sentiments. McMinn, too, was inclined to agree with them, but they confused him; he wanted to be loyal to Pally Gray.

'We'll leave my thoughts on the subject until the meetin',' the ex-provost said.

'You tasted power, Pally. It was local, but it was sweet.' Williamson noticed his other listeners and looked at them as well as Pally Gray as he continued. 'Ye got used to lettin' contradictions slip in by the back door. First time around ye probably sent them back. Second time? Maybe aye, maybe no. But they were turnin' up every day. *Bound* to get in sometime.'

'Your attitude's destroyin' this party,' Pally Gray said, shaking his head at a younger man's political passion. 'I don't think ye know much about it. A wee industrial town like this, hemmed in by Tory farmers, lairds' tenants, bijoy villages colonized by yuppies, all voters natural to interests other than ours – we haven't a chance if what we're offerin' 's the folk-socialism of yesteryear. We haven't moved wi' the times ...'

Williamson interrupted Pally Gray's account. 'He wants us to move wi' the times! They're Tory times! Our responsibility's to contest them, Pally!'

'I'm a bit tired, Rick. I saw us win the seat in forty-five, and then again the next time. An' every ward in the burgh. Tasted the great party triumphs, ye see, Rick, an' for the past ten years I've watched the clock turned back. Or that was how it seemed. In actual fact, the Tories make time work on their side. I'm too old to sit down an' think how to capture the clock, Rick. Mussonwell's jobs, though, Tory jobs that they are, are first of all *jobs*. So keep yer eye on the immediate issue.' Pally Gray looked up from his chair in silent appeal.

'He's admitting that he's historically embarrassed by party failures,' Williamson said.

'Embarrassed isn't the word!' Pally Gray said vehemently. 'Nor's failures! I'm heartsick of Tory successes!'

'Historically' was a concept on the edge of McMinn's intelligence, but he liked the sound of it. To him it carried the satisfactions of reading a page in the book he kept by his bedside. Still, it pained him to hear Pally Gray announce, 'If the people don't have work, I don't care who provides it.' Mussonwell was a cipher to McMinn, a token of the detestable. 'I'll take the jobs,' Pally Gray said. 'That's the way the shortcake breaks.'

'Our country's timid,' Williamson said. 'It's as simple as that.' McMinn felt the urge to speak. Once or twice he'd opened his mouth and gagged on silence. 'We've had Scottish nationalism as an organized political movement for over sixty years,' Williamson said to his audience, 'and not one nationalist's died for the cause. It hasn't killed anybody either. I'm as much against violence as the next man, but the facts speak for themselves. Westminsterism's cryin' out for the bum's rush. But what do we do? We don't even take ourselves seriously. Only twenty-five per cent of Scotland votes Tory,' he said, as if it was hard for him to believe his own statistics, 'an' it's folk tryin' to be English who call the shots? It's out of order. Anywhere else we'd be out on the streets!'

'Calm down, Rick,' someone said.

'Give the man a pint,' said another.

'What's involved?' Pally Gray said. 'Think about it, then ask yerselves if yer willin'. I know politics. I don't know anythin' about guerrilla warfare, bombs in railway stations, or ambushes at the bridge. An' at my age, I don't want to know!'

McMinn anguished on his inability to force words from his mouth. He caught a glimpse of someone nudging his neighbour then nodding in McMinn's direction as if he noticed that something was wrong. What started as a heated conversation between Pally Gray and Williamson was now a general argument involving the entire bar-room.

'I say Rick's talkin' good sense. Lowers the spirits, maybe, but . . . '

'Away an' behave yersel'!'

'I'm no' arguin' for complete independence,' Williamson stated. 'Devolution, but wi' budgetary powers, would do for a start . . . '

'Fat chance!' someone shouted.

'Nationalism's just the flavour of the month,' Pally Gray said dismissively.

'Oh, aye? Nearly everybody here likes the taste, then,' a voice shouted from the bar.

'Is this the meetin'? Or are we goin' through?' a voice complained.

On his own initiative, the barman pulled the plug on the fruit machine. The man playing it stood back with affront as its merry sounds of musical paydirt faded to an electronic hum and then silence. Its lights flashed. He shook the machine, then kicked it.

'If ye don't keep your voices down,' someone shouted, in a tone of admonitory amusement, 'Special Branch'll be all over us!'

'Face facts!' Williamson said loudly. 'Opposition should be *opposition!*'

Voices buzzed around McMinn: they formed an audible blur. His collar felt tight. Pally Gray was looking at him with concern.

'Independence would help this country to grow up,' a mild-voiced woman said.

'Add the word "democratic" before "opposition",' her friend said, 'and I'm with you all the way!'

'All right, Keith?' Pally Gray said to McMinn through the heated babble.

'The Union's a joke!'

'Pally's right, though. I don't see me as a plainclothes rifleman.'

'Civil disobedience!' another shouted, his intervention provoking more arguments.

McMinn thought his own independence a miserable state of affairs. He had something to say on the subject of independence. It was wedged at the back of his throat. Fantasy eloquence toiled in an effort to master his vocal cords. Pally Gray was looking at him again. Something was said to Rick Williamson, and McMinn looked at the electrician. Men nearby rose to their feet. Two women got up at another table. The entire Labour Party Club seemed closing in on him. Fingers not his own were working to loosen his collar. The lights went out.

He woke up at two in the morning wondering how he had got into his bed in the first place. He could hear voices downstairs and recognized Pally Gray's. He switched on the bedside lamp. His book got in the way of his fumbling hand and fell to the floor. He sat up, dazed, perplexed, recollecting the argumentative evening. He had heard ding-dong verbal battles there before, but nothing like as combative. Still, it had been building up for weeks. All it took was Mussonwell to light the blue touch-paper and stand back.

'Movement upstairs,' Rick Williamson said.

'Aye, well, we'll give him a minute,' Pally Gray advised. He tipped whisky into Rick's glass. 'Ever wondered which way Dr Broadie votes?' Pally said. 'I've asked him. Says it's a secret between him an' the ballot box. I've never liked it when I don't know a man's politics.'

'Maybe he hasn't got any. It's been known.'

'I've enjoyed this *quiet* talk, Rick.'

'Me, too, Pally. Hope Toddle doesn't mind my fag smoke all over his livin' room.'

'I'll see what's doin' upstairs,' Pally Gray said.

'Should I slip away?'

'Don't be daft. I might need a runner. Mind what Broadie said. "If ye need me, call right away." I've too much drink taken to drive.'

Pally Gray climbed the stairs like the old man he was. McMinn was in his dressing-gown, shaking his head. 'I heard it was you, Pally,' he said. 'What happened?'

'One of these turns of yours, Keith. Feelin' better?'

'No' bad,' McMinn said. 'Who were ye talkin' to?'

'Rick. He kept me company. Broadie's been an' gone. Says there's nothin' to worry about, but if ye need him, ye know the way. I'll spend the night, if ye like,' Pally offered.

'No need,' McMinn said. 'Nowhere for ye to sleep, anyway.'

'I could sleep next door.'

McMinn thought for a moment. 'I haven't been in it, since . . . och, you know since when, Pally. I could murder a cup of tea. Would ye do the honours? Maybe Rick'd like one.'

'We've been on the hard stuff,' Pally Gray said.

'Oh, aye? What about the waterworks?'

'I can see *you're* back to normal!' Pally Gray said. 'Down the stairs wi' ye. Tea an' a bite to eat'll see ye right.'

Pally Gray and Rick Williamson left about half an hour later. When they'd gone, McMinn tidied away the glasses and tea-cups and placed what was left of Pally Gray's whisky in the sideboard – 'Don't be daft,' the old man had said, 'keep it for the next time I'm here.' He pulled out the electric plugs, then switched off the downstairs lights. Once upstairs, he washed: he brushed his teeth, rinsed the basin, tidied the towels on the rail. He unlocked the door to his parents' room. Inside, in the dark, he told them about Mr Mussonwell and the fifty jobs at the old Pokey Works that might soon be turned into a factory for the production of deodorized insoles.

'Big arguments tonight, Dad. All about devolution, independence and where the Party's goin'. I don't know what to think,' he said. 'Honest, I don't know. Pally held his own. Rick Williamson went at it hammer an' tongs. I didn't know where I was.'

Mulwhevin

Norman Makower, a man in his sixties, set a spry and vigorous pace over that rugged, steep and remote hill country. Bob Scarfe followed him with what looked like the imitated energy of a disciple or subordinate. When the path was broad enough, he strode alongside Makower, resuming a conversation that the demands of the terrain had curtailed. Earlier in the hike the wiry young man's ginger beard had caught the drift of a spider's web which he encountered when the path led through a grove of meanly leafed hawthorns. It left an irritating tickle on his chin at which he scratched and rubbed.

Twenty and sometimes as much as a hundred yards behind them, Joan Bolton struggled with nature's inconsiderate inclines, puddles and outcrops, and her increasingly bad temper. Like her boyfriend, Bob Scarfe, she was in her late twenties, but her gait was stooped and clumsy, her breathing loud and gasping and somehow the load on her back seemed heavier. 'Wait for me!' She had called on them to give her a chance to catch up at least a dozen times during the past hour, but they had not heard the petulant, impatient voice behind them. She found it hard not to take her eyes off her boots. She could hardly believe that she had allowed herself to be coaxed into such uncharacteristic footwear. Worse, she remembered that when she bought them she had actually looked forward to the great outdoors and to fresh air and the clean, Scottish scenery.

About half an hour later, Makower stopped and pointed to a hill. His arm described an arc as it traversed the sky, leading from Mulwhevin to the house that bore the same name and which stood in its shadow.

Joan caught up with them. She slung her rucksack to the ground and flopped down beside it.

'Mulwhevin!' Makower shouted with grandiose enthusiasm.

Joan had heard that name several times over the past few weeks, but it was only when she met Makower early that morning when they set out from Manchester in Bob's car that she discovered who Bob had heard it from.

She was suspicious of Makower's look-we-have-arrived tone of voice. For a start, the house was at least a mile away, albeit downhill on the floor of the valley. But Joan had learned over the last three hours that the Galloway landscape tended to go up when you expected it to go down, and that there were obstacles usually of a wet or otherwise impassable nature between her and the sight towards which she was headed.

They walked on and in her efforts to keep up with them Joan went over on her ankle. 'Wait! Oh, wait, will you?' she screamed at them. 'I've twisted my ankle!'

Makower put his hands on his hips and shook his head.

'Is it sore?' Bob asked.

Joan groaned and Bob helped her to her feet. 'Try a little weight on it,' he said. She hobbled a few steps. 'There's nothing seriously wrong if you can walk on it,' Bob said, annoyed at the delay.

'Limp,' Joan said, correcting him, as Bob walked off with Makower.

Renovated inside and out, modernized and white-washed, the farmhouse of Mulwhevin (as it had once been) now belonged to the remnants of the pre-war 'Cambridge Socialist Picnic Society'. Founded in 1934 by a group of undergraduates, the society had long since jettisoned its original name. Most of its founding members were dead, or they had refused to follow the guidance of Thomas Drinkwater, also deceased, who had transformed what had thrived as a simple fraternity of ramblers. Only Norman Makower, Professor Peregrine Eaves and his wife, Mildred, were left of that Cambridge generation of walkers. From green strolls through East Anglia, voraciously contemporary in their time, they had progressed to the pagan philosophy of Thomas Drinkwater.

Professor Eaves waved to Makower and his young companions as they approached the house. 'Oh, goody!' his wife said, with a skip. 'They're here! Norman! Nor-man!'

Joan staggered to a halt and unburdened herself of her rucksack. She looked on as Makower introduced Bob to the Eaveses. She shook hands with them herself and then realized that Mulwhevin was not quite so remote as she had been led to believe. 'There's a road,' she said, dismayed by the sight of a parked Range Rover. 'Look, Bob, a road!' Not that it was very much of a road, more like a track, but it was obviously hospitable to being motored over. 'Norman, why did we have to leave Bob's car at that farm, and then *walk*?'

Makower smiled. He was all brown wrinkles and his own white teeth. Joan understood Mildred's tight-lipped expression as disdainful.

'Joan feels a trifle put out. She "twisted her ankle",' Makower said in audible inverted commas. 'But you can't understand a place,' he explained to Joan, 'unless you get the feel of it right into your legs and lungs. Isn't that right?'

Perry and Mildred Eaves were full of earnest agreement.

'I think Joan's ankle might benefit from a rub,' Bob said quickly, his eyes appealing for help as Joan, having thought of possible treatment for herself, hobbled towards the kitchen door.

'Embrocation!' Mildred Eaves shouted after him. 'Cupboard opposite the Aga, top shelf, right-hand side!' She waited until the couple were indoors. 'A twisted ankle is not a good sign,' she said. 'We know all about "twisted ankles". Where on earth do you find them, Norman?'

Makower filled his chest with deep gulps of the fresh Galloway air. 'Don't you think she's suitable? She's certainly very pretty, and I think she goes extremely well with young Bob. And Bob's the most promising young man I've come across in years. He's a student at one of my evening institutes. Awfully well read. Spiritually *eager*,' he said with conviction. 'She isn't, yet. But I have hopes.'

'Yes, I rather like the look of Bob,' Professor Eaves said, 'but I can't help remembering the other occasions on which you've held these "hopes" of yours, Norman.' He grinned at his memory of Makower's 'young people'. 'And where are they now? I ask you, Norman – where?'

'Others arrived yet?' Makower asked.

'Geoff's here. Not that Susannah's with him, of course – that would've been too much to hope for,' Mildred said. 'He'll be back before din-dins.'

Makower looked at the mountain as if hoping to catch a glimpse of Geoff Huntingdon. 'One began to despair of Susannah a long time ago.'

'The Whigham boys are here,' Mildred said, interrupting Makower's thoughts.

'Jolly good, the Whigham boys!' Makower shouted. He expanded his chest, stretched his arms, and swallowed a deep draught of air. 'It's wonderful to be back again! I toast you, Thomas Drinkwater! I toast you in the clean air of Devanou!'

Invigorated, Makower opened his arms to catch Mildred and he held her close. Professor Eaves, tall, spindly, his Derby tweed breeches unbuttoned at the shins, embraced them both within the circumference of his long arms. They laughed and hugged each other as Mildred's drying laundry flapped on the clothes-lines beside them.

'They're kissing each other,' Joan said, leaning back on a chair to look out of the kitchen window. Bob rubbed more foul-smelling herbal liniment on her ankle. 'How much do you know about these people?'

'There,' Bob said, kissing Joan's injury. 'That'll make it better.'

Joan recoiled from the scent of the oily paste with which her foot and ankle had been anointed. 'Yah! What'd *that* taste like?'

As a young woman of her generation whose concerns tended towards the radical, Joan Bolton was inclined to believe what she had read and heard about the benefits of a vegetarian diet. So far, her only contribution to a climate which emphasized jogging, healthy food and abstemiousness was to have cut down to ten cigarettes a day. Wine or anything stronger she was seldom able to afford on her salary as a part-time, temporary lecturer in Victorian Studies.

Favourably disposed to dinner without meat as she was, the effect of Norman Makower, Professor and Mrs Eaves and the two Whigham brothers aroused in Joan something like a necessity to deplore the bean stew, brown rice and salad on the table. A cigarette would have brought the house down. But the urge to produce a cigarette and light it with carefree ostentation was almost irresistible. She felt an urge to ask what had happened to the wine. The conversation was not so much above her head as beneath her contempt.

'I would have given everything I have to have been in Taos when Lawrence was there,' Mildred Eaves said. 'Perry and I made our own private pilgrimage, of course. The sense of energy in that place was absolutely electrifying!' she said with tense, violent conviction.

'*Anywhere* Lawrence was at the time,' Bob Scarfe said, a remark that struck Joan as so slyly and unreasonably ingratiating that she found herself looking with extreme disrespect at the butter-bean on her fork.

'We have his legacy. Never lose sight of it,' Makower said. 'And you, Joan? What do you think of Lawrence?'

'Male chauvinism, justified by an unreal craving for ecstasy and significance, and putting the cause back by years.'

'Indeed? What cause?' Mildred asked. 'Or do you mean feminism? Well, how very interesting, but hardly new to *us*.'

'Negative erudition – that's Lawrence,' Joan said.

'Negative erudition?' Professor Eaves was puzzled. The phrase was unfamiliar, and he felt he should have heard it before.

'What is "negative erudition"?' one of the Whigham brothers asked, looking at his mentors as if accusing them of failing to keep his education up-to-date.

'A person said to be negatively erudite is one of which it is fair to claim that he knows a lot about zilch,' Joan said. 'I've noticed that they're usually male.'

Joan's dismissal of D. H. Lawrence brought down on her head a tirade of proselytizing and protest. She had not felt so vulnerable since announcing that she was leaving the Marxist Women's Criticism Seminar. Bob put his fork down as if what Joan said had ruined his appetite. She felt outnumbered and exceptional. She was dying for a smoke.

'Ankle all right now?' Bob asked her as she washed the dishes.

'I know you told me that maybe I'd find them a bit cranky, but you didn't say they were your gurus.' Joan's rubber-gloved hands splashed among the suds and crockery. 'They're off their rockers!'

'Yes, well, you certainly succeeded in embarrassing me,' Bob said.

'What about the Whighams?'

'What about them?'

'They give me the willies. Creeps,' she said with emancipated malice. 'Now where are you going?'

'We're having an extremely important discussion,' Bob said, crossing the spacious rural kitchen.

'I could do with some help!'

While Joan was drying up, both Whighams came into the kitchen for a glass of water. In their thirties, they were short-haired, open-faced, tanned and exactly the same height. Both wore their shirt collars neatly overlaid on the lapels of their linen jackets. 'Am I missing anything through there?' Joan asked with thinly disguised sarcasm.

'Norman has been reading to us,' one Whigham said, his difficulty in speaking caused either by shyness or by a feeling that Joan was not worthy of being spoken to.

Identical dress and what seemed identical movements led Joan to ask, 'Are you twins?'

'No,' the other Whigham said.

They walked over the kitchen floor, each appearing to hold his tumbler in the same way as the other.

At 9.30, in the studious sitting room which the occupants of the house called the Library, Mildred Eaves closed the notebook in which she had been writing.

'Time for beddy-byes,' she said gaily.

'Up the wooden hill,' her husband said, closing his book.

The Whighams rose from their sofa and returned their books to the shelves. 'Good night,' said one. 'Good night,' said the other.

'What time does this household get up in the mornings?' Joan asked, the exodus from the room having made it clear that it went to bed at an unconventionally early hour.

Geoffrey looked at her suspiciously over his reading glasses and then looked at Norman Makower.

'We go to bed within the first hour of darkness,' Makower said. 'And we rise with the first hour of light.' Makower stood up, his finger keeping his place in his book. Mulwhevin was barely visible in the dusklight, but its flat-topped immensity could be felt as a lowering, geographical presence. As a mountain, it was not so much high as simply massive. 'It is the home of a god,' Makower said to Joan, who, had joined him at the window. 'And of a goddess, too,' he added, looking into her face for signs of how she reacted to this information. ' "Women's rights", as you call them, are a social thing, and as such they are very temporal indeed. Important, yes; I grant that they may seem to you to be of very great immediate concern. But ask yourself this: what is eternal? The male principle of the world, and the female principle of the world – *these* are eternal. They are of the spirit as well as of the body. They are the explanations and causes of everything in the world. Devanou and Creva,' he said, turning to smile briefly at Geoff Huntingdon.

'It's been an exhausting day,' Joan said. 'I think I'll hit the sack.'

'They're up there. I assure you,' Makower said. 'Devanou and Creva.'

'Lawrence was an ideological bigot, but he wasn't a vegetarian. I just thought I'd let you know,' Joan said.

Makower laughed, but Geoff Huntingdon seemed alarmed and angry, as if bothered by a recurrence of attitudes and antagonisms that he had met with before.

'Lawrence is no more to us than a major clue,' Geoffrey said. 'Thomas Drinkwater built on Lawrence to some extent, yes; but above all he built on his own staggering synthesis of a lifetime's research.'

'And a remarkable discovery,' Makower said, 'into the secrets of which Miss Bolton has yet to be initiated. Thomas Drinkwater is a new name to Miss Bolton. Nor is she quite in the necessary state of readiness to be illuminated on that subject, Geoff, as I'm sure you'll agree.'

'Only too willingly, Norman, I do assure you,' Geoff Huntingdon said.

On the stairs, Bob said, 'You're so plainly averse, so downright opposed. All that facial cynicism and bad nature. Joan, if only you'd listen, and think!'

'It's all hokum!' she said in a vindictive whisper. 'And who's this Thomas Drinkwater anyway?'

Mildred Eaves was waiting for them, decently house-coated, at her bedroom door. 'I'm afraid you put your belongings in the wrong room, dearie. My fault, I'm sure. I should have been on hand to show you.'

Joan ignored Mildred, but once inside what she had taken to be her room, she found her rucksack gone. Her walking clothes had been removed from the bed over which she had thrown them before dinner, and the clothes she had put in the chest of drawers had vanished. Mildred was whispering to Bob in the hallway.

'Where have you put my things?'

'In your room, girlie. In there.'

Bob went into the bedroom which Joan as his girlfriend of four months' duration had assumed she was sharing with him. Bob closed the door.

'Next door to ours,' Mildred said, pointing to Joan's room.

She was too angry at Bob to bother contesting with Mildred the issue of where she was to sleep or the underhand manner in which her possessions had been moved from one room to another. She sat on the edge of her bed in a state of bemused wrath. Her affection for Bob had turned sour. Joan was old enough to have been betrayed and mistreated several times before, but Bob's sub-intellectual mysteries and condescensions were wounding, and the more hurtful for being almost comically beyond her comprehension. She dragged deeply on a cigarette, flicking her ash into a wastepaper basket.

In the morning, she looked out of her bedroom window and watched the last strips of mist on the swampy flats of the valley. It was six o'clock and she imagined she must be at least an hour late for breakfast. Light was still pale in the valley, but to her right, where there was a broad opening in the hills that faced Mulwhevin, the sky was bright and blue.

The Whighams were bathing together in Tormure Loch, about two hundred yards away. The ragged lake was surrounded by tufts of rough grass and reed beds. Both Whighams appeared to be naked. Joan shivered at the thought of that cold immersion in which the Whighams seemed playfully delighted, if their agile jumping and splashing were anything to go by.

Still in her night clothes, Joan knocked on Bob's door and opened it without waiting for an answer. He sat on the floor, meditating in the lotus position. Taken aback by this novelty, Joan said, 'Honest, Bob, I don't know whether to laugh or cry.' He looked up as she passed him. She took another look at the Whighams from Bob's window. 'You knew last night that my stuff had been moved. Why didn't you tell me?'

Bob came out of his contemplation with a moan, as if re-entering the world. He had trouble drawing his legs from under himself.

'Got bad cramps, dear?'

'I was thinking.'

'I felt humiliated! I felt dirtied! I've a mind of my own and I don't like being told what to do by people like that!'

Bob tried to stand up and ended up hopping on the leg that was less cramped than the other.

'What a state to get into!'

'Please, Joan, try to relax! Try to take it seriously!' Bob said from the bed, on which he lay, trying to bring the life back to his legs, both of which he rubbed.

'I spent half the night lying awake and trying to take *you* seriously,' Joan said vehemently. 'And I failed! Dismally!' She slammed Bob's bedroom door as loudly as she could in the hope of letting those in the house know that she had sacked Bob from her affections.

Joan washed and dressed and before she worked up the courage to face the others she looked to see what the Whighams were doing. To her shivering amazement it looked as if they were rubbing each other with mud from the shallow bed of the loch. Bob ran from the house, a towel in his hand, and his bare feet toeing through the stumps of rough pasturage. His pale nudity sprinted towards the silvery-blue mirror of Tormure Loch. 'If bare-buff swimming in that lake's in the house rules,' she said to herself, 'well, just let them try it.'

In the kitchen, Norman Makower carried on singing while Joan complained about the idiocy of courting double pneumonia, ideological witchcraft and a prevailing atmosphere of intellectual fraudulence and moral terrorism which encouraged a total disregard of a person's beliefs and preferences.

' "*Ol' man river, he keeps on rollin'*," ' Makower boomed in a faked baritone voice, to the tittering glee of Mildred Eaves.

Joan had interrupted a conversation between Professor Eaves and Geoffrey Huntingdon. Both of them listened to her without interest, their expressions suggesting to Joan that they were more appalled by her bad manners in interrupting them than in the individuality that she tried to assert.

'You haven't listened to a word. Have you?' Joan said.

To prove that they hadn't, Geoffrey resumed what he had been saying to the Professor. 'Susannah ran out of the aptitude to accept wisdom. She fell back on anything and everything easy to accept without having to question the essentials. I keep telling her, Perry: one has to defy this spiritless, corrupt, noxious, centreless society.'

'I couldn't agree more,' Professor Eaves said with a glance that asked if Geoffrey wanted more tea.

' "*He don't say nothin', he keeps on rollin'* . . . " '

Both naked Whighams ran through the kitchen. Wet slip-slops quacked on the tiled floor. 'Wonderful!' one said. It took him four attempts to get over the W. 'Awfully invigorating,' the other said.

'And wonderful to the wonderful Whighams!' Makower bellowed with oratorical cheerfulness.

A pinkish, half-dry Bob Scarfe dashed through the kitchen apparently disguised as a towel carrying a man's shape.

'Virile,' Professor Eaves said with a sigh. 'Ah, yes. Virile!'

'Is there any chance of breakfast?' Joan shouted, stamping her foot to make sure her tantrum caught their attention.

While Joan ate and Bob and the Whighams changed upstairs, the others gathered in the Library. 'I can imagine what's passing through your mind,' Makower said to Geoffrey. 'Susannah's rejection of us made us all extremely sad, as you know. But I feel so strongly that Bob must be encouraged. We can't let him down. We're all getting older. I'm as fond of the dear Whigham boys as the rest of you, but I honestly don't foresee them perpetuating Thomas's discoveries . . .' The others agreed with this remark of Makower's. He looked towards the mountain. 'So unlike the contribution made by their beloved parents. Yes, well,' he said after a mournful pause. 'Bob strikes me as a different kettle of fish entirely. Geoffrey, I'm asking you to advise us. Do you, for instance, see any point in hoping that Joan might come round to a more receptive state of mind?'

'Like the rest of us, I think we ought to try, for Bob's sake as much as her own.'

'For *our* sakes,' Mildred said.

'If not Joan, then someone else,' Perry Eaves said. 'I mean, is Bob likely to *want* her, in view of what seem to be her peculiarly damning convictions?'

'She has no convictions,' Mildred said flatly.

'She's intelligent,' Geoffrey said, although neither Mildred nor her husband thought this opinion of Joan worthy of being taken seriously. 'Yes, a prickly, argumentative, contemporary kind of intelligence, I grant you.'

'Vulgarly quick-witted,' Mildred said decisively.

'In that case, intelligent enough for us to consider being a little more candid with her. Were we to lay our evidence before her, we might see a quite remarkable change of heart,' Geoffrey said.

'We all know only too well what Thomas would have said to *that*,' Makower said, asserting his voice above the disapproval of the others. 'There must first be receptivity and good will. *Then* the truth of what we possess can be shown to her. "Our knowledge must fall as a blessing on that steadfastness of spiritual need which has come here to seek it," ' he quoted. His words came from the handwritten book which Thomas Drinkwater composed for their guidance in the weeks before his death. 'We must simply hope that she stays here long enough for the magic of Mulwhevin to convince her. Devanou and Creva have their own powers of persuasion. We must put our trust in them,' Makower said, eliciting their agreement.

Bob came into the kitchen looking for the others. 'They're in the Library,' Joan said. 'No, wait a minute! I'm not finished with you. I came here for a holiday, and now you're all dressed up to go and climb that mountain and leave me here with a twisted ankle.'

'Isn't it better yet?'

'No, it isn't. If anything, it's worse. It hurts.'

'Please, I want you to try, Joan. I want you to try to understand them. More than that I can't tell you, but I'*m* convinced,' Bob said earnestly.

'Some sort of very strange ritual or belief's being hatched here. I want to know what you've got yourself into.'

'I can't tell you,' Bob said, innocent with frustration.

'You're making me feel frightened!'

'There's nothing to be frightened of!' Bob said. 'I just can't tell you yet!'

He took Joan's hand and pulled her towards him, but she pushed him away. 'I feel tricked! I feel duped, and I feel used! Don't touch me,' she said, refusing the hand that Bob offered to her. 'I can't stand this place!'

'Please, give it a few days more. I'm pleading with you, Joan. Mulwhevin's very important to me. Very,' he said.

By eight o'clock Joan was alone in the house. She drank tea and inspected the photographs hanging in the Library. There was a portrait of Thomas Drinkwater and she scrutinized it carefully, hoping to find an understanding of his character from his bland but serious face. About all she could tell from Drinkwater's features was that he had been well brought up and lived much of his life out-of-doors. Had his collar been turned round the other way, he could have been a parson with an active interest in wild-flowers or ornithology.

There were photographs taken on outings of the Cambridge Socialist Picnic Society in its heyday. Khaki-shorted young pipe-smokers stood beside full-skirted young ladies and a few in tailored slacks, some of whom held flowers, others books. Joan grunted with amusement. As far as she was concerned, they were pre-war malcontents, genteel rebels who had passed through their misspent idealisms in much the same way as she had done the galleries of Florence. There was a disturbing charm to these pictures of young men and women who had shared in the modish political passions of the 1930s. It was disturbing because she could imagine the convictions of the past decade, in which she had shared, being looked back on with the same superiority of hindsight as futile, amusing and a bit on the silly side – a tongue-in-cheek nostalgia for the 1960s and 1970s.

Whatever the disappointments, transformations and global upheavals through which the people in the photographs had lived – and, statistically, some of these young men must have died of them – Joan found it inexplicable how a possibly virtuous faith in the brotherhood of man could have been corrupted into occult vegetarianism and some sort of lunatic religiosity associated with a mountain, which is what she had decided the tenets of Makower and his cronies amounted to. That short, unsmiling figure in the middle, she reckoned, must be Thomas Drinkwater in his early twenties, a diminutive king among his well-bred *Wandervögel*.

From books she had seen in the houses of a few of her friends, Joan was already familiar with the kind of reading with which Mulwhevin's shelves were generously stocked. It all testified to a toehold on a corner of the same hungering primitivism, a need that was intuitive or fashionable for violent explanations of Man and Nature. There were books on the religions, cults, witchcrafts and mythologies of all continents. They underlined Joan's suspicion that if Mildred Eaves were not the Bad Fairy in person, then she might be her sister. There were studies and descriptions of what seemed to be every religion except Christianity. Joan was no believer, but she wondered what God had done to warrant exclusion from Mulwhevin's library.

Varnished or painted floors; rugs with a touch of the wigwam about them; big, solid, timbery pieces of furniture, like mock-ups made by giant carpenters – Mulwhevin's interior looked philosophically appropriate. When she had finished ridiculing the furnishings to herself, Joan went outside and wandered around the yard and outhouses. A door in the old stable block was very padlocked and forbidden and its windows were shuttered. She was in a mood to think of a locked door and shuttered windows as sinister. From the outside, the house of Mulwhevin looked what it was – a traditional farmhouse of the southwest of Scotland that had been acquired by owners with money enough to improve and extend it. Strange – a farmyard but not a hen in sight, no dog, no beasts and no signs of agricultural work or dirt.

After a search that proved there wasn't a tin of ham in the kitchen cupboards, Joan tested her ankle. It felt better and she risked the idea of a walk. She packed her cheese sandwiches in a plastic supermarket bag and set off.

She followed the course of a stream that flowed into Tormure Loch. Light and shadow chased each other across the lower, grassy slopes of Mulwhevin. After an hour she reached a diminutive waterfall and sat down to eat her sandwiches beside its hydraulic trickle. It was moments like these that Bob's description of Mulwhevin, repeated from Makower, had led Joan to look forward to her fortnight in Galloway. She sunned herself and listened to bees in the heather. As if unwilling to be caught in the act of anything so natural, she looked to see that no one she knew was about before taking her boots and socks off and paddling her feet in the stream.

Mildred looked very angry as Joan sauntered across the kitchen. 'Make yourself useful,' Mildred snapped with the peppery command of an elderly woman who had bossed the young in a score of communal kitchens. 'If nothing else, you could at least wash the lettuce.'

'I washed up after breakfast, and I washed up last night,' Joan said, rebutting Mildred's assault on her domestic virtues. 'You wash the lettuce.'

'No floors swept, no wood brought in, no bread baked, your crumbs all over the table and the teapot full of dregs!' Mildred listed. 'And you haven't even made your bed. Am I making it quite clear what is expected of you?' Mildred said, wiping her hands on her pinafore.

'I'm on holiday!'

'Well, if you think that a year's waste can be swept away by what you call a "holiday", then all I can say is that it's perfectly typical of your sort of mentality.'

'I came here on holiday!'

'You came, girlie, because Bob asked you to come, and Norman invited Bob,' Mildred said, making it clear that she was too wise to tolerate any other explanation. 'One washes lettuce under a running tap!' Mildred yanked the plug from the sink which Joan had begun to fill with water. 'Nor does one chop lettuce! One tears it!'

Mildred grabbed the lettuce and Joan grabbed it back. 'This one chops it! It's a Crystal Heart!'

'I don't care what it is – one tears it, like this,' and Mildred pulled the lettuce once more from Joan's hands. Her lean, brown, veinous arms tensed with venerable muscularity as she ripped the heart from the lettuce. Joan dreaded to think what Mildred could have done with the Manchester telephone directory.

'I want meat!' Joan thrust her face so close to Mildred's that the old woman dropped the lettuce. 'Sausages! Mutton!' She used her words like projectiles, much as an angry apostate might have yelled blasphemies at a captive believer. 'Steak! Small, tasty mammals!'

Each spitefully enunciated cut or kind of animal flesh drove Mildred farther across the room. 'Pork! Bacon! Chops!'

Mildred's discomposure obliged her to sit down.

'I'm sorry, Mildred, but I didn't mean all that. No, let me do it,' she said, trying to take the wooden spoon with which Mildred had begun half-heartedly to stir her avocado paste.

'No!' Mildred said.

'Honestly, Mildred, I'm not in the least bit hostile to vegetarian food. I don't know what came over me. I suppose I want to go home. It hasn't been much fun for me, you know. It's a long way to come to find out that a boyfriend I was really fond of ... well, to find out he isn't what I thought he was.'

'From the very moment I set eyes on you, limping along the path, I could tell that you would never be sympathetic to us,' Mildred said. 'Freud noticed something that is *very* true.'

'I knew it! I knew it! "There are no accidents." '

'Why, then, if you know that, must you pretend that your "twisted ankle" is some sort of insignificant physical injury?'

'Insignificant? It was *sore*.'

'It is not physical, girlie,' Mildred said with broad, malicious assurance.

'That's it! I'm leaving! I can do without cranks!'

It took Joan only a few minutes of livid haste to stuff her rucksack with her belongings. Then she sat down for an hour expecting that Bob would come upstairs to persuade her to stay. She was determined to leave, but there seemed something irresponsible in throwing away four months of her affections without giving Bob the opportunity to explain what had happened to him. There was a knock on the door. 'It's open!' she shouted. When she saw Professor Eaves, and not Bob, Joan tugged on a strap of her loaded rucksack and fastened it shut.

'We've been having a discussion,' Perry Eaves said with hand-rubbing nervousness.

'You would have.'

'There's no precedent for it. Indeed, it's even against what our teacher, Thomas Drinkwater, laid down as procedure. Some of us are still far from convinced that we're doing the right thing. But we're old now,' he said sadly, 'and you and Bob are young. It's not that we're afraid of dying, Miss Bolton. But we're agreed that it would be awfully selfish were we to allow certain truths in our possession to die with us. Would you please stay a little longer?'

'I don't want to hurt anyone's feelings, but I've been neurotic ever since I got here. Even the furniture's against me,' Joan said.

'Long enough only for an explanation,' Professor Eaves said.

'How long's that?'

'Not very long.'

Curious to know what had seduced Bob's earnest mind, Joan agreed to wait. 'All right. Tell me all about it.'

'No, it must come to you from the mouth of a woman. I'll have to send Mildred to tell you.' From the door, he added, 'I'm grateful that you've given us this chance, Miss Bolton.'

After Professor Eaves had gone, Joan heard distant voices raised in argument. The internal walls of the house were very thick. She knew that for the sound to travel so far they must be practically shouting at each other. She identified the voices by intonation rather than through decipherable sentences. It was fifteen minutes before Mildred arrived.

Mildred looked as if the argument downstairs had shaken her and that she had gathered her wits together through an effort of will in order to perform a task that she found disagreeable.

'Thirty years ago, Thomas Drinkwater discovered a large and

ornately carved slab of stone on the very top of Mulwhevin,' Mildred said.

'And in long flowing robes he brought this tablet down from the mountain . . . '

'Sit down! Bob is deeply ashamed of you. He is extremely upset.'

'I don't have to listen to this,' Joan said, reaching for her rucksack.

'Nor do I particularly want to tell you,' Mildred said. 'In fact, I am very much against telling you.'

Joan sat down again, while Mildred moved a vase and its dried grasses along the cast-iron mantelpiece, finding a spot on which to lean her elbow.

'It took several years to unravel the meaning of the Mulwhevin Stone. Thomas was very expert in these things. With the assistance of my husband, with the late Percy Whigham, and with the aid of Norman's knowledge of pagan iconography, the significance of the Mulwhevin Stone finally became clear. On it are depicted Devanou, a deity of a Pictish tribe which lived in these parts, and Creva, his consort – Man and Woman; Male and Female. The carvings are what might be called erotic in nature. At first, we considered it as no more than an archaeological discovery and of little or no significance to our own immediate lives. In that we were wrong. During the act of love, on top of the mountain, Thomas and his wife, Marcia, *saw* Devanou, and they *saw* Creva.'

Joan looked doubtful. 'And you believed them?'

'One took what they said seriously, without actually "believing" it,' Mildred said. 'Thomas persuaded us to look for ourselves. *I* saw Devanou and Creva. And then the true meaning of the Mulwhevin Stone became quite unavoidable. Mulwhevin is the house of Devanou and Creva. Since that night we have been quite different people,' Mildred said, trying to sound matter-of-fact, but the awesomeness of what she believed to have been her experience trembled in her voice. 'A most utterly new and transforming energy came into us.'

Joan felt like laughing at the serene conviction in what Mildred was saying. 'Yes, well, whatever turns you on, Mildred . . . '

'I was not speaking of some cheap, sexual thrill! There are other places in the world like Mulwhevin, places where spiritual, erotic and intellectual energy become tangible, and from which mortals may draw strength. These places are more than doors into the pagan past. They are ways into our true selves. And that is what Bob offers you – to put you in touch with a reality that is beyond what you refer to with chilling triteness as "life". You would be deities,' Mildred said almost casually, implying that she knew what she was saying from firsthand experience and that her knowledge could only be contradicted by a fool.

'No, thank you,' Joan said. 'Do you think someone could drive me as far as the main road?'

Mildred did not look disappointed. Joan picked up her rucksack and went downstairs.

The table was set for eight. At one end a chair had been raised on a box so that it dominated the other places, while at the opposite end a chair had been similarly elevated, although it was a foot lower than the chair at the top. Stoneware plates and stoneware goblets were set at each place. Even the handles of the cutlery were stoneware. The tablecloth was a bridal white. Presumably, Joan thought, this has been laid out for the thwarted nuptial feast, and Devanou sits at the top, and Creva at the other end.

The door from the kitchen to the yard was locked. She went to the front door that opened to a view of Mulwhevin. It was locked too. 'They're in the Library,' Mildred said. She had been watching Joan from the stairs.

All six men stood before the large stone fireplace. Each man wore a large and exaggerated animal mask. They were recognizable by their shapes and clothes. They looked bigger in their masks; they looked proud and dominating. Startled at first, Joan soon recovered from her initial fright until she felt capable of the insolence which the spectacle deserved. She named them in turn: 'Bob, Norman, Geoffrey, Whigham One, Whigham Two – or is that Whigham One? – Professor Eaves . . . '

Bob approached her with outstretched arms. He wore the head of a goat. 'Don't come near me!' Joan said, backing off from Bob's advance. 'I don't blame your wife one bit,' she said to the Fox. 'No wonder she got fed up with this lot.' Geoffrey bowed his fox head as if his lips trembled beneath the painted mouth of his mask. 'She realized it was pagan junk, that's why!'

Twin stags stared at her, their brown eyes beneath sculpted lids. Norman Makower, his equine head caught in a permanent suggestion of a whinny, said, 'You are denying yourself a very great deal.

The difference between you and Geoffrey's wife is that Susannah knows what she has turned her back on, and you do not.' The Fox nodded in agreement.

Of them all, Perry Eaves's long-eared Hare looked the most ridiculous. 'Don't think you frighten me. I couldn't be afraid of anything so pathetic,' Joan said dismissively.

'Would it help if Bob were to speak to you in private?' Norman Makower's horse mask added an extra sonority to his already resonant voice.

'I don't want to speak to her. I reject her,' the Goat said emotionally.

Mildred walked across the room, wearing no mask. Were it not for her pleated shin-length tweed skirt, slippers and thick walking socks, she would have looked like a housekeeper whom no eccentricity distressed. She asked her husband to get out of the way while she lit the fire.

'I won't let you down again,' Bob said to them. 'I promise that you won't be subjected to this kind of indignity ever again.'

One of the Whighams sat down, exhausted by the events of the past couple of hours. Perry Eaves took his mask off. Disgusted with their failure to convince Joan, he threw his mask on the floor, and then sat down.

'The Cambridge Socialist Picnic Society,' Joan said. It sounded almost like a question probing through the forty years that had passed since the photographs on the walls of the Library were taken in those defunct summers of turbulent promise. 'What happened to you?' Norman Makower sat down beside the Professor. 'Too well off, pampered all your lives, and with nothing to believe in or look for except a justification for your sexuality . . . ' she said to him.

'Get out!' Makower shouted at Joan with a ferocity that tensed even Mildred Eaves into an expectation of something worse than verbal violence.

'Then somebody please open the door,' Joan said calmly.

Joan had been walking for ten minutes along the track from the house before she stopped to look at Mulwhevin. It was seven o'clock and the summit of the mountain was still clearly outlined against the blue evening sky. She could not make her mind up if the older of these well-educated devotees of strange, antique deities were preposterous in the manner of English eccentrics or if they had been crazed by the magnitude of the secret they believed themselves to have discovered. Millions, she knew, hungered for the satisfactions of the supernatural, the magical and the arcane, and were entertained by the inexplicable and the demonic. Perhaps their lives had attained such a reasonable security within a framework of a not-inconceivable apocalypse that they enjoyed being aroused or frightened by the dark and the imagined intervention of the ghosts of extinct peoples which it was only too easy to suppose were hidden by starless nights on high, lonely outcrops of wilderness.

The farther she walked away from it, the more the house of Mulwhevin looked situated in a normal remoteness. It looked pretty and rural with its suggestions of a hard agricultural livelihood. The sun in the west was still high enough at that time of year for its last blush of cool radiance to enliven the pigment of the house's white-washed walls. She looked again at the mountain. Even as the sun spilled over its long ridge she could find no special mischief or benevolence in how it looked. It exerted its evening mood of squat, immovable splendour. As a seat of deities in which it was possible for men and women once to have placed their faith, it was imaginable; but it was not believable.

Several trucks and cars passed her on the main road without stopping. It was getting late. Joan had only a hazy idea of the geography of where she was. She had never looked at a map of the region and she had never been there before. She felt strangely and sadly free. She thumbed an approaching car. Its driver drew up twenty yards ahead of her. She ran towards it, her ankle free of ache and stiffness, her rucksack bobbing on her back. 'What,' she asked herself, 'does he, or she, believe?'

'I'm going to Dumfries,' the woman who drove the car said. 'Is that any use to you?'

'It sounds lovely,' Joan said.

More Than Half the Way

Rent was low, life was quiet in the country. It suited Harriet Mortimer to live there. Her small, inexpensive cottage was comfortable and no more. She had perfected her thirty-three years of widowhood in its few rooms. When her son Christopher left home it was like the addition of one last touch to her fastidious grief.

First he had gone to university and then to London. By now he was nearer, in a town fifty miles north. He was as tall as his father had been and he had the same appearance of an athlete who had given up his regimen and on whom late nights, tobacco and alcohol were beginning to catch up. Neither of them had been particularly athletic, and, now, Christopher was a decade older than the age his father was when he had been killed in the last weeks of war by frightened German boys, almost, Harriet had been told, by mistake. She had looked at her son on his sixteenth birthday and thought of these German teenagers and relished the dispiriting, European irony. Her husband, Gareth Mortimer, a war poet, would have approved of how Harriet noticed these coincidences that cumulate into a grotesquely amusing sadness, a grin before terror. It was a mystifying circumstance for Harriet and her son that he was now ten years older than his father had ever been. She could see Gareth in Christopher, her husband shadowed in her son who was now thickening at the waist. Her tall Sunday visitor wore his face set in a projection of gentle bemusement. He looked as if he acknowledged the world through the weariness of an amiably melancholic man older than his years. Those who knew he was the son of Gareth Mortimer were quick to read a wonderingly profound sensitivity into his range of expressions. He never swore; he did not raise his voice or lose his temper. His saddening eyes were easily distracted by the sight of something vague in the distance.

Reports of those cut down in chance explosions –
For ever more now, they are nocturnal roses
In abstract gardens whitening with loss.

These lines from one of Gareth's poems often came into Harriet's head. It was an unpublished poem and she kept it along with many others in a locked drawer of his old desk – it was not to be defaced by trite suggestions of 'prophetic'. She saw these roses – white, red – like kind but agonizing clenched fists raging with demented compassion. Gareth was a night-rose, as she, and many others were too. Sometimes she felt almost as if she had counted them all, one by one, counting casualties as insomniacs count sheep.

She coughed on a cigarette as she craned out of her living room window at the spot where the lane bent round towards the turn-off from the main road. Christopher was a few minutes late. She pushed herself between a sideboard and the bay of the window and waited for the sight of his car's snout as it turned the corner under the dark interwoven spread of the branches of wintry trees. Even from that distance she could tell the branches were still dripping after the early rain. She knew her house, and the trees immediately around it, the way an expert knows his chosen subject. There were no people in that knowledge other than Christopher. Her clothes were carelessly chosen. She did not wear them to look attractive. They were loose clothes, indeterminate middle- and late-twentieth-century clothes. These clothes she had worn for years, the cigarette she always had in her hand or dangling from her lips, made her look incompetent, perpetually shaken and as if dowdiness had been chosen as her only suitable appearance.

No one used the lane except on week days. There was the butcher's van, the grocer's van, the baker's van, the fishmonger's van once a fortnight, and the coal-merchant's lorry once a month. Each brought and delivered her small, thrifty orders. Christopher's car squeezed over these previous runnels in the February mud. He waved before he got out, as he always did, and she went from the window to the front door. It always happened that the sound of the door opening coincided with the slam of the car door closing. A careful man, Christopher watched his shoes on the muddy path from which the gravel had long been washed away. Harriet came down one welcoming pace on the doorstep, because – it is a paraphrase of a love poem – you go forwards to those you love although as you wait for them it seems they have a greater distance to cover before they reach you. She took pleasure in affirming the meanings of her husband's poems.

As soon as they were inside, Harriet went to the kitchen to super-vise their Sunday lunch. Christopher hung his coat in the hall and after saying things about traffic and weather went into the living room. Every time he went in there the room and its furniture met him with the force of a small shock. The room never changed. It was the same mixture of everything in its place and slow dilapidation. Wear and tear were more conspicuous than familiarity. Breathing its air was a different sensation from anything he had known in any other room he had been in. The room was specific; it was as particu-lar as the right answer in a lengthy calculation. He said, through the open door, 'Do you still have my old rocking-horse?'

He waited for an answer, hearing a pot lid rattled on the work-surface by the sink. He went over to the window and looked out at the small, untended lawn now smeared with winter, where he had spent years playing under his mother's eye. Harriet appeared at the living room door in an apron and with an oven-glove on one hand. 'Of course, I still have it. Why do you ask?'

'They've become trendy,' he explained. 'A man I met during the week was saying they fetch a small fortune in the antique trade.'

'Trendy?' she asked.

'Going with the trend. Up to the latest fashion.'

'Oh, I see. But you don't want to sell ours?'

'I thought it might interest you,' he humoured.

She shrugged. 'I suppose it does.' She went back to the kitchen and Christopher followed. 'What's wrong with new ones? Don't they make them any longer?'

'I've no idea.'

'Then don't suggest I should sell ours. You know why.'

'I wasn't,' he said. 'Absolutely not.'

Warmed by the old Aga, they sat eating Sunday lunch in the kitchen. Since his mid-twenties, with his growing salary, Christopher had been bringing a bottle of wine on his Sunday visits. It added the encouragement Harriet needed to make Sunday into more of an occasion. It didn't show in her dress though it reflected in how lunch itself was served, on wedding-present china on a white tablecloth instead of the waxed gingham patterned kitchen table-covering rubbed away to the canvas on each corner and in crosses where it had been folded too often.

'Another new suit?' she asked.

'Why not?' he said, defending himself with a widening smile.

'You're becoming quite the dandy . . . '

'A large wardrobe impresses the clients. Theirs, of course, are supposed to impress *me*.'

Harriet enjoyed the moving pictures in her mind in which men like film stars of the late 1930s and early 1940s vied with each other in a competition of sartorial elegance. It was a world she had virtually forgotten and it amused her to think that Christopher starred in its latest version of fashion.

'How about Hayward's widow? Any developments there?'

'None,' said Harriet, seriously. 'I'm *adamant*. And they won't find me giving in. You won't see *me* going on television.' It was what Christopher expected to hear. Always, though, in spite of being prepared for it, that tone of bitterness, edged fuzzily in her voice, disturbed him enough to make him back down from a subject he did not want to leave alone. 'I won't be that kind of a representative of the dead.'

'You're probably right,' Christopher said slowly. 'You should do what you think best.' He had always found it difficult to talk to his mother on any subject connected with his father or his father's poetry. Harriet either clamped up in morose hostility or told him severely to talk about something else. 'You ought to be pleased with the interest they're showing . . . ' He hesitated on this unfamiliar ground. 'You should be, you know.'

'I'm neither pleased or displeased,' his mother said. From the way Harriet looked at him, Christopher could sense she was asking herself what his motive was for raising questions which he, more than anyone else, knew she did not like to hear. When he turned round to face her, after putting their plates in the sink, she said, 'Do you know what I wish they'd stop doing? I wish they'd not keep on saying, "What kind of poet would he have become *if* . . .?" ' It was more of her own thoughts on Gareth Mortimer than she was in the habit of saying, even to her son.

'Perhaps you ought not to read what these people write about him.'

'Florence Hayward keeps *sending* me these things,' and Harriet was almost irate in the way she suggested she didn't want the cuttings and reviews and publications that arrived in the post from Roger Hayward's widow. 'She probably *knows* I don't like Roger

Hayward's work. I think his poems are brutal. He wrote like someone who was actually *glad* to be in a war.'

'They say authors often don't read the reviews of their books.
Perhaps their widows ought to do the same.'

Harriet began to show signs of her customary reluctance to speak
of herself and the parsimonious way she had administered Gareth
Mortimer's literary estate. She was surprised, and worried, that
Christopher should suddenly start to take more of an interest in it.
His casual tone of voice took her by surprise, too. It was a long way
from his respectful silences of the past.

'The most I'll admit to,' said Harriet, announcing that this was the
end of what she would say on the subject, 'is disappointment –
disappointment in people preferring Roger Hayward's poems to
your father's.'

'You haven't helped by refusing to co-operate, though, have you?'

'I've given them permission to use his poems.'

'What about the unpublished ones you won't let *anyone* see? Or his
letters? His manuscripts?'

'Why should I? They're mine. They're even *about* me.'

'Shall I do the dishes?' he asked.

'Why, all of a sudden, are you so interested in your father's
poetry?'

'I don't know.' They looked at each other in silence. 'It's you,' he
said.

'Me?'

'It seems mean.'

'Only because you don't understand.'

'I was re-reading them the other night. Engineers do read sometimes, you know. And you're right. My father's poems are totally
different from Hayward's.'

'Everyone *says* they're different. The "trend", however,' she
sneered, 'is for cruelty. Hayward was a poetic gangster.'

'And it's because they're different you've refused to co-operate in
their programme ...'

'Christopher, it's *my business*,' she protested. 'I've devoted my life
to what's best for your father's work.'

'And what's best for any writer's work, surely, is publication ...'

'They have *enough*.'

'... of *all* of it.'

'I'm only possessive of what's *mine*.'

'And I'm his son,' he said quietly, finding it hard to believe he had drawn his mother as far as he had without the subtle probing he had felt would have been necessary.

'You're my son, too.' Christopher nodded, taking back most of what he'd said before. 'And you'll admit it yourself, you're hardly an expert in poetry let alone his. You must leave me to look after what I know most about.'

Christopher knew how difficult it was for him to think of himself as Gareth Mortimer's son. He had never seen his father and his father had never seen him. He was like a biological memory. Or a story his mother told him when he was a child and which he could never quite forget. His father seemed fictitious. He was a resented absentee, who'd left printed relics. He'd left behind more than love, but things – not objects exactly, but words, things made of words – in which he was preserved, his voiceprint pickled in print.

'They've asked *you*,' his mother said to his back, as he stood before the sink, his hands in water, 'to go on that programme.'

'How did you know?'

'*I guessed*.'

'You know I won't if you don't want me to.'

'You promise you won't do it?'

'Yes. I promise.'

'Good.'

'What good would I be anyway? It's not as if I know very much about him.'

'And they don't either.'

'When I was at school, I tried to boast about him. They hadn't even heard of him. What really cut a dash was that my father had been killed in the war. The fact that he had, so to speak, written about his own death before it happened, was of no distinction whatsoever.'

Harriet sent him way from the sink. He went into the living room and sat down as the clouds cleared patchily from the sky and the wind blew harder through the trees that surrounded Harriet's house. He was glad his mother had refused to have anything to do with the programme Hayward's widow had pestered a producer into undertaking. Apart from whatever dignity there is in refusing to publicize yourself, Harriet's grief, her glamourless devotion, were ill-suited to any kind of exposure. He could hardly understand it himself. He remembered all the times he had seen her working at his father's desk. Papers had been left in it and others had been returned by the Army. She had scrutinized each sheet a thousand times. It was a composite memory in which he was various young ages while each picture that flicked through it came with a glint of weather and various shades of daylight and dusk. 'Mummy's busy,' she'd say if he interrupted her. 'What are you writing?' he'd ask. 'A book,' Harriet would say. 'I'm writing a book about your father.' For all he knew now, she was still writing it. She would always be writing it. How could a man who had been dead for so long continue to cause such trouble?

> *Imaginary o'clock, time for the dead*
> *To laugh their heads off in infinity*
> *Where, hiding out, they're really in your head . . .*

Even Christopher had his father's lines stuck in his brain like neural pests. As a child he had known well enough that his father was a poet. Harriet had proudly shown him his books. People had thought him famous enough to visit Harriet and ask questions. They were coolly received, given tea, told nothing, and sent away. She was more self-confident then in her customary loose suits and carelessly groomed hair. When he first read Gareth Mortimer's two thin books he hadn't understood a word. They were so thin, hardly like real books at all. Harriet gave him copies of his own on his sixteenth birthday and when he was at university someone had published the *Collected Poems*. Gareth Mortimer's publisher lost patience with Harriet's delays, which had become increasingly short-tempered. He commissioned a young critic and poet to do the best he could, and, though Harriet had seen him a few times, their meetings had been far from placid. It was a mis-named volume which its editor introduced by lamenting the 'improbable possessiveness' of a woman he named as 'Gareth's widow'. Harriet was infuriated by a usage of her husband's first name which she couldn't be persuaded to accept as a literary convention. 'He didn't *know* him,' she shouted. 'He was only nine when your father died,' she said to her son.

Christopher stood up and sighed as these memories ended. He went into his mother's room. Something of his father was in him; but he had no means of identifying it. On his father's desk were diaries, notebooks, papers, letters and poems – materials of Harriet's book, the book she might never finish. Other papers were neatly filed in thin folders on the shelves of the two bookcases with locked glass doors which also preserved his father's library. This time he stood back from the desk and looked at it without disturbing any of the relics that lay on its surface or were hidden in its drawers. He knew what was there – pens, ink bottles, unused sheets of paper; a pair of gloves, and a cigarette-box with a broken clasp and a box of matches more than three decades old, one of which he'd struck when he was about fourteen and then held until the experimental fire burned his finger; gum, a toothbrush for cleaning his typewriter, pencils, envelopes, postage stamps, that, like the old coins there – big, brown pennies, solid threepenny-bits – were of another age; and a photograph of Harriet, twenty-one years old. She slept in sight of these things in the desk. Gareth Mortimer had never seen that room. He'd never been in it. He'd never seen the house or known it existed, though Christopher had thought that if his father had seen it, then he would have known what it was his poems prophesied. Harriet curated the room like an exhibit in the house where the poet had worked, looking out, season by season, into the bedraggled ranks of birch trees. Her room did not seem to be in 1978 but farther back in the era she lived in. It was a summery wartime when spirits were high. Christopher could not *see* 1940, or 1941, or 1942, or any of these years. Yet he felt them present in Harriet's house and they were like shy pets that take to corners when strangers come in.

They sat in the living room. Coffee dregs were cold in their cups. A clock in its wooden case tocked as if determined to unwind itself as quickly as it could into a dead stop of sudden quiet that would reveal everything they were unable to say to each other. Ash collapsed in the grate; hot powders shifted in glows and the fire drew back into its embers and vanished in grey as if the light had been exhausted in them. It was like all their winter Sundays, that moment. It grew darker outside, bit by bit, in sudden stages instead of smoothly. Harriet threw her smoked stubs into the fire, one by one.

'With what you two have in common,' Christopher said, 'it strikes me as inevitable that you'll meet' – and he paused before the name – 'Florence Hayward. Without her, you'd be unique.'

'If she so much as knocked on my door,' Harriet said with a scowl on her lips, 'I wouldn't let her in.'

Firelight – what was left of it – blotched Harriet's face as she sat back in her chair. She slid into the growing darkness of the room. It was a reply of sorts, and it silenced Christopher, who, after a few moments, said, 'Is there anything you need?'

'No.'

'I'll have someone rewire the place in the spring. It's high time. You know, I worry about you out here miles from nowhere and the fire brigade and with this old-fashioned wiring.' He couldn't see his mother's face. 'You were lucky to miss a burst pipe this winter.'

'So practical, Christopher,' she said, almost laughing. 'I don't understand how you could have turned out to be so practical.'

'Yes. I know. Unlike my father. Unpoetical,' he said with a tone of resignation.

'The publisher says I *should*,' she said. 'He says I've a responsibility to *him*. If I prepare a bigger edition then it will sell more and help Gareth. And he says I haven't been helpful so far, have I? It's only fair to come clean *now*, he says. What does he mean by "now"? That I should have forgotten him anyway? I don't know what to do.' Everyone involved in her dilemma seemed to have been dismissed – Christopher, Florence Hayward, editors, publishers, producers – everyone except Gareth. 'You know,' she confided, leaning into what light was left in the fire, 'I've been so faithful. I've never known a man since, and I never knew one before. But they don't understand.'

Despite his embarrassment, Christopher was eager to hear more of his mother's desperate fidelity. He had always known it, but attached no significance to it. But she withdrew into the dark again as if she had already said too much. 'There are poems they've never seen,' she said, from the darkness on the other side of the firelight. 'Poems he wrote and never printed. He showed me everything he wrote. Or he sent them to me when he was away. I can hardly believe he wrote so much in such a short time. There are more poems in my room than there are in the *Collected Poems*. Better poems, too. There were half a dozen that arrived after he was dead. He never saw you, but he wrote about you, too. You, me, and your father ... Why do other people want them? They have nothing to do with them. They're mine. Private things.'

'Well, as you know, I don't really have a taste in poetry ... '

'Don't you think they'd leave me in peace? *They* think of me as a quaint, eccentric little widow who can't bear to let her love letters out of her sight.'

He had never realized before how forcefully she detested anyone other than herself who had an interest in Gareth Mortimer's poems. She hated anyone who had ever read them. In the silence that followed, four lines Christopher knew by heart went through his mind.

> *A choir of widows hired a hall*
> *To sing to their new sisters.*
> *Their lovely songs could not console*
> *Eavesdropping widowers.*

They made him feel like a widower.

'Harriet, dear Harriet,' said Harriet, mimicking a letter from Hayward's widow, 'do, please, send me a chapter of your book. I'm so looking forward to reading about your life with Gareth, and written by *you*, who, like me, was so lucky to have met and married one of the finest poets of our time.' She paused, breathless with the venom of how she had delivered her impersonation of a woman she had never heard speak. 'But she's *different*.'

'I haven't read her book,' said Christopher.

'Oh, do, *please*. It will show you *exactly* what I mean. There's no love in it.'

'Mother, she remarried . . . She's, well . . . temperamentally, she *is* different. She isn't even called Hayward any more.'

'It's how she signs her letters to *me*.'

'Is it?'

'And it's how she signed her introduction to Roger Hayward's *Collected Poems* with the frontispiece and footnotes. And *her* book.'

'She hadn't remarried by then.'

'All and sundry who ever wanted to rummage through Roger Hayward's papers have been given *carte blanche*. She even,' Harriet cried with disbelief, 'sold them to a *library* for a very fat sum. Anyone who wants to read Hayward's papers has to go to Texas, for God's sake. Texas!'

'I know what's in father's desk . . . '

'You were *meant* to look.'

'That stuff's better not kept, surely . . . It's – well, it *is* morbid.'

'They'll get nothing from me,' Harriet said. He knew that even if Harriet wanted to appear personally on that programme, or introduce a new, full edition of Gareth Mortimer's poems, she couldn't.

Something like a promise she had made years ago stood in her way. To go against it now would turn her life into a mistake, or a lie.

Christopher leaned over to the fire and poked it. He placed small kindling over what promising coals survived in it. When that lit and began to burn he put a larger piece of wood on top. 'It's hardly normal,' he said. 'You're denying those who have a legitimate and probably quite enthusiastic interest in his work.'

'They can have what they like when I'm dead.'

'That's hardly a very helpful way of looking at it. By then I'll be the one who decides, and I'll always want to do what you'd have done.'

'Your father's is the only important poetic output over which someone who loved him has complete control. If it had been up to him, *he* would have published it, of course. But it isn't. It's up to *me*.'

'I don't know anything about poetry,' Christopher said, as, with an old-fashioned pair of tongs, he placed small pieces of coal on the brightening fire. For several minutes more he raked in the bucket by the hearth for suitably sized larger pieces and then worked them into the burning design he was artificing out of black coal and flame. He sat back again, rubbing his hands. 'You know I don't like driving in the dark,' he said.

'Do you want some tea before you go?'

'I'd better make a start.'

'I'd like you to hear something first.'

Christopher hesitated. 'You may have said too much already.'

'Gareth met Hayward. Only once. They didn't like each other. Hayward mentions it in his journal. She printed it in her book. Well, she's a liar. She's worse than that. She's a fraud. Gareth wrote to me. He said Hayward told him he'd been unfaithful to her, and she to him. She was living with someone else. And Hayward knew it. He didn't even mind. You see, they weren't like us. They were nothing like Gareth and me. But she wrote very little of *that* sort.'

Harriet got up and went through to her room. A few seconds of being alone in the living room forced Christopher to get on his feet and do something. He switched on a lamp, one that stood near the window. Harriet, he knew, hated bright lights. He was drawing the curtains when she came back.

She sat down and opened a folder. It lay on her lap showing sheets of paper, some handwritten, others typewritten. 'He wrote this on the day he heard Hayward had been killed.' He heard his mother laugh under her breath. It was a laugh no one was meant to hear, one that people keep for the recognition of ironies which, for some reason, are usually detected in private. 'If I edited an edition with notes, with chunks quoted out of letters, this would do Florence Hayward no good at all. Hayward didn't mind, you know. He was just as unfaithful. He was quite famous in the war years. He said in his journal that he found Gareth "tedious".'

'Can I see it?'

Harriet shook her head.

'Then why produce whatever it is ...? I'm not really interested in their marriage.'

Harriet read the poem aloud.

> *Her infidelities have been confirmed,*
> *Though he, who's been unfaithful, won't complain*
> *Of tittle-tattle in the mess, where, warmed*
> *On Scotch-and-soda, staring at the rain*
> *He sees our regimental roses die*
> *In the storm-winds of autumn. 'Talk to me,'*
> *He says, then says, 'The rule of verse is – lie;*
> *Then try to get away with it. History –*
> *Now that's a harder game.' I like verse sweet*
> *And in its sweetness doomed to speak the truth*
> *Of how we feel when our two bodies meet*
> *Mysteriously confused by love and youth.*
>
> *But that was years ago, another life.*
> *Then we had words like love, son, and wife.*
> *Now there is nothing. Could she understand*
> *That ringless finger on his severed hand?*

'Perhaps,' said Christopher, 'it would be an idea if you were to read me his poems more often.'

'One day,' she said, 'I'd like to hear *you* read them.'

He felt himself tall, unmarried in an expensive coat and a man who was about to return to his apartment along a smooth motorway. He felt himself to be a successful, unheroic representative of the late 1970s, as much as his father had been characteristic of the casualties of a war, and whose voice, in his poems, whispered its spokesman-ship on behalf of the dead – that poet of absences, of civilian memories confronting him in military depots, during training routines, on landing-ships, on battlefields.

'You never knew me,' she said, 'when I was happy.' It sounded as if Harriet spoke from far away in a place where'd she lived before he was born.

'Why did you do it?'

'And I'll keep on doing it,' Harriet said, in the same voice. 'I can't bear the thought of not being in love with him.' She laughed her under-her-breath laugh, a series of arrested breaths. 'For all I know that might be how Florence Hayward feels too, except that she doesn't possess the habit of honesty. Are you sure you can't stay?' she asked, like a girlfriend.

'I'll stay next week. It's the best I can do,' he added, to her upturned face. 'I don't like to think of you living here on your own . . . Letting the fire go out, practically in the dark with all those books and papers on your lap. You let the house get too cold sometimes.' He looked at his watch. It was new. She hadn't seen it before. She looked up at him approvingly. 'I'd better go then.'

'Fifty miles,' she said.

'Yes.' He smiled. 'I can do it in an hour, quite easily.'

Harriet walked with her son to his car. The raggedy front lawn was yellowed by electric light from the open door. Harriet waved him off, thinking – it was a paraphrase of a love poem – that when someone left, it seemed you walked more than half the way with him, except that in the poem it was 'her'.

The Earl of Hell's Waistcoat

Augusta Boswell didn't think of herself as a lucky woman. So when she opened a book in the secondhand dealer's in Edinburgh and saw clearly that it had come from the library of the only man with whom she had ever been in love, her feelings were those of good fortune modified by heart-rending surprise.

It was twenty years since she had last seen Erskine Gibb Geddes's elaborate bookplate. At one time it had been familiar from scores of books borrowed or consulted in his rooms in the Cambridge college where he'd been a Fellow. From early in the eighteenth century his family had enjoyed increasing mercantile success in Dundee. Around 1910 these interests had been sold off. Erskine Gibb Geddes's branch of the family settled into a gentrified life in Perthshire. Others emigrated to ranches in Montana and Texas or to pastoral properties in New South Wales. Trade was celebrated on the engraved bookplate by a two-masted vessel, perhaps too fancifully galleon-like to be taken seriously, with a pile of books on the right-hand side, and the façade of the Geddes's family house on the other. It had been engraved to Erskine's brief by Joan Hassall as far back as 1947 when he was ten – 'The best birthday present I ever had,' was how he'd referred to it.

The book was Eve Blantyre Simpson's *Folklore in Lowland Scotland*. As well as Erskine's bookplate there were marginalia, endpaper annotations in his small, neat, scholarly and still perfectly legible pencilled handwriting. The bookplate jolted her. Notes in his own hand, however, intensified the recognition and she felt momentarily feeble and drained. She held the book against her and supported herself against the shelves with her other hand. She was the only customer in that part of the shop, and out of sight of the proprietor. She wiped an eye with a handkerchief and let the effects of sorrowful serendipity – its griefs and pleasures – wear off.

'Do you, by any chance, have others? With this bookplate?' she asked the proprietor's back. 'Mr Hogarth, have you more where this came from, please?'

'Oh, Dr Boswell. Nice day again,' he said, waving his arms in an apology of absentmindedness. 'You caught me in a deep dwam.' It was hard to tell if his impression of being busily preoccupied elsewhere was a genuine reflection of bookish concentration or a ploy calculated to disguise his financial interest in his stock. He looked at the bookplate. 'Delightful. Worth having for the plate alone,' he said.

'But did you acquire any more from the same source?' She was impatient. Although considered an academic oddity at five feet tall in any of her large selection of brogue shoes, tweed two-pieces and symbolic Celtic jewellery, Dr Boswell was known equally for her forthright manner. 'Do you have *others?*'

'I have.'

'I'll take them.'

'There's rather a lot,' Hogarth said on a rippling laugh that was supposed to make Dr Boswell say, 'How many?' with a shudder at the possible cost.

'Work out a price. Ring me at my department. If I'm not there leave a note of the sum with my secretary.'

'It'll take a wee while, that will,' an assistant said with thin-voiced disbelief.

'Are you sure you're not being . . . a bit impulsive, Dr Boswell?'

'Quite sure.'

'We're talking three, four hundred vols here. Some very tasty items. Not a few rarities. I gave a decent price, to, I believe, the sister of the deceased. Are you quite sure?' Hogarth asked in his slow, sly tones.

'And if I'm buying the rest, then I don't suppose you'll mind if I take this with me?'

'Oh, well, if you're sure, then I suppose so,' Hogarth said grudgingly.

'A very carnaptious wee woman,' Hogarth said to the young man, who was also his son, although it's doubtful if even regular customers knew of the relationship.

'A really cracking sale. One fell swoop!'

'Dr *Augusta* Boswell!'

'I look forward to seeing her signature on a cheque!'

'That toxic wee spinster's *loaded*. And one day, there's every chance her executors will bear the firm of Hogarth in mind after she's kicked off her clogs, son. Then they'll come back,' he said lyrically. 'Well, let's get weaving! Sooner packed, soonest paid for.'

'What about the price, Dad?'

'Ach, you think of a figure. Go on, say a sum, son.'

'One thousand five hundred!' the son shouted triumphantly.

'Och, away! Nearer four! Let's say 3,685.'

'What did you pay for them?'

'Money and fair words!'

When Augusta Boswell first met Erskine Gibb Geddes in 1961 she'd just come down from St Andrews to Cambridge to do her doctorate. Erskine, who'd completed his only two years before, was assigned as her supervisor. He was twenty-eight; she was twenty-one. She was diminutive, brilliant, dotty and charming; he was lanky, thin, already with a slight stoop, ascetic, an elegant, scholarly recluse, pale, fair-haired, inward and melancholy. What they had in common was means – New Town old wealth behind Augusta Boswell, lapsed Dundonian commerce turned into estates and serious finance (about which he need never concern himself) bolstering Erskine Gibb Geddes's bibliographical demands on life. They were two of a kind. They shared a devotion to the early history of Britain, Arthurian legends, early literatures and languages, druidism, the fairy faith of the Celtic lands, folklore and archaeology. From each animated, industrious, successful and sometimes ruthless family had emerged a gentle scholar for whom getting and spending meant nothing at all. On Augusta's side of the matter it was love at first sight.

But for a woman as lively as Augusta was in her younger years Erskine's apparent frailty and obsessive study made it hard going.

'You're not *just* my supervisor. We're friends, too, aren't we?'

'I wish you'd put this to one side, instead of pressing me with it.' He spoke slowly and carefully.

'Why are you so opposed to coming with me on my field trip?'

'Irregularities of that sort are usually found out. One way or another the culprits are discovered.'

' "Culprits?" I'm not suggesting anything criminal.'

'I have my book to finish.'

'Is it possible that you're scared to cross the walls of the college for fear of the outside world?'

'Nonsense!'

'You hardly *ever* go *anywhere*, Erskine!'

'Then, yes, if one has an ivory tower, one tends to prefer it.'

'I don't just "admire your mind".'

'Well, I admire yours. Your work is outstanding.'

'I think you're as fond of me as I am of you, but you can't say or do anything about it. Erskine, we're two extremely fortunate people. Youth, money, talent . . . Why do you have to define yourself as monastic and saintly?'

He turned to look at her for the first time in that conversation. 'I think I'm frightened of being found out.'

'I don't understand,' she said, scared on her own account in case of what he might say next.

'I think it's to do with money. I've no idea what I'm worth, but also, I've never experienced want. I was considered too delicate for school and educated privately. I don't know much about "out there". I'm not just shy and timid. I've never known desire.'

'And for me? What do you feel for me?'

'Affection. Interest. Concern. Admiration.' He said these words with difficulty, pausing between them, then turning his head away once more, as if distracted by the shrub that wavered in the wind outside his window.

'Are you homosexual?'

'No, Augusta,' he said quietly. 'I'm not.'

Hogarth could have asked three times as much and Augusta Boswell would have paid it. Her inherited house, and its inherited furniture and inherited pictures, were backed up by invisible, inherited where-withal.

Surrounded by those of Erskine Gibb Geddes's books which his sister had sold to Hogarth, Augusta found herself in a more unsettling dimension of the past than she had experienced before. It was different from her memories of their times together, especially that first summer trip which he'd come round to sharing with her. Trains and buses appalled him. Sensitive, unworldly, and coddled, he was terrified of ordinary life. They'd travelled to a score of different, interesting sites, in a Rolls-Royce hired complete with driver. They looked an unusual couple leaving a Rolls-Royce dressed for walking, she in shorts, each with a light rucksack and heavy hiking boots, as they set out for places associated with lore and legend. She sketched, photographed and took notes, while he spouted erudition in full flight like a man released from years of self-confinement in which silence and tutorial whispers were the only events. 'I know what you are,' she remembered him saying, as if the phrase took weeks to put together. 'You're a *scamp* of scholarship.'

'It's not quite how I think of myself. It must be my height.'

She remembered, too, the moment when he said, 'Should we try kissing?' and how she said, 'I knew I was right to wait until *you* asked. It didn't take as long as I thought.'

A week later – she was lightly amused as well as happy – he realized that he'd discovered want and desire. Weeks later, in his rooms in Cambridge, he said, 'Love-making isn't the least bit "literary", is it? Or do you think so?'

'Is it meant to be? Just because numberless poets have gone on about it in countless rhapsodies doesn't make it "literary". My father didn't have a "literary" bone in his body, nor my mother, but they managed to produce me. Did you want it to be "literary"?'

'I like it a lot, but there's an animal absurdity to it which really does puzzle me when I think about how poetic it's supposed to be.'

On another occasion: 'Not a lot goes on here without certain Fellows getting wind of it,' he said. 'I don't foresee a scandal, but it could be mentioned, and I'd be expected to do something about it.'

'Such as?'

'Resign my Fellowship.'

'Would you?'

'I wouldn't like that. Why don't you move into a flat or a house? Then we could be together more often, and propriety would be served as far as here's concerned.'

But faced with piles of Erskine's books wasn't the same as remembering him. The sensation was different. He'd died too long ago for her grief to be unbearable. There were days and nights to remember, pleasant things, which, if the hopes in them had been dashed in the mid–1960s, were enough to remind her that the person she'd become was not the person she was before. But his books ... They were objects of his life, and more meaningful than her gorgeously expensive engagement ring and two brooches, a silk scarf and his British Museum library ticket, or the receipt for a room in a Bloomsbury hotel where they'd spent four nights in 1964. She'd read many of these books and possessed many of them in her own library; but they competed strangely with her treasured relics – two brooches still worn, as well as the Jacqmar silk scarf – and stood on a plane of significance similar to Erskine's letters to her, even the last few dozen of them. They were more secretive, but of her own past, too, where the language now seemed different and the realm in which they'd lived seemed to have a different name. They were from the time of her body. Looking at his handwritten marginalia, his notes on fly-leaves and endpapers, felt like a discovery of the truths that lurked in what she'd forgotten, or misremembered. Or else she'd altered them in the intimacy of time as she pursued a desperate need to keep the past vivid and alive.

Each evening when she returned from the university she devoted herself to compiling a coherent summary of Erskine's notes and marginalia. They were in a more personal, more subjective, more candid style than that of his only publication. *Pre-Christian Faiths and Beliefs in Northern Europe*, the foundations for which had been his doctoral thesis, had become something like an acknowledged major work by 1990, but the reviews after its appearance in 1967 – it was in keeping with Erskine's luck that it should finally come out eight months after his death – had been contentious, nit-pickingly pedantic, and, in their last paragraphs, dismissive. Old-guard scholars, deep in retirement, on the verge of it, or half-dead, lashed out at the innovative and original.

But other things had been noted in Erskine's books, too. In several volumes he'd copied a folk rhyme. They were all dated 1965, when he was ill, and had moved back to the house in Perthshire, the house whose façade was engraved on his bookplate. It was

> *I stood upon Eyemouth fort,*
> *And guess ye what I saw?*
> *Fernieside and Flemington,*
> *Newhouses and Cocklaw;*
> *The fairy fouk o' Fosterland,*
> *The witches o' Edincraw,*
> *The bogle-bo o' Billy Myre,*
> *Wha kills our bairns a'.*

It would have read as a routine and undisturbing memorandum had he not repeated it in several books, and had he not underlined the last two lines, and had the date been earlier than 1965, when he knew that he was a dying man. They had spoken of having children. She detested the idea of her family being continued by cousins for whose crass ambitions in law, politics and high finance she had nothing but contempt. At first, the thought of paternity filled Erskine with terror; but then, before he met Augusta Boswell, before she changed his life, the idea of love reduced him to elegant stuttering and lassitude. She was in two minds about her influence on his life. Had he never met her, had she suffered love in timid solitude, would he have been alive still? Had he, by nature, by something more profound than mere temperament, been chosen for a life of scholarly solitariness, which she, intrusively, and fatally, had shattered with passion and love? Or was that bairn-killing bogle-bo merely a metaphor for disease, death, and the sundering of all contentments and futures before they could cross from dreams to reality?

> The bogle-bo o' Billy Myre,
> Wha kills our bairns a'.

It was how he tended to read folk poetry; but she was unconvinced. Or, rather, it was how she, too, read folk poetry, but not that particular poem.

When they were lovers, but before marriage and children entered their conversations and prospects, she'd felt contempt and consternation for Erskine's self-pitying remorse for his substantial but indefinable wealth. It seemed to pollute him, as if he lived in a vision in which his unearned circumstances existed in constant contrast with the poverty, hardships and deprivation of so many others. 'I am very wealthy,' she said. She was naked at the time and half-sitting on her desk in the bedroom of her flat. 'Indeed, I've inherited a fortune. You, too, are very wealthy. Indeed, you've inherited a fortune, too, perhaps of the more nebulous, less discloseable kind than my own, but a great, a very great, deal. So, I have a fortune, and you have a fortune. To you this is a state of affairs which promises absolute misery.' He tried to interrupt but Augusta would have none of it. 'Do you know a single don in your college, or my college, or *any* college, in Cambridge, or Oxford, or in *any* university, who wouldn't give his or her eye teeth for a *fraction* our our combined resources?'

'Oh, well, I mean, if you put it like that . . . I . . . well . . . No, I . . .'

'I've seen poor people. They don't deserve it, no more than we deserve to be rich. But, *I can't help it, and neither can you.*' She was sure the memory was accurate; she was certain she was trying to recall the episode with total honesty and clarity. All the same, she wondered if she'd taken advantage of his quiet, broken, pusillanimous temperament. Or was she overstating to herself now how fierce, forthright and scornful she was with him? 'I'm like you. I'm just like you in some ways. I'm frightened of what I've got, who I am, and of how what I've got makes me who I am, to even *want* to be political. I back out of it. I tell myself the world's got nothing to do with me. There are times when I actually believe I'm above all that mess and noise, all that chasing about in search of money, or something to eat, or amusement, or whatever . . . But I'm not above it. I like to think I am, but I'm not.'

How long did it take for them to get round to talking about the future and what they could do in a life together? Time-scales concertina'd in her mind. No sooner did she remember one significant incident and what was said than it seemed that the next, the step forward, happened a few minutes later, when she knew it took weeks, or months. So – 'What I find myself imagining,' he said, 'is *independent* scholarship. We could live at Lindorack. Of course, from the point of view of publication, and reputation, a university post is very much to be desired. How about you? Do you have your mind set on a university career? Have you dreamt of the crowning glory of a Chair?'

'I know Lindorack's yours. But what about your sister, who lives there?' she asked.

'You don't know Daphne very well. But I think you know enough to feel that she wouldn't be any trouble. Well, yes . . . Actually, Daphne's part of what's been on my mind. Marriage appears to be very low on her list of priorities. She seems interested only in running the estate – and in her painting. She likes you. She'd be delighted if we populated the place with little Geddeses.'

'I'd like that, too.'

'But there's your thesis, and your book.'

'Am I planning to write a book?'

'Your research is too good not to!'

'I can write it at Lindorack.'

'You've about a year's work to finish. And you can't go anywhere until you've completed it,' he said.

Other rhymes and poems on the endpapers and flyleaves of his books were, she decided, of his own composition.

> *It is dark. It is very dark.*
> *Black as the Earl of Hell's waistcoat.*
> *Dark, dark as opposite. Dark as the is-not.*

That, too, was dated in the months of his dying. He'd always been in the habit of saying things like, 'Talk about blank? Talk about there being nothing in the stupid man's mind! It must be as black as the Earl of Hell's waistcoat in there.' She'd forgotten that. It came back with a jolt. All these years of remembering and that tic-simile hadn't once got through!

Her library overlooked the square. The electric pale green of the trees didn't witness her reading-lamp go out until long after revellers had passed by with their shouts and laughter.

> *Let love accumulate, more, more, and more,*
> *And ours be happy children and delight,*

she read on a flyleaf. As poetry it was probably poor, old-fashioned stuff, but she was agreeably hurt that Erskine had tried to write it, even at a time when the imperative of his heart-felt sentiment was utterly without hope – the date showed that. But after all those years weeping was impossible, with or without another glass from a second bottle of Sauternes. 'Is that really true, Augusta? Sweet wines are "unfashionable"?'

'I read it in a newspaper last Sunday.'

'But dry wines don't taste as nice!' he protested.

'Hedonism isn't supposed to be you.'

'All right with fish, I suppose, but . . .'

'My theory is that dry wine is a puritanical reflex in a pleasure-seeking decade.'

It was at her bedroom window at around 3 a.m. that August night that Augusta Boswell became a nocturnal person and discovered the sad pleasures of the moon. The long, walled garden behind her house was adequately looked after by a Mr Paterson, whom she rarely saw or thought about and who was paid every Friday by Mrs McLennan, who did the housework three days a week. Balmy weather, a clear and starry sky, and the moon, with only the faintest rustle of leaves, drew her to go outside. She took her bottle of wine, put on a hat from a peg by the kitchen door, and took a large torch from a drawer.

For several minutes she stared at the sky's astral remoteness, its lunar immensity, its universal, dwarfing scale that humbled whoever contemplated it while comforting the observer's loneliness. She felt alone with the grandeur of time, to which every life that is or ever was adds a pathetic pittance. She sat down on a chair by a garden table. It wasn't bright enough to read. Flowers were almost colourless, trees grey-green. It felt like a personal outdoors although overlooked by other houses. At that hour almost all were in darkness save for a few hall lights and some in which late parties were still in full swing. They were far enough away to be silent. People had come home from late performances accompanied by friends, strangers and artists of one kind or another. From the unlit window of a bedroom in a high flat a man was rapidly dressing when he noticed a tiny woman in a broad-brimmed hat apparently moonbathing. In another flat a woman had dashed into a room to find the text of a play in order to illustrate once and for all the hideous deviations perpetrated by a director, who, in the sitting room, was defending his integrity to a dozen people as well oiled as himself. She switched the light off and looked out. She saw a small woman in a towelling bath-robe and wide-brimmed hat holding a torch on a book. Or that it is what she decided she saw after a good two minutes of scrutinizing the unnerving nocturnal vagueness of the sight. A hand reached out for a glass that sat beside a bottle on a table.

On a dozen consecutive nights after that, at approximately the same time, the same woman excused herself from her guests to look out of the high window. She saw the same woman in the wide-brimmed hat. On the third night the lighting arrangements had clearly been improved by the introduction of a desk lamp led from the kitchen on an extended cable. There was a pile of books, a bottle, a glass, and sometimes the woman wrote on a pad. She didn't mention it to her guests. More than once the woman at the garden table appeared only to be basking in the moonlight in that uncharacteristically sustained run of fine weather.

But Dr Boswell was hard at work. She'd decided that *Pre-Christian Faiths and Beliefs in Northern Europe* was due for a revision only she could perform. She was drafting a chapter in the form of an appendix in which Erskine's marginalia and other notes would be interpreted. Daphne Geddes had been written to seeking her permission and asking for her help. Augusta also asked why she'd sold her brother's books, if she'd sold all of them, and if his notebooks and other papers were still at Lindorack.

Three months before he died, Augusta moved in to Lindorack to help Daphne with nursing and caring for Erskine. Her thesis had been completed, examined, and her degree awarded.

'I know there's no hope. I accept what the doctors say. But I'd sooner live the rest of my life as Mrs Geddes than Dr Boswell. But he won't hear of it. He says that I must learn to live without him, and that having loved truly once, then I should feel free to love again. How could he? How could he say such a thing?'

'I think he's right. But can you imagine how surprised I am that my brother, of all people, could have turned out to be so wise about something like that? You've changed him. He loves you like I never thought he'd love anyone. No one's loved me like that. Nor have I. Just once, you know, is very, very lucky. And being that sort of person, twice is far from impossible. I think that's what he's telling you, and that for him to marry you when he's so close to dying would be sinfully selfish of him.'

'There would be a legal document revoking my rights to his property. Everything would be left to you.'

'I can't help you, Augusta. I'll do nothing to persuade him. I believe what he says is true. Much as I like you. And I didn't expect to. When he told me of your plans to live here, I felt threatened by them, until I met you and realized what a different man he'd become. You've no idea how sorry I am, and how disappointed I feel about life and what can happen. My father was hardly ever here. He seems to have spent most of his time in the United States. My mother was a confirmed alcoholic by the time I was ten. We were brought up by aunts and tutors, nannies and housekeepers. Has he told you all this?'

'I think I know most of it.'

'I'm so glad you're here, and I wish everything could be different. But I've been wishing for that ever since I could think for myself.'

The weather turned to cloud, rain and starless chill. Augusta Boswell paced the rooms and stairs of her large house cursing the climate for being as black as the Earl of Hell's waistcoat and cold with it. Daphne Geddes's reply was on the telephone answering machine. It had been preserved there for several days. 'Please come and see me as soon as you can,' Daphne's voice said. 'I had to sell Lindorack. I live in a cottage not far from it, though. I had to sell a lot of his books. I didn't have room for them and I needed the money. I couldn't bring myself to tell you because I knew how you'd feel. Can you forgive me? My dear Augusta.' There was a long pause. Augusta could sense the choked hesitancy in Daphne's voice; it felt like a vivid emotion struggling against judgementless, neutral, passive technology. 'Please come soon. I still have his papers and quite a lot of his books.' She repeated her telephone number. It was after midnight, but Augusta picked up the phone and dialled, suspecting that Daphne, too, was a woman for whom sleep was elusive.

Attendance at Erskine's funeral was meagre. The only relatives apart from Daphne were an aunt in her seventies and a slightly younger uncle. Several tenants and employees, a representative of the family's lawyers, and one from the bank, made up the rest of the numbers.

'You can stay for as long as you like,' Daphne said later.

'Just a little while. A cousin and his wife are living in my house in Edinburgh. I've already told them to be out by the end of the month. Harsh, but necessary. They don't understand.'

'Will you look for a job?'

'Universities are about all I'm fit for. Not that there's much demand for what I do.'

'I feel as if I've been orphaned twice over.' Augusta remembered the quiet, puzzled anger in Daphne's voice as she was driven north from Edinburgh. Bridges, motorways, flyovers and speeding cars and trucks made it hard to believe in the early history and customs of the people who once lived on the damaged countryside over which she travelled.

'You seem very calm and determined,' Daphne had said.

'No. It's clear to me that I'll never get what I wanted most. Now it's sunk in, I have to accept that I've no choice but to live without that side to what people call "happiness".'

'What ages were your parents when they died?' Daphne asked.

'My father was sixty, and my mother sixty-one. Why do you ask?'

'Not exactly long-lived. My father was forty-four, my mother forty-seven. Erskine was thirty-five. I'm a year older than him. But from an actuarial point of view, my prospects look pretty dire. I'm afraid to ask you to be my friend in case you end up burying me beside Erskine. Or if my presence on a regular footing discourages you from meeting someone else. Men probably find you attractive.'

'You're not exactly plain. And you've got height on your side.'

'Please, stay as long as you like.'

'Just for a little while.'

'I've been wooed,' Daphne said, as if surprised at her disclosure. 'Several times. Chinless wonders, most of them. Awfully good at fly-fishing and from *very* good families, but skint, and good for next to nothing. Am I desperate? Am I frustrated? And to these questions I've had to answer with a truthful, "No, I'm not." Sauternes will make me fat, eventually,' she said, 'assuming I get that far.' She examined the bottle. 'Each time I replenish the stocks, I'll think of Erskine and probably cry buckets.'

'He wouldn't drink anything else.'

'What will I put on his stone, Augusta? "Beloved son of" rings false and horrid.'

'Name, dates, and then "scholar".'

'Then "beloved brother" and "beloved fiancé".'

'That's very unusual.'

'I think we should.'

'Yes.'

'Or does it tie a stone around your neck?'

'No. I'm so grateful that my name will be on the stone, too. Thank you.'

'You could hardly have insisted. So, congratulations, me. I've done something thoughtful and unselfish!'

Daphne's cottage was small, the sort of house in which a gardener at Lindorack might have lived, or a gamekeeper. It had a small garden, lazily kept; the house was too close to trees to have other than a darkly cramped outlook. A ladies' bicycle with a large basket before the handlebars lay against a wall beside a rusting rake and an unemptied wheelbarrow full of discoloured weeds. Roses were running wild for lack of pruning, their leaves spotted with lumps of fibrous black. Woodwork looked in need of paint. The porch was dusty. On each side were columns of unused plantpots piled inside each other. The impression was of a demoralized resident within.

They embraced, and Augusta found herself the consoling one, applying her handkerchief to Daphne's tears. 'I have to tell the driver whether to wait, or when, or if, to come back. I thought I'd stay for a few days, if I could, and if you'd like me to,' she said as Daphne shook, wept and nodded. 'Is it all right for me to stay?' Daphne nodded and Augusta went back to the car, told the driver she'd phone his firm in due course, and was handed her suitcase and several boxfiles of papers, which Augusta handed back to the driver, who brought them into the house.

It was six years since they'd last met and visited Erskine's grave. 'There's a lot you'll want to know,' Daphne said. In six years she'd aged markedly. Her appearance wasn't helped by her clothes – a homemade cardigan over a thick polo-necked jumper, a tweed skirt, the waist of which she hitched up every few minutes, ancient ankle-boot slippers which zipped, and wrinkled wool stockings. Her hair was greyer. She looked older than sixty.

'I'd always assumed that the Geddes family fortune was rock solid,' Augusta said. 'I recognize the shelves.'

'I ripped them out. I thought they wouldn't be missed but there was a very nasty letter from their lawyer to my lawyer. I knew I needed shelves, for heaven's sake!'

'You should have told me much, much sooner,' Augusta said.

'I bought it from the Forestry Commission,' Daphne said as Augusta looked at the packed little sitting room. 'I'm not entirely indigent. I've 50,000 left over to provide an income. I can just about get by. I've gin if you'd like a drink.' Augusta looked surprised. 'I don't have any Sauternes.' There was a look in Daphne's eyes which expressed painfully the remorse of someone who knew what she should be providing, but couldn't. 'They didn't have it in the village shop. They'd nothing like that.'

'Don't blame yourself. *I* should have thought of it. I could have brought a case of Sauternes without any trouble.'

'Gin's no good?' The loss of self-confidence was obvious in how Daphne's voice trembled with guilt-ridden timidity.

'I think you've been through sheer hell.'

Daphne shrugged. 'I've had two years to get used to it,' she said lightly. 'I've a room which makes a decent little studio. No central heating, of course, but then Lindorack's was pretty unreliable. Do you remember? And when I think of the bills! I could live for over a year on the likes of that!'

'Have you been all right? I wish you'd *told* me!'

'Please, please, dear Augusta, you really are my only friend, you know. Don't be angry with me! I've been dreading this! It's been like having the guiltiest secret. Sure you won't have gin?'

'Absolutely certain. But what happened?'

'Well, like you I thought everything was taken care of and 100 per cent dependable. Then I'd a letter from the bank saying could their Mr So-and-So come and see me next Wednesday at 11 a.m. and I wrote back saying, "Yes, fine." The man came with two briefcases, there was so much paperwork. None of it made sense to me apart from the highly explicit conclusion – *my* share of the Geddes's millions had taken a bad knock.'

'But I read the property supplement in *The Scotsman*. Lindorack wasn't advertised.'

'Naturally. I wouldn't let them. I'd my pride to think of.'

'Didn't you have any warning? I thought you ran the estate yourself.'

'Not the investments. These were what went under. The legal bill for pursuing the chance of mismanagement or something dodgy was *enormous*. Oh, all the estate involved was throwing relatively minor sums of money at it. The blow came out of the blue. Not much pride left now, my dear. None, in fact. But I've settled in quite nicely. I'll have a gin if you won't,' she said with signs of impatience.

'No. Phone a taxi. If your village shop hasn't heard of Sauternes, then we must be able to get it in Dunkeld, surely.' She held Daphne's hand and raised it from the half-empty gin bottle. 'Regular consumer of this stuff, are you?'

'If you're so stuck on Sauternes, then I dare say you're a regular consumer of *that*,' Daphne answered defiantly.

'Very regular. Indeed, practically addicted to it. When I say I drink nothing else, I mean nothing else. Now ring for the taxi.'

After dinner, Daphne said, 'I used to be a competent woman. Now I feel silly and useless. You, though, have become practical.'

'Actually, I think I'm off my rocker.'

'Oh?'

'When the weather's fine I sit in my garden until I'm too pissed to concentrate.'

'Hardly a symptom of madness, whatever else it suggests.'

'I forgot to mention that this occurs between midnight and the early hours. You see, I feel myself to be in very close touch with

Erskine, through his books, his handwriting, and the moon and stars.'

'I see,' Daphne said.

'No, you don't "see". Nothing occult is behind what I've just said. It's a personal phenomenon to do with the exact physical circumstances which induce the inexplicable but indispensable thrills of a peculiarly intellectual kind of remembrance. And you can believe or disbelieve that as you see fit. Don't ask me to explain it any further because I couldn't do it.'

'All right. If you say so. But I don't understand.'

'The forecast's pretty promising. You'll see for yourself. You might even join me if you're of a mind to.'

'Yes, well, I don't sleep much.'

'I didn't think you did. How much did Hogarth give you for the books?'

'Five hundred.'

'He robbed you. Then he robbed me. Had I known, I'd gladly have bought them from you.'

'What difference does the moon make? I mean, this sitting out that you do. What happens?'

'I don't hear voices, if that's what you're driving at. Nor see visions either. What "happens" is in here.' She tapped her head. 'Are you really, really sure that you want to live here?'

'But why at *night*?'

'Look, it simply makes a difference. Let's leave it at that. A place like this is too much of a come-down! I don't want to rub it in, Daphne, but the Boswell funds are in a healthy state of growth and my house is too big for two, never mind just me on my ownie-oh. At least, think about it.'

'From Lindorack to charity is worse than from Lindorack to here,' Daphne said.

'Add what you get from selling this dump to your 50,000 and the income would give you all the spending money you need. What I offer is bed, board, and a remarkably efficient cental heating system. To say nothing of the agreeable smell of polished furniture and a relative absence of grime.'

'When we last met you were talking about a professorship. Did you get it?'

'No. They gave it to a world-class halfwit from Oxford with whom I'm at loggerheads. We don't even speak.'

'Why?'

'Because he lives in Oxford and commutes. As well as that, he's a dope. Now, I think living in Edinburgh would be good for you. It might give you a chance to show your work more. You haven't done much about punting your paintings around. Have you?'

'Haven't much felt like it for years. Too many disappointments. I don't know, Augusta. I'm grateful. It's very kind and considerate of you. But I'd like to rest my bones here, beside Erskine.'

'So would I. If it's permissible. If it can be arranged.'

'I couldn't possibly object. And wouldn't. I can fix it.'

'You've no intention of popping off in the near future, I take it?' Augusta asked, suppressing a lady-like Sauternes-repeat.

'I'm a dreadful mess, aren't I? No, I don't feel like dying.'

'Nor me. I've useful work to do,' Augusta said. 'I intend to nag my head of department into a resignation.'

'I don't visit his grave as often as I used to. As often as I should,' Daphne said.

'Isn't it bad for you to live so close to Lindorack and not in it?'

'Well, I see it – rooftops, anyway – when I bike down to the village. Yes, always with a wrench on the old heart-strings. Of course.'

'Very, very acceptable Sauternes,' Augusta said. 'And I'm fussy.'

'Yes, very.'

'If you die first, I'd see to the necessary arrangements, to the letter. I promise. And if I die first . . .'

'I promise, Augusta.'

'And these are promises as readily kept from Edinburgh as here . . .'

'I've said I'll give it serious thought, and I will. You on one side of Erskine, and me on the other. It's only right. It fulfils perfectly what's written on his stone. It makes everything ring true – sad, but true. But maybe not so sad. Anything so true, and loyal, and unforgotten, can't be entirely sad.'

'Personally speaking, I find it miserable beyond words, but, as you say, true, loyal and unforgotten. However, I've lived with it for twenty-five years, so I can grin and bear it for as long as I've got left. But then, I'm that bit younger than you. It's gone midnight and the weather looks quite nice. Shall we sit out?'

They sat on two old chairs on which generations of servants had parked themselves in the kitchens of Lindorack. They held hands and talked about Erskine Gibb Geddes. From time to time Augusta inserted a question or remark to which Daphne replied by saying, 'I'm thinking about it.' After an hour she started to say things like 'I've one of two reservations to clear up with myself, but only I can do that. So why don't you leave me to it?'

'About the only subject on which the lousy schools I was sent to were any good was the stars. One school in particular. I knew all the names. I thought I'd forgotten them, but last month, when I started sitting out, I realized that I hadn't. I seem to have an excellent memory.'

'No one taught the stars to *me*.'

'Erskine knew about them.'

'We always had different tutors.'

Augusta pressed gently on Daphne's hand. 'Think about Erskine.'

'I am.'

'Very soon, it might become moon-blue, silver, starry, and celestial,' Augusta said matter-of-factly. 'But don't be frightened. It's not at all like the Earl of Hell's waistcoat.'

'No,' Daphne said, with a laugh. 'Not at all.'

'But first, I want to make a toast,' Augusta said tipsily, in her won't-take-no-for-an-answer manner.

'A toast?'

'To the sky.'

'To the sky!'

'To the sky!'

And the moon giggled, having seen everything, not once, but many times.

The Race of the Sword

Two middle-aged acrobats played backgammon in the chintzy sitting room of Mrs Lambie's guest house. They were the leading and oldest members of the Six Flying Fontanas. Age accorded them managerial and choreographic status, apart from a few leaps and bounds and invitations for audiences to show their appreciation. One was Egyptian, the other Bulgarian.

Jock McCulloch parked the district council's stately, over-maintained and under-employed Daimler with the care and precision it deserved. As he stood in Mrs Lambie's hall, he removed a black leather glove from his right hand and slapped it several times into the palm of the glove still worn on his left. He listened for signs of life as he peeled off the remaining glove, and then consulted his watch. Excited exclamations in a foreign tongue drew him to the sitting-room door. He doffed his municipal driver's cap on the way, scowling with respect at the taxidermed salmon in its glass case, a wag-at-the-wa' clock, a full-length mirror in an ornate black frame in which he looked like the perfect portrait of himself, and an oil-painting of an imaginary Highland scene.

Tugging the sleeves of his uniform and clearing his throat, McCulloch waited for the backgammon players to notice him. Years of military service had taken him to many countries, so he knew tric-trac when he saw it. 'Soon,' said an elderly acrobat. 'Soon.' He pointed to the clock on the mantelpiece.

Paying no attention to how McCulloch's considerable bulk blocked off half the doorway, younger acrobats pushed past him, skipping and laughing. They wore uniform pink leotards and tights. He made a quick eye-count. 'Are you the *Six* Flying Fontanas?' he asked emphatically.

No one answered. One of the three young women rushed past on her way out of the room. 'There's no hurry!' McCulloch shouted after her, rasping with irony.

'Ten minutes! Give us ten minutes!' the Egyptian backgammon player said, yelling above heated conversations in three languages.

McCulloch showed him five fingers. 'I say ten minutes, he shows me fingers! Ten!' the Egyptian shouted indignantly, showing the fingers of both hands.

'There are eight of you! How am I? . . . Five minutes! Chop-chop! Savvy? Capisci? Comprendo, pal? *Five!*'

'Is that you, Mr McCulloch?' Mrs Lambie appeared behind her miniature reception desk, wiping her hands on a tea-towel. 'I made a dreadful mistake this morning,' she confided. 'Two of them don't eat bacon on religious grounds.' She covered her face with her towel.

'Now, now, don't you be embarrassed, Mrs Lambie.'

'And that's a new uniform, if I'm not mistaken. My, you really suit it. I keep telling my brother, "If you skimp on a few pounds there, and there, what happens? The town ends up looking like a back-water, and a lot worse off than it is".'

'A bit of a mixed bag,' McCulloch said, lowering his voice as he expressed his low opinion of the Fontanas. 'And these Six Flying Fontanas are eight.'

'Oh,' she said, noticing McCulloch's chauffeur's driving boots, shaped to fit over his substantial calf muscles. 'It must have taken ages to bring out a polish like that.'

'And you,' he said, returning the compliment, 'keep your house in first-rate ornamental condition. Ornamental,' he said, savouring the ground consonants before swallowing them. 'Your house is a joy to behold.'

'I've plenty of broth in the pot,' she said invitingly. 'A good plate of soup would set you up for the rest of the day,' she said. 'It'll be a very busy day for you.'

Soup, at eleven in the morning? Helen Lambie's being a bit forward, McCulloch thought.

'Last week it was men from the Scottish Office, beavering away in the back of the car on what they called "laptops". And when they weren't, they were calling HQ on portable radio-telephones. Today it's acrobats, Miss Ida St John, and God alone knows who else. All one to me.'

'A nice plate of broth?'

'I've a human pyramid to transport at eleven sharp,' he said apologetically.

'Then I'll put it in a Thermos flask for you.'

'If it's no trouble . . .'

'A bachelor like you can't be trusted to look after yourself. And I hope you'll say hello to my brother for me.'

'Oh, I'll be seeing the provost all right.'

'Convener,' she corrected. 'It's a long time since Dereholm was a burgh.'

'Still is, by my reckoning, Mrs Lambie.'

Each Flying Fontana carried a gold Lurex hold-all. McCulloch glowered in fascination as the tumblers stowed their garish bags in the Daimler's boot. 'It'll be a hellish crush,' he said, with no hint of apology. 'Blame yourselves. I expected six.' Six younger acrobats piled into the rear of the car. McCulloch grimaced at the intensity of the perfume worn by the three young women. The Egyptian sat in the front, and the tiny Bulgarian sat on his knee, carrying the backgammon set in its ancient box.

The route to the Memorial Park went along the street in which the parade was beginning to assemble. Dereholm Silver Band tuned up in the yard of the monumental mason who was its leader and conductor. Boy Scouts, Girl Guides, Sea Scouts, Brownies, Cubs, the Boys' Brigade, the Army Cadet Corps and the local company of the Territorial Army formed ranks in a confusion of shouted orders and consulted instructions. McCulloch slowed to walking pace as he approached 'C' Company. He lowered his window as Company Sergeant-Major Guthrie trotted up to him, leaving a young officer in a posture of hopeless abandonment.

'Heh, Wally. These are the Six Flying Fontanas, an' they're to tag on wi' your lot.'

'Oh, aye?' he said, looking in. 'Ye canny count, then.' He held his nose. 'Stinks like a whore's armpits, Jock.'

'Give it max, Wally. Bags o' swank,' McCulloch said, driving away. Under his breath, he muttered, 'Fix bayonets. God, give me strength.'

'You live here?' the small Bulgarian asked.

'God's own country,' McCulloch snapped, suspending the conversation for ever.

A man in grey flannels and a black blazer was waiting at the entrance to a small marquee allotted to the Flying Fontanas in case of rain. He sported a badge bearing his name and stating that he represented the authority of the Regional Leisure Services, Recreation and Arts Department. Three workmen were walking away, each bearing a wooden mallet and a handful of excess tent pegs. 'All present and correct?' McCulloch asked.

'There are eight of them,' the confused official said.

'Exactly what I said myself. Six somersaulters and two backgammon addicts.

'Backgammon?'

'Backgammon.'

McCulloch heard the parade go by from the alley beside the town hall, which was no longer the town hall, but the local government offices of Dereholm district council. Still, in Dereholm it was called the town hall. He browsed through his newspaper and repolished the interior woodwork. Each year the Fair Day seemed bigger and different. From the external balcony to the town hall the convener of the regional council, assorted officials and elected members of the regional and district councils, the Lord Lieutenant, several Members of Parliament, a Member of the European Parliament, local gentry and invited guests were taking the salute. The Silver Band went by. The pipes and drums of 'C' Company droned and rattled with satisfying vigour. As martial music receded, the competitors in the five-mile race strolled past in their tracksuits. McCulloch glanced up from his paper and saw a crane carrying a film crew. The race was first run in 1510 at the command of King James IV, who died with most of his army at the battle of Flodden three years later. Royal command laid down that the race be run each year for the right to carry the sword that the King endowed as the prize. In McCulloch's younger days the race attracted only local men and boys. For some reason – money – it now drew some of the best runners in Britain. Athletes who had competed in the Olympic Games were in the parade, which McCulloch made no effort to watch. Not only that, but women could compete, and a graduated class of runners, male and female, known as veterans.

He had never come close to winning it, but in 1960, when he was twenty, and on his first leave home, he finished tenth. In these days a young man in Dereholm was a nobody if he failed to possess a blue bonnet presented to competitors who finished in the first ten. A blue bonnet entitled the lucky recipient to join James IV's bodyguard the next time he visited the district, which, McCulloch mused, was unlikely in the foreseeable future, and, if Flodden was anything to go by, not much of an inducement anyway. The winner of the Dereholm

Sword was also entitled to hunt with the King's party, and those of his successors, the kings and queens of Scotland, and, for one complete year, from July to July, to enjoy hunting and fishing privileges on the royal estates. Such worthwhile benefits had long since faded into antiquity, or, rather, had been purchased by businessmen and hoteliers with head offices in London, Chicago, Frankfurt and Tokyo. Apart from a couple of golf courses, James IV's hunting park was now an adjunct of territory owned by international exponents of agri-industry, and there was nothing on it worth hunting, other than, perhaps, its present proprietors, whom no one had ever seen, and who, in all likelihood, had never seen what they owned.

McCulloch watched the crowd disperse in the wake of the parade's backmarkers. Those who came from around Dereholm walked at a lazy pace. Their expressions were filled with innocent but half-stifled expectations. Their observation of visitors and incomers left them touched with sardonic wonder. Their conversations were communicated as much by winks, nods and facial inventions as by words. A complete sentence was a rarity. McCulloch had noted in recent years how the strangers drawn to Dereholm's Fair Day were taller and more brightly dressed than the locals. They were better looking; they even looked cleaner. They seemed more adept at enjoyment without having to smoke forty a day or drink themselves into a stupor. McCulloch found the contrast deplorable and saddening; but he was prepared to smile at it. After all, if there was one thing he was good at, it was loyalty.

He nosed the Daimler round to the front of the town hall. Local people were nimbly obedient in getting out of his way. Over the generations it seems never to have crossed their minds that their taxes pay for such symbols of authority as the official car. According to his reliable presentation watch – a gift from his regiment – the time was 11.28 precisely. Across the road, the clock on the County Hotel said 5.15. It's been stuck at that hour since VJ Day, when a party of revellers made such a racket that it was said to have stopped the clock. The provost of the time decreed it would be symbolic for the County Hotel clock to remain for ever fixed at that hour. So be it. For ever fixed it has been and remains so to this very moment. There used to be a clock on the Odeon-style façade of the Dereholm and District Co-operative Society's shop, which once had pretensions to being almost a department store. Now it's a DIY emporium and lawn-mower repair centre. A round discoloured hole in the middle of its off-white stuccoed late-1920s frieze shows where the public timepiece used to lodge. The town hall clock was a mere two minutes slow, but McCulloch knew that by later in the day the accuracy of its measurement of time would have slipped further from its hands.

The lame town hall porter hobbled down the broad steps to the Daimler. He waved to someone at the door, who waved to someone in the foyer, who waved to someone at the top of the internal staircase, who waved to a porter at the door of the James IV Room, who, in a rough parody of Ruritanian urgency, waved to someone else to say that the cars were arriving.

'For a burgh chronometer,' McCulloch said, looking up at the imposing dial, 'that's an insult to each and every poll-tax payer in Dereholm.'

'Horology's not my department,' the prim cripple piped. 'And we haven't been a burgh in quite some years. Also, its real name is the community charge.'

'If you're so fucking clever, Mr Anster, how come you're just the town hall porter?'

'*Not* town hall. *District council offices.*'

'From Flying Fontanas to flying fucking farce,' McCulloch growled.

'I'm happy enough,' Mr Anster said.

'Who winds it?'

'Mr Mitchell is in charge of the clock. Oh, he collects clocks. It's his hobby. If anyone can fix that big clock up there, it's the assistant finance executive. You can bet your boots on that, Mr McCulloch.'

'Wonder what makes him tick?' McCulloch said.

'What's that?'

'Cutbacks, setbacks, drawbacks, hatchbacks, fumbling bloody fullbacks, and now flashbacks,' McCulloch snorted. He stared hard at the impressive, inaccurate clock on the fantasy baronial tower of the town hall.

With the casual pomp of those who know they are waited on, that nothing can, or should, start without them, and with the good humour of elected representatives confident that their accents are holding up in genteel company, the convener and his party descended the broad steps to the pavement. A few cynical locals, with a taste for the preposterous, had waited to see this formidable sight – the dignified descent of the official party.

'No, sir,' McCulloch said quietly to Mrs Lambie's brother, 'ladies, Lord Lieutenant and generals first.'

'I was just checking that everything was all right inside,' Mr Waugh – pronounced Woff – the convener said in a whisper. He was put out and pouting, but forced an affable grin over his square, bald face. 'After you, Lady Formakin.' Her ladyship got in, followed by Mrs Woff – spelled Waugh – the Lord Lieutenant, and the general.

Other cars – they were the regional council's cars – now drove up in a line. The convener looked deeply satisfied with this clockwork timing. 'You'll be more appropriate,' McCulloch whispered, 'in the front, beside me.'

'I know that,' Waugh said in an irate whisper. 'Everyone comfortable?' he asked of his guests in the rear. 'Good, good. Good. Splendid.'

'Well?' the convener said when McCulloch showed no signs of starting.

'It says here,' McCulloch answered, holding his sheet of instructions, 'motorcade to the Memorial Park.'

'And?'

'No point shooting off before the other cars are ready, Mr Waugh. Sir.' McCulloch was a few years younger than Waugh, but he could remember the convener when he was an apprentice grocer in the sawdust-on-the-wooden-floor, cheese-smelling, bacon-smelling premises of Allardyce and Fisher, a shop whose passing was lamented by everyone in Dereholm over forty-five. With the years, Waugh, not a tall man, had grown square rather than fat, or, rather, his lavish adipose had squared instead of rounding him. He had acquired, too, the polished bald head associated with professional grocers. Also, he had picked up a genial command of public speaking which struck local observers as sinister. His eloquence gave them the opportunity to disagree with everything he said. They didn't vote for his politics in Dereholm itself, but they did in the area round about which made it Dereholm district council. Now he was convener of the regional council, and had been for eight years.

'Are ye well, Provost?'

'Fine,' said the convener.

'A good day for it.'

'Fine. Fine. And it's convener. Convener. Convener,' he repeated. 'A good Scottish term.'

'Aye, right. Oh, your sister passes on her hello. She struck me this morning as looking remarkably well.'

'My sister?'

'My earlier assignment was the transportation of the Six Flying Fontanas – actually, there're eight of them – from Mrs Lambie's guest house. It was a great shame about Jack Lambie. A great shame.'

'At long last!' the convener said in an angrily conspiratorial whisper. A police motorcyclist pulled out from a side-street in front of the Daimler. Two more materialized, one on each side of the advancing official car, at the head of the motorcade.

'God, give me strength,' McCulloch said. 'They're cheerin' ye!' Crowds at the entrance to the Memorial Park waved and shouted as the cars drove past.

McCulloch returned to the town hall as soon as his passengers were deposited outside the official marquee ('Invited Guests Only' it said on a notice, guarded by two commissionaires from regional HQ, and a police sergeant). No sooner had he drawn up than the head of Regional Leisure Services, Recreation and Arts sprinted down the town hall steps to the car, and no sooner had he put his hand on the rear door-handle when a squeakingly deferential cry from Mr Anster called him back to take a phone call.

The head of etcetera was agitated. He was overcome by arrangements already made but which might go wrong, arrangements that were still to be made, and arrangements that should have been made but might not have been. McCulloch noticed, however, that the cares of office didn't oppress Mr Beattie to the point where he forgot to delight in his self-authored prestige. Instead of taking a companionable seat beside the driver, Donald E. Beattie, MA, MPhil, MBIM, etc., reclined in the back, long legs stretched out, scanning the street in hope of recognition.

Few cars were heading out of Dereholm, but traffic approaching the town was heavy. Locals from the outlying housing estates were walking to the fair, or travelling by bicycle, or waiting at bus-stops – they looked like refugees. Once past the speed limit, McCulloch put his foot down and the Daimler whooshed. Mr Beattie slid open the glass panel that separated passengers from the driver. 'For heaven's sake, we'll have sirens behind us in no time!'

McCulloch leant back with a well-rehearsed movement and slid the panel shut. He switched on his end of the intercom. 'Simply press the button beside you, Mr Beattie, and you may speak to me in perfect safety. But to fling open the panel like that' – the Daimler purred at seventy-five mph down a straight mile – 'could give a driver a very bad fright and see the car in a ditch.'

'Slow down, for God's sake!' Beattie shouted as the Daimler touched ninety.

'Miss St John's train arrives at 12.23. Our minimum speed required to reach there in good time is seventy mph average. I questioned the timetabling at the office, sir. Fat lot of good it did, or ever did. But don't worry. I'll get you there without the embarrassment of a delay. Oh, and another thing. Miss Ida St John is opposed to smoking. So I'd put that out before it stinks the car, sir. I heard her say on television. Or did I read it? Anyway, she's a spokesperson for the Anti-Smoking Campaign.'

'I won't be talked to like that! You're overstepping the mark! What's your name? What's your name?' But McCulloch had switched off. He watched Beattie in his mirror as he put out his cigarette and tried to waft away his smoke.

Dereholm's Daimler arrived a few minutes before the train bringing Ida St John to the station nearest the town. There used to be a station at Dereholm itself, but the line was closed thirty years ago when the country first began to dismantle itself. That was prior to the present governmental strategy, which is selling the best bits off to the highest bidder. Local fans and a few press photographers were waiting in the expectation of autographs and pictures. The head of this and that got out of the Daimler and informed a policeman of who he was. A space was cleared so that Mr Beattie could walk in comfort to the platform. A film crew readied itself for action as soon as the train appeared. They were part of a team covering what the *Dereholm Advertiser* called 'A Typical Day in the Life of Ida St John'. That week, she was number eight in the charts. McCulloch had already seen a detachment of the crew at work in Dereholm that morning. He watched the jostling of fans as the pop star showed herself, holding on exaggeratedly to her alleged fiancé on one side and her mother on the other. It was a touch calculated by Ida St John's management and publicists to look down-home and folksy, for, if Ida St John wasn't local, at least she was Scots, with a real name that certainly wasn't Ida St John (pronounced Sinjin).

When his obsequious profession demanded it, McCulloch could be smart to the jump in opening a door with accomplished gentlemanly expertise. He nodded, but with something like grim disbelief, at the singer's mother, a woman of around his own age, whom the garments of unexpected affluence transformed from an ordinary dish-washer and provider of plain meals into a demented would-be dowager. 'Other door, sir?' he asked the boyfriend. 'Oh, well, it's entirely up to you,' he added as the young man – how can anyone *get away with* dressing like that? – disregarded McCulloch's proffered protocol and fell into the car, telling his would-be mother-in-law to move up the bed a bit. 'Front or back?' he asked Mr Beattie. 'It's all one to me.' McCulloch sounded as if his professional principles had been wiped out by the vulgarity of his passengers.

'Miss St John? Everyone? Quite comfortable?' Beattie inquired. McCulloch winced at Beattie's merry deference.

Beattie jumped in beside the driver, looking anxiously at his watch. Dozens of Ida St John's fans trotted after the car as it pulled out of the station's small forecourt.

'She's smoking!' Beattie said with quiet rage.

'Really? My God, she is, too.'

'You told me she didn't smoke.'

'Showbiz types who'd kicked the weed – I saw them on television,' McCulloch said. 'I'm sure I did. Belt up, Mr Beattie.'

'I beg your pardon? Oh, the seat-belt.'

Policemen and stewards were hard-pressed to hold back the crowds while the convener welcomed Ida St John and presented her to selected dignitaries. From a mobile crane the film crew panned over stalls, tents, booths, ice-cream vans and itinerant catering outlets. People from all over and just up the road milled round entertainers on stilts, clowns on mono-bikes, a fire-eater, jugglers, the Flying Fontanas, tracksuited athletes, and other livestock. Children were queueing to have their faces painted, for the donkey rides, the go-karting track, sideshows and merry-go-rounds, the chair-o-plane rides. McCulloch couldn't help but be impressed. Not only was this the biggest Fair Day ever, but it was jam-packed with novelties, and the noise was deafening. Clearly the regional council and the district council had pulled out the stops and gone for broke in an

effort to thrust Dereholm's fair day into the last decade of the twentieth century.

High-ups in the official marquee were making a start on assorted
alcohols and an abundant spread of victuals. There was a slight smell
of strawberries mixed in with the aroma of grass cut the day before.
McCulloch drove slowly away before he could be commandeered for
an unscheduled errand. There were enough drivers on hand. Idlers,
tourists, agricultural types on their annual day out made way for the
imposing vehicle. Some locals looked dismayed by the scale and
contemporaneity of what was happening. Women stood close to
stalls hawking traditional fare – home baking, crochet work, pickles,
potted plants – as if seeking security in the solaces of the past. Hand-
thrown pottery, second-hand LPs, potted herbs and paperbacks were
being touted by ageing hippies from a range of stalls set up under a
banner proclaiming the New Age. From 1960 McCulloch remembered a beer tent and half-a-dozen stalls run by the Women's Rural
Institute. In their saffron robes, following bells and a drum, chanting
disciples of Hare Krishna streamed across McCulloch's path. He was
too astonished to complain. Members of Militant Tendency and the
Socialist Workers' Party, shadowed by two policemen, carried placards saying BAN THE TORY POLL TAX.

After a few minutes on the open road, McCulloch stopped and
reversed into the entrance of a farm lane. From under his seat he
brought out Mrs Lambie's Thermos flask. He poured some of the
soup into the top that formed a cup. He blew on it several times
before taking his first sip. Viscous liquid rippled over chunks of
vegetables and barley. By God, it was good. He smacked his lips. The
windscreen steamed. It was the stuff to stick to a man's ribs. It
crossed his mind that it might be in his interest to return the flask
that evening. Truculence, deviousness and sheer force of personality
could see to it that he got off early enough. Fair Night usually kept
him busy until the early hours. High-placed drunks and their giggling or threatening wives had to be ferried home. A very few drinks
were all it took to make the convener magnanimous and offer the car
and its driver to persons whom McCulloch thought it beneath his
dignity to carry. There was a lot to be said for Mrs Lambie, and her
soup was but one accomplishment in her favour. She might be over
fifty, he thought, but she's trim. She's a widow and set up nicely with
a guest house. Jack Lambie must have left her comfortably off. He

had known her since childhood. As a former sergeant in the King's Own Scottish Borderers, McCulloch knew that his broad-shouldered dependability was an asset, but his bank account was a disgrace. He was also aware that he was charmless, fierce and lonely; he commanded fear more than respect, and respect more than affection. He finished his soup in a bad mood.

Sir Fergus Karrochan stood waiting at the door of his ancestral home as the Daimler crunched over the weedy gravel of the drive. All year round, the elderly baronet wore a bracken-brown tweed suit. Inherited field-glasses hung round the old man's neck; they'd seen service in two world wars, several colonial uprisings and countless race meetings.

'Aye, Colonel, sir, and how are you this fine day?'

'Tickety-boo, McCulloch. Tickety-boo.' There was no beating about the bush with Sir Fergus. His father had been an eccentric campaigner for Scottish Home Rule and addressed many an empty church hall on the subject. His principles had prevented Sir Fergus from attending an English public school. Anglicized mannerisms and other quirks of the Scottish gentry had been kept from Sir Fergus for as long as possible, and it had almost broken the old patriot's heart when his son opted for Sandhurst and a military career. Another consequence of his upbringing, however, was that Sir Fergus had a very low opinion of the political classes. As far as McCulloch was concerned, the old boy was in a class of his own.

'Get down to business,' the knight said, as they headed in the direction of Dereholm.

'Hutchinson, at eight to one, looks an interesting sort of a wager to me,' McCulloch offered.

'No local lads?'

'None wi' a snowball's chance in hell, sir.'

'An' what's appealin' about Hutchinson?'

'He's engaged to a Dereholm girl,' McCulloch said. 'Sentiment's not worth money. I'm thinking of the girl – Deirdre Craigie, eldest daughter of Fred Craigie, ironmonger. A hard man to please is Fred. His daughter takes after him. Young Mr Hutchinson will give full value.'

'Fifty quid on your man, then,' Sir Fergus said. He took a swig from a hip-flask. He passed it to the driver. McCulloch looked reluctant. 'Go on, ye daft big sergeant. Make life more excitin' for other folk on the road.'

McCulloch knocked back a gulp of antique whisky. Split-second heartburn soured his face, then an acrid pleasure warmed it into a broad smile. 'Would ye like me to perform the usual services, sir?'

'Aye, if ye please. Good God,' Sir Fergus said, wiping an eye, 'other than Old Mother Farquhar' – he referred to his housekeeper – 'I haven't spoken to a soul in a month. Good God Almighty!' he exclaimed as he caught his first sight of the fair. 'A big dipper! Next year they'll need a bigger park! Where do they come from?' A flock of sheep looked transfixed by the sight of the fair, or else they'd scented the whiff of a thousand hot-dogs.

'There are 550 entrants this year,' McCulloch said. 'They call it "fun-running". A great boost to the bed-and-breakfast trade. The place is chock-a-block wi' the brotherhood of the tracksuit and the nifty wee shoes in all shades and sizes. There are eighty-five women in the field, including eight grannies. The oldest man's seventy-four. I almost felt obliged to enter myself. By the way, sir, my instructions are to show you into the official marquee and attract the eye of the regional convener.'

'I've come for the race,' Sir Fergus protested. 'I said so when I accepted the invitation.'

'You're the oldest living winner of the race,' McCulloch pointed out. 'Waugh wants to show you off.' He guided the old man by the elbow towards the sound of tented chatter and the smell of food and drink.

'Not my natural habitat. Do me a favour, McCulloch, and take me to the wrong tent.'

'Like last year? I got a bloody good telling off.' Plates were piled on tables. Waitresses in black twin-sets and white aprons, bussed in from the main town of the region, were sliding fragments of salmon, chicken and salads into buckets. Anything that looked as if it hadn't been touched, McCulloch noticed, was being kept to one side to be divided up later as perks. When he turned round it was in time to see Sir Fergus's agile departure.

Boisterous locals had taken over the beer tent. A few tourists persisted at the long, animated bar. Sheer weight of numbers and the local accent were against them. McCulloch caught up with Sir Fergus, who would have nothing to do with the thought of going back to the official marquee. He guided him to the bar, where a space was cleared for service. It was hard to know why it was called the beer tent, for a large majority were drinking whisky, although, to be fair, they had a pint of beer in the other hand. McCulloch ordered and helped Sir Fergus carry his drinks to a table. Nearby the Egyptian and his small Bulgarian partner sat over their backgammon, watched by several men betting on the outcome. McCulloch put down a quickly finished drink. 'I'll be back for you when it's time for the start,' he said. He waved to Mrs Bell, who waved back from behind the bar, meaning that, as always, Sir Fergus was guaranteed a steady replenishment of drink without having to fight for it each time he drained his glass.

With a whoop, the Flying Fontanas undid their pyramid in a cascade of somersaults. McCulloch watched as other leaps followed this loudly applauded stunt. 'What do you make of it?' he asked an acquaintance.

'Ach, we used to do better than that on the way to school every mornin'.'

He looked in on the sheep-dog trials. 'Pretty fair, John?' he said to a policeman he knew.

'Pretty fair, Jock,' the constable said. 'But this is what I've been waiting for. These dogs are the bees' knees.' Two police dog-handlers entered the roped-off arena. A bearded man in a raincoat tied round the waist with rope took up position twenty yards from the dogs and their uniformed handlers. One of his arms was heavily bandaged with sacking. 'Watch this,' said the constable.

The handlers released the animal as the raggedy make-believe criminal in the false beard broke into a run. The dog raced to its target, leapt, and seized the unprotected forearm of the disguised policeman, who, like someone seriously cheated, howled and called for help. The handlers whistled and called and the crowd jeered. 'Pretty fair, John? Yon's the sort of beast that turns its nose up at lampposts, then pishes on yer leg.'

Old Etonian intonations buckled and droned in the electric woom of the loudspeaker system at the show-jumping arena. The jumping was a relatively recent addition to the pageantry of Dereholm's Fair Day. It reflected the prosperity of farmers, and also the demands of families with second houses in the area. Cottages had been thrown on the market as depopulation took its toll, some of it caused by cottage-hunters and their agents offering sums that local people couldn't refuse.

'Why does English-English aye sound like it's in pain?' a crony of McCulloch's asked him at the edge of the show-jumping ground. Several young men were ogling the legs and backsides of young women in jodhpurs.

'Once you've banked your first million,' McCulloch said to a young man beside him, 'you'd have a chance there.' He turned to his crony. 'They can't help it, Harry. Forked tongues.'

'White settlers,' Harry stated with distaste. 'Time's comin', Jock, when we'll jump the reservation an' burn these buggers out.'

'Calm down, Harry. Ye're a bit auld for pillagin'. Where's the honest man?'

'Big blue Merc. Over there,' he answered, pointing. 'Far end.'

Betting was strictly forbidden by the rules under which the race was now run. McCulloch pressed through the crowds, keeping his eyes open for signs of anyone looking as if they'd a job for him to do. He soon found the bookmaker's car. A couple of punters were leaving, having just placed their bets. If there was anything illegal about the activity, the police were turning a blind eye. McCulloch transacted his business through the open rear window. 'Fifty pounds on number 134, Hutchinson. Odds still eight to one?'

A man smelling of hair-cream took the money and furnished the paperwork.

'And a tenner for me on the same.'

The bookmaker interrupted his employee with a nudge. 'The larger bet's Sir Fergus's?' he asked.

'It is,' McCulloch said.

'Ah, yes. I thought I recognized you. Sir Fergus well, I hope?'

'In the pink.'

'Good. Good. Say "good luck" to him for me, and give him my best wishes,' the bookmaker said.

'I'll do that,' McCulloch said. To the assistant, he asked, 'Same place back here for the winnings?'

'We'll be here,' the man said with a grin.

'You'd bloody better be.'

Sir Fergus was where McCulloch left him, but engaged in an animatedly anti-political discussion with men of slurred speech. McCulloch's uniformed arrival dispersed them. 'Arrangements made,' he said. He showed the betting slips. 'Shall we, sir?' He offered his arm. Sir Fergus groaned as he rose to his feet. 'Are you up to it?'

'Tickety-boo, Sergeant McCulloch! Looking forward to it. In very good fettle.'

Runners were already filing into the starting funnel. They bobbed, trotted and chatted, thirty or forty abreast. McCulloch's appearance, and a few barked requests, worked wonders on the crowd of spectators in their way. He led Sir Fergus to the miniature stand erected by the Regional Works Department for the benefit of the convener and his invited guests.

'Not to worry, Colonel,' McCulloch whispered when he saw Sir Fergus's reaction to the stepped wooden edifice and the people already beginning to fill its spaces. 'Just you tell Waugh that you need me. Eyes not what they were. Feeling a bit feeble these days. Sergeant McCulloch's your necessary mainstay. Get the picture?'

'Will do, Sergeant.'

'Good man, Colonel.'

Several men stared wrathfully at McCulloch as he shepherded Sir Fergus into the stand. One of them was Mr Beattie. Another was the convener himself, who'd settled in nicely beside Ida St John. McCulloch pointed out to himself that no one would notice Sir Fergus had been drinking. Wine and whisky fumes were practically audible. Sensing it was the best tactic, McCulloch went out of his way to catch the convener's eye. It wasn't difficult – the convener was watching him with menacing tenacity. In no time flat the convener was shaking Sir Fergus's hand and introducing him to whoever was in range.

'Got to sit down soon,' Sir Fergus said. 'Old pins playing up. Eyes not what they were. Feeling a bit wonky. Need my major-domo here. Good man this McCulloch. Known him for years. One of my own, y'know. I'll sit down with the sergeant and he'll see I'm looked after. Won't you, McCulloch?' he said sharply.

'Certainly, sir,' McCulloch said, with a hint of self-sacrifice. 'All right with you, sir?' he asked the convener.

'Yes, perfectly appropriate,' Waugh – pronounced Woff – said with bad grace. The square, bald, immoderately perspiring convener made his way back to his place, telling everyone who Sir Fergus was. 'Won the Race of the Sword in 1939. Oldest surviving winner.'

Officials fidgeted and held the runners back, then ran out of the funnel as soon as they saw the starter mount his plinth. Sir Fergus bounced on his bench. 'Oh aye, sir, we mind that feeling well,' McCulloch said. 'Not that I ever did better than tenth place. But a blue bonnet's a blue bonnet. Or it used to be. Yon's a devalued beret if ye ask me. These days,' he added.

In his red blazer, white cap, white flannels and Athletic Association tie, the starter steadied himself on his dais, raised his pistol, and fired. A great cheer rose from the crowd. Much of this enthusiasm was directed at two officials in blazers and flannels who hadn't got out of the starting funnel in time and were carried along at a sprint for 300 yards before being able to drop out. As soon as the grandmothers trotted by – there was such a big cheer for them that one twisted her ankle and fell – the crowd dispersed, knowing that they'd more than twenty minutes to fill with food, drink and amusement before the leading runners fought it out at the finish.

Most of the convener's party high-tailed it back to their marquee. McCulloch, though, peered through Sir Fergus's binoculars at a point where the runners came back into view. 'Number 258?'

'Cassidy,' Sir Fergus read from his programme. 'Of Dublin.'

'A fancied entrant. In the lead. I recognize Berrisford.'

'Nottingham. Won last year.'

'The Kenyan. Also highly fancied.'

'Go on, take a tot.'

'Oh, aye, thank you, sir.'

'Hutchinson?'

'Not sure. Hard to make out. There's a big chasing pack.' He laid the field-glasses down. 'Won't see more until they show on that hill, sir.'

'That's a very good little hill, McCulloch. You see, there's a bigger hill comes after it. In my memory of the race, it's very important to get to the top of the second hill first. There's that blind corner, you see. And if you put a spurt on round it you can be yards ahead of the next man and that's bloody dispiriting if it's you. Believe me. I learned that the hard way. The man in the lead at the top of Wanno Hill's the man who bloody well *ought* to win it – if, that is, he's got the legs for the downhill and flat that follow. D'ye remember, McCulloch?'

'I mind it fine, sir.'

'Hutchinson?'

'Sir Fergus, we're banking on Fred Craigie's advice. He's a blue bonnet five times over. He knows that course like the feel o' his willie.'

'Ye know, Sergeant, I sometimes think ye're a bit hard on the here and now. Ye're like me. Yesterday feels like the best proposition. My old dad mixed up yesterday with the future. I was never sure if he was trying to turn the clock back or wind it forward at a great rate of hours.' McCulloch winced; he was embarrassed. 'But I very well remember that it was neither history nor politics which disappointed him. It was time. What he resented was that he was born when he was and not several hundred years before. It wasn't even England. That was what he blamed just about everything on – England. Of course, I hold no brief for the English – ghastly types on the whole, man, ghastly types. Good God, d'ye remember Aden? Eh? Bloody awful!'

'Cassidy still leads at the top of Wee Law. Berrisford. The Kenyan. Two or three others. Can't see . . . oh yes, Hutchinson. Definitely him. Twenty yards off the leaders. Looks good, sir,' McCulloch said.

'Splendid, splendid,' the old knight said wearily. 'Do ye agree wi' me? Ye're a bit stuck in the past, McCulloch . . .'

'Cassidy still there. Berrisford. The Kenyan. Oh, yes, if you ask me, Hutchinson's been told all about the course.'

'It isn't fair to the young. Men like us represent something that's dead and gone, Sergeant. It was a corpse before we even got to it, but we didn't know. You won't be able to see Wanno Hill from here,' Sir Fergus said, looking behind him and seeing empty benches and nothing else.

'Easily solved,' McCulloch said. 'We go to the top row. I'll just look over the back of the stand. I'll have a clear view of Wanno.'

McCulloch clambered up the steps. There was no one else there other than a woman who looked bored witless and was reading a book. Sir Fergus followed him and sat down beside McCulloch's boots while the driver peered over the top of the mini-stand. 'Grand view,' he said. 'They'll run from behind the timber in a couple of minutes.'

'You should take stock of yourself,' Sir Fergus said, landing a thump on McCulloch's leg. 'Driving's a proper job for you. You're very good at it. But you should try harder to keep up with the times, man. That's what it's all about. Time. *Time*,' he repeated emphatically. 'And I don't mean the bloody race. I mean life. I mean being alive and kicking and getting the best from breath. To be a happy man, McCulloch, you might even find it necessary to be selfish once in a while. Give up the idea of service. Stop being one of nature's sergeants.'

McCulloch stood with the glasses trained on the summit of the ridge known as Wanno Hill, but he'd been listening. Although perplexed, embarrassed, and feeling that Sir Fergus had become a distinct liability, he wondered if what the old soldier said might have a bearing on Mrs Lambie, her soup, her competence, her immaculate appearance, her guest house, its turnover. 'Thank ye kindly for these remarks, sir,' he said.

'Not at all. Not at all,' Sir Fergus said, batting McCulloch once more on the leg. 'You're a man who *needs* advice.'

McCulloch nearly choked. It was a long way from how he thought of himself.

Focusing the field-glasses was like clearing the fog of his existence. 'Oh . . . oh . . . oh, yes, Hutchinson's a good'un. Two, three, four, five . . . He's ahead!' He looked down at Sir Fergus, who, looking up, smiled. 'We'll see nothing else until they're over there.' McCulloch pointed west.

'I know,' the old man said quietly. 'I know. About four minutes before we'll see them. They'll come out of the fir trees on to the flat. You'll see them for half a minute. Then they'll be hidden by the cemetery wall. Then 800 yards on the flat to the tape. Same course since 1510. Or so they say. Legend becomes history and history legend. Or so it seems to me, McCulloch.'

The convener and his guests were beginning to return to the stand. Crowds drifted back to line the last few hundred yards of the course. Time-keepers, result-takers and other officials took up their positions.

'We seek you here, we seek you there, we seek you every-bloody-where!' Mr Beattie, the director of Leisure Services, Recreation and Arts, shouted at McCulloch. 'Where the hell have you *been*?'

'You didn't seek me here, then, Mr Beattie, for here's where I've been these past twenty minutes, looking after Sir Fergus, as agreed with the convener.'

'I've had scouts out looking for you for at least *an hour*!'

'Sorry about your scouts, Mr Beattie. White-stick cases, are they? I'm not exactly inconspicuous.'

'Sergeant McCulloch's been doing a grand job looking after me,' Sir Fergus said. 'What matters is the race, and he's been keeping me informed.'

'Oh, never mind! I'll get someone else,' Beattie said and walked away.

'See what we're up against? No disrespect, Colonel, but you can take the present and stuff it. There's more like him where he came from, believe me.'

'Nasty piece of work,' Sir Fergus said.

'Hutchinson! The Kenyan! Berrisford! God's holy socks, sir, but if he's still got the legs for it, we're in wi' a chance! Here, take a look.'

Sir Fergus stood up, and peered off the edge of the stand through his field-glasses until the leading runners were blanked out by the cemetery wall. 'But it's all to do still,' he said resignedly to McCulloch. He trained the binoculars at the point where the athletes would emerge. There was no containing the old boy when they did. He'd been betting on the Race of the Sword for decades and for the first time in dozens of passages of substantial wagers his man looked to be sprinting home. All along the finishing stretch, thickly lined with spectators, loud cheering rose in pitch as the English and Kenyan runners strained to beat each other and pass Hutchinson. McCulloch growled with sheer sentiment at the thought of a young Edinburgh man's love for a Dereholm girl surpassing whatever motives fired his nearest rivals. Form was overcome. The result struck McCulloch as a victory for local mischief. Hutchinson, the winner by only a few yards, was soon mobbed by back-slappers and hand-shakers. Columns of also-rans but high-scorers soon congested the finishing area. Young women in tracksuits handed out cans of drink manufac-tured by this year's sponsors. The film crew tried to be everywhere at once. First-aid volunteers deal it with cases of collapse. Stewards led the finished runners to the tents where their belongings were stowed.

Sir Fergus looked as jiggered as some of the athletes. 'Who are these people?' he asked McCulloch, who was helping him descend the steps of the stand.

'I understand they're what they call "radical feminists", sir. They want to know why there are only eighty-five women in the race.

Fancy that, for here's me wondering why so much as one was let near it. All right, now?'

'Be as good as new the minute I set eyes on fifty quid to win at eight to one, old boy.'

Most of the crowd had scattered to other sources of amusement, although there were groups of locals who waited to jeer plodding acquaintances. Others, women with small children, middle-aged and elderly men and women, hung on like camp followers anxious to discover if their loved ones had survived the battle. It was simpler in McCulloch's day, when forty was considered a big field. It was even easier in Sir Fergus's, when twenty or thirty local lads and men turned out and not a trained athlete among them.

The chauffeur deposited Sir Fergus back to his table in the beer tent, then set off to collect the winnings. Pastor Sam Casement preached fire, brimstone and eternal damnation outside the official marquee to a giggling Ida St John. Placards bearing the ireful commandments of the New Reformation were held up by docile disciples. The convener looked abject and angry. He was talking seriously to the chief constable, who, when he saw McCulloch, broke off the conversation, and told a policeman in civvies to follow him.

'Fine day, eh, Inspector?'

'Willie Brock.'

'Aye, Willie. Thought I'd take a leak.'

'Don't come the old soldier. I've to collect the boss's winnings and you know where.'

'Aye. Right. Hutchinson?'

'The CC went to school with Craigie the Nails. Beautiful wee love story. Don't you think so? Dereholm lass's beau wins the big race?'

There was a small crowd around the blue Merc parked discreetly now behind the vans, caravans and trucks of the traders and showmen. A law-abiding citizen – a stranger, obviously – had dragged a policeman to witness these disgraceful transactions. By the looks of it the constable wanted to know nothing about it. He wanted to know even less when he saw Willie Brock. Asked what he should do, Brock said to the constable, 'Take him away. The man's causing an obstruction. Any time now it'll be an affray.'

'It's good to have friends,' McCulloch said. 'Now, now, lads, make way there,' McCulloch said, jumping the queue. They knew him and let him in first. 'It breaks my heart,' McCulloch said to the hair-oiled assistant bookmaker, handing him his betting slips.

'Sir Fergus's lucky day,' the bookmaker said from the other side of the car. McCulloch noticed that the large leather bag from which the money was taken was attached to the bookmaker's wrist by a chain. The man struggled with indigestion. 'I made the big mistake of eating a pizza. Worst pizza in the world.'

'What's a pizza?' McCulloch asked. 'Come on, pay up the dosh before the rush starts.' Counting his money, he said to Brock, 'Will I wait and walk you home?'

'You'd better do that. I want a word.' Later, as they walked back, he continued: 'You're in the shit, Jock. I don't know what you've done to that half-wit Beattie, but he's after your scalp for his teepee, old son. Square-heid Waugh couldn't agree more, either. I overheard a conversation. You've blotted your copybook.'

'Not for the first time, Willie,' McCulloch said as a competitor from the caber-tossing competition dented the bell at the trial of strength. 'Ding-bloody-dong,' McCulloch said. 'Mind if we stop while I try this?'

McCulloch paid his fifty pence, took the hammer, and with a great shout brought it down on the big metal switch to the spring, which sent the weight flying into what was left of the bell. 'Feel better after that,' he said to Brock. He looked at the pink fluffy bear put into his hands as a prize, then gave it to a small girl whose mouth was fastened with candy-floss, who, otherwise, looked delighted, until her sister starting screaming because she didn't have one. 'God, give me strength,' McCulloch muttered. 'I canny win.'

When he got back to Memorial Park from taking Sir Fergus home, hordes of people were beginning to leave. Coaches and cars queued at the main public gate. Anyone on foot was likely to be local. But there were few of them. They would stay on among the tents and stalls, or leaning on ropes and barriers, or clamouring in the beer tent, until the last moment of entertainment had passed. Even then, small boys would hang on to watch the tents come down and the traders and showmen dismantle their booths and machinery. When it was late and dark, there would be drunks staggering and falling about, wondering what in God's name had happened to Saturday.

McCulloch drew up in front of the official marquee, got out, and stood in a pose that was natural to him, one in which massive propriety and disrespect were combined. His stomach rumbled. He was reminded of Helen Lambie's excellent broth. His reverie of soup and Mrs Lambie was interrupted by Mr Maguire, one of Mr Beattie's minions. 'Slight change of plan. You've to take Miss St John to the County Hotel.'

'Oh, really?'

'She wants to have a wee lie down and then get changed,' the regional employee confided proudly, meaning that he had been spoken to directly by the famous songster. Cheers went up from inside the beer tent next door. Mr Maguire, the District Librarian, winced. 'Oh, dear,' he said.

'Half an hour later than last year,' McCulloch said.

'What is?'

'That is,' he said, nodding towards the beer tent.

'I was appointed just under a year ago . . . '

'Miss St John on her own or with Mummy and fancy man?' McCulloch said like an interrogator.

'Oh, I don't know. I assume . . . '

'Never assume. Details are important in this job. Find out, sunshine.'

Several policemen forced their way into the beer tent. 'Oh, my goodness!' said Mr Maguire, running off.

More policemen burst into the beer tent. A few locals crawled out under the flaps and a policeman who attempted to follow them by the same route was hauled back by his ankles. 'What goes?' McCulloch asked a man who'd got out of the tent.

'A bad loser. That's what goes. Claims he should've won the bale-throwin' competition. Says that the man that won cheated. Says he used an unlawful arm action. Unlawful arm action?' the man said with consternation. 'Unlawful arm action? How can ye stick a hayfork in a bale, an' hoist it, wi' an "unlawful arm action"? Whit law?' he asked, scratching his head in disbelief.

'A very strange law,' McCulloch said. 'A law that states that when some men get pished they get poisonous an' need a fight. But as we all know, the law's an ass. Still, there's a lot who enjoy a good barney.'

McCulloch's next drive was a silent one, from his point of view. Inspector Brock's alert was at the front of his mind. In the back of the car were Convener Waugh, his wife (a lady not often allowed to appear in public), and Ida St John. The driver was on his best behaviour. When he dropped the convener and his wife at the town hall, he was smartly out of the car to open the door. It registered with McCulloch that the convener went out of his way to ignore him and that Mrs Waugh's gratitude for the slightest signs of courtesy rankled on her husband. The County Hotel was a hundred yards up the road on the other side. Ida St John's boyfriend was giving an interview to press and television on the front steps. 'My bags are still in your car,' she said accusingly to McCulloch.

'Of course they are,' he said. 'I hadn't forgotten, madam.' There was a delay between 'forgotten' and 'madam', the timing of which was second nature to McCulloch, but Ida St John was equally quick to hear it.

'There's something about your face,' she said.

'I beg your pardon, ma'am, I'm sure.'

'I'm talking about your fucking *smirk*.'

'Smirk, ma'am?'

'*Smirk!*'

McCulloch passed the bags belonging to Ida St John and her entourage to a porter who stood beside the manager of the hotel. 'It's just my face, ma'am. I always look like this when I'm enjoying myself,' McCulloch said with heavily loaded insincerity. He would have said more but she took the manager's arm and entered Dereholm's best – only – decent hotel, a place of solid, old-fashioned comfort, on at least three rooms of which no expense had been spared in the past couple of months.

Outside the beer tent those who hadn't been arrested looked on as those who had were bundled into police vans.

'All that trouble and expense to make a first-rate tourist attraction,' Mitchell, the district deputy finance executive, said sadly. 'And what happens? There's always a rough element to let the side down and give us a bad name.'

Tents were coming down. Trestle-tables, stalls, sideshows, were being dismantled, so many of them that McCulloch was reminded of how big Fair Day had grown.

'I hear you look after the town hall clock.'

'That's not all I do, I assure you. It was the same last year,' Mitchell said in his customary tones of modest lamentation.

'That's what I mean. It's the same every year. They should make it a proper event. Now *that* would be a real tourist draw.'

'You couldn't give me a run into town, could you?'

'I await Mr Beattie.'

'Oh. Well. I see. But, if you ask me, most of today's problems can be traced back to region sticking its nose in what should be a district matter pure and simple. And you're a district driver, Mr McCulloch.'

'There used to be a man who knew the town hall clock backwards,' McCulloch said. 'Aye. It kept accurate time, and its ding-dongs were mellow.'

'Alec Drummond retired years ago. Poor old soul,' Mitchell whimpered. 'Walks with a zimmer now. Hardly gets about at all.'

'It says ten on the face, but chimes nine,' McCulloch said.

'Don't think I'm too proud to take advice,' Mitchell said, close to pleading with the driver, 'but clocks are highly temperamental. They get used to people. It just hasn't got used to me yet. But it will. I'll see to that.'

'Ah, Mr Beattie. Mr Mitchell here would appreciate a lift.'

'You know perfectly well, Mitchell, that assistant officers don't have access to number one vehicles today. Addresses and directions once we're mobile,' he said curtly to the driver, holding a door open as dignitaries slid into the rear.

McCulloch pointed to a district council van which drew up to collect the Flying Fontanas, after negotiating a course between workmen gathering litter and throwing black plastic refuse bags into the grinding vehicles of the Environmental Health Department. 'He'll take you,' he said to Mitchell, 'if ye' can put up wi' the smell o' sweat, embrocation, an' God knows what else, including backgammon.'

It was 8.30 before McCulloch parked the Daimler behind the town hall beside the other official cars. Instead of joining his fellow drivers in a room in the basement, he sat down in Mr Anster's glassed-off porter's office with a view of the main door, the impressive hall and the broad Victorian sweep of the staircase. At one time the Dereholm Burgh Library had been on the ground floor. Inset in alcoves, their marble shoes five feet from the ground, were Robert Burns, Sir Walter Scott, Nisbet MacLellan Neill (the 'Dereholm Poet') and William Shakespeare. 'It could've been worse,' he said, inspecting his packet of sandwiches. 'Much worse.'

'You won't hear me complaining,' Mr Anster said.

'We most certainly will not,' McCulloch said. 'You? Complain? You're the man who said the bloody poll tax was the best thing since sliced bread.'

'Wages at time-and-a-half till six. Then double time till midnight. Then triple time after! Oh no, I'm not complaining. That's David Loudon. See? An' him nearly twenty minutes late.'

'Who?'

'Prospective SNP candidate.'

'Should be ashamed to show his face.'

'Do you vote Nationalist?' Anster asked anxiously.

'I don't vote for anybody. I don't vote full stop, Mr Anster. It's not that I'm without convictions. But I've seen too many politicians at close range for the big X not to look like an offence to the humble pencil. But I'm worried. In 1922 the librarian of this burgh wrote a book about the Dereholm foot-race, a copy of which happens to be a proud possession of mine. It's a book full of lore, legend and sheer information. That statue of the immortal Robert Burns has just put me in mind of the issue. For I've heard that the present district librarian is of a mind to revise the volume and bring it up to date. Now that would be a very handy and useful undertaking, I agree. On the other hand, Mr Anster, it can hardly pass without comment that the district librarian is a native of Manchester and bloody speaks like it. All right, perhaps that doesn't matter as much as I think it does. But the man's a pasty-faced physical nonentity whose only athletic accomplishment is the occasional bowel movement. Mr Anster, I saw him this afternoon. He didn't so much as grace the event with half an eye. What does the Race of the Sword mean to a man like that? I'll tell you in crisp, plain words. Damn all! Or per- haps the chance of recommending himself to his superiors.'

'It's a lovely piece of ham is this, but I wish I'd some mustard.'

'Long before TV personalities, hi-fi stereo systems, and the internal combustion engine, Englishmen never showed themselves round here unless armed to the teeth and intent on nasty business. In those days the race counted for something. It was local. Yes, thank you, I'll join you in a small refreshment,' McCulloch said, seeing cans of beer on Mr Anster's table and helping himself while the porter choked back an instinctive complaint. 'And now what? I'll tell you.' The noise of an opening can caught the ear of a policeman guarding the foot of the big staircase. 'Dereholm an' just about every place like it's soiled itself stupid in an effort to get on the tourist map. We're not ourselves any longer. Whoever the hell we were, we're somebody else from now on. Change? Indeed, change, Mr Anster. We've been changed witless. A man was talking to me today on the subject of time. I know what time I want. Seventeen-hundred-and-bloody-six. Turn the bloody clock back!'

Anster didn't like McCulloch's conversation. He didn't like McCulloch. 'I just don't understand you, Jock. Surely a celebrity like that must be the high point of your driving year?'

'If you're referring to Ida St John, then, dear Christ, Anster, ye haveny been listenin' tae a word I've been sayin', ye foolish wee lickspittle.' The porter backed involuntarily away. 'Anster, the high point of my year was a flask of broth made by Mrs Helen Lambie.'

'The convener's sister?'

'A very fine broth. Very fine. Excellent. I couldn't praise that woman's soup too highly. And her house is a treat, even littered up at present as it is with sweaty pink tights belonging to eight tumblers who've the cheek to call themselves the *Six* Flying Fontanas.'

'Did you see the menu? Wonderful,' Anster said. 'Smoked salmon. Venison . . . '

'Would that, by any chance, be the official result?' McCulloch directed his eyes at what looked like a typed list lying on the porter's table.

'Computerized print-out,' Anster said with what sounded like pride in the technological advances of the human species.

McCulloch lifted it and the sheets unfolded into a length of paper that stretched from his raised hand to the floor. 'Dear God,' he said angrily. 'It's like a bloody phone book.' Reading down the list he couldn't help but gag when he saw that the first woman to cross the finishing line covered the course faster than he had when he won his blue bonnet back in 1960. Her time was almost a minute faster than Sir Fergus Karrochan's when he won the race in 1939. 'No trouble, I hope, with the radical feminists?'

'Who's worried about them, when we've marksmen on the roof?' Anster said. 'Och, mustard *makes* a ham sandwich.' He looked sadly at the bread in his hand.

'Armed?'

'Security precautions.'

'Security precautions?'

'The Irish.'

'The Irish!' McCulloch pondered, aghast on his own exclamation. 'See what I mean? The English were aye bad enough, but now we've marksmen on the roof because o' the Irish!'

'There's a general here, an' four other high-rankin' officers . . .'

A round of applause indicated that speeches were being made in the ballroom. After a short silence the hand-clapping started up again, accompanied by cheers and a few zealous whistles.

'Oh, it's the presentation,' Anster said reverentially. 'The sword . . .'

'I'd guessed that, ye daft doorman.'

Lesser rounds of applause described the subsequent awards, blue bonnets and the scrolls that went with them. 'If anybody's looking for me, Anster, I'll be in the motor out front. I'll bring the old dame round. Oh, and by the way,' he said from the door of the porter's glass booth, 'it's not just a sword nowadays. There's also a substantial sum. Private room, fat envelope, convener's compliments and congratulations, and very under-the-counter.'

Baronial, floodlit, and solid with the authority of years, the town hall's architecture looked as if it resisted the festive lighting and bunting in which it had been dressed up. Flags strung across the street and along its length from one municipal lamppost to the next made an impression on the atmosphere of economic decline, but not a big one. McCulloch sat in the car and let the town's annual bout of street-life pass before him. Young men, already well-primed, staggered in the direction of the Fair Dance – an event quite different from the after-dinner ball about to commence in the town hall. Young women and assorted tourists were already there, wondering when the young men of the town would turn up. Those staffing the bar readied themselves for the rush that would follow the unhurried, reasonable orders they were already serving. McCulloch could visualize it. As groups of men passed the car, and groups of women, he grinned at the thought of the big rounds that would soon be shouted at the bar staff. 'Eight pintsa heavy, four lager an' three double vodkas an' Coke! Sorry! *Nine* pintsa heavy, *five* lager, an' *four* double vodkas an' Coke!' If nothing else, no outsider would find it possible to accuse them of meanness. Unstinting alcoholic generosity would be the order of the night.

At 10.30 Mr Anster brought McCulloch his first passengers. They were two ancient widowers. Former provosts of the burgh, they lived in a home for the elderly on the edge of town. Both were the worse for wear, speechless, half-asleep and slack-jawed. It was a run which did not detain McCulloch for long.

He was 200 yards from the town hall on his return when the Daimler began to cough. One tremor followed another. Mechanical spasms and unnatural vibrations turned quickly into a state of near-immobile paroxysm. Worse, there were people on the streets watching this sub-performance of expensive engineering. Nothing delights pedestrians, catchers of buses, owners of small third-hand vehicles, so much as the sight and sounds of an exclusive automobile in its death-throes or a fit of the staggers. McCulloch could feel his comfortable, uniformed, municipal prestige plummet close to the depths of humiliation and unemployment. There was nothing for it but get out and push. A dozen bystanders cheered and rushed to help.

Deflated by this disappointing experience, McCulloch flopped into a chair in Mr Anster's booth and loosened his black tie and the neck of his white shirt. 'It's a mite early for taking your ease,' the porter said.

'Daimler's buggered,' the driver said passionately.

'You've a job in ten minutes.'

'Other cars, other drivers,' McCulloch said.

'You'd better report it right away,' Anster said, limping across his office, his tone expressing his fear of dire consequences.

Conversational overspill from the ball now in high progress to the strangulated tempos of an all-purpose Scottish country dance band dotted the staircase and the spacious landings beneath gloomy portraits of Victorian provosts. McCulloch made his way through clusters of gowns and tuxedos, groups of deep-dyed Lowlanders in Highland evening wear, readjusting his collar and tie. They parted to allow his uniformed bulk and misanthropic scowl to pass without so much as an excuse-me or I-beg-your-pardon crossing his lips. It took several enquiries before he found Mr Beattie at a crowded table where a waitress was adding more glasses to a surface already crowded with winking liquids.

'What is it, McCulloch?'

'The district council's Daimler, Mr Beattie, is on the blink.'

'Oh, for God's sake! Have you any idea of the inconvenience? . . .'

'Your regional drivers can handle it. Mr Anster'll just have to rejig his timetables.'

'Can't you repair it?'

'Not a hope. It'll no' go. It's a very old car. If you ask me, it's had its day.'

'If it was up to me, McCulloch, I'd have you sacked on the spot. Dismissed. Do you understand me? Sacked, forthwith. Get out of my sight!' Beattie whispered venomously, half-rising from his chair in a display of executive wrath. 'Out!'

McCulloch crossed the ethnic revelry of the dance-floor with booted strides. At the door he looked back on the processional athleticism of a hundred couples engaged in the Gay Gordons. A hundred others were busily occupied at their tables with elbow-bending, chin-wagging and laughter. Waiters and waitresses were noting and delivering orders as if under instructions to take no prisoners.

'There's a Euro-MP,' McCulloch said to Anster, 'who can't stand up, and the Flying Fontanas are living up to their name. Drink,' he said, 'is being poured like it gets made illegal at dawn.' Cheers and whistles interrupted him. 'That'll be Ida St John. It looked as if she'd been persuaded to give them a song. The band had their cowboy hats handy. They're ready to slip into country 'n' western mode.' By the time he'd said Ida St John the porter was rushing at a limping sprint for the stairs. 'Here's me ready to puke an ' you can't wait to hear the overpaid bitch! You've let me down, Anster!' Members of the constabulary were dashing upstairs too, as if it were something they could tell their grandchildren.

McCulloch lifted Anster's telephone and dialled. 'Mrs Lambie? Jock McCulloch here . . . Helen. Yes. Thank you. I know it's late, but I thought I should tell you that the acrobats might be quite some time yet before they turn up on your doorstep . . . Yes, a hectic day, but over now for yours truly. District council car's broken down. I thought I'd pop round with your Thermos. If that's all right . . . Oh, yes, delicious! Best broth I've tasted in a long time. No, there's no telling when it'll be over . . . Well, of course, if it would save you sitting up on your own . . .'

McCulloch set off for Mrs Lambie's guest house bearing a plastic bag containing the Thermos flask and a few personal possessions he had been in the habit of keeping in the Daimler. Drunk women argued with drunk men. Sober women argued with drunk men. Sober men argued with drunk women. A few boozed individuals were probably still trying to get home from the excesses of the beer tent earlier in the day. Lights spilled, throbbed and changed colour outside the recently built community leisure centre, where the dance that anyone could go to was being held. From the other side of the street policemen in a patrol car kept a lazy eye on a group of young people gathered there.

Pubs could remain open on Fair Night until two in the morning. This magnanimous extension of legal drinking hours was exploited for all it was worth by those middle-aged and over for whom the decibels of the groups playing at the dance were an abomination. Many stood drinking and talking on the pavements. Pastor Sam Casement and his righteous followers marched in front of the out-doors drinkers broadcasting the good news that they were imbibing sinful alcohol dangerously close to the Sabbath. Radical feminists took issue with the pastor and his evangelical die-hards, but by now they were in too good a humour to argue with their usual ferocity. Local tactics were to buy them all a drink and agree with everything they said. Besides, it wasn't long since they'd just kicked the shit out of several young men from the Militant Tendency whose line of erotic discourse struck them as lamentably misogynistic. As he reached the King James IV McCulloch was hailed by men who knew him.

'Settle an argument, Jock,' Company Sergeant-Major Guthrie said. 'Now, am I right? No one knows what happened to the original sword . . .'

'That's a stupid piece of cutlery that means nothing . . .'

'But, Jock, the original sword . . . Long gone. Am I right?'

'Long gone,' McCulloch said.

'He's read the book,' Wally Guthrie said to a tourist. 'Jock, what happened to it?'

'It's at the bottom of the Tweed or the Till. Who knows? "Says Tweed to Till," ' McCulloch recited,

> 'What gars ye rin sae still?
> Says Twill to Tweed,
> Though ye rin wi' speed

An I rin slaw,
For ae man that ye droun
I droun twa.'

'Battle of Flodden,' McCulloch explained. 'But there was a perfect replica after that. It went to America in 1770 when the man who had it in safekeeping emigrated and took the sword with him.'

'Where's the motor, Jock?'

'Off the road. Broken, diseased, senile, or pissed off – I don't give a piddle in the tinker's bucket. It's fed up to the back teeth wi' pop stars, politicians, uppish top brass, fat conveners an' their snake-faced womenfolk.'

'Then have a drink, Jock!'

'No, thank you.'

'Aw, come on!'

'Not tonight, gentlemen.'

All was quiet on Helen Lambie's leafy street where large houses amounted to a stone statement of the middle-class prosperity of a former age. Some houses were in darkness. A few residents would be at the town hall's Fair Night ball. Others were either tucked up for the night or watching TV behind drawn curtains. As a boy McCulloch had delivered newspapers there. With a twelve-year-old's perceptiveness it had registered on him that it was a part of town very different from where he lived. In those days a guest house like Mrs Lambie's would have been out of the question. It would have contradicted the street's estimate of its respectability. Now, too, several houses had been divided into apartments for those who felt it necessary to live in that part of town but couldn't afford it. At any rate, it was the first time he'd paid a social call in that district of Dereholm. He could still remember delivering newspapers in all weathers at seven in the morning.

He rang the bell, a satisfyingly old-fashioned fitting which had to be pulled hard until the caller heard a brassy resonance from within. Mrs Lambie was dressed in a kimono of which the dominant colour was green. 'Thank goodness it's you, Jock. I don't know what I'd have done . . .'

At the far end of the hall, at the foot of the stairs, an ageing Egyptian tumbler attempted to guide his friend, the dwarfish Bulgarian, over the first step. For the umpteenth time both collapsed together and fell in a giggling heap.

'Pour souls,' Mrs Lambie said. 'They weren't invited, there being eight of them, but billed as six. But I don't think they really wanted to go anyway.'

'Compulsive backgammon players,' McCulloch said. 'And very, very drunk.'

'Funny sort of drink,' she said. 'Smells like sweeties. They put water in it and it goes like milk.'

'That'll be ouzo, or raki,' McCulloch said with man-of-the-world expertise. 'A potent brew. Not much on offer in these parts. They must've brought it with them. Now, now, Abdhul, no trouble, please,' he said, lifting the Egyptian by the scruff of his neck, his other hand on the Bulgarian's. 'Which rooms, Helen?'

'End of the upstairs hall, Jock, last door on the left.'

McCulloch dragged the unsteady duo up the carpeted stairs. 'Oh, careful, Jock!' Mrs Lambie said when McCulloch raised the Bulgarian two feet off a step to hoist that semi-conscious lightweight into upwards and forwards motion.

'Leave it to me, Helen,' he said firmly.

'I phoned the town hall. They said just the six and no management or hangers-on. They were very strict. I said my brother would . . .'

'Just you leave it to me.' McCulloch tugged and heaved them to the top of the stairs as Mrs Lambie followed. She went ahead and opened a bedroom door. 'Now then, one at a time, for comfort's sake,' McCulloch said. The Egyptian uttered several rapid, slurred sentences in a language strange to McCulloch. 'That's enough of that, m'lad,' the driver said, leading him to fall face down on his bed. He went back for the small Bulgarian, lifted him into his arms, and plonked him on the bed next to his friend. 'That's enough tric-trac for one night,' McCulloch said to the prostrate former acrobats. 'And don't pee the bed. I'd leave the bathroom door open and the light on if I were you,' he said to Mrs Lambie.

'Oh!'

'Haven't seen one of these in years, Helen,' McCulloch said as she produced a chamber pot from a drawer in a sideboard, 'but a very wise precaution.'

'Shouldn't you put them into their pyjamas, Jock?'

'If it's not against their religion, it's certainly against mine,' he said. 'We'll leave them to stew. Sleeping beauties,' he said as he closed the door on them. 'When the other six'll turn up's anybody's guess,' he said as they went downstairs to Mrs Lambie's part of the house on the ground floor. 'They were hard at it when I left. Nor can I imagine that they'll be sober. Alcohol was being lashed around as if it cost a penny a bottle. You know, Helen,' he said, pulling off his driver's gloves, 'I seem to have been in one uniform or another for most of my life. Now I've passed my half-century I think I deserve full civilian status.' He sat down in the armchair which Mrs Lambie pointed to. 'A busy day. A very busy day,' he said.

'Then here's a tonic for it,' she sat, pouring whisky. 'Water?'

'Oh, plenty of water,' he said, seeing there was plenty of whisky in the tumbler as well. 'The district motor's broken down. Quite possibly a write-off,' he said. 'I ought to tell you – I'm in bad odour with my employers, Helen. On Monday morning I'll be handing in my notice.'

'Oh, but I'm sure my brother could sort things out, if I asked him . . .'

'No, you don't understand. Me and the convener don't hit it off. We never have done. We go back too far, you see. It's a tricky thing to explain. How can I put it?' He thought for a moment. 'It's like this. We were at the school together. He's a couple of years older, but we mind each other too well. And he's convener of the regional council, and I'm the driver of the district council's official car. Twenty-seven years as a soldier was no waste of my life, but neither is the rank of sergeant a great achievement. I held that rank for many years. My efforts to obtain a commission and better my career always came to nothing. I know why. As Sir Fergus Karrochan said to me this afternoon, I'm one of nature's sergeants. I was type-cast by the age of twenty-five, and I did it myself. Top soldier. I made myself indispensable to a line of junior officers who were inept when they came to me at first but worthy of their uniforms when they left to move a rung up the ladder. I'm sorry. I'm being indiscreet and personal. It's been a hard day.' He drank half the contents of his tumbler in a single swill. 'Ach,' he sighed, 'that's better.'

'But what'll you do, Jock?'

'I haven't a clue, Helen. Everything that comes to mind just looks demeaning. You must admit, I'm not qualified for much else other than commissionaire outside the front door of a big city hotel, or night watchman . . . When you were young, Helen, you never said "Woff", and neither did he . . .'

'I still don't. He thinks it sounds better.'

McCulloch drained his glass and she rushed to refill it. The clock in the hall chimed midnight. 'Survivors are chucked out come two in the morning. Drunks tactfully shepherded off the premises before then if they start to get embarrassing. It could be a long wait, so go easy on the hard stuff.'

'When you came home on your first leave, in your uniform . . . I don't suppose you remember?'

'Oh, I remember my first leave, quite clearly.'

'You'd run in the race . . .'

'Tenth place, just enough for a blue bonnet. I was never a hot shot at the running.'

'Aye, well, you gave me a dance that night, and I liked it.'

'I did?'

'Then you went off and got drunk.'

'Did I?'

'So your memory's not as good as you think, Jock McCulloch.' There was a distant accusation in her voice. 'The man I married didn't take to drink till he was very nearly forty. He'd lived for his business. God knows, I couldn't say he lived for me.' She sipped her drink.

'Are you saying something along the lines of being sweet on me when we were young?' McCulloch asked with an unsureness that broke through his self-confident manner.

'And you're telling me you didn't have an inkling?'

He was uncomfortable, confused, and nervous. Either his life was about to change for the better, or, were it too late now, for the worse. 'You know, I've never been a great man for the booze. I was teased for it in the sergeants' mess. So it's ironic that I should have taken too much that night over thirty years ago. I was full of my own swank and swagger that night.'

'Blind and daft as well, then,' she said sharply, 'because I gave you the glad eye like a vamp on heat.'

'Spot on. Blind and daft. That's me when it comes to women.'

'You didn't meet *anyone*?'

'Can't say that I did, Helen. Can't say that I did.' He looked at her looking at him. 'I could say that there was you when we were young, but it wouldn't be truthful. My mind was full of one idea, to get out of Dereholm and away from my folks and everything else. I thought I'd come back a colonel at the very least, and retire in style. It would be a damn lie if I said I gave you more than a minute's thought, Helen. But you've been on my mind all day. That *is* true. If you like,' he said, getting to his feet, 'I can sit next door and wait for the Fontanas . . .'

'Sit down, for heaven's sake!'

He fell back into his chair. 'I thought you'd maybe had about enough of my stupidity . . .'

'I wouldn't be running a guest house if I'd been left high and dry. It's hard work, Jock, but a livelihood.' Seeing the puzzlement on his face, she said, 'Marriage. It's not too late. You've been on *my* mind.'

'Since this morning?' he asked, meaning the suddenness of what was being proposed. 'Is it a leap year?'

'Considerably longer.'

'Your brother'll throw a fit.'

'Woff-woff to him, then.'

McCulloch got up and poured himself a drink at the sideboard. 'Don't do *that* to me,' she said.

'I need it for my nerves,' he said. 'They're shot all to hell.'

'What are you? A confirmed bachelor, or a daft, shy man?'

'Right now I'm hardly sure of *who* I am, Helen.'

'Is it that bad?'

'I think I'm very happy, but I don't know how to say it. I don't know what to say.'

'Come over here,' she said, standing up to meet him.

There was a loud thud on the ceiling. 'An old Flying Fontana, no longer capable of flight,' McCulloch said looking up at the ceiling.

'The big fat one.'

'We wouldn't have heard the wee man. Shall I go and take a look?'

'Maybe you'd better,' she said.

He was on the stairs when the doorbell rang. 'Must be obnoxious to have been sent home this long before two,' he said to Mrs Lambie in the hall.

A young female Fontana stood on the doorstep holding the hand of a young man whom McCulloch didn't know. As soon as he'd opened the door a car drew off. McCulloch rested the palm of his hand on the young man's chest, guiding the young lady inside with the other. 'But I'm asked in for a drink,' the young man complained.

'Not in this house,' McCulloch said morally, and closed the heavy front door. He turned round to see the young woman swaying on stockinged feet holding her shoes. She turned round expecting to see the young man. He not being present, other than as fists hammering on the front door, she threw a shoe at McCulloch to the accompaniment of a broadside of bad language which, being in Italian, was lost on McCulloch and his fiancée of a few minutes.

'Oh, I think we're in for a night of it,' Mrs Lambie said. 'Black coffee, then off to your bed,' she said to the acrobat. The doorbell rang again, followed by urgent battering.

'But the car's gone!' the young man shouted.

'Walk it!'

'I'm asked in!'

McCulloch showed him his fist.

'Raffaella! We'll go somewhere else!' the young man called. 'Raffaella!'

'The girl's past it. You're a bit blown yourself, son.'

'Then call a taxi.' McCulloch grinned at this demand. 'I said, call a taxi!' the young man repeated, losing his step for an instant, and resteadying himself.

'A taxi? On Fair Night?'

'Phone the district council offices then!' the young man insisted.

'How about the police station?'

'Call a car!'

'Giddy-up, son. Tally-ho,' McCulloch said with whispered toxicity, then closed the door with a slam that sent the young man into a tuxedoed reel.

The young Fontana sat slumped with her head on the kitchen table. 'A fur coat, in this weather,' Mrs Lambie said. 'No wonder she passed out.'

McCulloch lifted the unconscious gymnast in his arms, recoiling from the aroma of liquor. 'Lead the way, Helen.'

'One down, five to go,' they said in the sitting room. They held each other for a moment.

'So,' McCulloch said. 'Will you marry me?'

'I thought it was good as arranged.'

'That's what I thought, too, but I've been finding it hard to believe.

I'm not in two minds. I'm just a bit jittery about the changes involved. To say nothing of Arbourlie Street, your house, the guest house, and you being a catch, and me being an unemployed driver. Tongues will wag.'

'When did tongues do anything else?'

'I bring you very little other than a sergeant's pension and many years of being incapable of suffering fools gladly. And I know it. I'm a fair way to being preposterous. For your sake, I recommend that we don't rush this.'

Car doors slammed in the narrow drive. 'Brace yourself, Jock. That'll be more of them.'

Grateful for the interruption, and extremely annoyed by it, McCulloch strode to the front door as one o'clock chimed on the wag-at-the-wa' clock in the hall. Clearly, the convener was on the crest of alcoholic merriment. He was supported by a regional driver. It was obvious, too, that he was as unpleasantly surprised by McCulloch's presence as McCulloch was by Waugh's. Whose shock was the greater? It was hard to tell.

'You'd better step inside,' McCulloch said hesitantly.

'I think I'd better,' the convener answered.

'Helen, it's your brother!' McCulloch called, but she was already in the hall.

'Maggie went home over an hour ago,' the convener said to his sister, shaking off his driver's arm in favour of independent unsteadiness. 'I'm on my way to a party at Donald Beattie's . . .'

'The convener would like the bathroom,' the driver said.

'I'm perfectly capable of asking for the bathroom under my own steam!' Waugh protested as he strode up the hall to where he knew one was. 'I'll see you in a minute,' he said threateningly to McCulloch.

'Caught short. All that hand-shaking and cheerie-bying must've put it out of his mind,' the driver explained. 'They're saying things about you, Jock.'

'My notice goes in first thing on Monday morning.'

'It's been a lovely day for it,' the driver said. 'Still going strong at the town hall when we left. Private party at Mr Beattie's for the inner sanctum.'

'Seen any flying Fontanas?' Mrs Lambie asked.

'Beg your pardon?'

'Acrobats,' McCulloch said. 'Swarthy types. Probably plastered, if their pals are anything to go by.'

On his irate march back from the bathroom Convener Waugh – pronounced Woff – knocked over a small table and a pot-plant. He looked stupidly at the mess for a few seconds. 'What are *you* doing here, then?' he shouted to McCulloch from one end of the hall to the other.

'Helping your sister put drunk acrobats to bed,' McCulloch said. 'And I think you'd better zip up your fly, Mr Waugh,' he added – pronounced Wawch.

'Oh.'

'Forbes, Jock McCulloch is my fiancé.'

It took a moment to sink in.

'What are you gloatin' at?' McCulloch rasped at the regional driver.

'Nothing, Jock.' But the gloat on the driver's face had by now settled into a fixed and exaggerated Lowland anticipation of a first-rate anecdote.

'Sis, did I hear you right? Have you any idea who you're getting involved with? What more can I say?' the convener said, like a broken man. 'He's . . . he's . . . he's *Jock McCulloch*, for God's sake! It's an *affront*! Never, never, in . . .' Legs spaced apart, arms raised slightly above waist level, dribble on the knee of one trouser leg, taking a deep breath, the convener was about to launch himself into automatic eloquence. 'Never, never, have I encountered . . . a minor employee . . . whose attitude, whose in-sub-ord-in-ation' – he was well rehearsed in the art of de-slurring long words when inebriated; all that was needed was slow, emphatic speech, keeping a steady eye on the listeners – 'whose in-so-lence, makes him un-pop-ul-ar, with every-one he comes into con-tact *with*.' Here the arms went up in a big, oratorical body-gesture.

'He's very popular with *me*.' The convener's sister picked up what was left of the pot and its plant. 'You were always the same, Forbes. Wherever you go you leave a mess for somebody else to clear up.'

McCulloch stood throughout Waugh's speech in silence, his head half-bowed, holding the inner front door open.

'Airs and graces of a field marshal, but he's a humble show-fer, a show-ferr, out of a job!' the convener yelled. 'Look, I can't stand here and argue the toss. Do you know who's waiting in the car? Ida St

John, that's who. None other. To whom *he*'s been rude. He's been rude to me. He's been in-so-lent to just about *everybody*! You'll keep this bloody well under wraps,' Waugh said to his driver, poking him in his uniformed chest, 'or I'll have your guts for garters. You,' he said to McCulloch at the door, 'you haven't heard the last of it.'

'Waugh, Woff, Wiff, Waff, Wuff, Weff, whatever you call yourself, have you any Flying Flaming Fontanas out there? Are they, do you know, on the way to Beattie's? If they are, then tell them to bide there until the morning, because this door is being shut, closed and locked.'

'Don't you speak to me like that!'

'Clear off!'

'Did you hear that?'

'He speaks for me, too. Go away, Forbes,' Mrs Lambie said.

McCulloch closed one door and then the other. They listened to car doors shut and the car draw away. 'Should we give them another hour?'

'If not, then they might break the door down.'

'I'd spare keys, but people walked off with them, so I'd the locks changed.'

'Very prudential and correct,' McCulloch said. 'I'll be happy to sit up. When they're all accounted for I'll doze on the sitting room couch. But you should get to your bed.' She looked at him closely. 'I've some thinking to do. One or two matters could do with a spot of pondering.' They held on to each other in the hall and McCulloch glimpsed their lonely partnership reflected in the big mirror where, that morning, he'd seen himself full-length in uniformed perfection. 'I think it's time to call it a day,' he said into her ear. 'Just one more interruption and I don't think I could be responsible.'

'There's some of that soup left, if you're peckish.'

'Oh? That would be wonderful!'

The Political Piano

The countryside of the Scottish Borders was wearing its winter tweeds. Here and there, on the pastures, patches of unmelted snow, decorated with frost, formed their crusty tiaras on clumps of rough grass. Snowdrops grew along the line of the rusted iron fence that escorted the long drive to the house of Alois Hanka, the Czechoslovak composer, who had settled there with his wife.

On the hills, snow was impressively pure against a blue sky. To meditate on that beautiful house, its pleasing proportions, and on the farms dotted over the lower slopes of the hills, was to think of an older but visually benign civilization at peace in a benevolent wilderness.

As they sat in their parked car, looking at the countryside, and at Hanka's house, Lucy Williams said, 'Is it Georgian? I've never been in Scotland before. Is there such a thing as "Scottish Georgian?" '

'Something like that,' Paul Salmon said. He heard what Lucy said without taking it in. His thoughts were turning over the practical opportunities which the delightful house and its pastoral setting offered him. 'It really makes its point.' He smiled with satisfaction. 'No need to say very much on the soundtrack about a house like that. Thirty seconds of careful planning and all anybody'd think about is money, and more money. And how did Hanka get it? Nervous?' he asked Lucy Williams.

'Very,' she said, although Paul Salmon failed to notice that her single, spoken word expressed her distrust of him.

Paul Salmon made television profiles of celebrities in the arts. At one time he had been a senior producer on the staff of a television company. Now he was freelance, successful, and busy.

Former associates and acquaintances of Hanka's, a few in London, two or three in New York, some in Los Angeles, others in Paris, Geneva and Rome, had suggested to Salmon that the composer was hardly likely to co-operate in the making of Salmon's film. Confidence, which Salmon possessed the way other people have degrees and qualifications, had led him to start work on the film without

Hanka's participation. A contract had been signed with a television company which was attracted by what was already known of Hanka's controversial past. Money had been spent on travel and research.

A bigger budget was almost guaranteed now that Hanka had surprised Salmon by agreeing to see him, expressing in his reply to Salmon's letter a willingness to help, mentioning old photographs and manuscripts. For the film-maker, it was a scoop. For years, the reclusive composer had refused to see journalists, interviewers and broadcasters, and now he was opening his front door.

'Even if he turns nasty, there's nothing he can do to stop me filming the outside of the house,' Salmon said to his girlfriend as they approached the front of Hanka's home. 'It says so much!'

'You could make a picture say anything,' Lucy Williams said derisively.

'So? I'm a film-maker!'

Alois Hanka was affable and welcoming. He was a small, round man in his mid-seventies. He looked to be in excellent health; his skin was unwrinkled, smooth, tight and plump. His eyes were a clear blue-grey and he did not wear spectacles. His hair, though, was thin and white. He wore a tweed suit, the colours of which imitated the countryside. A waistcoat drew attention to his corpulence. For a man of his years and size – he was five foot four and fat – he appeared unusually elegant, fastidiously dressed and well.

'I once met a cousin of yours,' Hanka said to Salmon, after he had shown the couple into a sitting room, introduced them to Mrs Hanka, and exchanged courtesies about the comfort of their long drive.

'A cousin of *mine*?' Salmon was seriously surprised.

'Mousse. Salmon Mousse!'

Hanka laughed loudly at his feeble joke. 'And do you know the Smoked-Salmons?' He laughed even more vigorously.

No one else laughed. Mrs Hanka shoved her husband, and he squealed as if it hurt.

'He thinks he has a sense of humour, but he is mistaken,' Mrs Hanka said in a mid-European accent, more marked in her voice than it was in the composer's. If anything, there was a slight intonation of American in Hanka's voice, and a queer suggestion of a

Scottish accent, barely perceptible – no more than a dash of the spoken colouring of his adopted country.

Mrs Hanka presented the disconcerting appearance of having been taller than she was now. Hers was a presence of withered beauty. She was slender and precise, but the straightness of her back looked like the willed demeanour of someone who had once been beautiful and elegant and whose temperament did not accommodate itself to the inconveniences of age. Her face was wrinkled vividly. But she was still graceful, her hair carefully ordered, her suit smart and its jacket waisted. The brooch that held a silk scarf to her neck was distinctive and antique.

'Hanka-chief,' the composer said, still smarting from his wife's chastising push, sniffing sadly, like a clown, and pointing to himself as the victim of his own jest. Then he waved his arms as if to dispel any taint of juvenile merriment from his chintzy sitting room, driving jokes out by the tall, ornately draped and swagged windows.

'Why is sweet wine so unfashionable?' he said to Lucy Williams, who had been invited by Mrs Hanka to say what she would like to drink, and had asked for a dry sherry. 'Why so severe and dry? Why not sweet? Sweet is joy! Here, in Scotland, they call whisky "nippy sweeties". These Scots people eat sweeties all the time. Eat cakes. They die like flies! But maybe they die happy!'

'Don't believe him,' Mrs Hanka said censoriously. 'Alois is in love with his "nippy sweeties". You must not believe a word he says,' she added, to Paul Salmon.

'He's come to hear me tell the truth, and you say, "Don't believe a word he says!" ' Hanka appealed to Salmon with a shrug and a wide gesture of arms, which might have meant 'Women! Wives! They're impossible!' And then Hanka winked, which could have been a hint of the composer's conviction that Salmon might try as hard as he liked, but he would not lead Hanka to say any more about his life than he wanted to disclose.

After small-talk about the house, an inspection of views from the sitting room windows, the indication of landmarks, Hanka said privately to Salmon, 'Lunch might be another hour, so maybe we should go for a walk, and talk about your film.' In a louder voice, he said, 'Would you like to see my garden?'

'Put on your coat if you go out,' Mrs Hanka said severely, her expression suggesting to Lucy Williams that Hanka had a long history of underclad walks in his garden. 'And your scarf and gloves.' Confidingly, she said to Lucy, 'He is a little boy – to be looked after, all the time, looked after.'

When the two men were in the hall, Mrs Hanka said, 'Your Mr Salmon is very tall.'

'Six feet and an inch.'

'Over six feet! Five foot four and over six feet together!' Mrs Hanka clapped her hands and laughed.

'We're not ready yet,' Hanka said in the hall. 'Before I go anywhere, there's an inspection. Coat, hat, gloves, shoes ... Do you know the joke? Spectacles, testicles, watch and wallet? No? Where have you been? You English! I have my watch. No wallet – won't need it. Don't wear glasses, thank God, because I eat carrots. Will I need my testicles, Mr Salmon? No? Maybe I'll take them off and leave them in the cupboard, but then I'd forget where I put them. "Alois! What do you mean, you have lost them?" ' he said, singing an imitation of his wife's imagined alarm.

Salmon was amused by Hanka's good-natured crudity. No one though, had forewarned him of the composer's manic humours. He wondered how one of Hanka's jests would look and sound on his film.

'Ah, here's my sergeant-major,' Hanka said, as Mrs Hanka came from the sitting room to check that her husband was dressed for the weather.

Although Salmon was too far away to hear her whisper in any language, Mrs Hanka took the precaution of speaking in German. 'I don't trust him. Remember, Alois – he is not your friend. He is handsome, English and sensitive, but I think he is cunning. He will be deferential and nice, but he might try to trap you. Be careful what you say.'

Hanka nodded his agreement and kissed her on the cheek.

'It is not only when men grow old, when their work is over, that they turn to their gardens,' Hanka said as the two men walked together. 'It is when they know that they are mature that they realize the peace and pleasure to be found in making things grow, and the great delight of being responsible for beautiful flowers and fresh vegetables. Oh, I love to eat. Most of all, I love my own fresh vegetables ...'

'I'm thinking of the film, in a way that'll present a complete portrait . . .'

'Yes, Mr Salmon, I know the questions you want to ask me,' Hanka said.

There was an article about you last year, more or less saying that you've written "the music of capitalism", and he tied this up . . .' Salmon's voice became unsure; it wavered as he stumbled on the unexpected difficulty of what he wanted to say. 'Your work during the war, and then that long stint in Hollywood.'

'I'm not any kind of an *ist*! *Isms*! These damned *isms* get everywhere!' Hanka said angrily, swatting the air energetically as if attacked by a swarm of insect isms. Visible breath flowed from them in the cold January air. 'Maybe they got into some people's music, but they didn't get into mine!'

'Did you read Lambourn's article about you?'

'Was it a long article? Do you know what Joseph Conrad said about reviews and articles? "Dear boy, I only ze measures zem!" ' Hanka said, overdoing his mimicry. 'Good music in Poland. Penderecki, Baird, Lutosławski . . .'

'Wooto?'

'OK, Lootosłavski. I am European. I pronounce. I speak languages. I am not English.'

'I suppose it's preferable for an artist of any kind to be on the truthful side of history. But it's not always possible, is it? Would you agree? Is that how you see it?' Salmon said, unnerved by the intensifying grimace with which Hanka greeted each question.

'History doesn't have any sides! That's how I see it!'

Hanka opened the door to a planthouse that was built against the south-facing wall of the garden.

'I see what you mean,' Salmon said 'You were understating when you said you were an enthusiastic gardener. Marvellous!' he said, impressed by the size of the planthouse. 'Interesting to look at, yes. I'd like to film you in here, if it's all right with you.' He looked around for a minute. Then you don't accept Lambourn's view that your career's disabled by a profoundly right-wing political stance?' Salmon asked.

'Right-wing, left-wing, no, I wouldn't. I'm a wishy-washy liberal, that's what I've been, always, even before there was the phrase. No, I'm a wishy-washy *survivor*! Like all liberals, I'm a coward, and I admit it. Thank God for liberals! Can you see me as a soldier? History!' Hanka shouted with a violent upward jerk of his arms, as if the word exploded. He looked at the ground and sneered; the word 'history' writhed in the thin dust of the path between the beds of the planthouse. 'I'll tell you what history is. It's the political piano, and the noise it makes is *lies*! I am like Greta Garbo. "I want to be alone," ' he said, with an absurd shake of his hips.

'Yes, I was coming to that. I'll have to ask you why you've chosen to live up here, in Scotland, and why you hardly ever see anyone . . .'

'Dear, young Mr Salmon, there are five million people or more in Scotland! It's old. It's not going to run away. There are no earthquakes in Scotland. Malaria's unheard of. So far as I know, there have been no nasty camps in Scotland. There were prisoner-of-war camps – and do you know? Would you believe it? The prisoners come back to visit their old friends in the villages. Even the wild animals aren't so wild! As for "nippy sweeties," ' he said, his face broadening on a grin, 'they don't even need grapes to make it!'

Salmon was unruffled by Hanka's preliminary evasions of the questions suggested to him. He was too enthusiastic for Hanka the man of talk, the man of gestures, that movable, expressive face, to be perplexed by what sounded like a lack of candour. If he could coax Hanka to speak on the film in what seemed to be his natural idiom, the composer would be a knockout.

Hanka looked at him over a plantpot which had been inspected for first signs of growth breaking the surface of the compost. 'I wonder how D-minor can be political. Or E-flat. Oh, those poor notes!'

'The film would give you a terrific chance to put your own case,' Salmon said. 'You could clear up what's been said and written about you.'

'You haven't asked me yet. You haven't said, "Mr Hanka, why did you work for the Germans?" ' Hanka put the plantpot back on its table, and picked up another. 'All these are lilies. Did you know that the water-lily has more DNA than man himself, more than you have? No? It's true. The lilium is the most beautiful and significant of all the flowers. And in these parts, I am *famous* for my lilies. And my asparagus!' He kissed his fingers in appreciation of the good taste of asparagus, and blew the kiss to Salmon. 'A retired general of the British Army comes here, and I tell him about lilies. *Royalty* has eaten my asparagus in a house not ten miles from here. Do *they* care if I conducted Mozart, at concerts, to an audience of German soldiers, most of whom didn't even want to be there?'

'I think I can imagine your predicament at the time, and maybe how you feel about it now, but it surely isn't as easy to dismiss as you make it seem. *You did it,*' Salmon said emphatically, but with less triumph and judgemental sternness than he had rehearsed. 'Your career and reputation are absolutely steeped in controversy. Hardly a single work of yours has been performed ever since it came to light that you conducted German orchestras during the war. If you aren't frank on film, it'll show,' he warned.

'I don't deny anything,' Hanka said.

'It's just as well,' Salmon said.

In the house, Mrs Hanka and Lucy Williams visited the kitchen, where the Hankas' housekeeper was preparing lunch. Mrs Hanka pointed out treasured possessions in various rooms – china, furniture, ornaments and paintings. In the room where Hanka worked, Lucy asked if she could play his piano. Mrs Hanka nodded with approval at her playing.

'Where did you study?'

'Just at school, and with a private teacher, but I've practically given it up. I don't even have a piano.'

'Alois says, "Why should I write music? No one performs it any more. I am writing symphonies of silence." '

They wandered through the house. 'He was very thrifty. After the war; we had nothing, nothing. During the war we had next to nothing, but who cared then, so long as you were alive. In bed you could pretend that everything was normal and no one anywhere was being hurt. Even that became impossible, and you didn't even have that any more. But in America, Alois worked, and worked, and if I wanted to buy something, it was always, "How much is it? Good God, no, that's too much!" He was a squirrel with money! And how he worked! Italy, Switzerland, Paris, London – he was some success in those days. I know what your friend, Mr Salmon, wants to talk to him about,' Mrs Hanka said, her voice austere with suspicion. 'Maybe you think we don't deserve to live in such a nice house, and so peacefully,' she said bitterly.

Mrs Hanka fitted a hand with a glove before trying to lift a log for the sitting room fire. The task was too strenuous for her and Lucy interceded, taking large logs from the fireside basket and placing them on the fire. She helped the kneeling Mrs Hanka to her feet. It was a courtesy Mrs Hanka seemed pleased with.

'If all your husband did was conduct an orchestra, then I don't find that so very terrible,' Lucy said, 'although I'd probably feel differently if I were Czech, and my family had suffered. Paul thinks it's pretty damning, though. I don't think Paul's cruel, or means to be, but he could be in spite of himself – all he's after are a few episodes to spice up a film and give it an edge, make it look "important". And money, of course: Paul's very interested in money.'

'Are you saying that your Mr Salmon might not be fair to Alois?'

'I'm saying, Mrs Hanka, that Paul's superficial. I've known him just a couple of months, but for someone who's making a film about a composer, you'd think Paul would know a bit about music, or have a decent record collection. About all he's got is party music, and a few token classics. God knows why, but he's got two LPs of the band of the Coldstream Guards. He can *talk* about anyone you like, Bach, Berg and Bartók, and he gets carried away about modern jazz, but he hasn't any records and he can't read a note let alone play an instrument.'

'If there is one thing Hanka can do, it is talk,' Mrs Hanka said, sitting back in her chair, looking relieved at Lucy's picture of Paul Salmon as shallow. 'I can rely on my Alois to explain to Mr Salmon everything that he needs to know.'

'I wouldn't be too sure,' Lucy said. 'Paul has contacts in Germany, and they've unearthed an old German propaganda film from some archive or other.' A tremor of fright showed on Mrs Hanka's face, followed quickly by a deliberately impassive stare. 'It's obviously your husband on the film conducting a German Army orchestra. When he acknowledges the applause, takes a bow and accepts the flowers, he looks as if he's enjoying it. I've seen it and it doesn't look good.'

'And it didn't feel good at the time,' the old woman said fiercely.

Mrs Hanka fidgeted in her chair. She put down her sherry glass and pulled a handkerchief from her sleeve. Wiping the sticky wine from her fingers looked like the action of a woman who was used to keeping her self-control, or retrieving its temporary loss through an act of calculated fastidiousness.

'I didn't mean to upset you, but I felt that you ought to know.'

'Why apologize to me? You weren't even born!'

'If he was *forced* to work for the Germans, then why doesn't he say it?' Lucy asked as Mrs Hanka dabbed at the smallest of tears with her handkerchief.

Very few people knew the real reason why Alois Hanka accepted the invitation of the German authorities in Prague and conducted and directed what started out as a joint Czech-German orchestra. Gradually, the Czech musicians dwindled in numbers. After only a month, no German civilian players remained, and the entire ensemble consisted of musicians in uniform.

'Because I made you guess that he did not want to work for them, does not mean that he was forced, Miss Williams,' Mrs Hanka said with difficultly.

'I don't understand.'

'It was a cultural lie. It was to look good. It was to look friendly. But they didn't mean it, and neither did Alois. I shall tell what happened. Alois is not proud of his secret.'

'But people have known for years,' Lucy said.

'I mean why he worked for them, not just that he did. What he is saying to Mr Salmon, I don't know; but I am tired of all this silence. Alois would like people to believe that because only music was involved, then there was no harm. Maybe he used to believe it himself, but I think he is tired of it, too. I am not Czech, you see, although I had citizenship there, from not long after I married Alois. My father was Austrian, my mother came from East Prussia, which is where they lived, although I was born in Vienna. Our home was in East Prussia. I met Hanka in Vienna. He wasn't a Nazi, he was never a Nazi, nor was I ever a Nazi. After we were married, 12 November 1935, we went to Prague – Hanka's city, his home, and I loved it. I was happy there. We kept it quiet that I was really a German. I did not *claim* to be anything else, but when I got my Czechoslovakian papers, I was proud. My father, you see – *he* was a Nazi – more German than the Germans, because of my mother, and her family, and business. Alois? He despised all politics. When we met, he didn't like me too much at first, because I said I was thinking of becoming a Communist; but I never did, you see, because of Hanka. After Czechoslovakia is occupied, then the war, the German authorities discover who I am, my family, my father, my mother; and they ask Hanka to work for them. He had a name as a composer and a conductor. His early compositions were admired. Not the most

famous, but everyone respected him ... He was talked about.
People liked him. He knows what they know about me and so he
accepts. He knows because they told him, but they don't say anything about what might happen to me, or to Alois, if he refuses. Alois
asks them, but all they do is smile. I said to him, "No, never!" He
says, "Why not, it's harmless?" But he made an arrangement with
them. They stop thinking of Hanka's wife as a traitor German, a
woman who hates her mother and father. So, you see, the shame is
mine. Hanka did it to save me, but he tells no one. Instead, he says: "I
wave a little stick, I keep time, I tell when the cellos come in. What's
wrong with that?" And I still nag him, and I indulge in little extrava-
gances that he says we can't afford, even now, when we can. "I am a
soldier in the army of St Cecilia!" he says, but he doesn't know how
stupid he makes himself seem, Miss Williams. Because of me, he has
this terrible thing on his conscience. And now you'll tell your Mr
Salmon, although if I took a whole day to explain, if we talk for a
week, you will not understand,' Mrs Hanka said with cold passion.

'I won't tell Paul if you don't want me to,' Lucy said.

In the garden, Paul Salmon turned up the collar of his coat against
the weather, wishing that he was inside by the fire. Hanka said, 'You
say you'll give me fair play? There's no such thing! In the twentieth
century?' he said, shrill with theatrical disbelief.

'I can't turn my back on the evidence,' Salmon said petulantly. 'As
well as the old archive footage, we've even found a list of officers
invited to one of the concerts.'

'*I* didn't invite them!'

'Five of them were convicted as war criminals,' Salmon stated.

'So? The man who shot Abraham Lincoln in the theatre was guilty
– but they didn't execute the cast, did they? Did they hang the
leading lady? Did they shoot the author? Maybe you want to dig up
Mozart's bones and burn them?'

'But you performed the concerts,' Salmon said, exasperated with
Hanka's refusals to submit to how damaging the evidence would
look on the screen.

'Fiddlers played in the cafés the German soldiers went to, but
nobody branded them as traitors!'

'That isn't the same thing, and you know it,' Salmon said, risking
the sound of anger. 'All over Europe, artists, of one kind or another,
didn't wait to find out what the Germans might ask them to do. They

got away. They went abroad. Those who stayed, many of them, most of them, refused to have anything to do with the Nazis. Some of them suffered for it.'

'I am so very sorry – I am guilty of being alive. Forgive me, Mr Salmon, for not being dead. My own music was forbidden by the German authorities, you know. I used to play it in my head. I knew other composers who did the same. No one has forbidden my music in this country, or anywhere else, but it isn't played! I have no children and I have no philosophies – that's me, Hanka. Does it matter to your film that I wash the dishes? That I have always been faithful to my wife? No? Ah, poor Webern!'

'Webern . . .?'

'Do you like Webern's music?'

'No, not a lot, some, but . . .' Salmon was caught off-balance by Hanka's sudden change of direction. His discomfort was worsened by Hanka's closeness to him, the challenging earnestness with which the composer stared at him.

'He was shot by an American soldier who thought he was a black-marketeer making his escape! And he wasn't. He was Anton Webern! He was modern music with a bullet in his back. Poor Anton! And that poor soldier! Even if all the music he knew was his own whistle, what a responsibility!'

'So, what was said?' Mrs Hanka asked in the hall, where her husband sat on a stool and his wife helped him off with his heavy outdoor shoes.

'You've heard of British fair play, this thing the world has never seen? Mr Salmon is full of it – promises, you never heard such promises! But his worst fault is banality, and after that comes ignorance. He knows as much about music as a rabbit.'

'Mr Salmon is a divorced person, aged thirty-six, and Miss Lucy Williams sleeps with him,' Mrs Hanka said. 'She is so nice, Alois, but she is not a happy woman. She told me that her Mr Salmon knows nothing about music.'

'What else did you talk about, other than who is sleeping with who?'

'About you, Alois; and about me. I told her the truth, but I trust her, and she will not tell her Mr Salmon.'

'The goody-goodies, they'll be coming in the windows! Ah, no, what have you done, Eva?'

'Shh. Not so loud,' she said. 'I have lived with my shame for a long time, Alois. We're old now. What harm can it do to tell the truth? Don't let me die ashamed, Alois.'

'But they'll *make* you feel guilty,' Hanka said.

'I did not want to do it. Did I ask? Did I plead with you for my life?'

'You stupid, brave woman, you would have done anything to have stopped me working for them. You were ashamed of *me*, for working to save you, and you were ashamed of yourself for being German, for something you couldn't help. I took your shame away from you, Eva! I waved the historical wand, I played the political piano, but all the time I was saying, "No, no, no!" Maybe you're too German to understand that "No" can be in your heart but not in your mouth.' He stood up. 'She'll tell him. If she sleeps with him, she'll tell him,' Hanka said. 'Who'll understand? No one!'

'It doesn't matter,' his wife said, smartening the sleeve of his jacket. 'I could not have asked you to work for them to save me. I could not have asked it, and did not need to. Can you imagine how much I have cherished what you did for me, and yet how I have hated myself that it was because of me that you had to make that choice? That is why I feel so guilty. You made yourself look like the enemy of so many people, because of me, not because of music.'

Paul Salmon stood before the fire, warming himself and looking displeased. He had been annoyed by Lucy's refusal to tell him what she had been talking about with Mrs Hanka.

'Go on, you can tell him!' Hanka shouted to the young woman as he walked past her on his way to the dining room. 'Tell him now, because he can't wait, then come and eat!'

Mrs Hanka followed her husband. She turned and opened her arms to Lucy Williams, and shrugged, as if to say, 'That man, Hanka, what am I to do with him?'